LOVE ON THE RUN

The moonlight revealed brown eyes in which Kalina saw only love and tenderness. She pressed all five of Max's fingers against her lips, kissing the tip of each. Cursing, he tore his hand from hers, and then he was kissing her on the mouth, this time not the sweet touch one gives a child but the hard, sensual man-to-woman meeting of flesh.

They sank deep into the straw and his lips darted to her eyes, her cheeks, her nose, her forehead — any part of her that was not covered by her coat. She locked her hands together behind his neck, willing him to go on, pressing herself against him.

But springing to his feet, he hurled himself into the open door, clutching both sides to keep from falling out the moving train. He sobbed as if in pain. "Kalina, I'm a beast, I didn't mean — "

"Please," she murmured. "I want it too, Max."

Her blood was singing, every nerve in her body was alive. This was love. All the rich and handsome men in Pennsylvania were not for her. *Wait for me*, Max had said. One day he too would be rich . . .

SILK AND STEEL

RITA BALKEY

ZEBRA BOOKS
KENSINGTON PUBLISHING CORP.

ZEBRA BOOKS

are published by

Kensington Publishing Corp.
475 Park Avenue South
New York, NY 10016

First printing: December 1986

Printed in the United States of America

To the nuns of St. Peter's School at Twenty-Eighth and to Sarah on Pittsburgh's then sooty South Side, one block from the steel mills and the Monongahela River, who imbued a little slum kid with the love of learning, of history, and of America,

And—

To the nuns of St. Joseph's Home for Orphans on Troy Hill Road, Number 1366, overlooking the Allegheny River and even more steel mills, who taught me that in America anything is possible.

I sincerely, with heartfelt thanks, dedicate this book.

Part One
America

Cinderella dressed in yellow
Went uptown to meet her fellow.
How many kisses did she get?
One, two, three, four . . .

— American rope-skipping rhyme.

Chapter One

At the first melodic chime from the tower of Trinity Church, Kalina Olkonsky lifted her head and smiled. Eagerly, she knotted the last thread on the day's last pair of knee pants, bit it off with sharp white teeth, and added the pants to the pile on the floor, patting the garment firmly in place with her two hands. They'd keep some little boy warm this winter, she thought, with satisfaction.

Jabbing her needle into the collar of her black frock, she darted to the narrow window and threw it up as far as it would go. Curving her workworn hands on the splintery sill, Kalina leaned way out, her slim body almost bent in half, to inhale the frigid New York air. In the hours since the sun had slid behind the rooftops of Manhattan, the cold had deepened, and the furious daylong wind had stilled, as if reverently awaiting the snow.

"One, Holy Mother of God. Two, Holy Mother of God."

Her counting was pious in the old Polish way—a prayer for each stroke of the bell. Her lightly accented voice was soft lest she waken her ailing aunt, who slept fitfully on the narrow cot tucked into a shadowy corner of the small room.

The last reverberating echo soared into the clouds. Nine o'clock. Three hours till midnight.

Flinging out her arms, the immigrant girl embraced the

9

air. The American air. The sweet, sweet air of freedom. Supple muscles, cramped from hunching all day in a wooden chair over the sweatshop pants, responded avidly, for the blood of youth was strong in her veins. Sixteen-year-old Kalina felt the heart within her leap with joy and anticipation.

A new year! A new century!

Like a new baby, she thought, a new century is fresh from the womb of time, plump with health and promise. It was a whole new chance for dreams to come true.

"Kalina!"

A petulant voice from the cot sliced into her reverie.

"Yes, Aunt Litka." Kalina's voice was mild, patient, dutiful.

"How many pants today?"

"Three dozen, Aunt." She paused a moment. "That's a whole dollar, Aunt."

"Ho!" The voice strengthened. "Zuska would have done four dozen."

The sick woman's unwonted exertion brought on a paroxysm of strangled coughing, and, frightened, the girl ran to the tall bureau to pour a cup of water from the pitcher. She sank to her knees by the cot. Her aunt drank but abruptly spit it out with surprising force for one so weak, soaking the pillow beneath her as well as the top of her worn flannel gown.

"Pfui! Bilge! Little wonder when they draw it right out of that sewer of an East River."

Kalina was silent. She had heard it all before. Nothing pleased the woman now. She smiled and, as one would a fretful child, cradled the gray head in her arm and forced a few more drops of water between the fever-cracked lips.

Eventually, the spasm subsided, and Litka leaned back on the wet pillow, weak as a kitten. Kalina dipped a cloth in a saucer of cool water and tenderly bathed her aunt's sweating face.

"Hear the bells, Aunt. It'll soon be 1900."

But Aunt Litka was beyond caring. Her eyes were closed and she seemed to sleep. Kalina rubbed at dried bits of blood on the old woman's lips. Hemorrhaging again, Kalina thought, dismayed. It was only a matter of time. She must be patient, she must pray. Death would bring her own deliverance.

Carefully, Kalina slipped her arm from beneath Aunt Litka's neck, and rising, turned once more toward the window. Sounds came from Mulberry Street. Happy sounds. People talking, laughing, singing.

Life lay outside the window. Inside was only death.

"Close the window, girl. I'm dying of the cold."

Obediently, Kalina shut out the world and leaned against the cold glass, swallowing the knot of tears that filled her throat and threatened to cut off her breath.

"How many pants you say?"

"Three dozen, Aunt," she replied tonelessly. Three dozen black cotton trousers, all seams sewed with the neat, tiny stitches her aunt had schooled her in.

Kalina rubbed the thumb and finger of her right hand together, feeling the roughness. Like sandpaper, she thought bitterly. She had never mastered the slippery thimble and managed to prick her finger a hundred times each day, it seemed.

"Zuska would have done maybe five—" The nagging woman stopped to cough again, but this time Kalina did not rush forward.

"Yes, Aunt," she said with some heat. "But Zuska is not here."

Bitter words danced on Kalina's tongue, but she compressed her lips to keep from lashing out.

"Zuska, Zuska, Zuska." It was Litka's favorite word, a name she said more than any other.

Litka's daughter and Kalina's cousin, Zuska Olkonsky was two years older than Kalina and, to hear Litka tell it, was swifter, better, cleverer at almost everything. Especially at growing up, Kalina mused. At twelve, when Kalina's breasts were mere oversized warts sticking out on her bony ribs, Zuska had sprouted in truly miraculous fashion plump half-moons, firm and ripe as early apples.

At sixteen, on fire to get on with life, cousin Zuska had

run off to Pennsylvania with a wickedly handsome Italian street peddler twice her age. Three months later a postal card had come to Mulberry Street. *I am well, expecting child, will send money.*

Two years passed, but no money, no more postal cards. From anywhere. There was sure to be a child, however, Kalina thought. A son, of course—fat, bouncing, and beautiful. Zuska would do that well too. A less clever person like Kalina would have a daughter. Daughters are never as welcome as sons.

"Kalina, light the samovar, you lazy girl!"

Contritely, Kalina shook her head, banishing bitter thoughts. Wafting a quick and silent prayer of repentance heavenward, she skipped across the dark room and lit the stub of candle in its saucer on the table. Her aunt was raving again. There was no samovar in the Mulberry Street tenement. The woman was back in Poland, imagining herself in the manor house where a great fire always burned in a stone pit as wide as the room and a gleaming samovar simmered from dawn till midnight.

Kalina remembered too. With a pang, she evoked the cozy fire-lit sitting room. There had always been a crowd, men, women, children, old ones and young together, circling the white porcelain stove and copper samovar, drinking bottomless cups of black Russian tea.

The candlelight, though flickering and weak, quieted the dying one, and, lifting the teapot from the table, Kalina peered intently, but with no real hope, at the mat of soggy tea leaves nestling forlornly at the bottom.

Had she used them four times, or only thrice? She racked her brain. She cast her dark eyes on the cold grate. No fire, not even a few sticks to make one. She gazed around the room, but there was nothing left to burn. Bureau, table, chair, cot. She sighed. Tomorrow she would run down to the river and pick up a bucketful of coal from the tracks.

Teapot to chest, Kalina flew out the door and down the wooden stairs to the flat just below, where there was not only a fire but a perpetually boiling kettle. Mrs. Anna

Cipriani, her husband Tony, and the three eldest of their numerous brood manufactured slippers from wool, which had to be ironed into the proper curved shapes after sewing. Three heavy flatirons sat on the stove, ready at all times. Alongside, a tall, blue-enameled pot brewed strong, black, aromatic coffee, and a cast-iron kettle simmered merrily.

Kalina rarely saw any bread or cheese or food of any kind. What there was got eaten, she surmised, minutes after it arrived. The Ciprianis, old and young, apparently sustained life on rich, black coffee, though sometimes it was laced with milk. Despite the seeming lack of nourishment, however, the Italian woman was fat and unfailingly good-humored. At sight of the Polish girl in the open door, she shifted this year's baby from one breast to the other and flashed a wide smile. Two black-eyed girls sat on the floor, cunning fingers busily threading strips of grosgrain ribbon through brightly colored squares of felt. A boy of ten bent over an ironing board, deftly shaping the slippers handed up to him by his sisters.

What appeared to be several bundles of rags lay screaming on the double bed. These were "rent babies," Kalina knew, infants who were cared for by Mama Cipriani and fed from her copiously flowing breasts while their parents worked in sweatshops.

"*Buon Capodanno!*" The woman bellowed a hearty holiday greeting as Kalina headed for the stove.

"Happy New Year to you also, Mrs. Cipriani," Kalina screamed back over the clamor, adding in the Polish way, "and the peace of God be with you this night and always."

The woman turned back to the squalling baby, and Kalina lifted the kettle and filled her pot. The water turned a dingy gray. Energetically, she jiggled the pot, but the worn-out tea leaves swirled round and round like dead leaves in a rain-filled gutter.

Swallowing what little pride years of poverty had left her, Kalina said, "Mrs. Cipriani, please, can you spare a spoonful of tea? I'll give it back tomorrow when I get my dollar from Mr. Lutz for the pants."

13

The Italian woman turned from the bed where she had laid down one infant and picked up another. "No tea, *caro*. Coffee maybe?"

Kalina shook her head. "Aunt Litka despises coffee."

There was a loud laugh, then a crack on a blanketed bottom as a tiny mouth clamped on a long, brown nipple.

Watching, Kalina forgot her troubles for a moment, her heart quickening at the sight. Like a painting, she reflected. Madonna and child. The Ciprianis had arrived from Italy six years ago, and despite their unending toil, the family was still uproariously happy at being in America.

"How is the poor dying one upstairs?" The melodic Latin voice was lyric with compassion.

Kalina shrugged. "Well enough. Been sleeping on and off all day. That herb you gave me to put in her tea is very potent. I am most grateful."

After a moment, the girl turned away. She was loath to leave this steamy, people-warm place. Mama Cipriani touched her arm. "You talk so fine. You be a lady someday."

Impulsively, the Polish girl kissed the fat, sweaty cheek. "You are the *true* lady, Mama Cipriani."

As she bounded back upstairs, words from out of the past echoed in Kalina's brain. Words from Poland. "In America you will be a great lady. You will marry a fine man, rich and handsome and of good family. You will never be hungry or cold or despised."

Mama's lovely face had been white with sorrow, her black eyes brilliant with unshed tears as she bade a sad farewell to ten-year-old Kalina, off to America. The other side of the world.

Upstairs, the candle had guttered, and as she struck a match and dug with her fingers for the wick, Kalina reflected on her mother's parting words. Thanks to six long years of Litka's English lessons, the Olkonsky cousins could talk like ladies. Grammar perfect too, no slang or vulgar profanity like the other kids on the street.

Besides the grammar, there were readings from library

novels, lessons in deportment, moral training, and politics. One would have thought the Polish girls were heiresses and their aunt a governess on a landed estate. "The Queens of Mulberry Street," the neighbors snickered behind their backs. Imagine! Lowly Polacks—greenhorns—fresh off the boat at Ellis Island—acting so hoity-toity!

Completely forgetting her earlier impatience with her aunt, Kalina now thought with affection of the blooming woman who had braved the steerage passage for the sake of her two charges—her own golden-haired Zuska and her sister Hania's bastard child. Litka's own hair had been abundant and richly brown, but now—

"Zuska!" Her aunt was sitting bolt upright, dark blue eyes aglitter with fever, the telltale roses of consumption crimson on her sunken cheeks. "The samovar is boiling, I want my tea."

She spoke in Polish, and the girl's heart plummeted. When she got like this, it took hours to calm her down. Wordlessly, with no thought but to give the sufferer much-needed rest, Kalina dropped a sprig of Mama Cipriani's narcotic herb into a cup, spooned in a quantity of sugar, and covered them both with hot water from the teapot. Kneeling once again by her aunt's cot, she held the cup and watched expectantly as Litka drank. The hot brew stayed down, thank the Virgin, but bright red blood spewed from the sufferer's mouth, turning the edge of the thin blanket into a ribbon of scarlet.

Now she would sleep, Kalina knew from past experience. As before, she cradled the fever-racked head to her girlish bosom, gazing tearfully at the sparse gray hair. Hard times and disease had caused Litka's rich, brown hair to vanish seemingly overnight. Kalina crooned songs of her native village.

Kasha, get the horses, Yasha, pump the water. Yasha, he is singing, Kasha, she is crying.

It was a silly song about lovers quarreling, but it seemed to soothe her aunt. The girl's voice was sweet and low and, as she heard her own voice sing the old words and haunting melody, she herself was lost to the grim reality of Mulberry

15

Street. The magic of music transported her back to a happier time.

Market Day. Fresh straw covers the rough floor of the farm cart. Humps of long green cucumbers, round brown onions, new potatoes with the earth still upon them weigh down the creaky vehicle. The horses prance, impatient to be gone. Proudly they toss their long manes which the women have braided with spring flowers. The old cook Anya, her seamed faced haloed by a red-dyed babushka, lifts the little Kalina onto the plank seat. Then springing up herself, spry as a colt, her gnarled hands grab the reins, and, with a shrill cluck at the beasts, they ride to Jaslo on the rutted dirt road.

The inky Polish sky turns first purple, then pink, then a bright, warm, wonderful gold.

For one long delicious moment Kalina rested her head on Litka's barely moving breast, forgetting everything, even Zuska's heartless desertion of them both.

After a time she rose, and moving to the bureau, lifted the candle to the cracked mirror hanging over the once-elegant chest of drawers. The soft light imparted a remote beauty to her young features, reminiscent of the faded portraits on the walls of the manor house where she was born and spent her first ten years.

She was not pretty in the conventional sense, she was acutely aware that she had none of Zuska's full-blown ripe wheat look that caused men's heads to swivel as she passed.

She cocked her head coquettishly, admitting with some lack of modesty that there *was* a distinction, an elusive aristocratic kind of look, as befitted the daughter of Pan Mikolai. She saw an elegance to the cap of velvety black hair captured by the thick braid that hung down her back to her tailbone. If one were to judge by the pictures in the Sunday rotogravure, her well-defined widow's peak was quite the rage. Heavy brows arched gracefully like birds in flight, cheekbones rested high and bony, nose a millimeter too long perhaps.

Kalina Olkonsky grinned at herself. She was a damn

16

good-looking girl.

"My God, girl, you look more like Hania every day! If only you'd fill out," Aunt Litka had remarked just the other day. Like her mother Hania, Kalina's eyes were the deep purplish-black hue of the sloe berries that lined the Carpathian countryside.

"Your eyes are your fortune, girl," her aunt had continued, "but in the name of all the Saints, hold onto your virginity. Without it, you are nothing. Virginity is the jewel of the poor."

Good advice, she thought now, gazing soberly at herself, but even in America, rich, handsome men of good family didn't marry bastard daughters of Polish serving maids. Both Zuska and Kalina were fathered by the lecherous Pan Mikolai, who scattered his seed like spring wheat in the villages governed by the manor. The boys, if well formed, were given to the army, while the prettiest of the girls were fetched to the big house to pleasure the lord and his noble guests. A precious few made their way to America or across the mountains to Austria.

When Kalina was born, Hania, determined that her beautiful child should not fill Pan Mikolai's bed, had begun to save her kopecks. When the time came, there had been enough passage money for three of them. Hania's sister Litka would go, it was decided, taking the nubile girls, Hania would follow when the child in her womb was old enough to withstand the voyage.

The young woman and two girls had done well at first, rolling Havana cigars. But Litka soon fell ill from the tobacco aroma and they turned to finishing pants. That meant sewing on buttons, securing seam ends, and turning up hems. They ate well enough by Mulberry Street standards and put aside money each week for Hania's passage.

At day's end, after being cooped up in the stuffy room for twelve hours, Kalina was wild for the outdoors and often went round to the livery stables on Mott Street where the street vendors brought their dray horses for the night. A very old man with a bushy, gray beard and felt cap, who reminded her of Anya's husband Mashko, sat out in front

17

smoking a pipe. Man and girl would talk of Poland and America and he would give her lumps of sugar to feed the horses. She would lean on the warm, sweating flanks of the animals and dream. There was a boy too, about her age and tall, with flame-red hair and a face brown with freckles. He had given her apples to take home for Zuska and Aunt Litka.

Eventually, Hania wrote that her child was a boy and was not by Pan Mikolai. She called him Pepi, for Philip. She did not reveal the name of her lover. Aunt Litka, Zuska, and Kalina had saved thirty dollars for the passage, but before Litka could send the letter with the happy news, Zuska had run off with the money.

After that, with Zuska's labor gone, there was nothing but work. No more visits to the stable, no more sugar, no more apples, no more red-headed boy. Litka came down with a bad cold that hung on and on. In the second winter after Zuska's departure, she took to her bed.

A sharp rattle at the window sent Kalina flying across the room. She flung it open. Three stories below a knot of boys and girls buzzed round the lantern pole. The tallest of them swung back his arm, ready with a second handful of pebbles. At sight of Kalina, her long, black braid falling over the sill, he pulled off his cap to reveal a shock of whitish hair.

"Kalina, Kalina, come down," he shouted.

Furious at the racket, Kalina yelled back. "Joe Wagner, have you no respect for the dying?"

He grinned. "We're going downtown to see in the new century. Come on. Free beer and sausages."

"You know I can't, Joe." Her voice took on a wistful note.

"Aw, the old lady's gonna die anyway, whether you're here or not."

"Yeah," piped up a thin girl at his side. "The gallopin' consumption takes 'em quick. My ma died from it, and my little brother."

"Quick, it would be a mercy," Kalina whispered.

The rest of the gang joined in. "They're shooting fire-

18

works from a barge. We can stand on the bridge all together and watch. Think of all that food."

The girl at the window hesitated, arms upraised to lower the sash. It had begun to snow and the cold flakes fell on her face. Her black eyes were moist with longing. The street was alive. People hunched around bonfires, hands splayed to the flames. Children, bundled up like sausages against the cold, scooted in and out of the grown-ups' legs. Strains of gypsy violins drifted from the beer hall on the corner.

Kalina's young heart yearned to be a part of the good time. Her eyes shifted back to Joe. He was leader of the Swamp Angels, one of the myriad gangs that roamed the riverfront. They thieved, rolled drunks, even sold their bodies, both boys and girls, to buy food and tobacco and a nightly mug of beer. Many had no homes at all. The thin girl with the consumptive mother had left an abusive father and, like the rest, lived in the vast network of sewers under the New York streets.

Joe Wagner had been pestering Kalina for months to join the gang and be his special girl. But being Joe's girl meant losing her cherished virginity. That led inevitably to a full belly and another bastard child to add to the already swollen population.

She bent her elbows to lower the window. "No, Joe, I have to take my pants to Ludlow Street tonight."

"Ol' Lutz ain't there, nobody showed up at the shop for work, so he closed up for the night."

Summoning all her strength, Kalina banged the window shut and, dashing back to the bureau, furiously undid her braid and brushed the rich fall of hair until it shone with blue-black fire. There was no more noise at the window. Her stomach growled. She had had nothing to eat all day but a crust of stale bread and a cup of weak tea.

Brush in midair, she paused, torturing herself with thoughts of rich, garlicky sausage, deep gold-brown ale, sweet, sirupy cake. Setting down the brush, she slanted a glance at her aunt, who seemed to be in a profound slumber, her breathing deep and regular. If she ran all the way, she could get to Trinity Church in ten minutes, see some of the fun, load her apron pockets with goodies, and be back within the hour.

A wild exhilaration seized her. She would dress up as for a holiday. Pulling a long string of Litka's amber beads from the top drawer of the bureau, she wove it in and out of her loosened hair, securing it in several places with bits of scarlet ribbon. Another drawer yielded a voluminous, richly embroidered skirt and velvet bodice, carefully preserved in tissue for her aunt's burial. The skirt came barely to her ankles, but so much the better, she thought, to keep out of the mud and snow.

Kalina pulled the strings of the bodice extra tight to push up her slight bosom. Deciding against the fragile slippers that went with the outfit, she regretfully stepped into her battered street boots.

A fringed sheep's wool shawl, cut in a circle, went round her shoulders twice and reached to the top of the boots. It would hide the costume, she thought ruefully, but in the event she met a rich and handsome gentleman she could let it fall apart long enough for him to view her charms.

On the landing Kalina alerted Mama Cipriani that she would be gone an hour or so and asked her please to send one of the children to look in on her aunt.

"Sure t'ing," grinned the woman's husband, who sat by the stove, nursing a schooner of beer. "When you come back, we give you beer and you celebrate with us, huh?" His black Italian eyes glinted invitingly.

On Mulberry Street a band composed of accordion, fiddle, and drum thumped energetically on the sidewalk, picking up pennies thrown by admiring onlookers. "Should auld acquaintance be forgot" sounded from every direction in a jumble of accents — Italian, Irish, German, Serbian. Kalina managed a Polish rendition. She and Litka were the only Poles on the street and were viewed with contempt as "Polacks" by the others.

As she passed the saloon, a drunk lurched out of the doorway, mumbling, "This way, little girl, the party's in here." Eluding his grasp with the skill of long and repeated practice, Kalina darted toward the river.

Midway in the block a light glimmered from Mr. Lenz's butcher shop. Despite her rush, the hungry girl stopped to feast her eyes on the rows of fat sausages on hooks displayed in the window. Imagine how Aunt Litka's blue eyes would widen when she handed her a plateful of the sizzling little darlings.

The Dutchman's stocky form was bent over the cutting counter where he sliced at a haunch of beef with a wicked-looking knife. Suddenly, as if conscious of being watched, the man lifted his head and smilingly beckoned Kalina to come inside. Wiping his bloodied hands on his white apron, he rushed to open the door. His pale blue eyes glimmered with pleasure, and the butcher chattered nervously as she entered, his booted feet shuffling like a schoolboy's on the sawdust-covered floor.

"What an honor," he babbled, "to be visited on New Year's Eve by such a pretty young lady."

"Thank you for the compliment, Mr. Lenz," she replied primly, as her aunt had taught her. "I am on my way to the celebration by the Church; they're giving away free food."

Seeing his obvious delight at her company, Kalina remembered that Zuska had often come home with choice pieces of beef or pork and sometimes a piece of liverwurst that she had in her words "weaseled" out of the old man.

"Just smile and flirt a little." Her cousin's voice resounded in Kalina's brain.

Flashing her best smile, Kalina hopped up on the lard barrel. Slowly untying the knot of her shawl, she let it fall apart, bunching it up in her lap. Mr. Lenz beamed and leaned close, his little eyes squinting boldly at her girlish bosom. Kalina flushed but, minding Zuska's words, lowered her own eyelids modestly. It wouldn't hurt to be nice to the Dutchman. He was a longtime widower and had neither chick nor child.

Her virginity could scarcely be in any danger, she assured herself. The man must be fifty at the least.

Turning abruptly, he walked to a sink in a corner to wash the blood off his hands. The haunch lay big and red and inviting on the wooden counter. He took off his white cap, revealing a surprisingly thick thatch of iron-gray hair. Kalina giggled, the prospect of good rich meat making her giddy.

"What does the little Polish *mädel* desire tonight?" Mr. Lenz returned, working a towel over his hands and face. "A nice bit of steak?" A stubby finger pointed to the haunch.

Suddenly, the smell of fresh blood seemed suffocating to Kalina. Her eyes caught a large, round enamel pan under the chopping block. It was filled with snaky intestines with purplish clots in the folds. The ravenous hunger vanished and a sickening nausea rose in her stomach. She swayed on the barrel, reaching blindly for the edge of the wooden counter.

With a bound, the butcher was at her side, his thick arm girdling her waist, his thumbs digging into the soft flesh that lay exposed between the velvet bodice and the top of Aunt Litka's skirt.

"Please," she cried in a tiny voice, "do you have some tea?" She dared not think of what his hand was doing, as it crept up beneath the bodice. She felt him squeeze the underside of her breast. His fingertips were hot and rough. It was the first time that anyone but her mother had touched her there.

"Tea." The word was thick and strangled. "You bet, I got plenty tea. And coffee, too." Smoothly, he slid her off the barrel and across the sawdust. "It's upstairs."

Kalina shut her eyes, seeking to shut out what was happening. When she opened them again, she saw the wooden steps that led to his upstairs rooms. The hand on her breast pressed harder, she could not breathe. Terror drove out her nausea; with a jerk she pulled herself free and faced him.

"No. No, Mr. Lenz, please. I must get back to my aunt." His round visage was red, and his nostrils were opened wide. "Just give me some meat to take home to her. I'll pay you tomorrow when I take my pants—"

His strong butcher hands yanked her back to his body.

22

"You pay me now," he gritted. Then, with a grating laugh, "No credit."

It was like a nightmare. Kalina felt herself sinking toward the bloodied floor behind the high counter, the butcher kneeling over her, his knees straddling her prostrate form. He was fumbling with his trousers. She tried to get up, but his powerfully muscled legs held her as in a vise.

"Please, please, please, please." The frightened girl chanted the word like a prayer. But no prayer could help her now, she thought despairingly. The thing most dreaded in all the world, save death itself, was about to happen to her.

"Please sir, I am a virgin," she shrieked with all her strength.

The big face over hers lit up in a beatific smile. "A virgin for the New Year. *Wunderbar!*"

Her youthful vigor was no match for the old and experienced man who lay upon her like a leaden weight. Crazed, he ripped the bodice as he plunged his head into her breasts, nibbling first on one, then the other, like a starving man at a loaf of bread. Wet lips descended on hers, forcing her mouth wide open, and his hot tongue darted inside her mouth.

Writhing in revulsion, she forced her teeth down upon his tongue. With a cry of rage, the butcher hauled back a meaty hand to hit her on the cheek. "Be still, girl. The other one, the goldy-hair, she liked it very much."

Oh, the agony, the unspeakable irony, to lose her jewel of the poor to such a beast!

His hips were gyrating, and he was struggling with her long, heavy skirt. The stallion in the farmyard had moved like that when they brought him to the mare. The mare's scream had pierced the dawn.

Kalina became still, waiting for the pain.

But it never came. His engorged manhood never reached her maidenhead. Instead, all hell broke loose. There was a crashing of glass, and the sound of people running in the shop.

"Donnervetter! Thieves, rascals!" Her ravisher sprang up, pulling at his loosened trousers.

Scrambling up, Kalina reached for her shawl but could not find it. She must have left it on the lard barrel. She flattened herself against the wall, trying to become invisible, desperately holding her torn bodice together with her hands. She stared wide-eyed at the scurrying figures who darted about the small place, tearing sausages and wursts from the wall hooks, grabbing lamb legs, pork roasts. Two young girls got on either side of the beef haunch and lifted it to their shoulders, bearing it away like a log of wood. Even the lard barrel was tipped over and rolled out the door.

The hysterical butcher ran upstairs to fetch a long brown rifle which he pointed at the marauders. *"Heraus*, you rascals, or I shoot to kill."

A familiar voice sounded at Kalina's ear. "Is this yours?" Joe Wagner stood on the other side of the counter, holding Kalina's shawl high over the mess. His Dutchie face was crinkled up with laughter. Before she could reply, he threw the woolly thing at her head and, turning quick as a sewer rat, hurled himself at the butcher. The rifle shot hit the ceiling. Nimbly, Joe wrested the weapon from the older man and laid it on the chopping block.

He grinned at Kalina. "So-o-o, my pretty Polish virgin, Aunt Litka dying, huh? You can't come out tonight, huh?" With the same ease with which he had disarmed the butcher, he vaulted over the counter and kissed Kalina straight on the lips. "Well, I've got all the meat now, you little bastard." He made a lewd motion with his hips. "You know where to find me."

The Swamp Angels were gone as fast as they had come. Mr. Lenz rushed out into the dark street. "Po-lees, po-lees."

Huddled in the shawl, Kalina raced past the half-crazed man, down Mott Street to Mulberry, muttering frantic, incoherent prayers to the Virgin for sending the Swamp Angels to save her from mortal sin. Another few seconds . . . She banished the terrifying thought.

24

Trinity Church was striking eleven as she reached the battered steps of the tenement. The snow had deepened; tiny, ice-hard pellets stung her cheeks. The stoop and steps were thick with men, women, children, and babies waiting for the magic stroke of midnight. Mr. Cipriani leaned against the iron railing. His wife and older children were dancing on the sidewalk.

Aunt Litka! Who was watching Aunt Litka?

Kalina panicked. "Please, let me pass." No one moved. Hands reached out to pull her down to the steps. Mr. Cipriani grabbed her arm. "*Bene, bene*, it's the little Polish firecracker."

As she struggled to break away, a blue-coated policeman fastened on her other arm. She heard a woman shriek, "That's one of 'em, off'cer. I seen her runnin' out the butcher's. She's Joe Wagner's slut."

The copper placed two hands on Kalina's shoulders, swiveled toward the street. "OK, little gal. B'Jesus, can't you kids stop your thievin' even on New Year's Eve?"

"No-o-o. Not so. Kalina's a good girl. She take care of her sick aunt." Mama Cipriani's shrill voice soared over the din.

But nobody paid any attention. The shawl had slipped from Kalina's shoulders, exposing through the torn bodice a good part of her breast. She looked wild; indeed she looked like a slut. The iron hands on her shoulders pushed her inexorably away from the crowd. Suddenly a piercing whistle from the saloon brought everyone on the steps into the street, rushing off to see the new fun. In the melee, the copper's hands loosened, and, like a snake from under a rock, Kalina ducked under the blue arm and took off in the opposite direction.

Her only thought was to put distance between her and the police. Mrs. Cipriani, knowing her plight, would look in on Aunt Litka until she returned.

The Swamp Angels hid out from the police in the labyrinthine sewer pipes by the river. She would find her way there. In the spring, when torrential rains flooded the New York streets, a person could drown down there, but now, in the dead of winter, there would be but a thin layer of ice.

Somewhere in the inky maze of alleys near the river her shoe caught in a cellar grate and she fell headlong. She lay, momentarily stunned, but upon hearing shouts and whistles, darted up again. The crowds were thinner here, just a few people strolling by, bottles in their hands. The neighborhood consisted mainly of warehouses, all closed up tight for the holiday.

"Happy New Year." A vendor walked slowly behind his sway-backed horse. He tipped his snowy cap to her.

By the time Kalina reached the wide sewer opening, the sky was a curtain of white. The thick snow blanketed the dingy buildings and littered streets with a cleansing shroud. Shivering and sweating all at once, she slid gratefully inside the huge round pipe and leaned a long moment on the curving iron, adjusting her eyes to the gloom. The subterranean dark was relieved at intervals by the light that filtered through the street gratings. She had left the warm shawl in the copper's hands, and, now that she had stopped running, the icy damp pierced her to the bone. Vigorously, she began rubbing her cold hands together to restore the circulation, when something soft and furry brushed against her bare neck. Sharp claws dug into her shoulder.

A large, sleek rat fixed his beady eyes on hers.

With a shriek of purest terror, Kalina knocked the creature down and skittered along the slippery sewer bottom until she reached the river end. Between the end of the pipe and the riverfront lay a stretch of unevenly placed stones, all carpeted now with fresh snow. She picked her way across, gingerly, with downcast eyes, trying not to slip. There were lights on the wharf. Probably a saloon, but it would be warm inside.

She never saw the ragpicker's cart nor heard the driver's shout of "Look out" until she crashed into the wooden side. Her feet spun out from under her and she pitched headfirst. There was only the sharp crack of her head hitting the hard, wet stones, and the the snow, the night, the cart, all spiraled into blackness.

A strong, wonderfully gentle hand was cradling the back of her head, and a magnificent, bracing warmth coursed like a river through her frozen veins. Someone held a cup to her lips, a cup filled with a thick, golden liquid.

"Drink. C'mon. Another sip. Though, from the look of you, God knows, you're more starved than knocked out."

The hand circling the cup was brown and large and young. The brown came from a thick coating of freckles. Obediently, Kalina sipped, then jerked upward, choking and sputtering as the burning liquid seared her throat. The hand behind her head moved to her back and pressed forward gently but persistently until she was upright.

"C'mon, some more. Got to get the icicles out of your blood." The cup pushed against her lips so that she was forced to swallow. After three gulps, she pushed the cup away and a brown face came into view. Her eyes refused to focus and she closed them, fighting nausea.

"Brandy," she gasped. "It's brandy."

"The best, one hundred proof."

The hand on her back relaxed and Kalina sank backward until she rested on something soft like a feather mattress. In a moment the dizziness passed away, and she opened her eyes wide to gaze directly at her benefactor. The face was kind and broad and even more freckled than the hand. A wide mouth stretched into a full-lipped smile. A fire crackling behind her somewhere cast a reflected glow into eyes that were a deep, rich, comforting brown and were fringed by long, reddish lashes. More red hair sprang up in a feathery fuzz from the open-necked shirt. An orange-and-purple knitted cap was pulled down around his ears, cloaking what was bound to be a headful of thick hair of the same carroty hue.

"Well now, Miss," he said in mock politeness, "do you think you'll know me next time we meet?" The smile contracted into an equally mocking scowl. "Or are you maybe counting my freckles?"

That voice! She knew it, had heard it before. So deep, so kind. "I know you—" she broke off, the effort of speaking bringing an agonized pounding to her head. She moaned and tried to raise herself.

"Here now, back down. You've a nasty bump there. But no blood lost, praise the Lord. That bushel of hair you've got saved you, I guess."

"I'm Polish," she grunted. "We're all hard-headed."

But he was gone, out of her sight, talking fast and loud. "Don't move a muscle. Lie still. You'll have a hell of a headache for awhile. Now don't fall asleep on me. That's bad. I'll keep talking—"

Kalina lay quiet, enduring the pain, glorying in the heat from the unseen fire, liking the tingle of the brandy. She picked feebly at the scratchy wool blanket covering her, trying to reassure herself that she had not died and gone to heaven. On the ceiling, fat pipes radiated, spokelike, as from a furnace. They must be in the cellar of a warehouse or some other large building by the waterfront.

He was back. "I've got some soup, and some nice German Christmas bread loaded with as many nuts and raisins as I've got freckles."

He knelt beside her, holding in one hand a tin plate with several slices of cake, in the other a wooden bowl of steaming hot soup. Placing the plate on her blanketed belly, he steadied the bowl and started feeding her with a spoon.

She submitted meekly, as a child. Something in the boy—though the broad sweeping back and shoulders made him more a man—evoked memories of Hania, firelight, tea in the manor house. Must be Irish, she figured, with all that red hair and freckles. He exuded virility and ruddy health in stark contrast to the young men she knew like Joe Wagner and the Swamp Angels, who were for the most part as thin and brittle as graveyard wraiths.

There was the look and feel of the earth itself about this one. Like old Mashko—

Suddenly it came to her. "Max! You're Max!" She reared up, knocking the spoon from his hand. Soup spilled all over the blanket.

"Hey, don't do that!" Then, "Yeah, I'm Max. Been wondering how long it'd take before you remembered me." He swept off the cap and a torrent of red curls spilled out. They seemed to light up the cellar.

He laughed boisterously as a man does who is in love with life. "You're the little Polish girl who used to come begging for sugar and apples."

They chattered about Nick, the old man who used to sit in front of the stables, who had reminded her of Mashko. Kalina wolfed down a second bowl of soup and ate up all the cake.

"Nick died," Max told her, "and after that the place went downhill."

They were in a riverfront cigar factory, he told her, where he fired the furnace and cleaned out the ashes in exchange for a place to sleep and a dollar a week. He swung the mattress round so that she could see the furnace. The firebox was wide open and the pot of soup sat directly on the red-hot coals.

"Got to keep the fire going, even when there's nobody here," he said, "so's the pipes won't freeze up."

Max also worked the docks, picking up fruit, vegetables, and even meat that fell from barges and carts. Just as the kids on Mulberry Street picked up coal from the tracks. He had been out scavenging when she and the ragpicker's cart had collided.

An entire wall behind the furnace was lined with wooden cupboards, which in turn were packed with cans of beans and soup, loaves of bread, and tins of cake. Chip baskets of apples and potatoes sat in a corner. There was more food here than in Mrs. Konrad's grocery store on Mulberry Street. Kalina suspected that some of the food was "helped" in falling off the barges.

"You can't possibly eat it all yourself," she remarked. Her eyes were wide with wonder. She had never seen so much food in one place.

He laughed, reddening under the freckles. "Some I sell for cash. You don't pick up a bottle of brandy from a barge."

Max bent over the firebox, and Kalina caught her breath at the beauty of his rhythmic movements as he shoveled coal from a nearby pile. He had the natural grace of a young stallion. Banging the door shut, he washed his hands in a bucket and, walking to the chip baskets, picked up two red, shiny apples.

Kalina bit into the sweet-and-tart fruit, letting the juice run unheeded down her chin as a child does. Less than an hour ago, she'd almost been forced into unwanted, premature womanhood by the lustful butcher. Now, in this warm, cozy place with this gentle person, she wanted nothing more than to be the child she once had been.

Haltingly, she told Max about the robbery in the butcher shop and her narrow escape from jail. She did not tell him about her near rape, explaining her torn bodice as the result of her struggle with the police.

"Joe Wagner would rob his dying grandmother," was his laconic comment. "And kick her into the gutter to freeze to death."

"Do you belong to a gang?" she asked, wiping her chin with her sleeve.

The fiery head came up. "No! Max O'Hara's a lone wolf."

Kalina's headache was now a dull, not unpleasant throb. She tossed the blanket aside. "I must get back to Aunt Litka."

Max cast brown eyes at her torn bodice. "You can't walk the streets with your bosom hanging out."

Her face turned painfully red, and, quickly averting his gaze, he led her to a large wooden crate filled with a jumble of garments. Pulling them out, one at a time, he held them up for her inspection. She hid her surprise at the unexpected clothing store, figuring it came from the same place as the groceries. Thieving was a way of life in lower Manhattan; getting caught was the only crime.

While his back was turned to the furnace, Kalina slipped out of the Polish costume and into a white shirtwaist made of fine linen and a black, wool skirt that hugged her hips and flared out charmingly at the ankles. Noticing a cracked mirror on the side of a cupboard, she hastily braided her long hair, winding the amber beads in and out of the coils. She pulled the thick braid to the front, where it fell heavily across her breast.

"The skirt's too long," she mourned. "It'll drag in the snow."

"Never mind, just hold it up with one hand. Like this." Holding out a muscular arm, Max O'Hara flicked his hand stylishly downward, and, grabbing Kalina by the waist, he waltzed her round the cellar, a length of the long skirt held firmly between their clasped hands.

Kalina Olkonsky laughed as she had not laughed in years. She laughed so hard the tears ran down her cheeks. Her heart tripped like a hammer at the feel of his warm flesh on hers. She was in Jaslo again, Mashko's little blackbird, flying about the barnyard, free from care, radiant with health and dreams of the future.

Several more thrusts into the depths of the crate produced a lambskin hat and a long, dark-brown coat with black, silky fur on the collar and sleeves. Woolen gloves, marvelously warm and soft, completed her ensemble.

He stood back then and viewed his creation. She could be a "swell," he thought, one of the rich ladies whose pictures appeared in the papers. The proud, gleaming braid nestled in the soft wool of the coat, the furry cap caressed tiny, curving ear lobes. Her skin was like fine porcelain, and her black eyes were dancing with a kind of blue fire.

A man could drown in eyes like that, Max O'Hara thought, as the keen knife edge of desire stirred in his loins. At seventeen, the Irish-American street kid had known more than a few street women, some of them from Gotham Court where Kalina lived with her Aunt Litka. Some were younger than the Polish girl and fed their families with their bodies.

But, as Max gazed, enraptured, into the lustrous eyes of Kalina Olkonsky, he knew that she was not such a one. Innocence, pure and blinding, shone like a beacon from her face.

"Let's go down to Broadway and see the New Year in by the church," he said gruffly, clenching his fists to keep from pulling her to himself and covering her with kisses. "I'll take you home right after midnight, I promise." He pointed to an ancient brass clock ticking away on the cupboard above the mirror. "Just twenty minutes to go."

She brightened. "And I can bring home some food for Aunt Litka. Just as I started out to do." She watched as he donned a heavy ulster and cap. "But the coppers—" Her eyes were fearful.

"Ho! No cop's going to connect such a fine young lady with the Swamp Angels. Anyway, they'll have better things to do. On New Year's Eve, pickpockets will be as thick as flies on a dead horse."

The boy and girl ran down South Street to Pearl to Nassau, taking the middle of the streets where everybody else seemed to be. The only vehicles moving were the steel-track trolley cars. "We'll never make it in time," Kalina panted. Turning, Max swooped her up in his arms, hoisting her to his shoulders like a sack of potatoes. She gasped, clasping her gloved hands around his neck. Her face burned with embarrassment, but she quickly noticed that there were numerous piggy-backers, mostly children on their fathers' backs. She tried to forget about her black-stockinged legs sticking out, exposed to the knee. But she couldn't, any more than she could ignore the hard, warm clutch of Max's hands on her ankles.

Two full blocks from the church, the throng became so dense they were forced to stop. The snow had turned everything—buildings, people, lampposts—into a wonderland of white. Her gloved hands moved from his neck to his face, cupping his cheeks. "Put me down, Max," she begged. "We can see the clock from here."

He eased her to the ground, and they huddled close, his arm tight around her waist. A trolley ground to a halt and disgorged what seemed like a thousand merrymakers, all brandishing whistles, horns, and metal clappers that made an ear-splitting racket when shaken.

Max swore under his breath. "With all that noise, we'll never hear the chimes."

Someone handed Kalina a schooner of foaming beer. Yellow light streamed from a tavern festooned with holly and scarlet paper ribbons. She drank and handed the mug to Max, who took it, covering her hand with his as he raised the mug to his lips.

A portly man on Max's other side yelled, "My diamond stickpin's been hooked."

"Damn fool," muttered Max through beer-foamed lips. "Wearing jewelry in this thieving crowd."

But the man's cries were soon lost in the roar of the crowd as the gilded hands of the Trinity clock came together as one and the great, historic chimes rang out. Bells from countless steeples all over the teeming city between the rivers joined in the symphony. A tired, old nineteenth century sank into the grave of time; a new, glorious twentieth pushed out of the womb. The people thundered. Hoarse whistles sounded from tugs and steamers in the rivers, sirens wailed from the fireboats near the Battery.

As one voice, one throat, all sang out, "Should auld acquaintance be forgot," and "Happy New Year," and "Blessed New Century" sounded in a dozen languages.

Kalina Olkonsky, tears melting the snow on her cheeks, turned to the boy-man beside her, in whose arms she nestled. She lifted her lips for his kiss.

And when his flesh touched hers, it was as though the doors of Heaven itself had opened and flooded the earth with happiness.

Chapter Two

The snow had let up and in its place a clean, round, twentieth-century sun sailed proud and serene through the Manhattan heavens. The revelry had ceased, but for a faint remembrance echoing from the foghorns in the bay. Pealing church bells called the faithful of New York to early Mass.

Max and Kalina rounded the Hester Street bend and strode at a half-run up Mott to Mulberry, their crunching footsteps sounding in rhythm. The familiar streets were canyons of white behind whose walls the people slept into this holiday morning.

The girl took a firmer grip on the canvas bag of food swinging at her side. "Oh, Max, it's so late," she breathed, "I didn't mean to be gone all night."

"You deserved a night out. I'm sure your aunt will agree." He shifted his own huge bag of groceries from one shoulder to the other and reached for her free hand, giving it a quick squeeze through her thick glove. "That Italian woman downstairs knew the coppers were after you. She'll look in on your aunt. Stop fretting."

Giggling with relief at his reassurance, Kalina returned his squeeze. She sighed. "I feel just like Cinderella after the ball when Prince Charming came along and whisked her away from it all."

Max turned, his brown eyes puzzled. "Cinderella? Prince Charming? Who are they, people from Mulberry Street?"

She gaped in surprise. "Why—you know, the people in

34

the fairy story."

There was a silence, as Max dropped her hand and made a fuss about securing the knot on his bag. "I never heard a fairy story." He gave a short laugh to hide his embarrassment. "I never went to school and never learned how to read."

Hastily, she said, "I never went to school either, Max. Hardly anyone I know goes to regular school," She laughed too to keep him company. "If Aunt Litka hadn't drilled me and Zuska, I too would be illiterate."

But suddenly there was no more time to talk, for they had reached her tenement and were bounding up the rickety steps to the third floor. The girl's heart fairly sang as she pictured her aunt's sallow face brightening into a radiant smile when she saw the sausages and bread and cans and cans of soup and beans.

As she entered their little room, a clammy, penetrating cold chilled her face, flushed from running. Dropping her sack, Kalina ran immediately to the cot while Max lit the candle stub and walked to the cold grate, hoping to get a fire going. Since there was no fuel, he walked over to gaze down at the still form under the blood-stained blanket.

"See, what did I tell you? Sound asleep." He turned to the door. "I'll rustle up some wood, maybe a couple lumps of coal."

"No, wait." Her sharp cry brought him back. She bent low to peer into the still face, and a sickening, petrifying fear snaked into her belly. There was no movement, however slight, under the blanket. No up and down of breathing. Peeling off her gloves, she touched the marbled skin of Litka's cheek. "Bring the candle, Max," she said in a strangled voice.

But even before he held the tiny flame to the cold, blue lips, Kalina knew that no more words—nagging or kind—would emerge from Litka's mouth.

"Mama Hania," she cried in an agony of remorse that became an iron band across her heart. "Forgive your sinful daughter for killing your sister."

"You didn't kill her, silly girl. She died of the consump-

35

tion. Look at all the blood on her. She had a last enormous gusher of a hemorrhage."

Max straightened up to stand statuelike beside the sorrowful girl, racking his brain for remnants of childhood prayers. There had been few enough of such things in his rent-baby establishment. Years on the street had brought him face to face with death more often than he liked, but the tragedy, the awful finality of it, never failed to still his tongue and slow his heart for a moment or two.

Kalina was muttering in Polish, her fur-capped dark head resting on the unresponding breast of her dead Aunt Litka.

The door flew open and Mrs. Cipriani hurried in, reeking of stale beer, a soiled wrapper covering her ample form. "How is the little one, *caro*? I t'ink she sleep all night. I come in, couple times, but she all the time quiet—"

The woman halted as Kalina raised her grief-ravaged faced and turned it around. Emitting a doglike howl, Mrs. Cipriani sank into the sewing chair and whipped out a black rosary from the depths of the wrapper. At the window, Max stared stonily at the street. A sweet-potato vendor pushed his cart hopefully through the deserted street. A man stumbled out of the saloon where he had apparently slept the night. Life goes on, he thought, in the midst of death.

He had no words for Kalina. Time, not words, would heal. Time—and with luck—some love to go with it.

In a while, blessedly, Mrs. Cipriani took her weeping person downstairs, and Kalina rose from her knees. She was calmer now and proceeded to do what needed to be done. Aunt Litka had drilled her in it. There was a ritual. First, a long, thick lock of the departed's hair, snipped off neatly with clean scissors, must be wrapped in white linen and tied with black ribbon.

Zuska would have it in time, Kalina thought, as she laid the hair in the drawer. Provided she could be found. The amber beads, which had been in the family for generations, would also go to her cousin.

"She must be washed and dressed," she told Max,

tonelessly. "Please fetch the Polish costume from the cigar factory where I left it last night."

He shrugged into his coat. "Don't send for the death wagon till I come back. The police will stick her in a sack and throw her in a pauper's field trench." He kissed her lightly on the cheek. "I might be able to get her a decent coffin. That's the least."

When he had gone, Kalina fetched some water from the spigot on the landing and commenced with her sad duties of bathing and combing and fixing the stiffening limbs in graceful gestures. At the end, she took the wooden crucifix from the wall and placed it between the stiffening hands.

As it turned out, her new friend Max O'Hara provided more than a decent coffin for the beloved dead. With the magical ease with which he had produced the wonderful clothing and the food which her aunt never tasted, he showed up two hours later with a mortician and a shiny pine coffin sporting not only brass handles but angels painted on the inside of the lid. There would even be a priest to pray at the graveside, he promised, though his cash did not extend to a funeral Mass and flowers.

"Besides," he whispered, as they huddled over a new-laid fire while the mortician filled out official papers and arranged the body in the shrouded coffin, "the cops are still after you. Best bury your dead and get out of here. Fast."

Five o'clock saw them riding in a covered black hearse barouche pulled by two black horses. Shiny harness bells cleared the traffic, now thick in the ice-rutted streets. The Polish immigrant girl, on this her first time outside lower Manhattan, pressed her face against the little round window and gaped in wonder and astonishment. The rows and rows of neat brick houses entranced her. Each had its own square of snowy lawn, which Max assured her was a lovely green in summer. Iron fences, some intricately carved, guarded the sanctity of these homes, while happy, well-fed children stopped their play at the sight of the hearse, standing in respectful silence for the dead. Many crossed themselves piously, murmuring prayers for the poor dead soul passing by.

"So this is the *real* America!" exclaimed Kalina, turning to Max, who sat at her side, dressed like herself in sober black, which he had scrounged along with her clothes from the endless crates in his cellar. She sighed, "If only Aunt Litka could see it."

"Maybe she can," said Max, laughing, "a woman as good as she was must be up in Heaven by now, looking down." Then, "This is nothing, only Brooklyn. Wait till you see the cemetery."

"Why are you doing all this for me, Mr. O'Hara? you hardly know me."

Her question caught him unguarded, and now it was his turn to stare out the window. To his consternation, he found his eyes were brimming. "I'm not doing it for you at all. Or even for your Aunt Litka. I never knew my own ma, don't know if she's dead or alive, or even if she ever had a funeral."

With a quick movement, he buried his red head on her shoulder, abandoning himself to a long-buried grief.

Touched, Kalina caught his face in her two hands and lifted it for her kiss. She would ask no more questions. Now. There would be a lifetime for questions. Somehow, she knew that she and Max had set their feet together on a road that would go on forever.

Feathery snow filled the air as they turned into the pretty cemetery on Brooklyn's outskirts. Kalina's heart leaped at sight of the name carved on the wrought-iron gate. "St. Casimir, Patron Saint of Poland." In truth, the curving hills and arching trees, whose bare limbs bore the promise of green, could be in Litka's native land. As they walked to the vault where the body would be interred until the frozen ground could be worked, quick glances at passing tombs revealed good Polish names. Dmowski, Pilsudski, Mosicki.

Aunt Litka would not be lonely.

Max figured it would take at least three days to dispose

of his worldly goods and suggested that Kalina stay in the cellar with him during that time. Meeting her was just the push he needed, he assured her, to get him out of congested, poverty-ridden New York City where the vast majority of immigrants stopped their journey.

"Many never get up the guts to go into the richly laden, golden American West," he said.

"You mean we're going to California?" she asked, wide-eyed with excitement.

His quick, spontaneous laugh rumbled through the cellar. "No, silly, at least not for a few years. Pennsylvania. The steel mills in the state just below New York on the map belch out an awful lot of money along with all that smoke and soot. A man with muscle who doesn't mind working hard can make good money in places like Pittsburgh. Andrew Carnegie did."

"Andrew Carnegie?" she echoed, puzzled.

It was his turn to tell her a story she hadn't heard, one that he had heard on the street. Andrew Carnegie, he said, was a poor Scottish immigrant lad, who at fourteen was a runner in a bobbin factory but now, fifty years later, had become the richest, most powerful man in all America.

"The little guy was a shortie, only five-four, but he outsmarted men twice his size and amassed enough money to buy out railroads, iron foundries, and finally entire steel mills. He owns nearly all the steel in the country." Max's brown eyes shone with a kind of worship. "And now he's selling out so he can retire to a castle in Scotland, where he'll spend the rest of his life giving his money to the poor."

He had picked up all this information, he told an engrossed Kalina, from Wall Street where all the rich stockbrokers hung out.

"Sounds like the real America to me," Kalina said thoughtfully, "the one Aunt Litka was always talking about. But for a woman, she always told us, the best way is to marry rich and become a fine lady without working so hard."

In her turn, Kalina finished the story of Cinderella she started as they had walked home on New Year's Day in the snow. "She was despised but beautiful and sat in the ashes in ragged clothes until a fairy godmother came along and magically transformed her into a princess because she had been so good. She went to a ball and there she met Prince Charming, who fell immediately in love with her. And they lived happily ever after."

Kalina's slim body was enveloped in an oversize but warm flannel nightgown, and her thick black hair fell in disarray around her beautiful face. Impulsively, Max grabbed two fistfuls of the silky mass, but he could not utter the words that trembled on his tongue.

He said, merely, "I'll be rich one day, Kalina. Wait for me."

He kissed the feathery tips of her unbraided hair and she froze, hardly daring to breathe. She must not betray by the slightest movement that she shared his desire. In her own excitement, she yearned now to belong to this man. Not in some distant, uncertain future, but now, tonight. Each night he tucked her into the blankets on the feather mattress, and kissed her briefly on the lips as one does with a sleepy child. Then he hied himself off to his own mattress in a far corner of the cellar.

At sixteen Kalina Olkonsky from Mulberry Street was more woman than girl, and she knew in her heart that the time would come when she could yield her long-cherished "jewel of the poor" to Max O'Hara.

It was the third day in January and Kalina struggled to keep up with Max's stride as they hurried through the slushy streets. They were headed up Seventh Avenue toward the railroad station. A cruel wind from the river made her nose run.

"Can't we stop until I blow my nose?" she pleaded, snuffling.

"No," he said sternly. "Anyway, if you're to be my little brother, a runny nose looks all the better. All little brothers have runny noses."

Long, baggy trousers dragged below Kalina's battered

shoes, and a fringy scarf held a knitted cap down over her ears, hiding every scrap of hair. There was nothing to indicate that Kalina Olkonsky was not Karl O'Hara, which was what Max had christened her that morning, playfully sprinkling tap water on her head as he intoned Latin gibberish. Though scandalized at the blasphemy, the girl had taken it all meekly enough. For a horrible moment, though, she feared he would cut off her hair.

The disguise made good sense. Pretty young girls, so Max affirmed, placed their virtue, and their lives as well, in mortal danger when venturing out on public conveyances.

"The railroad cars are the worst," he finished, darkly.

Upon her expressed doubt that the railroad surely wouldn't be so careless with their female passengers and that surely there were uniformed conductors everywhere on the trains, Max grew angry. "Don't ask so many questions. Trust me."

Kalina sighed, willing to put her fate into his hands. In a matter of days they would be in the wide open spaces of Pennsylvania where a man and a woman could breathe the clean, fresh air of the real America.

The vast terminal swarmed with travelers, all intent on private journeys of their own. The interior of the place looked like a cathedral. Elaborate murals glorified the steep walls and the domed ceiling, chandeliers blazed with real electric globes that cast an ethereal light on magnificent stained-glass windows.

But there was no time to savor the beauty, for with a glance at the enormous clock high on the arched concourse, Max pushed her through a door marked Freight, and they were running along an endless line of boxcars strung together. Many of the cars were slatted, and Kalina saw cattle packed like fish in a can, lowing softly at their imprisonment. The flat, unwalled cars held long bars of steel or rounded iron pipes.

"Max," she spluttered, confused, "the coaches for the passengers are back there in the station."

"That's not for us." He yanked her, cruelly, by the arm.

41

"We're riding the rails."

"Rails?"

"Yeah, little brother, we're off to Pennsylvania in a boxcar. Now shut up and act dumb like I told you."

Dumb. She was to pretend she couldn't talk. Presently, he was lifting her into an empty boxcar spread with straw and smelling powerfully of manure. Max beamed. "Perfect. Now, don't forget, you never spoke a word in your life. You're a mute from birth."

In seconds, Kalina was under the straw, choking on the ammoniac smell of animal urine. She wondered why they had to ride this way, maybe Max didn't get as much money from his hoard as he had hoped. Maybe he'd spent it all on Litka's funeral. But no matter. She was rid of Mulberry Street and knee pants and on her way to places where rich and handsome men awaited her. Steel mills were not sweatshops, Max assured her. Andy Carnegie got rich, so could they.

A whistle sounded, a series of bells tinkled, there was a lurch. The intense emotional pitch of the last few days spiraled down inside her body. But the train wheels made a soporific click-click, and Max began to snore, so Kalina burrowed into the straw and fell asleep.

Another lurch brought her awake in the dark. A bar of pale moonlight filled the open door. It was very cold, and despite her bulky coat, Kalina shivered. How soon would they come to Pennsylvania? Her nose began to twitch and she sneezed, once, twice, a third time.

"Jesus!"

Max started up with an oath. A brawny arm struck her cheek so hard she yelled "Ouch." He clapped a hand on her mouth and pressed cruelly for a long minute.

"Okay," he breathed, finally letting go. "But don't do that again. Sometimes the dicks walk on the roofs listening for bums."

"Bums?" There were so many English words Aunt Litka never taught her.

"Sure. Vagabonds, tramps, drifters." His voice lost its hardness and he bent over to her face. "Sorry I hit you, kid, but we don't want to be turned out in the middle of nowhere."

The moonlight revealed brown eyes in which Kalina saw only love and tenderness. She pressed all five of his fingers against her lips, kissing the tip of each. Cursing, he tore his hand from hers, and then he was kissing her on the mouth, this time not the sweet touch one gives a child but a hard, sensual man-to-woman meeting of flesh.

They sank deep into the odorous straw and his lips darted to her eyes, her cheeks, her nose, her forehead—any part of her that was not covered by her coat. She locked her hands together behind his neck, willing him to go on, pressing herself against him.

But springing to his feet, he hurled himself into the open door, clutching both sides to keep from falling out the moving train. He sobbed as if in pain. "Kalina, I'm a beast, I didn't mean—"

"Please," she murmured. "I want it too, Max."

Her blood was singing, every nerve in her body was alive. This was love. Virginity was a poor, barren thing in the face of this vital, clamorous need. All the rich and handsome men in Pennsylvania were not for her. "Wait for me," Max had said. One day he too would be rich.

When she spoke, her voice was clear and firm. "Max, dearest, I want you too. All the way."

The light vanished as the train went into a tunnel. She heard the straw rustling at her side, and then he was upon her, feverishly digging her out of the straw, unbuttoning her bulky coat. Then his hands were on her breasts, and she was arching to him as women have done since time began.

All was silence but for the steady clicking of the train. The marvel of touching, she thought. It was nothing like anything she had ever imagined. Such joy could never be put into words. His body joined hers, and Kalina forgot about her "jewel of the poor."

She now possessed a jewel of incomparably more worth. Love.

At last, the consummation done, they fell asleep in each

other's arms.

Frigid sunlight streamed through the door when Kalina opened her eyes. The clicking had stopped; instead there was a grinding noise, then nothing. "Max." She poked him awake. "We've stopped. Maybe we're in Pennsylvania."

Alert as a forest animal, he bounded to the door.

"Must be a town," he said. "Looks like a water tower up ahead." He paused and, in the long silence that followed, she realized that he could not read the name on the tower. Pulling her coat tight about her, she scrambled to his side.

"Av-e-lon-i-a." She sounded out the syllables. "What a pretty name." She linked her arm to his, wrinkling her nose. "What's that awful smell?"

He sniffed. "Coal. That means we're in mining country. That means Pennsylvania."

The train lurched ahead, and, clutching the side of the car to keep from falling, the travelers gazed wonderingly as a tall, skeletal structure materialized out of the murk. Behind it three long rows of shacks, all a uniform dirty gray, straggled up the hillside like tired chicks after a mother hen. Except for the single window and the stick of chimney poking into the sky, they looked exactly, Kalina thought, like the cowsheds on Pan Mikolai's estate. The foothills of a brownish mountain range spotted with snow surrounded the town, imprisoning it in a dismal valley.

"Cheez-it, the dicks." Max shoved her brutally to the floor where they drew the straw over their heads and bodies.

A moment later there was a tremendous banging on the side of the car and a loud voice yelled, "I know you're in there, you tramps."

Max hauled the two of them up, and Kalina whimpered dutifully, trying to sound like a mute.

"We're going, we're going. Please don't hurt my little brother." Max scuttled into the doorway.

A big, swarthy man with a broad peasant face stood looking up at them. He looks Polish, Kalina thought suddenly. High cheekbones, long nose, little bump high on the bridge.

44

The dick grabbed Max by the leg. "Hold on there, kid. You two look pretty young to be riding the rails." He jerked on the leg, and Max pitched headfirst, letting go of Kalina.

Kalina lost her fright. The dick was Polish, no mistaking that accent. She must talk to the man, explain their plight. He would understand. But before she could utter a word, Max yanked her out, and she was tumbling after him down the steep embankment to the dirt road. The head scarf came loose, spilling out her hair. Blood from a cut lip filled her mouth and then she was running with Max along the frozen roadway past the skeletal building and rows of houses into a leafless apple orchard with gnarled branches. She quickly repaired the damage to her disguise, stuffing her hair with difficulty back under the cap.

"Whew!" Max exploded. "That was close! But he won't come after us. They've got a schedule to keep. They're loading up with coal here."

"Would we go to jail if they caught us?"

He laughed drily. "Hardly. They'd knock me about to teach me a lesson, but you—" He rolled his eyes. "I heard about a girl once who was caught in a boxcar. You don't want to hear about it."

They resumed their journey on foot, tramping westward by the sun when they caught it between the clouds and drizzle. More mining patches lay ahead, Max said, more rail stops. They would hop another freight bound for Pittsburgh. Luckily, the wind had stilled, but the freezing drizzle ultimately penetrated their layers of clothing and they sought shelter among the stiff stalks of weeds by a river that meandered at the base of the hills. Once again Kalina was struck by the resemblance to her native Poland and reflected that, though she loved America deeply, there would always be a place in her heart for her native land. She would never forget Poland, no more than a mother puts aside a child who has gone from her.

"I'm thirsty," she said and leaned over to drink from the sluggish, ice-choked river that looked exactly like the Wistoka this time of year. She quickly spat the water out in disgust.

"Sulphur," laughed Max. "From the coal deposits."

He pulled the brandy from his pocket and allowed her two swallows, but while it warmed her, it did not alleviate her raging thirst. So it was with enormous relief that she glimpsed another tall building emerging in the rain a mile or two up the tracks. By the time they reached the patch, a soggy dusk had settled on the gently swelling hills. She squinted to make out the lettering on the side of the building, which was a twin of the one in Avelonia.

Such long, poetic names, she thought wryly, for such ugly places. Stumbling ahead of Max, she spelled out "Shen-an-do-ah. Shenandoah Anthracite." Her heart stopped, and she read the sign again. It couldn't be! It was too wonderful to be happening! Surely she was only dreaming.

But it was! Max, and fate—and maybe the Virgin had a hand in it—had carried her to the very town from which Zuska had sent the postal card. Could there be two such towns with the beautiful name in Pennsylvania? She raced back to Max, who slumped, exhausted, against a tree, hitting his cold face with his bare hands in an effort to restore circulation.

She had never told him about Zuska, there had been so many things to talk about in the first, wonderful days together. Now he said, teasing, "Well, if she's half as pretty as you, I can't wait to meet her."

Max rubbed Kalina's cheeks against his own, which were hot and glowing from his self-administered massage. "C'mon, there's sure to be a saloon, no matter how small, in this Shenandoah. And where there's a saloon, there's a fire and something to eat."

Hope restoring their strength, they ran hand in hand toward the flickering lights of the town. Max panted, "How do you know she's still here? Maybe she's run off again."

Kalina did not reply, she was busy praying.

As they came closer, a noise like hell itself assaulted their ears, jolting the night with a pounding, jangling, grinding

46

clamor.

"Jesus," Max swore, "it's enough to wake the dead."

"Guess you get used to it," replied Kalina, not wanting to betray her own anxiety about coal mining. Here, she thought sadly, they were not likely to find the fabled streets of gold of the real America.

Close up, however, the place looked more inviting. Each tiny, uncurtained window framed a cozy, domestic scene. Kerosene lamps stood on oilcloth-covered tables, bulky shapes moved about inside. Women leaned over stoves where pots of succulent stews and soups simmered. Or so Kalina imagined in her desperate longing to see people once again, to be inside, toasting before a fire.

Midway in the first row of houses, on the near side of the noisy coal building, a woman was taking clothes off a line strung across the square of yard. Running forward, Kalina called out politely, "Good evening, Madam."

The woman looked up, her face in shadow, but there was no answering greeting, nor did she stop her work. Kalina leaned against the wooden fence separating the yard from the road and, on instinct, repeated her greeting in Polish.

"Dobre Vechyr."

This time the woman strode to the fence and replied, pleasantly, *"Dobre, dobre."*

Words spilled out as Kalina asked about Zuska. "A yellow-haired, girl, Polish, very pretty. I'm her cousin and have come all the way from New York to visit her."

The moon shifted from behind a cloud and Kalina saw the woman's face break into a wide, knowing smile. "Ho, that one!" Bending over the fence, she peered at Kalina, surveying her from head to foot. "Cousin, huh?" A short, dry laugh. "Looks like she rob the cradle."

With that, the Shenandoah woman, still chuckling, picked up her overflowing clothes basket and walked rapidly toward the house. With a cry of chagrin, Kalina suddenly remembered her masculine disguise.

As Max had promised, there was a saloon, distinguished from the other houses by its window, which was larger, and curtained heavily in green. The warm, crowded place also

47

sported bare electric globes in the ceiling. Unlike the Polish woman, the saloonkeeper was more than willing to talk of Zuska. "Yeah, you betcha I know her." He winked broadly. "Better ask, who doesn't know Zuska?"

He jerked a fat thumb behind him. "Third house from the end, Apple Blossom Lane. Second street up the hill."

"Apple Blossom Lane," hooted Max, as they started out the door. "Takes more than a pretty name to make a pretty place."

They found it easily enough, and the splintery door was opened by a tall, plump woman swathed in a dark-blue, very dirty wrapper. Not a trace of hair was visible under the tightly knotted babushka. Steely blue eyes raked the ragged-looking two on the wooden steps.

"Yah?" She said tiredly, and her eyes narrowed in contempt. She started to close the door. "No handouts. God knows I got barely enough—"

She got no further, for, at the sound of the voice she knew as well as her own, Kalina hurled herself against the soft bosom, desperately tearing off the concealing boy's cap and shaking loose her abundant black hair and crying out, "Zuska!"

Zuska wrapped her plump arms convulsively around the slim form in sopping wet clothes while at the same time she clutched a handful of glossy hair. After a frozen moment, Zuska shrieked, "Kalina, is it you? My little cousin, my dear little cousin, I never thought to see you in this world again."

Max had slithered past the two swaying, weeping girls and was already in the steamy kitchen, his booted feet planted wide before the blazing coal stove. "Do that inside," he yelled, and, laughing through the tears, Zuska shut the door and sat Kalina down in a wooden chair where she continued to weep, her head in her hands. But Zuska, ever the practical one, collected cups, spoons, sugar from the cupboard and, raising the window, reached into the box nailed outside to the sill for a mug of heavy cream. She poured three cups of coffee from a grease-blackened pot.

"Sit, sit," she called to Max, "You look ready to drop." Then, to her cousin, she said, "And you could be a chicken caught in a blizzard, skin and bones."

And you, who was once a ripe peach, look more like a pig ready for the slaughter. The words danced on Kalina's tongue, but instead she said, "This is Max O'Hara. We're on our way to Pittsburgh to get rich in the steel mills."

As if suddenly becoming aware of the masculine presence in her little house, Zuska tore off her kerchief and ran her fingers through golden hair piled in a careless heap on top of her shapely head. Grabbing Max's cold hand, she pumped it up and down in a vigorous American handshake. "O'Hara, is it?" She flashed the old, seductive smile. "I like Irishmen."

Her old, hearty laugh burst out. "But I'll respect Kalina's squatter's rights."

"You haven't changed," Kalina laughed in response to the banter. "Always the flirt." Then, shoving back the chair, she bent over the stove, shivering. "Zuska, I'm soaked. Do you have something I can wear?"

The bedroom was even smaller than the kitchen, with a slit of a window set smack in the middle of the back wall. Not much furniture, a sagging bed with chipped brass railings, a tall chifforobe, a low table, kerosene lamp. A hammock hung from hooks in the ceiling. Zuska turned up the lamp.

"The tipple and the saloon get electric lights," she said. "The rest of us in the company houses have to use oil."

"The tipple?"

"The big, gray building. You passed it. That's where the mined coal is sorted and loaded into boxcars."

So that was the noise; coal made an awful racket. Kalina found herself hoping that steel-making would be quieter.

Zuska slipped back into the kitchen, which was separated from the bedroom by a curtain. Kalina lost no time in slipping out of her wet garments and into one of her cousin's frocks. It proved to be too long, for her cousin was

49

inches taller, and fit her like a tent, but she hiked it up with a ribbon from the chifforobe. Further rummaging yielded woolen undergarments and several petticoats. Standing in front of the dusty mirror—everything in the room was clouded with a thick layer of coal soot—she brushed her hair with Zuska's brush and, pulling it back from her face, secured it with a bit of ribbon from the drawer that held nothing but ribbons and other fripperies. She'd braid her hair later; right now the aroma of food cooking was maddening to her famished stomach.

Her hand was on the dividing curtain when a sharp cry from the hammock brought her tearing over to peek inside at what looked at first like a bundle of rags but proved to be a child with a luxuriant topknot of dark-brown hair. She caught her breath. In the excitement at finding her long-lost cousin, she had completely forgotten the expected baby.

Lovely, soft, brown eyes gazed soberly back at the stranger. "Oh, you darling, you sweet, sweet darling," breathed Kalina. Scooping up the blanketed bundle into her arms, she dashed into the kitchen.

Zuska's pretty face darkened with annoyance. "Oh, damn. You woke her up."

"She's adorable," Kalina said, neglecting to add that her cousin had failed to tell her the child was in the bedroom. She sat down to a plate of fried potatoes and ham and eggs, cuddling the child against her body. "What's her name?"

"Dunia. My little remembrance." The mother's laugh was bitter. "Put her down, for God's sake, she can walk."

"No, I'll hold her while I eat." She liked the feel of the tiny body against her heart.

The child was still groggy from sleep and dug into Kalina's chest. Max cast an oblique glance at the child but said nothing and continued to eat voraciously. Zuska chattered like a blackbird while keeping the plates of her guests filled. Dunia was all that was left of her dream of love and riches promised by that no-good son of a bitch, Victor, she explained in an almost offhand manner. Her lover had lasted three months in the mine. One night he didn't come home.

"Took all the cash in the house, too, the bastard," she said, still in that cool, calm voice.

Kalina wondered if she could take such tragedy with the equanimity shown by her cousin. She hugged the child. "She's beautiful. Can she talk?"

"Sure. Mostly Italian though. I leave her with a family from Italy downstreet while I work. A woman with ten kids of her own, one more makes little difference."

"Like Mrs. Cipriani," Kalina murmured. She smoothed Dunia's thick, glossy hair. "She reminds me of Mama."

Unexpectedly, a look of naked pain made Zuska's blue eyes almost black. She bent her head to pour some coffee. "No, your mother Hania's hair was more like roasted chestnuts or that horse we all used to ride." Zuska cleared her throat before continuing. "Hania's hair was lighter, sunnier. But then in Poland there seemed to be a lot more sun." She threw back her head. "Any place is sunnier than this hellhole of a Shenandoah."

The anguish of homesickness in her cousin's voice sent a pang through Kalina's heart. She reminded herself that Zuska was only eighteen, her childhood was not that long ago. I must tell her that her own mother is dead, she thought with dread. She held a bit of bread to Dunia's mouth. The child bit into it, still grave and unsmiling.

Max, who had remained silent, wiped his plate with a chunk of store-bought bread, and rose, knocking over his chair in his haste. Picking it up, he said gruffly, "Think I'll mosey on down to the saloon while you two catch up on woman talk." He pecked at Kalina's cheek. "Don't wait up."

When he had gone, after refusing Zuska's offer of Victor's dry clothes, Zuska fetched a tin of cigarettes from the cupboard and lit up. She extended the tin to Kalina, who shook her head. Her cousin had developed the habit of smoking years ago when they were rolling cigars.

"So you finally left the old bitch, too," she remarked, through a cloud of smoke.

Kalina jerked her head up, awakening Dunia, who had fallen back to sleep. "Zuska, your mother's dead."

Dousing the cigarette into her coffee cup, Zuska replied smoothly, "Well, she's well out of it. This America is hell." The full lips trembled, and despite her seeming callousness, two shiny globes of tears slid down the full cheeks. She crossed herself in the Catholic way and bent her golden head to the table. Kalina talked softly about the elegant funeral in the Polish Catholic cemetery in Brooklyn and, setting Dunia on the floor by the stove, went into the bedroom to get the amber beads and the lock of Litka's hair.

Holding the gold-yellow beads to the lamplight, Zuska rippled them through her fingers. "Pretty," she said, "they should bring a good price in Pottsville."

The lock of her mother's hair she threw into the fire, where it sizzled for a moment, emitting a rancid smell. Then, returning to the table, she grasped Kalina by both shoulders. "Shocked, little cousin? Well, let me tell you, a few months in this back end of hell and you'll be surprised at nothing."

She stooped to pick up her child, thrust her back into a speechless Kalina's arms. "Try feeding this with beads."

"Oh, Zuska darling, don't talk like that." Kalina burst out at last, searching desperately for words to assuage her cousin's suffering. But she could only press Dunia's warm body to her own, in a small attempt to appease her own.

The rocking chair made tiny, cricketlike sounds on the worn linoleum. Dunia had been fast asleep for some time, but Kalina was reluctant to rise and carry her into the bedroom where Zuska was dressing. She'd been in there an awfully long time, Kalina reflected, she might be weeping or—hopefully—praying. But just as Kalina's own heavy lids were closing, her cousin reappeared, no longer the blowsy, tired, morose individual who had opened the door to her and Max. Elaborately gowned in scarlet wool trimmed in brown velvet, her magnificent hair wound into a triple coronet of braid, she was a curious blend of queenly majesty and sensuality. Heavy scent overpowered the lingering odor of ham and coffee.

The suspicions aroused by the woman in the yard and the saloonkeeper's leers were confirmed. Zuska Olkonsky was a lady of the night.

Even her cupid's bow lips, which needed nothing more to make them seductive, bore a heavy layer of rouge.

Without a glance at the sleeping Dunia, Zuska was at the door, shrugging into a black, woolen shawl.

"You and Max can have the bed," she said crisply. "I'll curl up in the kitchen on two chairs."

Kalina smiled. They had slept that way on Mulberry Street, giving the cot to Litka.

Zuska opened the door, then, hesitating, closed it again. She came back into the room, stood over the rocking chair like a witch in her black shawl. She whispered urgently, "There's no going back, little cousin, to Poland or anywhere. Even Mulberry Street will seem like heaven after a couple days in this dump. You can't still think that it's going to be as your mama and my mama said. We'll never be great ladies, you and I."

Then, like Max, she went out into the sooty dark, leaving Kalina alone with Dunia and her thoughts.

Utterly weary, Kalina threw a few lumps on the fire, found some napkins and changed the baby, and put her back into the hammock. Then she sat down in the kitchen to wait for Max. Dunia she did not expect till morning after her "workday" was over.

Deliberately, she banished ugly thoughts of Zuska and what she was doing. Her blood warmed at thoughts of Max and herself in the big bed. Their love-making in the boxcar had been hasty, they had both been hampered by heavy clothing. There had been no time for discovery, for leisurely kisses, all the things Kalina had imagined were involved in the marriage act. All that would come with time. She smiled expectantly. A few beers, some talk with the men, and her Max would rush back to her embrace. All that silly talk from Zuska about America not being the

53

heaven they'd all expected failed to depress her. Poor thing. No wonder she felt that way. Her man had abandoned her, forcing her into a dissolute life.

But Max would never leave his Kalina. He was no charming fly-by-night vendor. He was Max O'Hara, the kindest, sweetest, dearest man in all the world. He had proved himself.

A rush of cold air awakened her to Max's kiss. He reeked of beer and cigar smoke. "Max," she murmured, "Zuska says we can have her bed."

"I know," he mumbled, "I saw her at the saloon."

Carefully, Max banked the fire with cold ashes, then they slipped behind the curtain, and in less time than it takes to tell, were under Zuska's heavy quilts. The sheets smelled of being long unwashed, and the mattress sagged in the middle, but it was soft and comfortable. Kalina had found a flannel gown in the chifforobe, and Max slept in his underwear. They lay close, like a married couple, warming up, neither speaking. Finally, as if on cue, Max's arms tightened, and he lifted her face to his. His long, hard legs twined round her buttocks, drawing her close.

Kalina lifted the nightgown to circle her neck, then she tore the flannel over her head. Her body was bare and warm as toast. Unlike the first hurried coupling, this time brought no pain, only joy. The experienced Max was wonderfully gentle, knowing instinctively how to arouse his partner's virgin passions. Zuska and her Victor, Kalina thought sadly when she lay spent in her lover's arms, had never known love like this—sweet and whole and giving. That was the answer to it all.

The oil lamp flickered, then went out. The icy drizzle beat little tattoos on the window and the tin roof. Slipping out of Max's tight arms, Kalina bent over the hammock, satisfying herself that the child slept untroubled. Back in bed, she turned to Max, who had awakened.

"Max O'Hara," she said, "an odd combination of names. Max is German, O'Hara Irish. Which are you?"

He spoke into her neck, his words muffled, and she felt a pressure of his arms under her back. "Dunno. Irish, I think. Red hair and freckles could mean nothing else. A family called Schultz called me Max and then tacked on the O'Hara so's folks wouldn't think I belonged to them."

Astonished, she pulled back to look into his face although it was so dark she couldn't make out his expression. "Your parents, though, what were they?"

Almost angrily, he threw back the quilts and sat up, bending his head down between his raised knees as though preparing to weep. "I told you I don't know. I was a rent baby, left with a Dutchie family long before I could walk or talk. There was a little money from the folks who left me, but it ran out pretty fast, and then nobody ever came back for me."

"Oh, Max!" It was a cry of purest sympathy. Not to know your own mother, your own father. She reached out consoling arms.

But he pulled away. "Don't pity me. It made me strong. I was better off, I think. Most kids are sent out to work when they're eight or so to support their parents and a raft of brothers and sisters. I had only myself to worry about." Relenting, he pulled her to him once again, and they sat side by side on the mattress. "No sick Aunt Litka, no two-timing cousin Zuska."

"But now you have me," she muttered into his ear, but he seemed not to hear, for he raced on with a story common enough to crowded New York's immigrant sections. At nine, the Schultzes had put him to work over an ironing board, making slippers, but he had run off within weeks, preferring to live by his wits in the streets and sewers.

Kalina laughed, though her heart ached for the homeless lad he had been. "There must be more kids underneath New York than on top of it living in houses. Street Arabs, Aunt Litka called them, warning us to stay away from all of them."

She paused, then whispered, "All that stuff in the cellar was stolen, wasn't it?"

"Uh-huh."

He had fallen back on the pillow and pulled her back beneath the quilts. Little kisses rained on her face and neck and shoulders. Kalina gave herself up willingly to the fresh onslaught of passion until a vagrant thought caused her to pull away. "Max," she hissed, "all that money for the funeral. Where did it come from?"

The kisses continued, punctuated with words. "Remember the fatty on New Year's Eve who was yelling about his diamond stickpin? He was right to scream because it was valuable enough to buy a mighty fancy funeral."

There was no time for Kalina to absorb this shocking news, for his mouth was now hard on hers, his whole body was hard and demanding. She would think about it some other time, some time when her body wasn't all hot and pulsing.

Chapter Three

Pennsylvania, 1901

A painful jab in her soft buttock brought Kalina sharply awake. A gritty dawn outlined the window, casting a gray pall over the bedroom. She had dreamed of lying in a snowbank, but every time she had tried to lift herself from the cold, a swarthy railroad dick with a club shoved her back down with a hideous laugh.

Zuska stood over the bed, a broad smile on her freshly washed face. She is still so pretty, Kalina thought. Her long, yellow hair fell carelessly around her shoulders. She suddenly burst into song.

"Lover, lover, gone with the morn. Lover, Lover, where have you gone . . ."

It was a ditty from their village, sung by children at their games. Kalina whipped round, her hand flying out to touch an empty pillow, which still bore the indentation of her lover's head. Dunia was wailing lustily from her hammock.

"Get up, lazybones," Zuska yelled, grabbing Dunia and heading for the kitchen. "You can hold the kid while I stir up the fire."

Later, holding the cup of warm milk to Dunia's lips, Kalina said crossly, "Max got up early, before dawn even, to see about work at the mine. He mentioned it last night."

A hearty, derisive laugh from Zuska. "Yeah, sure. 'Gone with the morn, my lover has gone.' " Her cousin sang the maddening words while she moved briskly round the

57

kitchen, pumping water at the sink, brewing coffee, opening and closing the cupboard doors. Kalina longed to get up and slap the laughing face, but from past experience, knew that it would only encourage the teasing. She would sing the louder for it.

Of course Max had not deserted her. Zuska would laugh out the other side of her mouth when he came in that door. Finally, she burst out sharply, "You must think all men are rats like your famous Victor."

A whoop from the stove was followed by, "Ho, Kalina darling, at least my man stuck with me for three whole months. Your Irishman or Dutchman, whatever he is, just took time enough to fill your belly."

She glanced at Kalina's stomach, half-hidden by Dunia's body, and went into a paroxysm of laughter.

Kalina's face flamed. "What nonsense! We've only been together a couple times."

"You goose. It takes only once, believe me. Just one cockeyed minute out of your life, and you're done for."

While Kalina digested this startling information, a bowl of hot mush appeared on the table along with a jug of creamy milk and a bowl of lumpy brown sugar. "Here," said her cousin in a kindlier tone, "eat up. Things always look better on a full stomach."

As Kalina watched the plump but strong girl-woman feed and clothe her child for the day, she did not think her cousin "done for." In truth, she seemed quite happy as she sang and even danced about the dingy room, holding aloft the ecstatic and shrieking Dunia.

Her high, strong soprano rang out in warbling tones as though she were a prima donna in an opera. "Business was good last night, *chérie*. We'll have pork chops for supper. Fat and juicy." She winked broadly. "The butcher's a friend of mine. Maybe a cream pie, too, from the bakery."

Who's also a friend of yours, no doubt, Kalina mused. Suddenly she realized why her once-slim cousin had put on so much weight. She eats to fight off loneliness within, and smokes cigarettes, she thought. Wonder how many clients she took on last night. She broke off the revolting thought

58

to ask, "What kind of work can a woman do here, I mean besides — besides —" She stopped, unable to voice the word "prostitute."

Zuska dimpled. "The mine. That's all there is." Putting the breathless Dunia on the floor, she poked her cousin in the chest. "As for going into my line of work, you're far too skinny. But —" She cocked her head, frowning in thought. "A couple weeks' good eating and you just might give it a try."

"Stop that," Kalina gritted. "Tell me about the mine. What could I do there?"

"Pick."

"What's that?"

"They're called slate pickers." She flicked a thumb to the door. "That's what causes all that racket. They grind up the coal in machines, then it falls down a series of chutes to the ground, where it's loaded into boxcars. But first the slate — that's the part that won't burn — has to be picked out by hand."

Kalina brightened. "Sounds easy enough for me. Maybe Max and I can work at picking."

Her cousin gazed a long time out the grimy window at the dismal street. "Maybe," she said at last, "if you don't mind lungs full of soot and a permanent crook in your back."

Zuska went to Pottsville that same day, returning gayer than ever with the promised pork chops and a cream pie that, she avowed, had come from the big, fancy hotel there. The amber beads had found a generous purchaser, she reported with delight.

But there was no sign of Max, and no amount of looking out the window or opening the door to peer down Apple Blossom Lane past the rows of houses had brought him back. The cousins slept together, curled back to front like spoons in a drawer. It was just like old times, Zuska said, trying in vain to cheer up the despondent Kalina.

As day followed day and Max did not return, neither mentioned his name. Zuska's trips to Pottsville became more frequent and she was gone for longer periods, both night and day. Kalina's time and energies were consumed in caring for little Dunia.

"Pittsburgh," Zuska said, "that's where your Max has gone. Stay with me a month or two, get some meat on those bones of yours, then go after him."

Days became weeks. The snow vanished, the sun grew warmer overhead, and the voices of children sounded in the muddy lanes with the pretty names. Feathery leaves popped out on the scrawny trees, chattering birds went about their nest building, and Kalina decided that even Shenandoah, despite the constant noise and soot, was beautiful in the spring.

Some Italian children named Benvenuto pounded on the door, asking for Dunia. They were from the family who had cared for her before Kalina came. Happily, two-year-old Dunia joined them in the street at their eternal games of Ring around the Rosy and Run, Sheep, Run.

Kalina took to sitting on the sagging front steps, staring at the greening hills.

Then, Zuska left for three whole weeks, leaving plenty of cash in the drawer for Kalina with instructions to walk to the company store for food and supplies. Alone, Kalina found herself eating larger meals, baking breads and cakes, concocting rich desserts. Her angles became curves, and Zuska's frocks didn't seem as loose as before.

Paradoxically, Zuska had thinned down and took to wearing corsets. She looked, Kalina thought admiringly — but not with envy, for she loved her cousin dearly — like the portraits of Lillian Russell and other actresses she had seen in the New York papers. Like a goddess, sure of her beauty and power over men.

Kalina's anguish over Max's leaving — she still could not, even in her mind, call it desertion — began to diminish. The whole series of events, New Year's Eve, Aunt Litka's death and funeral, the flight to Pennsylvania, even their love-making, took on the semblance of a dream. It never happened, she told herself, any of it. She woke each morning in the lonely bedroom, half-expecting to be back on Mulberry Street in that cheerless third-floor room with a pile of factory pants awaiting her

But the immigrant girl was no romantic fool. Reality became harsher every day that passed, and Zuska did not return. Troubled, her money running out, Kalina voiced her fears to the storekeeper. "I think that something's happened to my cousin."

The man smiled, spoke kindly to her in Polish. "No, my dear child, nothing dreadful has happened. Your cousin was seen at the depot in Pottsville, boarding a train with an older man who appeared to be very rich."

The Pottsville Hotel was an imposing three-story wood and limestone structure planted on a knoll about a mile from the railroad depot, far enough from the locomotives and the mines to escape the thick soot that coated almost everything else. To Kalina it was grandiose, much larger than the manor of Pan Mikolai where she was born.

She paused at the foot of the winding gravel drive to catch her breath from the long walk and admire the vista of velvety lawn and neat bordering hedge. Yellow daffodils filled a circular bed. It was a feast for eyes accustomed to grimy company houses and coal tipples. A late March wind tugged at her long skirt and forced her gloved hand to her hat that threatened to fly off her pile of carefully braided hair.

Elegantly attired guests sat in wicker armchairs on the wide veranda that encircled the hotel. A few walked briskly back and forth, working off a hearty meal, she imagined. A woman with a pleasant face smiled from beneath a feathered hat. A man in a fur-trimmed coat tipped his hat to her, his eyes flashing. I must look like one of them, she reflected and, ignoring the butterflies in her stomach, walked boldly up the steps and through the polished front doors.

Immediately, the delicious aroma of roasting beef assailed her. Almost dinner time. The walk from the station had taken longer than she had thought. Settling Dunia with the Benvenutos had been a harrowing experience

61

taking the best part of an hour. The poor child was convinced that her aunt, like her mother, was about to leave her forever.

Once inside the palatial foyer, Kalina lost all anxiety in a confused, but delightful impression of dark leather chairs and long, cozy davenports set among dark, rich-looking furnishings. Not one, but three dazzling crystal chandeliers blazed overhead with electric lights. A man sitting in a deep chair sipped brandy from a snifter made of gold. He smiled directly at Kalina, showing two rows of yellow teeth.

"Yes, ma'am." The blond clerk behind the long counter cheerfully answered her question. "The Pottsville Hotel is in need of chambermaids." He pointed to a door at the far end of the lobby.

Murmuring a low "thank you," Kalina half-floated across the thick pile rug to seek out the manager. It was well over two hours before that personage could see her, she was told, so she sat, entranced, in a corner of the vast kitchen. A heavy-set Hungarian woman named Anya supervised a small army of helpers in preparing and serving enormous quantities of food. Everything was immaculate, no coal dust here. Everyone was smiling and polite, even the harried waitresses who swished importantly in and out of the swinging doors in white uniforms starched stiff as boards.

Zuska had been right about the mine tipple being no place for her. Or anybody, who wanted to live a reasonably long life. A dispirited line of old men, whey-faced children, and crook-backed girls and women sat on benches, bent over the chutes, picking, picking. Soot filled the place as though a volcano had just erupted. She had run out the back door as if the devil himself were on her tail.

Even now, remembering the grit, Kalina ran a tongue over her teeth.

"You speak English?" The question, spoken bluntly in a thick Hungarian accent, startled her. "I am Szabo, the manager here," he continued without waiting for her answer. She glanced up at a dark, slender man with a long, curving, well-oiled mustache.

"Yes," she said, standing up.

"Pretty," he remarked, "very, very, pretty. That's good."

Snapping black eyes raked her up and down as if she were a steer being examined for purchase. Suddenly, his hand whipped out to encircle her upper arm.

"Good muscles, too. That's good."

"I come from good stock," she said, defensively. "I've been educated, I can read and write—"

His upraised arm cut her off. "Okay. Start tomorrow. Six by the Angelus."

She used some of her dwindling cash for the horse car back to Shenandoah where she informed the Benvenutos that she would be gone all week at her job and would see Dunia on her one afternoon off. As the child flew into her arms, Kalina found herself wondering what she would do if Zuska, repenting, should return for her daughter. The prospect of losing the dear little girl after months of closeness devastated her. They were a family, she and Dunia. When she went to Pittsburgh to seek out Max, Dunia of course would go with her. Max would have to accept her as their own.

A chambie job paid four dollars and board and room. She figured rapidly in her head—two dollars to the Benvenutos for Dunia, one dollar for necessaries and clothing, one whole dollar to save for Pittsburgh. In six months she would have enough to ride the railroad in style and stay in a boarding house for at least a month.

Kalina's first weeks as a chambermaid were hectic and more exhausting than anything she had ever done. The knee pants work had been monotonous, but you got to sit down, at least. Here in this vast hotel, she found herself using muscles she didn't know she possessed. Up at five, a quick wash in the icy basin, a hearty breakfast in the steamy kitchen, then a long, long day of scrubbing spittoons, carpets, wood floors, toilets, windows, walls— anything Szabo decided was dirty. Though some distance from any mine or railroad, the omnipresent coal soot somehow found its way into the plush rooms of the vast place.

There were also linens, chamber pots, and dinner trays to be carted up and down the five flights of steps. Carpets were taken outside and hung on lines to be beaten with a wire whisk. Since every room had a fireplace, hoppers of coal must be furnished daily during the cold weather. Few boys and men were available for this work, most of them preferring to work in the better-paying mines.

The most detested job, however, was scrubbing out the encrusted spittle from the beautiful carpets with lye soap and stiff brush. She considered the habit of spitting tobacco one of the vilest in the world, and though cuspidors sat everywhere, the male guests, mostly traveling men, ignored them.

At nine o'clock, Kalina ate a hearty dinner in the kitchen, then wearily climbed the steps to her tiny, fifth-floor room where she fell promptly and profoundly asleep. A dining room girl named Hedy was her bedmate, but it was weeks before she spoke to her. The other side of the bed was empty when Kalina got there, and, in the morning when Kalina left for work, Hedy was fast asleep, having come to bed sometime in the night.

All Kalina ever saw was the head of yellow-gold hair crowning a pretty face, which was sweet in repose. The form under the blankets appeared to be slim and inviting.

The Polish girl's relations with Mr. Szabo and the staff were friendly. She liked people and was glad to be among so many who like herself were struggling for a better life.

Some of the kitchen boys winked at her now and then, smiling suggestively, but she did not encourage them. She had Max. There had been no word, but then, she told herself, he was illiterate and was too proud no doubt to ask someone else to do it for him.

One night in May she opened the door to find Hedy seated at the vanity table wielding a comb through her long tangle of hair, wincing and cursing like a barkeep at the knots.

powerful, like an emperor, the kind of head you see on ancient coins. Such a crown of rich coffee-brown she had not seen since leaving Jaslo.

Mashko had told her stories of the Cossacks, the fearless horsemen who rode their shaggy mounts from the steppes and hills to prey on helpless villages. She could hear the old man's voice even now in memory.

"Like savage minions from deepest hell, the horsemen thunder down upon the village, sabers flashing, burkas flying. Into the village square they ride. There the Cossacks satiate their lusts on any female over ten, impaling any who resist. Old men and women are cut down without mercy. Pretty girls and strong boys are strapped onto saddles and carried off to remote mountain lairs, never to be seen again, their fate only to be imagined with terror."

Her own experience with Cossacks was limited to a time when she was a child barely reaching her mother's knee. Cossacks had ridden into their village, right into the manor yard. But Pan Mikolai had given them fresh horses, meat, and wine, and they had gone off again without raping a single maid.

"Impressive, isn't he?" Szabo muttered at her side as she stood outside the kitchen door. "And rich, too. Owns coal mines, steel mills, God knows what else." He handed her a menu. "Go on over right away. His name's Murav."

"Me?" Kalina squeaked. "That's Hedy's table." She slanted a fearful glance at the man who was probably a Cossack in disguise.

"Do as I say," the manager hissed. "He specifically asked for you."

At that moment Hedy passed with a loaded tray, and winking at Kalina, mouthed silently, "big tipper." Knees shaking, Kalina walked toward the window, feeling somewhat like a Christian being thrown to the lions.

"Good morning, Mr. Murav. I trust you are well." It was what they were supposed to say, with spirit, but somehow it came out sounding stilted this time.

Half-rising from his chair, he nodded, acknowledging her greeting as if she were not a servant but a fellow diner.

Then, catching himself, he sat down again, self-consciously lifting his great beard to adjust his red cravat.

He can't be a Cossack, she thought calmly, he's too nervous. What would a real Cossack be doing in Pottsville, Pennsylvania? She was being a foolish girl, letting her bad memories govern her good sense.

But close up, seeing the heavy-set, muscular body, she felt something stir within her. A kind of warm, disturbing feeling. Something she hadn't felt since Max left.

"What are you, girl," he shot out abruptly in a gruff but unaccented voice. "Lithuanian, Russian, Greek?"

"Polish," she said mechanically, surprised at his flawless American speech but not surprised at the odd question. In America, everybody wanted to know, first off, what part of the "old country" you came from, what special immigrant group you belonged to.

She handed him the large menu printed on heavy cardboard and noted that the hands that took it were clean as a woman's with the nails trimmed neatly.

"May I suggest the ham, sir? Fresh cured from the country. Or you might prefer the sausage and hotcakes with syrup."

He scowled. "I can read," he snapped, adding, "which is more than you can do, I warrant." He thrust the menu back at her. "Some strawberries, big and fresh, a big bowl with cream on the side. Heavy cream."

Clenching her teeth to keep her anger at his insulting manner from erupting into words, Kalina bobbed her head and smiled brightly. As she turned to go, however, he clamped his big hand on her wrist, the sleeve of his coat pulling back to reveal a thick mat of brown hair on his arm.

His thumb moved from her wrist to circle the fourth finger of her left hand. "Unmarried. That's good."

His eyes flicked to hers, and a smile crossed his face. "Virgin, too, I bet, from the scared-rabbit look of you."

She flushed, lowering her eyes in confusion, but held back the quick retort that danced on her tongue. Apparently, waitresses were fair game for the male patrons. She would ask Hedy tonight how to deal with this kind of insulting behavior. What should she say? Surely her pretty bedmate was vastly experienced at fending off unwanted advances?

After a long, agonizing moment, he released her wrist. The smile was gone from his handsome face and he said again, with a little explosion of breath. "That's good. A man needs to know what he's got at the onset, before—"

He stopped, himself appearing confused, as if he had said more than he had intended.

Before what? she wondered.

Her head spinning from his bold talk and the intensity of the eyes that now seemed more a smoldering gold than hard brown, Kalina darted into the kitchen, like the scared rabbit he said she was, to fetch his breakfast. Szabo had said he had asked for her. But why? Was it her beauty or was there something else? Did he know her from somewhere? Or her family, perhaps?

As she walked back to the kitchen, she felt his eyes boring into her back like a hot poker. Kalina forced herself to calm down. If she were going to be a success at waiting tables, she would have to develop a thick skin with people like this Cossack.

What would he say if she told him she was not a virgin? Would the gold vanish from the probing eyes? Would they turn hard and cold again?

After a gargantuan breakfast came luncheon and dinner, all of which Kalina served the man whom she thought of in her mind as the Cossack. Through every meal, he watched her every move like a farmer appraising a brood mare, making her so nervous she nearly dropped the tray at one point.

It was dark, almost ten, before he finished his dinner. He seemed to take a long time with his dessert, a rich, caramelized custard in a heavy brown bowl, savoring each silver spoonful as if it were heavenly ambrosia.

He pushed back his chair and stood up, rolling up his napkin with great care and inserting it into the silver ring.

Kalina reached out a hand. "Don't bother, sir, we

launder the napkins each night."

Once more, as at breakfast, his hand darted over hers, the strong fingers encircling her wrist. "Polish, you say. Exactly where?"

"Jaslo. On the Wistoka."

He sucked in his breath, and for once the amber eyes showed true surprise, almost shock. After a long pause, he said quietly, "It all works out then. I seem to have hit pay dirt."

Seemingly oblivious to the diners at the next table, who were casting curious and amused glances at them, Murav touched her nose with his free hand, then moved up to trace the line of her dark, feathery brow.

"Good bloodlines. Intelligent eyes. If only you were literate. Murav's woman must be literate."

His eyes grew dreamy, and to her enormous relief, he dropped his hand from her face. "I could teach you, it would be a joy." The amber eyes glittered as with a fever. "I would be the potter, you the clay—no—more like fine marble, I would say." He took hold of her wrist again.

Thoroughly exasperated and red-faced at the loud snickers from the next table, Kalina snapped, "Unhand me sir. The waitress does not come with the price of the meal."

He laughed, releasing her. "Spirited too, marvelous."

"What's more," she went on, anger driving away fright, "I *can* read. I have read many books, perhaps more than you have. My Aunt Litka taught me at home along with other valuable lessons." Breathing deeply, Kalina threw back her shoulders and, with a great clatter, started piling the soiled dinnerware on her tray.

"I learned at an early age that courtesy and dignified behavior in public is the mark of a true lady," he answered.

Her tray full, she whipped around and shot back, "And the mark of a true gentleman as well!"

"Bravo," she heard him murmur softly.

"Be careful, they're all married," Hedy warned her that night. "But he sure doesn't sound like a man who's out for a good time. Why on earth would he want you to read?" she frowned. "And don't get any fancy notions about marriage. They all talk that way at first."

When Kalina tried to express her mixed-up feelings for the man, the girl turned over, sleepily. Of late, Hedy had been getting precious little sleep, tumbling into bed midway through the night. Kalina wondered, worrying a little, wanting to ask if maybe she had a serious beau. But Hedy had remarked that what she liked best about her bedmate was her knack for minding her own business.

In the morning, the Cossack was not at his table, Szabo reporting that the coal baron was touring the mining patches where trouble was brewing with the unions. The manager shook his head angrily. "Damn agitators. A strike's bad business for everyone."

Since it was her afternoon off and the day was fine, Kalina walked the five miles to Shenandoah to see Dunia, who was growing like the proverbial weed, seeming to thrive on the Benvenuto's care. She chattered busily in a mix of English and Italian; Kalina thought with shock that she would have to see more of the child or she would grow up with an Italian accent that might be difficult to erase. Being without an accent was terribly important in America and Kalina worked studiously to banish traces of her own.

"What's the hurry about this Pittsburgh," Mrs. Benvenuto inquired. "You no like your work?" To the woman, whose husband worked twelve hours underground, the Polish girl's job seemed like heaven.

"Oh, surely. But in the big city there'll be positions in fine houses where Dunia and I can be together."

The black eyes glinted slyly. "You find rich man to marry, pretty thing like you." She laughed her bubbly laugh, glanced ruefully at her own ample curves. "Once I was little too."

"Woman no good without a man," piped up her husband from the table where he was hand-rolling cigarettes.

A mental image of the Cossack Murav's leonine head flitted across Kalina's mind.

As she trudged back to the hotel in the dark spring night, enjoying the air despite the eternal coal smell, Kalina thought with irritation of the constant refrain from

71

almost everyone: marry a rich man. Was there no other way to happiness? Only a few months before, she had thought the same. But now, with the thrill of her own hard-earned money jingling in her pockets, she wondered if there could not be another way. Must a woman sell herself in marriage for the price of a roof, a bed, food on the table?

Were the poor always miserable? She treasured the echoes of laughter and the silly, loving talk of the Benvenuto menage. Eleven children, counting Dunia, two dogs, more cats than she could count, all seemed happy enough. But if there should be a strike, the little faces would grow thin, and Mrs. B. would regain her girlish figure soon enough.

Little Dunia, her heart's treasure, would have little energy to chatter in any language once the bread and meat were taken from the table.

Twenty-nine days later—Kalina was counting—Stefan Murav walked into the Pottsville lobby at dinner time, and after exchanging a few words with Szabo, stepped into the gilt elevator. The manager crooked a finger at Kalina, who had just come into the dining room. Murav wished dinner in his room, he said, and she was to serve him.

Anticipation through the Cossack's long absence turned suddenly, unaccountably, into fear. "We're short-handed, Mr. Szabo," she stuttered, "Hedy's sick. Can't one of the kitchen boys carry it up?"

"No, dammit," he yelled. "He wants *you*." Distractedly, he glanced into the dining room. "Where's that good-for-nothing Hedy, anyway?"

"In bed, something she ate, I think. She's been vomiting all day, can't even lift her head from the pillow, let alone carry a tray."

In the kitchen, Kalina loaded the serving cart. Oyster stew with extra butter, boiled salmon and capers, fried sweetbreads, cold sliced lamb with mint sauce, four kinds of spring vegetables, two bowls of greens. Enough food for a banquet, she reflected, marveling at the man's appetite.

On the way up in the elevator, she rehearsed her first words. *Good evening to you, Mr. Murav, I trust your trip was pleasant and profitable. Then—lovely weather, don't you think?*

What if he made a dishonorable advance? He had grabbed her wrist without so much as a by-your-leave that first morning. She recalled a conversation with Hedy.

"Had to fight my way out of the room many times," the girl had said, giggling.

"Murav's not that kind."

"Is there any other kind?"

For one so young, Kalina now reflected, Hedy was very cynical.

Inside Room 305 the walnut writing table was swamped with papers, the overflow sat on the floor in untidy piles. An ornate china lamp with a fringed shade cast a circle of gold light on the thick brown hair of the Cossack and she noted with faint surprise a distinct white streak down the middle where the part should be.

Closing the door quietly, Kalina waited behind the cart, but he did not speak or look up. He continued to write furiously with a black pen, jabbing frequently into a pot of ink.

She had been too quiet. He wouldn't appreciate a cold dinner. "Lovely weather, is it not?" she blurted out.

His head came up at that, and there was a look of almost comical astonishment on the imperial face. "Oh, it's you," he grunted.

"Where would you like your dinner, sir?" She was pleased at her composure. He was not nearly so disturbing as she remembered. She wheeled the cart toward the table.

Gold-brown eyes stared as if mesmerized. "Just leave the food on the cart. I don't want to muss my papers."

Laying his pen carefully on a scrap of blotter, he turned to face her fully. He wore a richly red silk dressing gown that had a rolled velvet collar of somewhat darker hue. The upright brass ashtray at his elbow was glutted with cigar butts, which gave off an expensive aroma. A nearly full

73

brandy bottle sat on the bedside chest.

Kalina lifted the cover from the oysters, whose unique odor filled the room immediately. He bared his teeth in a broad smile, and she noted their startling pearly whiteness. This one had never starved, that much she could tell.

Placing the casserole cover on the bottom shelf of the cart, Kalina turned to go. "Pull the bell cord when you're ready for dessert and coffee, sir."

"Stop calling me 'sir.' My name is Murav."

Then, more gently, "The room is clammy. Nothing like a long train ride to draw the heat from a man's blood." He glanced at the cold grate. "Do something with the fire."

Be nice, she thought and said sweetly "I'd be very happy to kindle your fire, Mr. Murav."

Chambies were supposed to make the fires, but without a thought to her starched apron, Kalina knelt on the black marble stones and quickly got a blaze going. Paper curls and kindling were already laid, and after applying a lighted match, she worked the bellows vigorously until the meager flames flared up. Pleased, she sat back on her haunches, savoring the heat, then rose up and turned around.

She ran into the Cossack, striking her forehead on his bearded chin. Instantly, he circled her with his arms and pulled her steadily toward his thick body. The man was taller than he seemed when sitting down, for her face was buried in his neck. There was a pleasing sensation of warmth and scent and a kind of spinning into a far-off lotus land of pure, delicious feeling.

Gradually, she felt an enormous heat. The room must be on fire, she thought with panic. But it was only the blood within her veins, for as he tugged her face from beneath his chin and covered it with wide-mouthed kisses, she felt the unmistakable mounting of desire.

He joined her hands behind his neck so that her breasts stretched beneath the apron, and then he was kissing her lips, in the fullness of Cossack passion.

The starched cap fell from her head, a wondrous, paralyzing delight seized her. Snatches of words chased each other in her brain. *Be nice to him. Big tip. Take care*

74

of yourself.

Alarmingly, his hands were on her buttocks, squeezing and pressing forward with ironlike strength.

Kalina, feeling the panicky burst of power a runner feels when turning into the last lap of a race, wrenched herself free and ran out of the room and up two flights of steps to her bedroom.

She flung herself beside the sleeping Hedy, who rolled over with a moan and opened two bloodshot eyes. "If I weren't too sick to laugh, Kalina, I'd laugh. So you're the lady who can take care of herself."

Two hours later, when she responded to 305's bell, Murav was sitting before the fire, feeding it lumps of coal, jabbing viciously with a poker. The room was stifling, the windows shut tight against the cool May night.

A crystal decanter sat amid the papers on the writing table, a scant inch of brandy lay at the bottom. He turned as she entered.

"You're back. Here's your hat." Rising, he picked the starched cap off the mantel and handed it to her.

"Thank you," she said stiffly, acting on Hedy's advice to pretend that nothing had happened but to "punch him in the gut if he tried it again."

He turned back to the fire as if unwilling to meet her gaze. Kalina stood, mute, twirling the cap nervously between her hands.

"What's your name?" he barked.

"Kalina, Mr. Murav." Her eyes were glued to his back, she was tensed for the slightest untoward movement.

"Kalina. And what else?"

"Kalina Olkonsky, Mr. Murav. Do you wish coffee now?"

"Olkonsky's your mother's name. Who's your father?"

Blood pumped into her face. "How dare you, you Cossack!" The hated word slipped out before she could stop herself.

With a whoop he turned round again and bounded to where she stood, touching her cheek with his fingers. "Ah hah! A bastard! *Nullia filia!*"

Nobody's daughter. It was the Latin term of contempt used by her countrymen. "I am Pan Mikolai's daughter," she said indignantly.

He laughed. "You and a hundred others, I imagine." He caught her elbows and she stepped back. "Never fear, my little Polish blackbird, I won't kiss you again." The irritating laugh again. "Despite your obvious enjoyment of the last one."

Releasing her arms, he leaned on the mantel, his eyes narrowed, in the manner of a man who is enjoying a delicious secret. "That little business when you brought my dinner was in a way of an experiment. A most pleasurable, and I might add, a most successful one. You passed with flying colors. Like the Cossack you think me to be, I do not value coldness in a wife."

Kalina moved quickly to the window in a desperate effort to escape the intensity of his gaze. But with a pantherlike movement, he was there, reaching past her to draw back the heavy curtain and shove the window open. The night air smelled of rain.

As they stood there, side by side, they could be husband and wife enjoying a quiet, after-dinner communion in the privacy of their bedroom. She waited for him to say the word "wife" again.

When he spoke, the bantering tone was gone, in its place was a new and curiously intimate seriousness. "While I was away, I did some investigating. It concerns a person with whom I intend to do business."

She felt his two heavy hands on her shoulders, but this time she did not flinch. "As you have guessed by now, Kalina Olkonsky, that person is you."

"Business! What business can you possibly have with me?" Her voice was faint; in truth, she feared that she might go into a "vapor" like the fine ladies of the hotel.

"Marriage. That most important of all commerce."

Incredulity, delight, joy, fear, and ultimately a raging anger consumed Kalina. He must think her the most naive, unlettered peasant girl, who, on being promised marriage, would jump under the blanket with him.

But before she could speak, his steely arms were once more at her waist like iron bands, and her back was tight against his body. She stiffened with renewed panic and tried to wriggle free.

He was speaking again, softly, gently. "My God, stop squirming, I don't intend to rape you." Then, abruptly, "Has this happened to you before?" His voice lowered. "Has another man gotten there before me?"

"It's really none of your concern," she said, testily.

"Oh, but it *is*, my feisty Pole." He grinned. "No matter, your passion earlier in my arms betrayed your secret. It would be a miracle if one as fetching as you had not been breached."

With that he released his iron grip, and Kalina bolted toward the door. Her hand was on the knob when she whipped around again. She must stop acting so rabbitlike. She was of noble blood. Aunt Litka's voice came sharply from the past. "Tell the truth. Be ashamed of nothing you have done in good faith and sincerity."

She had given herself to Max in love and trust. She would tell this Cossack the truth, and that would end this charade.

Her back against the door, she faced him. "I gave myself in love to a boy named Max O'Hara. He is gone, but I do not regret my actions. If you are looking for a virgin bride, Mr. Murav, I must disappoint you." She stared at him unflinchingly. "And if you want a pleasurable liaison to amuse you for a night or two, I suggest you look elsewhere."

Turning once again, she opened the door, but he was swiftly upon her, his hands on her shoulders, easing her gently back into the room.

Their eyes locked. "Surely you must have guessed by my probing questions that my intentions are most honorable. In my absence, I spent some time in New York, and it was simpler than you can imagine to find out all I needed to know about your childhood there." His hands tightened on her shoulders with a hurting pressure. "The police were most helpful as were your friends on Mulberry Street who all remembered the hoity-toity Litka Olkonsky and her two beautiful nieces."

His eyes grew soft. "I only guessed about the street boy, but I am mightily glad you told me."

Then he was saying the astonishing words, "I, Stefan Murav, ask Kalina Olkonsky, daughter of Hania and Pan Mikolai of Jaslo to be my wife."

She was speechless, uncertain whether to laugh, cry, or turn around and slap his insolent face. None of this was going as Hedy had said it would. It was not true that they never marry you, all they want is a little fun.

When she failed to answer at once, his voice grew sharp. "Murav asks no woman twice."

After a moment, he released her, and like a horse at the starting gate, she bolted out the door.

The heat from Hedy was so intense that Kalina threw back the covers. She had been praying steadily to the Virgin for guidance since leaving Murav. What had she done to encourage him? Perhaps her smile was too inviting, her walk too seductive.

The rain came finally, and now, at midnight, the soothing patter on the window lulled her into a kind of half-sleep, in which desultory thoughts swirled lazily around her brain. To marry—just like that—a man you hardly know—except that he is rich and devilishly good-looking. Maybe he's been sent by the Virgin, maybe he is the rich and handsome man her mother promised her back in Poland.

What about Dunia? No man wants another man's bastard child.

No, it was absurd. She would simply play along with the joke, stay clear of his bed, and that would be that.

Desperately, Kalina tried to summon the freckled face and red hair of the boy she had sworn to love forever. Wait for me, he had said. But with each passing day, the street kid who had been so kind and sweet and loving faded farther and farther into the past, like a dream of yesterday.

Three times in the night Hedy retched into the slop jar and three times Kalina got up to empty it in the toilet down the hall. The girl looked sick enough to die. During a respite from her vomiting, Kalina told her of Murav's proposal, laughing as if it were a joke.

But to Hedy it was no joke. "Marry him, marry him, marry him," she chanted. "But don't let him poke under your skirt until the priest ties you up tight in Latin."

The following day Room 305 teemed with men in black business suits, one and all puffing on cigars, all talking rapidly, all at once it seemed, and scribbling on bits of paper. As Kalina served and removed the tureens and platters, phrases buzzed around her head like flies in a barnyard. Stocks, bonds, dividends, shares, Wall Street. And names she'd seen in the Pittsburgh papers in the hotel lobby. Carnegie, Rockefeller, J. P. Morgan, Teddy Roosevelt, McKinley.

The men talked freely, oblivious to her presence. To them she was just another stick of furniture. As she pushed the last serving cart through the door, Murav slipped a folded paper into her apron pocket. In the corridor, she read, *Szabo told me about your cousin's child. I will adopt her as my own. Offer will be withdrawn at sundown tomorrow.*

That night, Hedy started to die. Her pretty face was unrecognizable from pain, her blue eyes rolled back vacantly in their sockets. Terrified, Kalina summoned the hotel physician. He grimaced at the filthy sheet. "Too late. Should have called me sooner." He raised a tired face to Kalina. "Seen her with any medicine bottles?"

She produced two brown glass bottles from under Hedy's sheet. "I saw her drink from these," she said. "She told me they were a family remedy for a stomach ache."

The doctor unscrewed the lids, sniffed, and shuddered. A smell akin to a thousand backed-up sewers permeated the little room. "Damn witch's brew," he exploded. Then, in blunt words he told the Polish girl that her roommate was perishing from induced abortion. But instead of being expelled from the womb, the unwanted child was putrefying in Hedy's young body.

The physician's morphine mercifully eased Hedy's last agonies. In the morning, her grieving family came from Loch Gryn to carry off their sad burden.

At noon, Kalina sat in Anya's kitchen sipping coffee laced with brandy, trying to undo the ravages of the sleepless night. The kindly cook talked softly, consolingly, her words running together like a phonograph record. "What a terrible way to die! Poor thing, she was so pretty, so young. God have mercy. Only the rich die old and happy. She did it for money, foolish girl. Just like your cousin Zuska, a dollar or two each time. Never used any of it on herself." The woman blew her nose into a huge handkerchief. "Hedy, I mean, not Zuska."

The bell rang on the big board. Kalina glanced up. 305. She dabbed at her puffy eyes with the corner of her apron.

Anya called after her as she left the kitchen. "Watch your step, little one, with your Cossack."

It was six o'clock when Kalina climbed the carpeted stairs to Room 305. The soft evening air resounded with church bells ringing the Angelus. Time for prayer. Bowing her head, Kalina prayed for heavenly guidance.

Her prayer done, she lifted her head and knocked on the door of Stefan Murav's bedroom. An anguished thought, so fleeting it seemed more a dream from the past, thrust swordlike into her heart.

Max, oh, Max!

She knocked, firmly, loudly. The door swung open at once as if he had been waiting just behind, and he stood there smiling, cocky, and handsome in his morning coat and striped trousers. Brilliant May sunshine filtered through the lacy curtains to make dancing patterns on the carpet.

"Stefan Murav," she said, lifting her eyes to his, "I will be most honored to become your wife."

Chapter Four

The private railroad coach was a vision of sapphire velvet and dark mahogany. Even the little windows which normally framed the sooty landscape were shrouded in cascades of lace and dark-red damask. Serene pastoral scenes in oil—trees, grass, running brooks, laughing children—adorned the walls. No effort had been spared to keep out the world for those privileged to travel in these opulent surroundings.

"I'd be content," Kalina murmured, "to spend our honeymoon right here." Sighing blissfully, she leaned her head against the starched white-lace antimacassar.

Stefan Muraf laughed indulgently at his bride. "Wait until you get an eyeful of the new Statler in Philadelphia. It's a royal palace." He covered her gloved hand with his own, possessively.

He left her then to consult with the steward concerning their catered luncheon, and Kalina closed her eyes, collecting her thoughts. If this were a dream, she prayed, let me not awaken. Ever. Tomorrow, she would surely write to Mama. America is all that you said, Mama Hania. A rich and handsome man has made me his wife. I am a fine lady and, soon as it can be arranged, you and my brother, little Pepi, will come to live with me.

The wonderful news would in a small way at least assuage for her dear mama the pain of Aunt Litka's death.

Wife of a steel tycoon. It was too much to absorb all at once. The very rails on which they rode were manufactured

in one of Stefan's mills. That's the way he spoke of them—
"my mills"—though in truth they belonged to the fabulous
Scotsman, Andrew Carnegie, Stefan's boss. "I'm top
man," he told her with pardonable pride.

The five-minute ceremony that united her with her
Cossack took place at St. Cecilia's rectory in Pottsville, a
dark-browed Italian priest pronouncing the sonorous Latin
with a finality that would have pleased poor, dead Hedy.
Szabo and a tearful Anya were witnesses.

As bride and groom raced to board the Philadelphia
Express, Kalina thought fleetingly of the weddings she
remembered from her native Jaslo. The village church
bulged with relatives and friends, some of whom had
journeyed through mountain passes and over trackless
meadows to wish good life and many children to the happy
pair. There was feasting, dancing, singing, sometimes last-
ing a full week.

Her heart ached. One must give up many things to live in
this blessed America. But one is given so much in return.
In Poland, she might now be warming the bed of Pan
Mikolai, whom she remembered as a much-wrinkled, lecherous old man with bad teeth.

Mr. Statler's posh marble palace masquerading as a
hotel overlooked Philadelphia's Rittenhouse Square and
made the Pottsville establishment seem like an overgrown
miner's shack. Their ten-o'clock supper was served in a
stunning, mirrored private banquet room by three uniformed waiters, whose aristocratic bearing struck awe in
Kalina's heart. Without exception, they were tall and
handsome and austere.

"I couldn't eat a thing," she protested to Murav as the
soup course arrived in a huge tureen brimming with
buttery cream and fat oysters. Hedy's grisly death and the
rush into marriage had left her with a nervous stomach.

"Eat up," he said shortly. But the amber eyes glinted
mischievously under the dazzling electric lights. "You'll
need sustenance for the night ahead of you."

Dutifully, she thrust spoonful after spoonful into her mouth and partook mechanically of the numerous courses that followed. Hours later, the fearful bride undressed in the gold-and-ivory dressing room attached to their suite, more than a little dizzy from the champagne the groom had plied her with.

In the frantic hours before the wedding, there had been time to purchase a neat and serviceable blue broadcloth afternoon costume but nothing else, so she slipped into the worn cotton shift she had worn to bed at Pottsville. When she emerged into the bedroom, she found Stefan awaiting her, stark naked, his torso white against the red of a capacious velvet armchair.

"Merciful heaven!" His thunderous exclamation was followed by an uproarious laugh. Then, whooping like a wild Indian from the prairies, he sprang from the chair and, grasping the almost threadbare nightgown, ripped it cleanly down the front, muttering as he did so, "Naked's the way I want you, my little one."

Three times on her bridal night, Murav possessed the body of his bride. The power and intensity of his love-making left her drained and limp as a rag doll a child has loved for many years. Her brief encounters with Max O'Hara had been sweet and tender with none of the blind lust that drove her husband into a semblance of animal rutting. She cowered under the onslaught, meek as a ewe set upon by the ram. He knew she was not virgin and said nothing, taking her passivity as expected bridal-night behavior.

He must truly be of Cossack blood, she thought. He had told her nothing of himself, his family, his forebears. She was still too fearful of him to ask him outright, boldly, as is a wife's natural right.

"End of summer, when all this politicking is over," he muttered in her ear before falling asleep at last, "we'll cruise the Mediterranean and I'll instruct you in the arts of pleasing a man in bed." They had come to Philadelphia for the honeymoon so that Stefan could attend the Republican Presidential Convention.

But sleep eluded Kalina, and she slid out from the silky sheet to walk, naked, to the window, drawing aside the curtain a scant inch to peer down into the square. The night air was cool, the electric street lanterns wore little fog halos. Strains of waltz music wafted up from the hotel ballroom, where she imagined fine ladies in brilliant gowns dancing round and round the polished floor with gentlemen in boiled shirts and cutaways. Carriage wheels rattled on the pavement, and occasionally the chugging breath of a motor car marred the lyric quality of the scene. Couples strolled about or sat on wrought-iron benches beneath leafy trees.

It was all hers, she thought with wonder. Kalina Olkonsky, who six months ago had been bending over kneepants in a grim Mulberry Street tenement, was part of the real America at last.

She dropped the curtain back into place and glanced at the little bedside clock. Only three. Hours before Stefan and she would join the Philadelphia crowds. Suddenly chilled, she slid back between the sheets and cuddled into the trough created by Stefan's bulk. Sighing, he turned and his heavy hand fell on her breast.

Swift, unheralded desire flamed within Kalina and with a cry of surprised rapture, she placed her cold hands on his warm buttocks. This time, the fourth, would be the charm.

When she received her husband's thrusting body once again, all maidenly reluctance vanished.

A brilliant June sun was slanting across the moss-green carpet when Stefan awakened her with a kiss. She bolted up, instinctively drawing the covers over her naked breasts. He bent over her, smelling of soap, his luxuriant beard damp and curly from the brush. He yanked the covers down. "These are mine, my dear, to gaze at, to kiss." He did so, pecking at each brown nipple as a bird tasting a worm.

He was fully dressed, and startled at having slept through his rising and bathing, she sprang out of bed.

"Stefan, you should have wakened me. I must dress."

He frowned from the mirror where he was fussing with his cravat. "But you're not going anywhere, sweet. As I explained, this trip is not primarily for pleasure, although"—he flashed a wicked grin—"after last night's performance I may revise my plans."

She flushed prettily, remembering her wanton abandon in his arms that last time. Was it possible that those animal cries had issued from her own mouth?

"The delegates arrive today," he went on, "I've got to mingle. If Roosevelt is nominated on the first ballot, my dear wife, then and only then, can we indulge our passions at leisure."

Despite her disappointment, Kalina breathed an inward sigh of relief. The bridal night had left her exhausted. "It sounds so important, Stefan. Will you ever run for president?"

His black brows shot toward the ceiling. "You goose!" Then, with a promise to send up breakfast to her, he was gone.

The *Philadelphia Inquirer* was tucked behind the silver coffeepot and as Kalina, swathed in her husband's scarlet dressing gown, lingered over breakfast, she read with interest the long articles portraying the leading candidates for the highest office in America. The current president William McKinley, so the editors opined, was safe for business. He was solid and experienced while his projected running mate, Theodore Roosevelt of New York, affectionately called Teddy by an adoring American public, the hero of the Spanish War, was too young and inexperienced to lead our country. Barely forty, he would do well to remain awhile as governor of New York. Such was the collective, considered opinion.

There were half-page photographs of the two leading candidates along with other, minor aspirants. Thickly mustached McKinley reminded Kalina of an older Murav while Teddy, the fabled Rough Rider, exuded a charismatic vitality even from the printed page.

She longed to be there with Stefan, to see it all, to be

part of a working democracy, but, sadly, she was aware that only loose women and suffragettes ever appeared at political rallies. Women could not cast votes, so what was the point of even being there?

The hours until luncheon she devoted to writing letters. A long one to her mother, short ones to Anya and Szabo, a note to Dunia to be read to her by anyone in Shenandoah who "had the English." At eight, dinner was brought to the suite, Stefan pleading that press of work forbade their dawdling in the dining room.

Afterward Stefan repaired to the writing desk while she sat in the red chair pretending to read a brand-new French romance the chambermaid had acquired for her. The silence was punctuated by the sound of the letter opener as she slit the book's uncut pages.

"Stefan," she said suddenly, "what's a trust?"

The dark head flew up from the desk. "Where on earth did you hear such a word?"

"I read it in the paper this morning. The editors think that McKinley will let the trusts run rampant and that such a thing will be harmful to the country."

He jabbed his pen into the inkwell. "Women should not read newspapers," he said testily. "It's all a pack of lies. But since you ask, a trust is a group of businessmen who band together to pool their skills, resources, and money to make their respective businesses more efficient and productive." He leaned back in his chair, continuing in a patient, lecturing tone. "A trust means bigger profits and more yield from the least amount of investment."

"Then why should the newspapers—"

He stood up then, clearly annoyed. "Come to bed, Kalina. This talk of business and politics is most unseemly in a woman of your position." He chuckled. "What's more to the point, it's distinctively dampening to my ardor."

Next morning there was no newspaper on her breakfast tray. She picked up the romance again to resume her page cutting when a stoop-shouldered little woman who said she was the hotel seamstress and had been sent by Mr. Murav to "run up" some dresses for the madame, knocked on the door.

Miraculously, it seemed, by day's end and with the deft assistance of numerous below-stairs helpers, she did just that, and the young Mrs. Murav possessed the semblance of a wardrobe. Three frocks had come right from the racks of Mr. Wanamaker's big department store but were so altered and enhanced by the seamstress that they could not be told from custom work.

Stefan was pleased. "These will do until we can do the thing properly," he said as she spun around the room in a dinner gown of sea-green chiffon with genuine Belgian lace inserts. The third night of their marriage, Stefan spent at the writing desk while Kalina fell asleep alone in the bed, her unquenched passion a smoldering fire within.

The following day was a hot, windy Tuesday, and he arranged for her to join a group of delegates' wives on a guided tour of historic Philadelphia. "No time for us, darling," he mourned. "The coalition for Roosevelt has run into trouble."

On the bus she was coupled with a Mrs. Moffatt from the state of Kansas, who chattered incessantly in a nasal Midwest drawl about any topic that came to mind: the weather, the buildings, the latest fashions. But not a word came from her mouth about the grave deliberations at Exposition Hall. When the omnibus was forced to stop for a parade of Roosevelt demonstrators crossing the intersection with their placards, she scowled, "What foolishness, don't they know that everything is decided way ahead of the convention?"

Wednesday and Thursday, Kalina resumed the tour, drinking in an America she had never seen. Independence Hall, Liberty Bell, Franklin's home. She boated on the Delaware, browsed in the hotel emporium, purchasing some gloves for herself and a bevy of colorful cravats for Stefan, feeling a thrill as she wrote in her bold, swirling letters "Mrs. Stefan Murav" in the charge book.

Thursday night, her husband burst into the room and scooped her into his arms, whirling her round and round the room in a mad dance. "Dah, dah, dah, *dah*," he warbled, in a powerful baritone. It was a ragged but recognizable rendition of the Blue Danube Waltz.

They fell into the armchair, laughing and breathless. "Remember this date, my dear bride," he said, "the twenty-first day of June, in the first year of the great twentieth century." Feverishly, he planted kisses on her hot face. "And the Danube is where it will start. Which is not blue at all, by the way, but muddy brown. Take it from one who's seen it."

"But I thought," she spluttered, "we were going to the Mediterranean for our honeymoon."

The amber eyes clouded with a kind of quick anger, and for the first time since the wedding Kalina felt her former fear of her Cossack resurge. But his voice was calm as he said, "My dear sweet child, I am not discussing our love cruise but war. War is coming, sure as snow in December and rain in April." His voice assumed a dramatic tone as an actor proclaiming on a stage. "And war, my child, means money."

He stood up so quickly that she slid off his lap onto the floor. His silken shirt was damp with sweat, and in Murav's face was the kind of excitement she had seen on men who race horses or dogs. She continued to sit on the floor, watching him in wonder, as he emptied the half-empty water decanter at one gulp.

"Money," he repeated, "War means money for Murav." A dreamy smile lit up his handsome face. "And Murav's wife of course."

Then, as she sat on the floor, knees tucked under her like the child he had called her, he told her about war. He remained standing, empty decanter in hand, and spoke like a preacher in a pulpit.

War gobbled up steel, he told her, steel for battleships, bullets, guns, cannons. The list was endless. He finished with the grand statement, "War and steel go together like the sun and the moon."

"But we just had a war," she protested, when he paused for breath. "With Spain."

He snorted. "McKinley's little so-called war was a mere

squabble in an alley between a couple of boys. I'm talking about a real war such as the world has never seen. A war, my dear child, which will encompass the entire globe."

Stunned, Kalina could say no more. Stefan spoke of war as others speak of joyful times—weddings, Easter, Christmas. War to the girl from Jaslo meant rape, slaughter, widows, orphans, starvation. War consumed young men as spiders eat flies—cruelly, mindlessly.

But amazingly, men enjoyed the scent of battle. Many went to become soldiers. Old Mashko had spun tales of war, concluding sadly, "To fight is part of human nature, there has always been war."

It must be so, she thought as she courted sleep that night after love. When the soldiers marched through the square in their scarlet uniforms and cockaded hats, the maids threw flowers and kisses. Many willingly offered themselves to a man in uniform. Stefan Murav was every inch a man and would naturally enjoy the thought of war.

Yet, in her memory, nobody had ever seemed to know exactly what the war was all about.

At Shenandoah, they interrupted their journey to Pittsburgh, where Stefan made his home, to pick up Dunia. One look at the dingy, poverty-cursed hamlet that had been her home scarce a week before made her once more grateful to Stefan to loving her, for saving her. All thought of challenging her husband's views vanished from Kalina's mind.

Strangely, it was he who revived the subject. Resuming their trip, they sat in the same luxurious coach that had carried them to Philadelphia. Dunia sat in Kalina's lap, chattering shrilly in Italian and English, deliriously happy at being reunited with her beloved aunt. She now considered Kalina as her mama, having all but forgotten Zuska.

In the seat directly across, Stefan beamed at the two. "Madonna and child," he said softly. Gold glints appeared in his eyes. "Have I told you how very beautiful you are?"

She crimsoned, pleased, and he leaned across the space

to place both hands on her knees. "About last night, my dear, and our discussion on war, I feel my ardent views troubled you."

"Men and women feel differently about war," she responded, her own eyes smiling. She giggled. "As they do about a great many things, I suppose."

How could she doubt him? He was perfect in every way. He had taken Dunia as his own with no reservations.

"I must teach the child proper English," she said absently, stroking Dunia's long, brown hair, which she suspected had not been washed or brushed for weeks. Vermin surely nested in the thick clots. "And clean her up." There had been scarce an hour between trains, barely time to ride to Shenandoah from Pottsville and back.

"War is a business," he said intently, willing her to understand.

"Like marriage," she said quickly, remembering his strange proposal.

His eyes softened. "In many ways, yes. Both are passionate encounters essential to life itself. Both may bring great misery as well as abundant joy." He paused dramatically as was his habit when instructing her. "Ultimately, my dear wife, money — nothing else — greases the wheels of both."

The rhythmic movement of the train had put Dunia to sleep, and placing the child on the seat beside her, Kalina pressed forward, taking Stefan's hands in hers. "Stefan, you are so clever, so completely admirable in every way. Yet I know nothing of your family while you seem to know everything about mine."

He stole a glance at the sleeping child, then in a low, almost passionless voice, Stefan told his story. Born into a landed Russian family, his family, comprised of his parents, his older sister Anusia and himself, had embarked for America in the early days of the War Between the States. He was three at the time, his sister seven.

"Father was a high-ranking officer of the Czar and wore a splendid scarlet and blue uniform. This was his." Reaching under his vest he drew out a short, pointed knife with an ornately carved head. "Anusia saved it when our ship foundered."

"Foundered?" She drew in her breath. Shipwreck was the terror that immigrants feared above all.

He seemed not to hear her, but continued to stare at Dunia almost distractedly. "When the voyage was almost over, just a few miles off the Atlantic coast of America a most terrible storm arose. Our parents were swept away, there were lifeboats only for the children."

Instinctively, Kalina knew that the man wanted no expression of sympathy on her part. The pain was old; any words of hers would serve only to revive it.

"How did you live?" she said flatly. "You were so young."

"Anusia." It was an incantation as one speaks the name of a saint. "After the first years in the county workhouse, of which my sister remembers much, I but little, she hired out at twelve." He looked up then, and the suffering in his eyes was plain. "She became a servant. She was always big for her age. And strong. The strongest woman I've ever known."

Women need to be strong, she thought, though appearing as fragile vessels. "Yet you speak as a gentleman," she said, wondering. "You were obviously educated."

"Anusia again. She saw to it that my unusual gifts were brought to the attention of her employers, and I was given instruction along with the young sons and daughters of the household." He sat back then, his hands behind his neck, a look of fond remembrance transforming his sculptured features. "Failing that, she used her pitiful wages to send me to the local school."

"Your sister must be a completely selfless person," Kalina exclaimed in wonder.

"She is that," pronounced Stefan proudly. "You will love her as I do."

When they met at last in the gloomy black-and-white tiled foyer of the house on Rutherford Drive, Kalina's first impression of Anusia Murav was one of austerity and great

91

dignity. Her sister-in-law towered by a head over Kalina, who herself was tall for a woman. Gleaming brown hair, so much like her brother's, was forced back from her sallow face and framed it like a veil. It was so smooth and taut it seemed painted on. She reminded Kalina of nuns she had known in Poland.

"But you are so young!" Anusia frowned.

"I am sixteen," Kalina stuttered, "seventeen in August."

"A child."

With great difficulty, Kalina suppressed a sigh of irritation. She was a woman, she had known a man's love. "I have not been a child since I left my native village," she said, quietly. "I have worked hard, made my own way —"

Stefan broke in with a bluff, "If one is to train up a wife, Anusia dearest, the younger the better. Kalina is most malleable. Her mind is quick."

Dunia was whisked off by a smiling maid called Wanda to upper regions and a proper bed, Wanda promising to clean her from head to toe with particular emphasis on the head.

Stefan disappeared as if by magic. At a nod from Anusia, Kalina followed the nunlike woman through a portiered arch into a parlor that was even gloomier than the foyer. It had that peculiar, musty smell that seldom-used rooms acquire.

"Sit, child," Anusia said in her toneless voice. Kalina perched uneasily on the rough edge of a horsehair davenport and automatically pulled the golden chain dangling from the brass-stemmed lamp on the adjacent table. She gasped with pleasure as a lush tropical scene, replete with palm trees and surging ocean, appeared on the curving glass shade.

Quick as a cat, Anusia sprang to snap off the light.

"The electric glare will fade the carpet," she stated, drily. But her calm tone was deceptive, for in that brief flash of light Kalina caught the same quick anger in Anusia's eyes that she had seen in Stefan. "The curtains in this room are never drawn," the woman went on sternly. "The windows face west, and the sun is cruel in the afternoon."

As with Stefan, Kalina felt as though she were a child in school, being lectured to. Anusia excused herself to see about some refreshments, and Kalina surveyed, as best she could in the half-dark, this small part of her new domain. A dim light emanated from a very small and thickly frosted lamp set on the mantel. The house seemed, from what she had seen, grander even than she had imagined. As was the fashion, furniture concealed most of the floor space, leaving no room at all in which two people could stand together in conversation.

One was forced to sit, in this crowded room, but hardly in comfort, for besides the scratchy horsehair sofa, Kalina saw only straight-backed chairs in gleaming wood, with uncushioned seats. Bric-a-brac abounded. She would have to keep Dunia out of here. What she could glimpse of the carpet was lovely, an intricate design of gold-and-crimson autumn leaves shot with graceful silver birds.

She rose to inspect the tall grandfather clock, which told the hours behind its upright coffin of burnished wood heavily embossed with cherubs and bunches of grapes. As she stood admiring it, the brass innards whirred and the chimes struck twelve measured notes.

Charming, Kalina thought. Her spirits lifted. The chimes reminded her of Trinity Church, and a pang of sadness struck her heart. Despite the meanness of their life there, she and Zuska and Aunt Litka had been happy on Mulberry Street.

The maid brought hot chocolate and cakes. Stefan rejoined them, and brother and sister talked in low tones of the political convention, making no attempt to involve Kalina. Stefan switched on the pretty lamp, and Anusia said nothing. In the brighter light Anusia appeared much older, the nunlike aspect giving way to plain, dull middle-age. The white streaks in the dark hair became stark. Except for the wonderful eyes and the imperious set of the head, there was little resemblance between brother and sister.

The warm room, the drone of voices, three cups of chocolate—all served to induce a powerful drowsiness in the young bride. She rose, yawned, and stretched. "I beg you to excuse me, Anusia dear and Stefan," she said, "but it's been a long day, and Dunia will be up with the birds at dawn."

Anusia turned from Stefan. "There is no need for you to rise with the child. Wanda will take superb care of her. She comes from a large Polish family, the eldest of ten."

"That's marvelous," Kalina said, "but it is most essential that I begin to teach her proper English."

"Nonsense." Rising swiftly, Anusia yanked on the velvet bell pull. "Wanda's English will suffice for now. When the need arises, I will engage a competent governess to supervise the child's education."

Unexpectedly, the stern nun's face softened, and she curved a protective arm across Kalina's shoulders. "Get a good night's sleep, dear. Tomorrow we will inaugurate your own program of studies."

"Studies," Kalina echoed, stupidly. What on earth did she need to study for?

The reply was swift and uncompromising. "One does not become the mistress of an establishment such as ours" — Anusia aimed a wide smile at her brother — "and the official hostess of a man like Stefan Murav without strenuous and assiduous preparation."

Wings of resentment beat in Kalina's breast as she followed the maid up the curving rosewood staircase and down a dark corridor into a bedroom the size of a small ballroom. Was she a bride or a schoolgirl? OK, she would go along for it would hardly be prudent to cause a ruckus at the outset. Once she was mistress here, however, things would change. No more lessons, no more dark places. A multitude of lights would burn both day and night.

But now they were approaching the bed, a massive, magnificent affair of feather quilts and silken counterpane, so high one climbed a little ladder at the side before one tumbled over the wooden rail and sank into a sea of wondrous comfort.

Hania's daughter, Stefan's wife, Anusia's protégée. Well, she thought as sleep overwhelmed her, she could manage to be all three.

"Mama, Mama!"

A squeaky clean and very excited Dunia in a charming, blue cotton dress broke away from Wanda to hurl herself at Kalina, who sat at a late breakfast in a sunny room off the kitchen. After a flurry of kisses, the child stood back, glanced quickly at the nurse, who nodded her white-capped head.

"Bwoo dress," Dunia lisped, spreading out the wide, floor-length skirt with two tiny hands.

"She couldn't wait to show off her new words," Wanda gushed in a clear, sweet voice with the slightest of Polish accents. What's more, Kalina noted with relief, the girl was pretty—no, more than that—she was attractive in that elusive, aristocratic way of many Poles. High cheekbones, long, thin nose, and deep-set blue eyes that had a way of looking directly at a person.

With the passing of the early weeks, Dunia's daily visits to Kalina were enlivened by more English words and sentences. Kalina's early fears about Wanda's ability vanished, but she sorely missed the intimacy that she and Dunia had developed in Shenandoah after Zuska left.

The bride herself had many new words to learn. *Mo-non-ga-hel-a*, the river with the lovely, tongue-twisting Indian name, the once pristine, but now mud-and-chemical-choked stream upon whose banks loomed the massive Carnegie Steel Works. Monongahela was the river to which her husband Stefan traveled each day to conduct his business. There were two other rivers, the *Al-le-ghen-y* and the *O-hi-o*.

The Allegheny flowed from the north to join its waters with the Monongahela, which came from the south. Together they made the great Ohio. This momentous juncture took place at Pittsburgh, to form the famous Point.

Basic knowledge for the wife of a steel man, so said Anusia. Relations between the sisters-in-law were far from unpleasant, but neither were they pleasant. Anusia rarely smiled except when Stefan was present. She never laughed. But little wonder, reflected Kalina, when one considers the woman's early suffering. One learns to laugh in childhood or not at all.

Along with the geography lessons, Anusia explained the basics of steel-making. Coal came from nearby mines, it was mixed with iron ore from Minnesota, then fired in white-hot furnaces to forge the wonderful, miraculous, shiny stuff that went into rails for trains, armorplate for ships, pipes for houses, and numberless other items.

Like bullets, cannons, and guns. Stefan's lesson in the hotel room remained vividly etched in Kalina's mind.

The hasty Philadelphia wardrobe was declared eminently unsuited to Pittsburgh society, so a seamstress was engaged and cloth was ordered. But when the bolts arrived, Kalina looked in vain for whites and pinks and yellows, all the lovely pastel hues she had dreamed of wearing, the flowery hues worn by the heroines in French romances.

"These somber browns and grays do not suit me," she wailed to Wanda, for whom she had developed an almost sisterly affection. "My complexion will take on a sallow tone."

Anusia's comment when she ventured to ask for brighter colors was terse. "You must manage to appear older than you are." Then, she added, sourly, "Gay colors are for women of the streets."

The older woman was right, Kalina conceded inwardly. In some ways, Stefan's sister was the mother who was far away in Poland. As one does not challenge the authority of a husband, so one heeds religiously the advice of a mother.

At day's end she was exhausted from the unending lessons and sore from being pinned and pummeled and twirled about by the dressmaker and her assistants. Falling upon her downy bed or lounging on the brocaded loveseat in her spacious bedroom and gazing at a moonlit prospect of garden and lawn and trees, Kalina scolded herself for any unworthy thoughts. She was the luckiest girl alive.

She dared not complain to Stefan in any event. On the rare occasions when he dined at home, the talk was all of steel production or rumbles of war in the Balkans or—his latest enthusiasm—the glider flights at Kitty Hawk.

His face glowed. "Some crazy geniuses called the Wright brothers. Mark my words, ladies, before any of us is very much older, men will take to the air like birds."

He paused to cut off the end of his cigar with a steel cutter shaped like a tiny guillotine. It was his favorite toy, and now he played with it, pushing it up and down, chuckling when the blade hit bottom.

"Warfare will be transformed," he said triumphantly.

But in the summer nights, as Kalina lay with her husband in the cavernous bed, there was no talk of war. There was only love. Although the longed-for Mediterranean honeymoon never materialized because of pressure of business, the young Polish girl was an apt pupil as the more experienced bridegroom led her forcefully but subtly to the heights of ecstasy in marriage. Many nights Kalina had reason to be grateful for the length of corridor separating them from Anusia and the maids.

Soon she would be with child. Such passion could not fail but impregnate her. Once she bore the Murav heir, Anusia's tyranny must come to a merciful end for the young bride. A woman who has borne a child is a woman, worthy to be mistress in her own house.

But to her dismay Kalina's womb remained stubbornly closed. As summer faded into autumn, she found herself spending long hours alone in the second-floor library, studying the books Anusia assigned or gazing morosely out the window at the carriages rattling by, bearing elegantly dressed ladies and gentlemen in splendid regalia to galas, operas, receptions, dances. Anusia had decreed that the young Mrs. Stefan Murav could not go into society until her wardrobe was completed down to the last pair of gloves, the last feathered hat.

At night, Kalina liked to pull the curtains and gaze, fascinated, at the firelit sky across the river. The bursts of flame seemed to her a great, constantly erupting volcano. The open hearths where the iron was melted into steel at temperatures beyond imagining stretched along the river banks as far as the eye could see. Hearths of hell, Wanda called them. Her father and three brothers worked in the mills, helping to forge the steel that came out of the gigantic blast furnaces.

Only at such times, as she gazed at the blood-red night sky, did Kalina permit herself to think of Max. *A man can make money in the mills.* How his brown eyes had glowed with supreme confidence! He was probably over there, in the mill, right across the river, in that living fire. A few short miles away, but it might as well be a continent, she reflected. Their paths would not cross again. The road upon which they had set their feet on a snowy New Year's Eve had diverged. She had gone one way, he another.

Rain—a heavy, persistent downpour—slashed against the library windows. Seeming to go on forever, it thudded on the slate roof of the big house and gurgled through the downspouts into the poplar-lined drive. One day was swallowed by the next in dismal procession. Stefan had been gone for a week, embroiled in some momentous doings in New York concerning the selling of the Carnegie Steel Works. "These things sometimes take years to accomplish," he'd said.

When Kalina complained about the bad weather, Anusia had announced, "October in Pittsburgh is always wet," as if giving the rain her permission to fall.

Now, on the fifth day of the rain, Kalina was seated at the long table before the tall window, writing letters. Years ago, Aunt Litka had set her and Zuska to copying laboriously from the models in manuals, but when she showed her first efforts to Anusia, her sister-in-law threw up her hands in horror.

"Stilted," she exclaimed, "Like something Mrs. George Washington might have written."

The immediate task at hand was to formulate an invitation to high tea to be held at the Murav residence, the date to be determined later. Five letters must be done neatly without a single blot. After numerous failures, three were finished, letter perfect, without a single smudge, and Kalina had started on the fourth when the wheels sounded in the wet driveway. She threw down her pen and flew down the stairs to the foyer.

"Stefan!" She ran like a child into his arms.

He smelled of rain and cigars and coal, but to her lonely heart it was the perfumes of Araby.

"My little, precious darling." The big man folded her into his arms and covered her face with kisses as if he would devour her. A raspy cough from Anusia cut short their affectionate reunion, and Stefan reached out to pull his sister into the circle of love.

To Anusia he said, "My dear sister, we've done it. We've pulled off the biggest coup in history. Every steel mill in the country with more than a handful of men is now part of one, big, happy family." He laughed uproariously. "We own them all."

Kalina caught a glimpse of Anusia's face. Pride and joy suffused the face, banishing the usual sallowness. The plain woman glowed like a girl in love. Why, she adores her brother, Kalina thought.

Releasing the two women, Stefan shucked off his raincoat and handed it to Wanda, who had hurried downstairs from the nursery at the commotion. Machinelike, Stefan rattled on. "It's to be called the United States Steel Company, and in a year when the crusty old Scotsman retires for good the top job will be mine."

Kalina had no time to digest this amazing news, for the coachman Andrew was bringing in armloads of boxes. There were gifts for everyone in the household down to the lowest scullery girl and gardener. Finally, he drew a thick, creamy envelope from his pocket and thrust it into his wife's hands. She opened it and shrieked with delight. It was an invitation to a reception in honor of Theodore Roosevelt, the candidate for vice-president of the United States. To be held at the home of Mr. and Mrs. Alexander Moore.

A party would follow an electioneering speech by "Teddy," and anyone who was anyone at all in Pittsburgh would be there. Stefan beamed at Kalina. "This is my first chance to show off my beautiful bride, and a party at

Lillian Russell's will launch you in style."

"Lillian Russell? The actress?" Kalina looked puzzled.

Anusia answered for her brother, her tone one of crisp disapproval. "Yes, the very same *actress*. She married Mr. Moore some years ago—her fourth marriage by the way—and has managed to set herself up as official arbiter of society in our town."

The elite of American industry would be there, and when Kalina wasn't standing for the dressmaker, a birdlike woman called Mrs. Raymond, she was memorizing from newspaper clippings and books all the big names, along with their photographs. Carnegie, Schwab, Rockefeller, Morgan.

Like all dressmakers, the Murav seamstress was full of gossipy information about what she called the "swells." Mrs. Moore was known as Diamond Li'l to an adoring public. "She's never seen without a bushel of diamonds," the woman babbled, "even wears 'em to bed, I hear."

No amount of pleading could, however, produce the kind of gown Kalina dreamed of—the kind she had seen in photographs of Diamond Li'l and other reigning beauties. Before her horrified eyes, a garish, bilious purple ball gown the color of overripe grapes took shape under the dressmaker's flying hands. It was accented with scarlet braid slithering like licorice candy down the front and sleeves.

"It's hideous," groaned Kalina.

"Nonsense, girl, you'll be a standout," snapped Anusia. "My Parisian sources tell me purple is the rage this season."

It was the first Kalina had heard of Anusia's Parisian sources.

"I understand that Mrs. J. Pierpont Morgan is much given to wearing purple," ventured Mrs. Raymond timidly. Whatever she thought, the penurious seamstress knew what side her own bread was buttered on. Anusia Murav was not one to be questioned by an underling.

To compound the horror, lacy ruffles were tacked on at the neck and hem. Anusia also suggested cascades of lace at the wrist, declaring, "lace is so genteel."

"Prosperity such as mankind has never known, and peace, sweet, beneficent peace will descend upon the earth."

Thousands applauded as Teddy Roosevelt boomed this hopeful sentiment over the packed auditorium. Stefan predicted exactly the opposite. War. But on the festive occasion to which she had looked forward with such great anticipation, Kalina was less interested in politics, be it peace or war, than in the dazzling ladies seated around her. The gowns that emerged from thrown-back coats of sable, mink, silver fox, and caracul were of rainbow hues. Whites, creamy beiges, sky or robin's egg blues, jonquil yellows, carnation pinks, rich, luscious violets.

No matter how far she craned her neck, she could spot not a single purple. Apparently the rage of Paris had yet to reach the banks of the Monongahela. Though the auditorium was stifling hot, Kalina kept her own sable coat tight about her.

Later, in the brilliantly lit salon of the Moore mansion, high atop a bluff over the river, she found no purple either. Anusia had played her for a fool. Stefan's sister, she was now convinced, was her implacable enemy. Her worst fears were confirmed by her husband's astonished glance as she walked out of the cloakroom. He had gone straight from his office to the auditorium and had not seen the gown.

"My God, Kalina," he exploded. "What in the name of all that's holy—"

"Anusia," she gritted between clenched teeth. But she could not say what was in her heart, for they were immediately beset by the crowd, and she was caught up in introductions, mouthing carefully the small talk that Anusia had rehearsed her in.

But when they came abreast of the candidate in the reception line, Kalina's timidity vanished before the irrepressible exuberance of the man. To one like this, she thought, purple was just another color, neither good nor

101

bad. His snapping eyes regarded people for what they are.

"You must visit Edith and me in Washington," Teddy thundered, pumping Kalina's hand as if he were drawing water from a well.

"Mr. Roosevelt seems very confident of election," she ventured to Stefan, but her husband had vanished, having been tugged away by a man with a gold-topped cane. Kalina stood alone at the tail end of the long reception line.

Mortified at her predicament, and appalled at the thought of approaching any of the tight little groups now forming around the room, she walked rapidly toward a doorway she thought might lead into a powder room. Her instinct proved correct, and once safely within the cloistered interior, she sat down before a mirror and fussed with her hair, which Anusia had braided so tightly it made her sloe black eyes slant up into slits. She dared not speak to the women going in and out, and for their part, after a quick glance at the girl in purple, none introduced herself.

Finally, when the uniformed maid began to look at her curiously, Kalina darted into one of the curtained-off commodes. As she sat tensely on the polished wooden seat, women came in and out chatting busily, and gradually she became aware through the babble of voices that the young Mrs. Murav was the main topic of discussion.

"The one in purple" . . . "after all this time, the old cock taking a bride" . . . "a child" . . . "where did he get her?" . . . "an orphan asylum?"

She started as the curtains were drawn aside. But it was only the maid. "Are you all right?"

"Yes." Red-faced, Kalina was forced to leave her sanctuary. But, despite the maid's stares, she resolved to remain in the lavatory until the evening ended.

"Mercy, so that's what you look like!"

The exclamation came from a slight young woman sitting in a velvet armchair. She was exquisite, a flower. Rich, creamy skin was brushed by nature with the most delicate rose. Her apple-green gown was cut very low, exposing a great deal of silky shoulder and neck before it plunged into a small but nicely curving bosom. A single spray of satiny apple blossoms was caught in hair the color of moonlight.

Two very blue and smiling eyes fixed themselves on a very embarrassed Kalina.

"I am Libby Hughes," she said without preamble. The voice, like its owner, was soft and elegant.

"Only child of Millard Hughes, general superintendent of the Carnegie Works," Kalina blurted out. She clapped hand to mouth. "I beg your pardon, Miss Hughes. I've read about you in the papers."

"Libby, please." The sweet smile only widened. "I am not offended, Kalina Murav. Once, I too was compelled by my governess to memorize names, faces, and biographies."

Extending her hand to grasp Kalina's, she drew her into an adjoining chair. "When your cad of a husband left you stranded out there, I came after you at my first opportunity." She laughed, a wonderfully light and easy sound. "But not soon enough, I fear, to keep you from hiding in the commode like a frightened child at her first dance."

Kalina's head dropped. "I am such a goose. If only Anusia had come with me, she would have seen how poor a choice she made in my gown." She was close to tears. How gauche she must appear before this fashionable, cultured, self-assured young woman.

"The esteemed Miss Murav never engages in society," Libby murmured. "And from the look of you, she wants to ensure that you won't either. She'd like nothing more than to mold you into a younger version of herself."

Kalina's head came up. "If only I could look like you!"

Impulsively Libby grasped her hand again. "Why on earth would you want to look like me when you can look like a smashing Kalina Murav?"

Astonished, Kalina gazed into blue eyes that had lost their merry look.

"I've learned from bitter experience," continued Libby, tartly, "the nefarious ways of your sister-in-law. You see, I was one of many girls who aspired to become Mrs. Stefan Murav." The blue eyes lost their sober look. "But all that's ancient history now. Our concern is with the present."

Pulling Kalina from the chair, Libby placed her in front of the mirrored wall. "Now hold still, very still," she commanded crisply. "Don't move a muscle. Don't even breathe. However much we might desire to change its dreadful hue, we must not get blood on your precious purple gown."

Extracting a dainty pair of silver scissors from her reticule, Libby began to snip at the waterfall of ruffles, patiently edging her way around the neck and wrists. In minutes, the entire frothy mess of lace surrounded Kalina's feet. Libby thrust out a gold-sandaled foot to kick it away. Impassively, but obviously suppressing a smile, the maid scooped it up. Apparently, Kalina thought wildly, this kind of thing is far from a rare occurrence in the lavatory.

Back on her haunches on the carpeted floor, Libby considered her next move. "Hmm. If only I dare cut the sleeves to display your lovely arms. But the seam would be ragged. In any case, the ruffles must go."

Soon the maid, who was grinning widely by this time, was engulfed in an armful of purple ruffles.

Kalina remained silent through it all, but her heart was beating like a bird who sees its cage door being opened after long imprisonment.

"*Voilà*," Libby fairly shouted. "Now we see more of Kalina Murav. And a very impressive 'more' it is to boot. One look at that swanlike neck of yours, my dear young friend, and no one will know if you're wearing purple or pink or green."

She called me friend, Kalina thought with joy.

It took a while longer to unbraid the tightly wound-up hair and arrange it into a gleaming topknot, securing it with silver pins Libby produced from her seemingly bottomless reticule. With the help of water from the spigot, her new friend's nimble fingers magically produced a mass of feathery curls to frame Kalina's alabaster brow and cheeks.

When all was done, she could only stare enraptured at her transformed mirror image. This is *me*, she thought, almost giddy with happiness. It was a revelation. Simple style, no frills, no lace. Nothing to distract from her dark, aristocratic beauty. Fashion may come and go, but one's own natural beauty remains a constant and reliable barometer for success.

Back in the salon, Libby steered a course straight for a circle that appeared at first to be completely male but that separated at their approach to reveal a statuesque blonde woman at the center.

"Our hostess," Libby hissed in Kalina's ear. "La Russell in the flesh, holding court."

By any standards the former stage celebrity was magnificent. A blue Gainsborough hat lavishly adorned with feathers topped obviously peroxided hair, but the face beneath it bore such disarming candor and open friendliness that Kalina had the swift impression of a woman liked by everybody.

Mrs. Moore flashed the brilliant smile that had enchanted audiences for decades. "Libby, my dear, who is this ravishing young person?"

"Mrs. Stefan Murav, Lillian."

The aging but still stunning actress, famed for her hourglass figure, extended a diamond-laden hand. Her grip was like a man's, firm and invigorating.

"Smashing, smashing," she murmured. Then, with a slight dimming of her eyes. "Ah, youth, youth."

Every polite phrase she had learned from Anusia flew out of Kalina's mind, and, forgetting to be sedate, she gushed, "I'm so excited to meet you actually, Mrs. Moore."

The beautiful head drew back and a hearty laugh issued from the heavily rouged mouth. "Please, don't be formal. Call me Li'l." After a promise to "have you to a soiree, just us girls," her rich stage contralto floated out over the vast room. "Jim Brady, come here."

Moments later, feeling much like Cinderella at the ball, Kalina found herself being escorted to supper by the notorious "Diamond Jim," friend, confidant, and reputed longtime lover of La Russell. Like the actress, his wealth was legendary, and he wore a ring on each of his ten fingers. Anusia had suggested that, like gay colors, the wearing of jewelry was vulgar and ostentatious. Instinctively, Kalina's gloved hand flew to her naked neck.

Seeing the gesture, the corpulent Mr. Brady leaned over her as they were being seated at the banquet table. "Such a neck," he said in a loud stage whisper, "is a tower of ivory without its needed battlements."

Some devil within prompted Kalina to reply, "I hear that your friend Mrs. Moore has diamonds stitched into her corsets."

His booming laugh echoed up and down the long table, and people lifted their faces to stare and laugh along infectiously. "Your wit matches your beauty, my precious child." Then, sobering, "Promise not to blush if I tell you I can verify the story." Spearing an olive, he popped it into her mouth, which was wide open with laughter.

Suddenly, as if a fairy godmother had waved a wand, the young Mrs. Murav was engaging in intelligent, witty, animated conversation not only with her famous companion but with the man on her other side as well as several women across the table.

Most of her attention was given, however, to simply dealing with the sumptuous viands that appeared in a seemingly endless stream under her nose. She had eaten nothing all day from excitement and so partook generously of the fish, meats, soups, and fruits and cheeses, finishing triumphantly with two helpings of a deliciously cold spumone ice cream, which she had heard about but never tasted.

Diamond Jim beamed. "I truly admire a woman who eats well."

"I understand," replied Kalina archly, "that it was the mutual love of good food that first attracted you to Miss Russell.

"Alas." The florid face assumed a mock tragic mien. "The two loves of my life."

The supper ending well after midnight, Mr. Brady led Kalina to a smaller room that was furnished in the popular Japanese style. Red and black tables sat close to the floor, and one sat on cushions instead of chairs. Stefan was there, deep in conversation with a group of men, all of whom were puffing nervously on long cigars. The room was gray with smoke. Despite the late hour, however, her hostess remained exuberant as she presented the young Mrs. Murav to Louise Carnegie and Amanda Morgan and then left the three of them to wait until their respective husbands had settled the world's affairs. Or at least those matters that concerned the newly formed United States Steel Company Trust.

After a long, appraising look at Kalina, Mrs. Carnegie remarked, "Adorable," and promptly fell asleep. Most likely near suffocation from the smoke, mused Kalina. The life of an industrialist's wife was not all cakes and ale.

Mrs. J. P. Morgan leaned forward to touch Kalina on the arm. "That purple, my child, is an inspiration. Most striking."

"Thank you," Kalina murmured. "It's taken from a Paris design. My dressmaker is most clever."

The woman, whose husband was reputed to be the richest man in the entire world, whose every word caused Wall Street to shake as from an earthquake, sighed with envy. "But on you, my child, anything would look stylish."

Kalina returned the smile with ease. She felt like a proud bird soaring over the earth. And Libby Hughes had worked the miracle. Dear Libby had given her the confidence she sorely needed. As for Anusia's reaction to the mutilated gown, she found to her surprise that she didn't give a hang!

Anusia's reign over her cowering sister-in-law had finally come to an end.

It was well past noon the following day when Wanda opened the bedroom door, her arms filled with a long, ribbon-bedecked box. Dear Stefan, Kalina thought, sleepily opening one eye to greet the maid. Last night, late as it was when they had climbed into the big bed, she had been vibrant with passion, responding eagerly to her husband's overtures. In the morning as usual, despite the rigors of the night, Stefan had departed early for the mill.

The box contained the expected long-stemmed roses of a unique silvery pink. But they were not from Stefan. A square white card tucked inside the tissue read simply, "From a secret, but very ardent admirer." Enchanted, Kalina buried her nose in the roses.

"Oh, Mrs. Murav, there's something else."

Wanda's exclamation drew her attention to a narrow velvet box deep inside the roses. In it reposed a nest of diamonds that, when pulled out, became a necklace. Stefan had not sent this. As she pressed the glittering circle against her bare neck, Kalina's pulse thumped convulsively and a telltale heat suffused her face.

". . . a tower of ivory without its needed battlements." "The audacious Mr. Brady of course," she murmured softly.

"And why should another man be sending you diamonds?" So absorbed was she in the diamonds that Kalina had not noticed the maid's disappearance and the entrance of Anusia. Her nemesis stood in the doorway, glowering.

Kalina's heart contracted but remembering her resolution to defy Anusia, she flashed a brilliant smile and in a brittle, cool voice, replied, "It is common knowledge that sending diamonds to ladies he admires is one of Mr. Brady's idiosyncrasies."

Anusias stiffened. "Stefan will not be pleased."

The woman was jealous! Delighted at the revelation, Kalina threw back the covers and bounded out of bed. She stood naked before the startled and very angry Anusia.

"On the contrary," purred Kalina, "if I know men, my husband will be most pleased, indeed flattered, that his little bride should be so honored by such a connoisseur of beauty."

Her instinct proved correct. After examining the necklace at length, Stefan Murav's face assumed a look of pleased satisfaction. But of course his wife could not keep the expensive gift, so he tucked it into his briefcase for personal delivery to Mr. Brady's residence, a transaction, he said with a wry smile, he did not quite trust his young and very naive wife to do for herself.

As for Anusia Murav, she endured the whole affair with suffering eyes and compressed lips. The sharp lines on either side of her thin mouth became little canyons.

The lioness had been bearded in her own den.

But then, no wonder the woman was so bitter, Kalina thought with sudden compassion. No one had ever sent Anusia diamonds.

The affair of the necklace and the mutilated gown was only the beginning. As the new bold character of her brother's bride began to manifest itself in myriad little ways, Anusia barely spoke, going about the house like a wraith. Relations became strained between the Murav women.

But in her newfound joy Kalina could find no room for sadness. Though she may have lost a mother substitute, she felt she had gained a friend.

Herself.

Chapter Five

Homestead, August 1901

At midnight, Max O'Hara left the red belly of the open hearth to plunge his head into the water trough outside. After a few delicious moments, he drew erect and shook himself like a dog. Cool droplets fell from his red head and naked chest. Six hours into the shift, six to go. Scorning the filthy cotton towel as well as the common tin dipper hooked onto the drinking bucket, he leaned against the brick wall. A knot of workers lounged in the yard, smoking cigarettes and dipping into tin lunchbuckets for onion and baloney sandwiches.

"Ho, Max! Come, eat!" Gus Koval's thick Dutchie voice soared over the din of the furnace. Max's best friend curved an arm toward himself. "I got fresh blood sausage from the butcher."

Max shook his head, liking the feel of the water falling from his head onto his hot face. He did not return the shout. Yelling consumed energy better saved for the furnace. He stood a moment longer before returning to the fire, savoring the mild August night, listening to the mill. An open hearth was both beautifully spectacular and dangerous. Like a much-loved woman, he mused, she sucked a man's lifeblood, she ate into his very soul.

The huge, shedlike building, higher than a four-story

house, cradled the giant, brick-lined womb where the crude iron ore was transmuted into steel. Being part of the miracle, especially in the awesome moment when the ladle tipped molten white-hot steel into the castings, showering flaming sparks on the puny men below, Max felt himself a king of sorcerers.

With all his heart, the young Irish American loved the open hearth. It was a thing alive. It even bore a name—Lucy—after the wife of a founding steel father. But he also feared it. Sometimes a chain broke, a ladle tipped too far, or a poor bastard with sweaty hands lost his grip and hot metal spewed death in all directions.

A roar like that of a hundred lions split his reverie, and along with the others, Max streaked into the mill. The hot steel was ready to pour. With a swiftness belying his bulk, Gus was at his friend's side. A tall crane, maneuvered by a man in a little cab far overhead, upended the gigantic ladle. Searing metal cascaded into the long ingot-shaped trough. Seemingly oblivious to the rain of fire, the small army of sweating men shoveled slag—the impurities that fell from the river of hot steel—into piles.

In the smoky dawn, a bone-weary Max trudged along the gritty cobblestones of Homestead, the Monongahela town that was the capital of the Carnegie Works. It was seven months since he had jumped the freight from Shenandoah. He had been hired right away. Six feet plus of hard muscle was exactly what the steel bosses wanted to man their string of furnaces. He had yet to meet his idol, however, the fabulous Scotsman, the autocrat of American steel.

"You've got a chance to make it good," the stove-gang boss assured him, "you ain't no hunky." The man's name was O'Brien. Max soon learned that here in Pittsburgh distinctions based on one's national origin made all the difference. "Hunkies," defined as Poles, Slovaks, Hungarians—anyone with middle European forebears—could never rise to be foreman, no matter how long or how hard he worked for Carnegie.

Renting a room in one of the gaunt frame houses stuck

111

onto the hillsides had been equally simple. Steelworkers' wives eked out their husbands' slave wages by keeping boarders, usually single men or men whose wives were still in Europe, awaiting passage money. Breakfast, lunch-bucket, and dinner were furnished along with as much warmth and family life the boarder desired. His room at the Leskos' cost Max three dollars a week, one third his pay.

Stopping for breath at the crest of the hill where River Road curved into Seventh, Max turned, as was his habit, to gaze at the sluggish river. A church bell sounded, shawled women poked through the gray streets to early Mass. Between the mills and the river, the train snaked along, its little windows aglow with yellow light.

He let out a breath. *Kalina*. That train might well be coming from Shenandoah. Three, four days from now, she could be behind those windows, ready to leap into his arms at the Pittsburgh station.

But quickly as it had come, he pushed the vagrant thought from his mind. He was not ready; his dear sweet Kalina must wait a little longer.

Though it was still early when he entered the house, Elena Lesko was already bent over the ironing board. Max bounded across the kitchen to hug her skinny frame to his own.

"Phew," his landlady exclaimed as he released her. "You need a wash-up." But her crimson face and sparkling eyes betrayed her pleasure at his touch. Of all her boarders, the New York Irishman was her favorite. Elena turned, set her cooling flatiron on the blazing coal stove, and picked up a hot one. "Mary'll have your breakfast in a minute."

Once robust and handsome, Elena Lesko was, at thirty, spare and gaunt with perpetual hollows under gray, deep-set eyes. She supported five little ones and a husband crippled in the mill with take-in laundry and boarders. The hard life had taken its toll.

"Okey, doke," Max grinned, placing his lunch bucket on the sink drainboard. Turning the iron spigot all the way, he splashed cold water on his face and hands, opening his shirt to rub the cake of hard, yellow soap on chest and upper arms. After a hasty drying on the roller towel, he sat down at table and started a silly banter with the two seated children sleepily awaiting their breakfast. They loved the silly talk, and they loved Max. Twelve-year-old Mary, the eldest and her mother's "right arm," was at the stove, frying meat.

"Blood sausage," she called out, "the Kovals sent it up."

The Kovals, who were childless, were longtime friends of the Leskos, the two men having worked as a team on Lucy Furnace and others until Stan Lesko's accident. *Accident* — Max thought bitterly as he speared a sizzling hunk of meat — hardly the word for what happened.

"Ho there, Max, another day, another dollar!" Stan Lesko entered the kitchen.

"Dollar sixty-five, old pal," Max corrected. "I get regular puddlers' wages now."

Mary Lesko plunked a plate filled with lardy fried potatoes and sausage in front of her father, then poured scalding coffee for the two men. Stan ate dexterously with two black-stockinged stumps, both of his hands having been crushed in a misaligned coupling just a year ago. Too poor to hire a lawyer to prove company negligence and collect compensation, he now pushed a vendor's cart through the narrow alleys of Homestead, hawking hot corn in winter, flavored ices in summer. The job didn't fetch much cash, but it kept him occupied and out of the house much of the day, leaving Elena to her own work.

"Crossing the river to Swissvale today," he said to his wife. "Mazzoni's orders."

Elena turned, iron in hand. "And will the high and mighty Mr. Mazzoni give the dime for the ferry?"

"Better over there," he said, ignoring her question. "People in Swissvale are Dutchie. Mazzoni says they'll buy anything from a cripple."

"Humph," Elena snorted, slamming the iron back onto the stove.

"He's right, Elena," Max said mildly. "Germans raised me like their own when my own folks abandoned me.

What's more"—he reached to ruffle Stan's yellow hair—
"they're partial to towheads."

Stan smiled his thanks to Max. Except for his stumps he
was still a fine figure of a man. Maybe with the river
between him and Mazzoni, he could free himself from
bondage to the Italian who controlled all the vendors on
this side. Maybe even, he thought hopefully, get his own
cart.

The bed Max fell into minutes later was still warm and
rumpled from Joe Petovsky, who slept in it while Max
worked. Joe worked days at Lucy Furnace. Like Max, he
was a puddler, the man who wielded the iron hook that
formed the ore into balls while it still flamed inside the
firebox.

The tiny room was heavy with yesterday's heat, but Max
resisted the impulse to push up the narrow gable window.
The reddish sky over the Carnegie Library cupola boded
another sultry day. He stared a long moment at the
substantial brick building, the generous gift of the fabulous Scotsman. What was it Gus said last night? If every
book in that damned library was a loaf of bread . . .

Slumber came instantly. But after a few seconds of
oblivion, Max jerked awake with a sense of having forgotten something. Something important. His tired brain
clicked into gear. The train. Kalina. He closed his eyes,
sank back again. Waves of longing and remorse pumped
blood into his veins. A man could labor all day, all night,
twelve, fourteen hours and more if a woman like his own
Kalina awaited him at home with a hot meal and a warm,
loving body.

No wonder, he thought wryly, these people have such
large families. His pulse quickened, remembering the feel
of her in his arms. Joe Petovsky was moving out next
week, having sent to Poland for his wife. Max had seventy-
five dollars in the Mellon Bank. Plenty for a train ticket
and a month's rent on a new place.

"Today," he muttered into the hot pillow. "I'll do it
today."

Bounding out of bed, he yelled down the steps. "Call me

at four, Mary. Got some business downtown."

The first dull boom failed to jar Max from his profound sleep. But when the second thunderous clap rattled the window, he raised up from bed and leaned over to push back the curtain. A thunderstorm, most like. But he saw no lightning. Must be something at the mill.

The mill!

He shoved the window open, stuck out his head. A woman was running pell-mell down the middle of the street. "Mrs. Janicek," he yelled, "what's up?"

Without halting her downhill plunge, the woman screamed, "Explosion. Real bad."

Instantly, the door to his room flew open, and there stood a very scared-looking Mary Lesko. "Max! Oh, God, Max!" she whimpered. "It's Lucy Furnace."

Pulling on his shoes and trousers, Max pelted dry-mouthed down toward the river. By the time he reached the foot of the hill, a small mob of frightened women and children surrounded the mill entrance. He raced past them between the buildings and into the cindery yard.

"A slip," the guard said, "Don't know how bad yet."

A slip. Max's heart went to his shoes. Something had gone wrong in that crucial moment of pouring when tons of molten steel chose not to follow the whims of its human masters. He headed toward the open hearth, ignoring the guard's warning shout of "Hey, you can't go in there!"

A clump of men stood at the foot of the smoking slag pile a few yards from the furnace door. A black-coated man huddled over a crumpled heap of what looked like a pile of burning rags instead of what had once been a living, breathing, human being. The doctor, his lined face impassive because he couldn't afford emotion, straightened up, and beckoned to the others to cover the corpse with a tarpaulin. That part which Max saw of the burned flesh resembled a piece of blood sausage.

"Joe?" he said, looking at the men.

"Nah," replied a burly worker. "Just a greenhorn. Hired

on last week, a dinkey man who had the bad luck to be in the wrong place at the wrong time."

A dinkey man pushed the little cars from furnace to furnace. "Where's Joe?" Max repeated. "Joe Petovsky, a puddler?"

The man shrugged, spread his hands in a gesture of helplessness, and walked away to hover over another smoldering body. An hour later, eight bodies had been identified. Joe Petovsky, whose wife was even now on a boat from Poland, was among the dead. A man named Mielchek had not been accounted for. He had been seen reporting to work that morning, the stove-gang boss had talked to him, so had others.

The superintendent, a man named Millard Hughes, a man with pale hands like a girl's and dressed in cool, blue-and-white-striped seersucker, announced at last that Yuri Mielchek had apparently perished inside the furnace. Like Joe, he was one of those who stirred the liquid fire with an iron rod, working it into little balls for testing. At the moment of explosion, he had slipped, most likely, and, being inches away from the white-hot soup, had been sucked in and consumed.

When Max entered the super's office, Millard Hughes looked up and said grimly, "Thanks for coming, Max. I asked for you because I know you for a cool head and a way with words." His bland face reddened. "Fact is, there's this hunky family who's got to be told. Officially." He dropped his eyes under Max's hostile stare.

"Mielchek, the poor bastard who died in the steel." Max bit off the words.

The older man flushed. Running the Homestead works for the Carnegie empire was challenging and remunerative, but at times like this, the middle-aged widower fervently wished he had never left schoolteaching. Lifting his eyes, he forged ahead in a steady, managerial voice. "Five kids, wife of course. In a house by the tracks."

"It's your job," Max said, tonelessly.

Hughes coughed nervously. "Something extra in your pay envelope, O'Hara, for doing this for me."

The Mielcheks lived in a row of hovels built in the eighties when smokestacks first poked into the sky over the Monongahela. Groups of four houses surrounded a common privy and an iron spigot that spewed out brackish water. The place was popularly known as Cesspool Alley. Stinging rain slanted into Max's face as he strode rapidly along the gravelly street where whey-faced kids played happily at their eternal games as if they were rich kids gambling on a spacious lawn.

The library clock chimed twelve as he knocked on the shanty door. Mrs. Mielchek, her head swathed in a black kerchief, walked slowly from the yard, a bucket of water swinging at her side. Sorrow darkened her broad features.

Bless the holy saints, breathed Max inwardly. She knows.

The woman spoke no English, so he stumbled through the interview in the kitchen with the little Slovak he had picked up. "Your man," he said, covering her work-rough hand with his own, "was liked by everyone. A hard worker."

He tried to think of the best way to say that a man's body was nothing, that a man's soul was what counted in the sight of God. The priest should be here, he thought with sudden anger. Where was the man, anyway? As he talked, the widow laid her head on the oilcloth-covered table, her sloping shoulders trembling in mute grief. Max was wondering what he would do if she became hysterical, when the door burst open and two very dirty children entered. They threw themselves at their mother, chattering in Slovak.

"*Nu, nu,*" the mother clucked, then got up to walk lightly to a cupboard where she pulled out a tin of lard and a loaf of home-baked bread. Working swiftly and talking softly to the children all the while, she sliced the bread, spread lard on the slices, sprinkled them with salt, and handed the product to the children. Munching greedily, the kids ran back outside, completely unaware that they were

117

now orphans.

"The company will pay seventy-five dollars for a funeral, Mrs. Mielchek," Max said, failing to add that since there was no body, the money could well be used for other purposes. At the mention of the money, the woman began to scream incoherently, standing in the middle of the small kitchen. She shook her fist at him menacingly. Then, God be praised, the door opened once more and two neighboring women came in to rescue him.

But the company would not pay, Max found out at midnight when he went to the stove-gang boss to pick up the seventy-five dollars.

"No body, no funeral, that's the policy," growled O'Brien. "Goddamn sons o' bitches."

A sick despair mingled with the rage already tearing Max apart. He and O'Brien talked about the accident, how the chains had needed fixing for a long time, how a greenhorn straight off the boat should not be asked to work twelve straight hours at the open hearth.

"Twelve?" O'Brien aimed a thick, brown jet at the spittoon. "Hell, those guys sometimes have to work straight through eighteen — twenty hours when the heat is tricky."

Next day, Sunday, Max strolled up Kensington Road, the topmost street on Homestead Hill. Two- and three-story brick and stone houses sat importantly behind sweeping green lawns and arching trees. A morning shower had cooled the August air and clouds still hung refreshingly over the hills.

"Number twenty-seven," Gus told him. Millard Hughes, he of the cowardly spirit and smooth hands, lived like a feudal lord in one of these awninged residences perched high above the belching smokestacks. Gus had been wary when Max told him what he planned to do.

"Go to his house and demand Mielchek's money? Christ, Max, you're signing your own death warrant."

"This is America," Max had snapped. "You don't kill a

118

man for demanding his rights."

They had been standing at the water trough, and Gus leaned forward to whisper. "They'll tag you for a union man, an agitator. That means either running you out of town or arranging an 'accident' for you."

But threats never kept the one-time New York street kid from doing what was right, and now, tall and handsome in freshly laundered Sunday shirt and trousers, a blue necktie setting off his crisp red curls, Max lifted the brass knocker of the super's white-pillared house. The heavy front door opened immediately, and a young girl in a crisp black-and-white uniform said, "Yes?"

Max noticed the absence of the expected "sir." He touched his tie, and dropped his hand. He must not appear nervous. "I wish to see Mr. Hughes."

The maid's black eyes flicked up and down contemptuously. "He's not at home. Anyway, he never sees workers here. You should make an appointment at his office." Backing into the foyer, she made to close the door.

Max thrust a quick foot into the doorway. "It's Sunday," he said patiently. "He's not at work."

The black eyes narrowed, half-frightened at this freckled giant. She was saved when a high, clear voice sounded from within the house. "Ask the gentleman to come in, Helen. I'll receive him in the library."

When Max was ushered into the spacious, book-lined room, his first impression of Libby Hughes was one of radiance. Her entire person seemed to shine as from a light within. Later, he would think her fragile, exquisite, lovely, slim, strong, the epitome of femininity, but now he was only transported as one might be by a masterful work of art. She could be twenty or thirty. Hard to tell. She was one of those moonlit creatures who simply laugh at the passing years.

She waited for him by an open window where snowy curtains billowed like little sails. A fresh, spicy garden scent caused him to exclaim even before she greeted him, "What is that wonderful aroma?"

She smiled. "White petunias. I grow them for the

119

fragrance."

"Oh. . . . I've come about Yuri Mielchek."

The blue eyes widened, questioning. She doesn't even know what I'm talking about, he thought.

"The man who was killed," he said, shortly, "in the furnace yesterday."

"Oh. I hadn't heard." She moved, graceful as a doe, to a bellpull by the fireplace. "May I offer you some coffee, Mister—?"

"O'Hara," he said calmly, collecting his wits. It was silly to be angry at the woman. This lovely, sheltered creature was not to blame for the hell within the mills. "Max O'Hara."

"Max," she laughed. "I've never known an O'Hara named Max. O'Haras tend to be Frank or Pat or Mike."

Witty, he thought, a sense of humor, but dammit, he could hardly deal with Libby Hughes man to man. It was her father he'd come to see.

When the bell brought no response, she excused herself to see to the coffee, giving her visitor an opportunity to examine the paneled room. Lining the walls were rows and rows of books, most of them bound in gold-and-brown hues. Gold lettering adorned the spines. A pungent leather odor mingled with the petunias. The smell of the rich, he mused with no bitterness. One day he would be as one of them.

Millard Hughes' daughter reentered with the maid and sat down in a deep, leather chair. "Please, Mr. O'Hara," she said, "be seated." The radiant smile appeared again, lighting up the sweet face. "I find talking easier with a cup in my hand."

Max chose a straight-backed wooden chair and took the proffered cup. He sipped, waiting for her to speak.

"I noticed you admiring our books," she said, "Do you read much?"

The maid offered him some little cakes on a plate, and left the room. "No," he responded quickly, twirling the rich cake in his big hand. "Twelve hours at the furnace don't—doesn't—leave much time for reading."

Outside of leaving Kalina behind in Shenandoah, Max's deepest grief was his continuing illiteracy. To ward off further talk of books, he plunged into the subject that had brought him here, drinking as elegantly from the dainty china cup as his big hands would permit.

"Mrs. Mielchek is entitled to her funeral money. It's the only decent thing to do." Thinking about the poor man banished his nervousness, and his voice rang with confidence.

Libby Hughes' pale eyelids fluttered, her polished ivory fingers whitened around the cup. "The funeral money is meant for just that. Funerals." She spoke in measured tones. "It should not be considered as a settlement."

"The payment of which would admit to obligation—let's call it blame—on the part of management." Stimulated by the rich coffee and driven to fresh anger by the woman's seemingly heartless response, Max set his cup back in the saucer so hard it nearly tipped over, and half-rose from his chair.

Her pale face became white as the chalky muslin that clung to her seductive curves. She did not answer immediately, and he waited, feasting his eyes on the fine line of brow and nose, the delicate but sensuous mouth. He was completely unaware that he had bent his big body forward until the full force of her heady scent assailed his nostrils.

She extended her hand to touch his arm, and Max O'Hara's lonely soul flamed into response. Unthinkingly, he smothered her hand in his. Making no move to break the contact, she said with feeling, "I am filled with compassion for the poor Mrs. Mielchek. Truly." The tiny lace ruffles at her breast heaved with suppressed emotion.

Max nodded, not trusting speech. He was loath to break the spell that had woven itself around them. At last, it was Libby Hughes who rose suddenly, fiercely. Darting to the mantel, she leaned her blond head on the marble, her back to him.

She spoke in muffled tones. "My father spends all his waking hours at the mill. It has become the wife he lost at my birth. These horrible deaths tear his heart out as they do mine." Turning, she faced him with tear-bright eyes. "It is the men who must help themselves. Men like you, Max O'Hara, who have both heart and intelligence. You must try again to establish a union. Only if you band together can you change the truly terrible conditions."

An illiterate, unschooled man cannot assume leadership, Max thought.

She seemed to him a suffering child, and Max yearned to leap from his chair and take her in his arms. His brown eyes must have reflected his sentiments for she quickly averted her gaze and half-ran back to her chair to fall down into its depths. "What's a mere woman to do," she cried, "I love my father and agonize for the workers."

"They crushed the union in 1892," he said coldly. "Do you want us to start the killing again? They tracked them down like dogs, with trained gunmen."

A silence followed. The afternoon had clouded up and spears of rain thrust at the open window. Max rose to close the sash, but she seemed not to see or hear the downpour. "Education," she said at last.

He stood beside her, resting his hand on the back of her chair. Libby Hughes spoke then of her work at the settlement house where she taught classes in English and helped immigrants prepare for the citizenship examination. Neither heard the front door open and close and were startled when Millard Hughes burst in upon them.

The superintendent gaped, obviously astonished to see a Lucy Furnace puddler drinking coffee, in his library, with his daughter. Libby bounded up to kiss her father on the cheek and take the bulging leather briefcase from his hands. He wore a sharp, blue linen suit with silk lapels, and Max noted with amusement that the man sported a newfangled narrow necktie like his own.

"Mr. O'Hara has come to inquire about a settlement for Mrs. Mielchek, Father," Libby said quickly.

Reopening the door he had just closed, Hughes waved his arm in a sweeping gesture. "The usual hearing will be held, O'Hara, but from what I've learned so far, it appears to be another case of worker negligence." His lips tightened. "Now get out of my house."

The glib dismissal touched a flame to the wick of Max's smoldering rage and, with an animal roar, he was upon the man, grasping the silken lapels with such force that the older man pitched forward and might have fallen had his daughter not rushed to clutch at his arms.

"Max!" she shrieked. "This won't help!"

"Keep out of this, girl," her father snapped, shoving her out of the way. Libby scrambled to the window, where she stood trembling.

Max released the man but stood his ground. "Those chains were bad, everybody knew it. Your stove-gang boss O'Brien reported it three times."

A white-faced, much-shaken Hughes smoothed his lapels and put his hand once again on the doorknob. "Leave before I call the police," he said in a low, threatening tone. Libby was sobbing quietly at the window, and leaving the door, her father walked toward her and enfolded her in his arms. Max watched them for a moment and then, knowing he was beaten for now, rushed blindly through the open doorway.

"Wait!" The girl left her father's arms to lead Max through the corridor past the green portiered parlor and into the white-tiled foyer. She dabbed at her tear-streaked face with a lacy handkerchief and opened the front door. Max walked out a few steps, his eyes falling on the bed of white petunias. Their pungent, rain-drenched fragrance pierced his heart. How can such beauty exist, he thought, alongside all the tragedy?

"You'll get wet," said Libby, casting her blue eyes upward anxiously. The rain pounded ferociously on the roof of the little portico.

He managed a crooked grin, though his heart felt ready to crack. "I need to cool off."

Both were silent, as the man and woman searched for something vital to say, some pleasantry that might restore the companionable feeling in the library. It was a feeling that neither, at this moment, could put into words. For Libby it was a resurgence of long-buried emotions. Whoever or whatever he was, wherever he came from, this brash Irishman had stirred her virgin heart as no other had done in all her twenty-eight years. She reached out to shake his hand.

"Come to my class in English," she said. "It meets every Tuesday night."

Max nodded, his heart too full for speech. Somehow she had guessed that he could neither read nor write. Turning abruptly, he hurtled down the steps to the street, pelting down Homestead Hill as if trying to escape the siren call of a life he could not hope to share.

Not for a very long time, if ever.

Monday morning, when the Mellon Bank opened its doors, Max withdrew his seventy-five dollars, and taking it to Cesspool Alley, told Mrs. Mielchek the company had decided that a funeral could be held without a body. Late that night, as he shoveled hot slag into a dinkey, he thought with a jolt that Kalina had been out of his mind for two whole days and nights. And with the days and weeks, his beloved girl from Mulberry Street took her place in his dreams of a life that would not come again.

A full-color map of the United States consumed an entire wall of the classroom, a large piece of gray slate another. Max worked his way to an empty chair in the back row, his eyes on the scuffed floor, acutely conscious of startled eyes. The news that the big Irishman was taking lessons from Miss Hughes would be all over Homestead by morning, the traditional grapevine working, like the steel mill, through the night. Once seated, he ignored the stares to watch the pretty teacher who stretched her slender form as she made large round letters on the slate.

"The pret-ty young girrrl is my sis-ter." She enunciated each word as she wrote, her sweet voice high and clear. Libby Hughes was more businesslike, but no less feminine than on Sunday, in a soft gray jacket and long, tubular skirt. A shirtwaist innocent of ruffles peeked out between wide lapels. She whipped around to face the class. "Now, let's all say it together."

The pupils, many of them old enough to be her father or even, in some cases, grandfather, parroted her words in a confused jumble of accents.

"The pret-ty young girrl is Miss Hughes," snickered a young man across the aisle, glancing wickedly at Max and putting a swarthy hand to his face to smother his laughter at his own wit. Max glowered at the man, and he fell silent.

Two hours later as they filed past the battered wooden desk, the teacher picked up a book from a pile on her desk. "Here's a book for you, Max," she said. "If you lose it, you pay two dollars."

Dumbly, he took it from her hand, unable to tear his eyes from her face. Her voice quivered ever so slightly as she continued, "This course is too advanced for you, I fear. Miss Stommel has a Thursday night class which is just beginning."

"I want this one," he said, finding his voice. "I can catch up." He refrained from adding that he had moved heaven and earth arranging things at the mill to be here tonight.

Promising Mary Lesko a dollar a week, he enlisted her aid in recognizing and reproducing the letters of the alphabet. The lessons went on, constantly, at breakfast, dinner, every moment he wasn't at the mill or at class. Instead of ridiculing him, as he had feared, the Lesko family regarded him with increased respect. One and all, they wondered that a grown man could work so hard at something that brought in no extra money.

In three weeks Max could read fluently from the book Miss Hughes had given him and could write whole sentences after a fashion in a sweeping, masculine hand.

"Maybe you can write a letter for me to my brother in Danzig," Stan Lesko joked. "He thinks I am a big capitalist." Max preened, replying that it would, of course, cost Stan a dollar, that being the going rate for letter writers in Homestead.

But it was his teacher's praise that made him soar. "Your progress has been spectacular," she caroled, dimpling in a way that set Max's heart to racing.

In September, she invited him to join a special, smaller class that met Friday nights in her home. For the one-time rent baby and small-time thief, the golden hours in the lamplit Hughes' library became all there was to life. The twelve hours at Lucy Furnace, the hurried meals at the Leskos', even the hours of fevered slumber in the room he now shared with a newly arrived greenhorn were simply to be endured.

If, in a rare moment, Kalina's face surfaced, Max assured himself that she was married to a miner by now. Or maybe a rich railroad man from the Pottsville Hotel, for he guessed that, like so many others, she would seek work there. A girl so pretty and so vibrant could not remain single long.

For himself, however, there could be no thought of marriage. He adored Millard Hughes' daughter; she was a goddess at whose feet he worshiped. A worm like Max O'Hara did not marry goddesses. He was not in love with her; rather, he was in love with learning. And Libby Hughes was his Muse.

She set them to reading the classics. "To imbue in your speech the lovely rhythms of our language," she explained.

And so, one late October evening, in the book-lined room where once he had been intoxicated by the smell of petunias but that now reeked of hair oil and sweat, Max recited with the others the immortal lines from Tennyson. "His strength was the strength of ten, Because his heart was pure."

The story of Sir Galahad, who alone saw the vision, who alone achieved the prize because he betrayed no man nor demeaned no woman, captured Max's imagination. Like the gallant knight, he too had a vision of greatness. But what shape that dream would take, he as yet had only a vagrant notion. Once he had read all the words behind those gleaming bindings on the shelves, he would know. That would be the talisman.

Ironically, it was the adulterous liaison between Lancelot and the aging Guinevere that intrigued the teacher. Libby's blue eyes glowed with passion as she told their tale. She bade them memorize the lines, "Man dreams of fame, while woman wakes to love."

"It's one of those philosophical lines that are bound to impress people at social gatherings," she said, twinkling.

The door opened just then and Millard Hughes called out, "A social gathering is exactly where you must be, my dear, next week at exactly this time."

Libby glanced up, blushing. "In truth, Father, we were so engrossed that I —"

"Forgot. I know." He smiled indulgently. His daughter's "good works" pleased the man immensely. It enhanced his image with the workers.

Later, walking home down the hill with a stocky widow named Olga who aspired to open a restaurant in town and felt that Miss Hughes' class imparted much-needed culture, Max chanted, "Man dreams of fame, while woman wakes to love."

"*Oy*, baloney," scoffed his companion in a comic mix of Slovak and English slang. "There's another line in the poem which is much wiser, much more true. 'Free love, free field, we love but while we may.' "

Max threw back his head and let his laughter roll into the autumn night. He sniffed the air. The smell of burning leaves almost choked out the soot, and he floated on the tide of his poetic dreaming. He squeezed Olga's plump shoulder with his big hand. If rumor was correct, she was the Guinevere of Homestead, not being overly faithful to her husband's memory.

"You are teacher's pet," Olga giggled, liking the squeeze. "That look in her eyes ain't only for the poem. She's mad for you, Irishman."

Blood pumped up into his neck and face. Max whirled, enraged that this coarse woman should put into words what belonged only in dreams. "You shut up, Olga Cesnik! Why you can't even think the way a woman like Libby Hughes thinks!"

Olga shrugged, laughing all the while. "Under all her finery, she's still a woman. And a mighty hungry one, if you ask me."

127

"Nobody asked you," Max snapped.

But he listened intently as Olga told him all she knew about the superintendent's daughter, cautioning him that it was all rumor, gleaned from the Hughes' household servants. Libby Hughes was thirty, if she was a day, a genuine old maid. Once, long ago, there had been a young man, but he had wanted to go West, and Libby had returned his ring.

"She'll never leave her father," Olga said with finality.

Chapter Six

The first winter of the twentieth century brought a kind of devastation to the upper Ohio Valley, that according to the oldest inhabitants, surpassed anything in memory. There seemed to be no respite from paralyzingly cold, mountainous snows, and murderous, shrieking gales. Ice jams blocked shipping on the rivers, ore barges were immobilized, and coal from mines could not be transported except by expensive boxcars. As a consequence, steel production almost came to a halt. Two of Homestead's fiery open hearths had to be banked.

Curiously, in the Murav mansion high above the Monongahela, the master of the house was far from crestfallen. "Shipping is down, rail profits are up," he told his wife one snowy December morning. "That's the beauty of a trust, my dear. Catastrophe in one division is easily offset by growth in another."

Kalina nodded, assuming the mildly intelligent look her husband liked to see on her face. She understood only, that despite the terrible weather and lack of production, they seemed to have more money than ever. The gown she wore this morning was a Worth of Paris original; her measurements had been sent to the designer's showrooms by cablegram.

Stefan merely glanced at the outrageous bill before stuffing it into a cubbyhole in his spacious oaken desk. Now, as she met his gaze in the dressing room mirror, Kalina felt the money well spent. Her husband stood

129

behind her, arms outflung as if wanting to embrace her but fearful of crushing the delicate fabric of the gown.

"Real gold thread," he marveled.

She smiled at his boyish pleasure. Husband and wife rarely conversed; there was never small talk of the weather, the children, furnishings of the house, viands for the meals. But of course, she reminded herself often, she had never known a father in the sense of family. Pan Mikolai was not her mother's husband; he had appeared only on special occasions in their living quarters.

The new wardrobe she had collected since the disastrous "purple" nightmare had done its part in transforming the timid immigrant girl into a self-assured, sophisticated society matron. Invitations in thick envelopes covered the table in the foyer. All of Pittsburgh was eager to have the Muravs for soirees, concerts, high teas, and grand balls. Kalina found her new life stimulating, for she had discovered in herself a new and previously untapped wit. She was rapidly becoming famous for her ability to converse with one and all, old and young, women and men. That she had her dear dead Aunt Litka to thank for her versatility, she was fully aware. The library books had proved a wise investment, she concluded. Not a night passed that Aunt Litka's soul was not included in her niece's prayers.

The only shadow on her happiness was her continuing failure to conceive and the absence of a letter from her mother, apprising her daughter of when she could come to America.

"We should hurry, Stefan," she said abruptly. "The way it's snowing, the motor car won't be able to get through the streets."

"We're using horses," he replied, shrugging into his black ulster. "They don't wear tires that skid and slide on ice."

"Good." She smiled up at him. "A carriage is much more romantic anyway, especially in the holiday season."

As she lifted her sable from the wardrobe, Stefan reached out to touch the golden dress where it molded his wife's abdomen. "What would make me happy is the sight of a tiny bulge right here."

Flinching as if from a blow, she cast her eyes down to the smoothly fitting fabric. "Your wish is no greater than mine," she whispered, half-running to the stairway. She was annoyed but was loath to show it. The way Stefan went on sometimes, one would think she was barren on purpose. "It's in the hands of God," she kept telling him.

"Who is this God?" he replied, jesting. "I'm the one who sleeps with you."

Downstairs, Anusia waited, her gaunt figure swathed in a brown that was neither rich nor dull, neither dark nor light, but a muddy hue that deepened the sallowness of her complexion. Stefan's sister, Kalina often thought crossly, seemed bent on obliterating all traces of feminine beauty in her person. Catching the gold shimmer beneath the mid-calf sable, the woman shrieked. "My dear girl, you are dressed most inappropriately for a visit to the mill."

"The fabric is hardier than it appears," Kalina replied mildly in a tone midway between mild and stern, a tone she had developed with her sister-in-law. "Stefan suggested I wear it. There's to be luncheon, then the theater, and after that a supper at the Carnegies'." She flashed an impish smile. "My Paris dress will be a sensation at every occasion and, being real gold, will certainly not wilt."

As their carriage crossed the Monongahela River bridge and headed for the mill, Murav lectured his women on the Bessemer furnace, the firing of which had inspired the day's festivities. An older type than the open hearth, it manufactured a stiffer, harder steel, a superior product in great demand for rails and armorplate for battleships.

"Ten inches thick," he boasted, so proud one would think he had invented it. "Bessemer steel can withstand the onslaught of the toughest cannonball."

"Libby Hughes, I understand, is to blow it in," Anusia interrupted.

Stefan nodded. "And rightly so, for it is to be called the Libby Furnace." He squeezed his wife's gloved hand. "The next Bessemer will be Kalina's."

Anusia turned her face to look morosely out the little

window. Poor thing, Kalina thought, as no one would ever send diamonds to Anusia, no furnace would ever be named after her. Her feelings toward her sister-in-law were mixed. There were many times when she tried to create a sense of companionship with the woman. They could become as sisters. But the older woman persistently rebuffed her advances.

Not so with Libby. The young Mrs. Murav had found a lifelong friend that night in Lillian Russell's lavatory. Just yesterday, the superintendent's daughter had been ecstatic over tea in the pleasant Hughes library. "Think of it," she said, laughing, "the Libby Furnace."

Privately, Kalina speculated that something more personal than having a furnace named after her was happening to her friend. In the past few months, Libby's pale radiance had intensified, becoming a splendor of being that one normally associates only with love. There had been no talk of a suitor or even a beau. Kalina did not probe. One of the precepts Aunt Litka had instilled in her charges was a respect for the privacy of others.

Kalina had never been to the mill and looked forward eagerly, if with some trepidation, to her first visit. When they arrived at the river, it was like a holiday. A red-and-white striped awning stretched from the gate to the alley fronting the long shedlike building, and heavy red cotton crash carpeted the cindery path, with off-duty workers forming a wall on both sides. Kalina found herself embarrassed by their stolid, expressionless faces, and their almost hostile stares.

She was now a "swell," she realized and was distinctly uncomfortable about it. Would she ever become accustomed to being one of the upper class?

Inside, the place was what she had expected: dark, somber, noisy, dusty, frightening. Men spent half their lives in here. The thought was sobering. Figures in ragged, crusty workclothes moved aside as the dignitaries passed, eyes white in soot-blackened faces. Some leaned on shovels, some pushed little carts. Stefan pointed out the mayor of the city and the governor of the state as they took their places in the group around the new furnace. The women huddled in their furs, the men smoked cigars, photographers set up tripods all around.

"We'll be in the rotogravure," Anusia snapped but did not look displeased. She even ventured a frosty smile.

A smattering of applause signaled the entrance of Millard Hughes and Libby. Andrew Carnegie made a little speech. Then Libby was handed a blowtorch, which she applied to some kindling soaked in kerosene and stuffed into a notch leading to the innards of the egg-shaped firepit.

There was an immediate roar as the fire whooshed up and all cried out "Hip, hip, hooray" three times in the traditional way.

Outside again, Kalina saw why there was such a crowd. Company men, handing out cigars, mingled with the workers, and in the alley between the mill and the railroad tracks, tin schooners of beer and thick, meat sandwiches were being dispensed from the back of a wagon.

Stefan left her side to join Carnegie and Hughes around the wagon where they busily pumped hands and handed out cigars. Kalina approached a thin, young woman with a baby in her arms. She was speaking in low tones to the child in Polish. The child was tightly swaddled in a clean, but flimsy blanket.

"How old is the infant?" Kalina asked in Polish.

The woman looked up, her pale face filled with fright and shock that a fine lady in a gold dress and sables should speak to her in her native tongue. She swallowed, then smiled tremulously. "Five months today."

"May I hold her?" With an impulsive gesture, Kalina extended her arms. Without a word, the mother handed her burden to the fine lady, and as she pushed aside the blanket to see the tiny face, Kalina exclaimed, "What beautiful brown eyes!"

"Her name is Hania," said the mother proudly.

Kalina's eyes filled with tears. "Hania is my mother's name. She's still in Poland."

"So is mine. I fear I will never see her in this world

again." The young mother gazed full-eyed at the fine lady and, seeing the tears, reached out a hand to touch the silky fur-clad arm. For that moment, they were as one.

Suddenly, Anusia was towering over them, her dark face a cloud of disapproval. "Stefan says we must leave at once for the luncheon."

Regretfully, Kalina placed the baby back in its mother's arms, thinking that the thin blanket was hardly warm enough for the cold morning.

A half-mile upriver Max O'Hara stepped out of Lucy Furnace to sit down on a snowy bench in the mill yard. He opened his tin lunch bucket and sniffed hungrily at the garlicky onion and liverwurst aroma. "Time to eat," he said to Gus, who had followed him out.

The heat had just been poured and they could take some time off while the cranemen swung the next ore feeding into place and the pit gang cleaned up the bricks.

Gus set his own bucket on the bench, unopened. "Have mine too. Free beer and roast beef down at the new Bessemer. Cigars too."

Max bit into a sandwich without looking up. "Nah. Damn swells. You go, bring me back some beer."

Gus ran through the alley, and flipping open his friend's lunch pail, Max helped himself to some of Mrs. Koval's homemade sausage. He chewed slowly, thoughtfully. How could he tell his partner the real reason he had scorned the "blowing in"? He could hardly say that seeing Libby Hughes in her native element, all decked out in furs and jewels and playing the grand lady would be to rub salt in an open wound. He needed no painful reminders of the gulf between him and his goddess.

When the big Dutchie came back, toting sandwiches, beer, and a pocketful of cigars, he was full of talk about the "hoitie-toities" at the big shindig. He waxed especially eloquently about a "tearing beauty dressed in gold like a fairy princess." He poked an elbow into Max's side. "And guess what, she's old Cossack Murav's bride."

When Gus reported in amazement that the beautiful dark-haired lady spoke Polish to John Kewalski's wife, Max merely remarked sourly, "Good for her. I guess there's one sure way for a Pole to move up the ladder."

As they rode into Pittsburgh to the theater, Anusia launched into a tirade at Kalina's behavior at the mill. "The idea, holding one of those filthy babies. Good way to pick up a disease."

But Stefan appeared pleased. "We should mingle more with the workers." He pinched Kalina's cold cheek. "I saw you, darling. It was charming. Perhaps you should get involved in some charity work. Ask Libby about it or Lillian Russell Moore. They're both very social-minded."

At the matinée, the audience seemed more interested in each other than in the play, a bit of froth from New York called *The Pink Lady*. Necks craned upward as the Hughes and Muravs entered the box they were sharing. Libby was resplendent in white velvet and pink roses, her moonlight hair piled high and interlaced with pink ribbons that streamed down her back.

"You look like an angel," Kalina whispered, squeezing her friend's hand. Libby flashed a glowing smile, and Kalina thanked God for the thousandth time for the gift of friendship and sisterly love she had found in the cultured young woman. Libby Hughes compensated in some degree for the loss of Zuska.

As their party emerged into the late winter afternoon, the cold sun was already behind the tall buildings and the usual five o'clock bustle prevailed. A parade of women, some in trousers and carrying placards, marched down the middle of the street, blocking traffic, singing, and shouting at passersby.

"Oh, look, suffragettes," Kalina exclaimed, taking a leaflet from an extended hand.

"Whores and prostitutes, the lot of them," Anusia said in a grating voice. She tore the paper from Kalina's hand and threw it into the gutter. But not before Kalina had read

135

the headline—"Women's Votes Mean an End to War."

Loath to make a fuss, Kalina remained silent, but as they climbed into the carriage, she cast a longing glance at the marchers. Exciting as her life had become, she increasingly had a sense that she was of little real use in the world. If only she would conceive!

At the buffet supper in the Carnegie mansion on Pittsburgh's fashionable East Side, Kalina walked past the elaborate display of rich foods. Her usual hearty appetite had deserted her, and she found herself thinking of the pinched face of the young mother at the mill this morning. Finally, selecting a bowl of bean soup and a thick slice of crusty bread, she sat down to eat alone at a little table. To her amazement, she heard herself mumbling—"There but for the grace of God go I."

"Praying, Kalina darling?" Libby pulled up a chair, her own plate filled with meat and fish. She cast a curious glance at Kalina's soup. "Fasting, perhaps, to increase your saintliness?"

Managing a wan smile, Kalina replied, "I keep seeing those people at the mill. They all looked so hungry. The way they went for those sandwiches . . ."

"I imagine many of them *are* hungry," her friend replied. "The bad weather's caused a lot of layoffs at the mill. But things are picking up. Father says the new Bessemer will make a difference."

Kalina swallowed a spoonful of the zesty soup, wishing she could send some of it to Hania's mother. She tried to imagine real hunger. Although a bastard and of the servant class, she had never gone without a meal in Pan Mikolai's house. "Stefan thinks I should do charity work," she said. "There was a woman down at the mill with a baby—"

"Oh, yes, I saw you talking to Mrs. Kewalski. She and her husband are very happy at finally getting a baby girl after three boys in a row. She's one of the mothers I visit regularly."

"You mean that child has four babies?" Kalina's brown eyes widened in disbelief.

"Homestead workers run to large families," Libby

grinned. "It's their wealth, I guess." The two friends were silent for a time, each busy with her own thoughts. Despite her resolve not to pry into Libby's private life, Kalina could not resist asking, "Libby, why don't you marry and have children of your own? Surely, men have asked you."

She held her breath. Would the girl be offended?

After another silence, Libby smiled. "For some of us, such happiness is long in coming." She looked up, and Kalina saw the radiance in the bright-blue eyes. "Have patience, dear friends, I may soon become one of your charmed circle."

Kalina leaned forward. "Who, who?"

But Libby merely laughed. "Not yet, not yet. But soon I will tell all."

After supper, Kalina walked with the others into a tiny music room where Louise Carnegie was to perform on the pipe organ. The enormous instrument took up three walls. The lone window was curtained, and a gas log burned cheerily. Folding chairs crowded the little space. As usual, Stefan had abandoned her for a lively, masculine conversation in the drawing room about battleships and armorplate. Soon dulcet organ sounds banished remnants of cigar smoke from the drawing room and the cloying scent of women's perfumed bodies.

Halfway into the concert, a terrifying faintness began to overwhelm Kalina. The day had been long, she had had little food, and there was an ominous churning in her stomach. Fortunately she had chosen a chair on the aisle, and, rising swiftly, she plunged blindly into the corridor, searching frantically for a door to the outside. She stumbled onto a little library and saw with relief that the gas log was unlit. The room was delightfully cool.

Sinking into a deep leather chair, she concentrated on settling her nausea. The soup had been too spicy; she decided it must have had some exotic kind of seasoning. Within minutes, she felt easier and closed her eyes. If she could manage to catch a few winks . . .

Suddenly, an unholy racket, sounding like a convention of wailing banshees, tore through the house. Bagpipes! She had forgotten that the Scotsman invariably treated his guests to a few selections from his native instrument.

Sleep being out of the question, she thought reading would take her mind off her stomach. She got up to fetch a book from the shelves, but no sooner was she on her feet again than an onslaught of fresh nausea gripped her. Bitter fluid rose into her mouth. Where was the lavatory? There wasn't a servant in sight.

Hand over mouth, Kalina rushed to the window, shoved the heavy curtains aside, and pushed the window up.

The crisp winter air hit her like a wet towel and she gulped spasmodically in a vain effort to stem the nausea. But to no avail. She bent her head far out over the sill and vomited into the shrubs against the house. Straightening up and feeling drained, she wiped her mouth with her lace-edged handkerchief.

"Too much to eat, lady?"

The voice was male, very close, and filled with sarcasm. Startled, Kalina found herself gazing directly into the leering face of a very large man crouching in the bushes.

"Oh-h!" Shaken from the vomiting and too embarrassed to say a word, she dropped her handkerchief in her confusion outside the sill and backed into the library. A second voice, this one from the other side of the window, hissed, "Here's your hankie, Mrs. Murav. Now go inside, and shut the window."

She took the soiled cloth from the grimy hand but remained at the window, staring out with stupefaction at the scene before her. The moon was bright, and she could clearly see that the entire slope of lawn to the iron fence and beyond into the street was black with men.

Some carried flaming torches, and the air reeked of kerosene fumes. And something else. Her heart flew into her throat. Whiskey! A deep, ominous muttering swept over the crowd. The sound reminded her of a pack of lions ready to spring.

At the very front, a young man, his blond head uncovered to the cold, his thin coat unbuttoned, embraced what appeared to be a wooden railroad tie. As she stood transfixed with fright, one of the men by the sill reached inside to bring the window down on her hands.

"Now get inside like I said, lady, or you'll get hurt."

The others must be told, Kalina thought with panic. If only those infernal bagpipes would cease! As she stumbled out the library door, the terrifyingly sharp sound of breaking glass brought an abrupt halt to the music. Kalina felt the floor beneath her tremble. The workers must be using the railroad tie as a battering ram on the front door.

All at once, it seemed, the corridor was filled. Men shouted, women shrieked. Yells from outside could be heard through the broken windows. "Come out Carnegie, bring your leftovers, my kids are starving." Then a chant began: 'We want work, we want work, we want work."

A thousand booted feet stomped on the manicured lawn.

Kalina returned to the closed library window to watch. Carnegie and Hughes were on the portico. The Scotsman raised his hand, and the mob grew quiet. This man owned them body and soul, he could hire and fire, he could kill or save. Stefan had crowded the women into Kalina's little library and joined the other men at the front door.

"There's no reason to be frightened," he told them. "Andy and I will reason with the men."

When he had gone, Kalina opened the window and perched on the sill, looking out. The workers surely meant them no harm. They were hungry. Hunger made you angry, violent. Those last weeks on Mulberry Street she had been hungry, and Max had saved her. *Max!* Could he be out there with the mob? Maybe holding a torch aloft or a pocketful of stones ready to be hurled at the mansion? No, her heart cried out. He idolized Andrew Carnegie; he could not bring himself to do harm to his fabulous Scotsman.

Kalina rarely allowed herself to think of Max. His name was never mentioned in the Murav household, Stefan having told her on their honeymoon that she must forget that part of her life, that her first lover, the man who had taken her maidenhead, was a fly-by-night Irishman who had simply taken what was offered by a foolish girl.

He was right of course, as he was about most things. She had left word with the postmaster both at Pottsville and Shenandoah that if a letter ever came for her to send it on to Pittsburgh. None ever came. No word from the redhead who had saved her from the New York police. The wonderfully kind boy who had stolen to give her aunt a decent funeral was out of her life forever.

And if indeed she should spot the carroty curls on a Pittsburgh street, what then? *What then?*

Carnegie's rough Scottish brogue sliced into the night. "I will not deal with savages wielding rams. Put down your weapons and go to your homes peacefully."

Millard Hughes, standing protectively a little in front of his boss, leaned over to talk softly to him, apparently urging him to hear the men out. The sullen rumbling swelled again and random shouts were heard: ". . . you making plenty money . . . we want our union . . ."

As before a chant began: "Union, union, union."

Carnegie remained silent. The blond young man in front with the railroad tie lowered his heavy burden to a thrusting position and took a few steps forward. The men surged behind him.

Kalina saw Carnegie's face whiten in the light of the portico lamp. He stepped back. "You are rabble. Get off my property." The man had no private guards or watchdogs on the place; Stefan had told her once that there was no need for that since Carnegie was beloved by his men.

The voice of Millard Hughes flew thinly over the crowd. "Your grievances will be heard through the proper channels—"

The workers surged inexorably toward the portico. The sunny-haired man with the battering ram took one step, then two. Carnegie and Hughes fell back into the doorway. Stefan Murav darted out from the foyer, and there was a loud, sharp crack like a firecracker. Then another. The men fell back.

To her horror, Kalina saw two black pistols in her husband's hands. Someone in the library screamed.

140

"He's shot him," yelled a voice outside. "The Cossack shot Kewalski."

A shrill clang in the street announced the arrival of the police.

An hour later, Kalina waited in the library with Anusia for Stefan to finish with the police and take them home. The rioters had been hauled off in wagons to jail. The dead man was in the county morgue. She stood, immobilized, in the middle of the room, staring mindlessly at a massive oil painting over the fireplace. A green-and-gold pastoral, it depicted a group of children romping in a field of yellow flowers. The sunshine and the flowers seemed unreal.

Stunned, she could only think, If only Stefan had warned the man—"stop, or I'll shoot"—anything—

But he hadn't said a word. Her husband, the man in whose arms she lay each night, had simply pulled the trigger and snuffed out a human life.

Weeping, Libby had confirmed her fears. "Yes, the man was the husband of the Polish girl with the baby Hania and three little boys. But, Kalina"—Libby's hand was on her arm, her sweet face anguished—"Stefan did what he had to do. The workers might have harmed Carnegie and my father."

"One must fight force with force," Anusia said crisply from the davenport.

Whipping round, Kalina spat out at her. "They had no guns." She broke down in fresh sobs.

"Come, dear." Libby pulled at her arm. "Father and I will take you home. Anusia too. Stefan may be a while yet."

"We will wait," Anusia said. "My brother will need us in his hour of trial." It was impossible to tell just how the woman felt about the whole affair for the dour face was the same she wore for every occasion.

In the carriage going home, Stefan did not appear as a man in any kind of travail. He was in need of nothing, apparently, but listeners. He talked feverishly, incessantly, about how he hoped the old Scot would listen to him now.

141

"If I told him once, I told him a thousand times, the only way to deal with agitators is to drive them out of town or clap them in jail and throw away the key."

He pounded on the glass that separated them from the driver. "Can't these nags go any faster?"

The police had offered them an escort, fearing reprisals in the street, but Stefan had imperiously declined, stating that he still had bullets in his guns. "I saw it coming, I saw it coming," he repeated, in the manner of a drunken man, but he was not drunk. He seemed, in his young wife's eyes, to be exhilarated with a delirium of happiness just as he had that night in Philadelphia when he had spun her round the hotel room, singing "The Blue Danube."

Many men joy in killing. Mashko's words echoed in her mind. Stefan Murav was such a man.

"Maybe," she ventured when he stopped for breath, "if you'd given them some food or hope—"

All she got from Stefan was an amused stare and a smothered "simpleton." Anusia snorted, "They spend their money in the saloons. Every last man of them was roaring drunk."

In her gold-and-white dressing room at last, Kalina slipped gratefully out of the gold dress. She would never wear it again. She would push it to the far back of her wardrobe, and one day, when Stefan had forgotten it, she would sell it. How many sausages, she wondered dully, how many loaves of bread would three hundred dollars buy?

She was slipping her cashmere sleeping gown over her head when she felt it being jerked upward forcefully. Stefan stood naked before her, the bunched-up gown in his hand. His face was blood-red, his amber eyes glittered with desire. "No gown this night, my lovely." His steely arms encircled her naked body, and she was being pushed toward the bed. Disdaining the ladder, he hoisted her into his arms and threw her onto the mattress.

Time after time through what was left of the night, Murav pounded his wife's body into the mattress. It was a pommeling fiercer than he had ever inflicted upon her.

Kalina lay stonelike beneath his heavy body. There could be no thought of returning his passion. He seemed to expect none.

One thought possessed her. She was married to a murderer. Her life was over.

"What time is it?"

It was more a croak than a question as Kalina struggled to consciousness the next morning. The curtains were still drawn, the house quiet. Stefan moved about the room, dressing quietly.

"You're awake." He came to the high bed and kissed her tenderly on the brow. His hand rested on her face for a moment. "You're clammy. Best stay in bed today."

He shrugged into his heavy coat and planted the felt derby he wore to the mill firmly on his springy brown hair. "Got to get to the mill before that drunken mob sobers up and makes more trouble. There wasn't room in the jail-house for all of them." Nervously, he combed his beard with his fingers. "We need to hire more guards, build more fences round the entire mill complex."

Kalina tried to sit up but fell back as a mist of blackness formed before her eyes. Stefan chuckled. "A little too much excitement for you last night, eh? I'll have some tea sent up." He ran his hand in little circles on her blanketed stomach. "Maybe you're with child."

She spoke through waves of nausea. "Stefan, what if I never have a child? Would it be so terrible?"

He was at the mirror again, securing the guns in their twin holsters under his coat. Yesterday she had not seen him pack them in his clothing; she had been too engrossed in the gold dress and her own appearance. If only she had not been so vain, Kewalski might still be alive.

"Never?" The handsome face in the mirror grew dark. "No, my dear ninny, it wouldn't be terrible. It would be tragic." He faced her once more. "That's the whole reason a man marries. Pleasure he can get from any chit. But legitimate children from a chosen womb is vital."

Heedless of the dizziness, Kalina bolted up. "Stefan, don't you love me? For myself?"

His hand lifted up as though to strike her, but as she watched, his face cleared, and striding back to the bed, he flung back the covers. "Quite an alluring sight, Kalina Olkonsky, one that draws me like a bee to a flower. I suck, I inject my seed, then I wait for fruit." He punched her, none too lightly, in the abdomen. "If my flower proves barren, then my manly vigor has been squandered. Like so much slag."

Kalina was aghast. "But what about love?" She pulled the blankets back up, covering her nakedness.

"Love!" He spat out the word as if it were a curse. "You read too many romantic novels. While I admit your flesh is sweeter by far than any I have ever tasted, you should know that I married you for your blood. Bastard or not, a whelp of Pan Mikolai's is not to be disdained."

Bending close, he hissed into her ear. "And you, my greedy little Polack, married me for my money."

His boisterous laugh echoed down the stairs and into the drive. Within minutes she heard him shout to the chauffeur and then the splutter of the motorcar as it pulled into the street.

Stunned, humiliated, Kalina lay in bed like a statue. Her blood seemed to become as ice. However much she loathed the man for his cruel words, she loathed herself all the more, for the truth of his words seared like a flaming sword into her heart. She *had* married him in a fit of panic after Hedy's death. She was no better than the harlot who sells her body for bread and frippery.

She had taken the easy way, the coward's way, no less than had poor Hedy.

But, oh, God, what torment lay ahead?

Wanda crept in with a tray, her broad, pretty face concerned. "Here's some of that black Russian tea you fancy, Madame. A cup of this will settle your stomach."

The genuine kindness in the girl's voice, especially after Murav's cruelty, released the floodgates, and scalding remorseful tears rolled down Kalina's cheek onto her neck.

She pointed to the lumped-up nightgown on the floor, and Wanda climbed up the ladder to slip it over the dark head. Then she held the cup to Kalina's trembling lips. The taste of the heavy brew and the posture of the maid brought back the harrowing memory of Aunt Litka the day before she died. Pushing the girl away, Kalina buried her face into the pillow and wept out her insupportable grief. If only she had a sprig of Mrs. Cipriani's soothing herb . . .

"Wanda," she said a long time later. The maid had moved discreetly to the window to allow the young wife her grief. "Where is Dunia?"

"With Susanna." She smiled. "They're sledding in the back garden."

Susanna was one of Wanda's younger sisters, whom Stefan had engaged to help with caring for the child. The girl was twelve and provided Zuska's daughter with sorely needed companionship. "Good," Kalina murmured. Then, "Have you any headache powders?"

"Miss Murav does. She is much afflicted with migraine."

When the girl had gone, Kalina rested and arranged her thoughts. First, she must be calm. What if she really were barren? Six months now and not a sign. Many women waited years. She had heard of cases where ten, twelve years elapsed before a child was born. It was God's will, not Murav's.

But now it was not *her* will to bear his child. It would be the child of a murderer.

A soft knock was followed immediately by the entrance of Anusia. Kalina looked up, annoyed as usual by the woman's habit of entering a room without invitation. But her annoyance gave way to astonishment for the old sourface was smiling. Widely. Two rows of brilliantly white teeth shone like pearls. The sallow face was a network of tiny laugh lines. In her long, bony hands she carried a book.

"Wanda reports that you are unwell and wish a powder." Her usually whiny voice dripped with sweetness and light. She sat down in a chair. Kalina noticed that, even at this early hour, she was starched and immaculate in the unvarying black skirt and white shirtwaist.

"Something I ate last night. The food at Carnegie's was very rich. It's nothing, I'm sure."

The heavy brows lifted, and the corners of Anusia's thin mouth curled upward. "Perhaps it is not the food my dear." The plain face became suffused with crimson as she stammered, "I don't know how much your mother or your aunt told you about such things, but—"

Unable to continue, her sister-in-law rose abruptly from the chair and threw the book on the bed. She stood stiffly alongside, twisting her handkerchief in her hands like a nervous schoolgirl. Picking up the book, Kalina glanced swiftly at the title, *Manual for Motherhood.*

Why, the woman is convinced I am with child, she thought. In an instant rush of feeling, all the resentments harbored for months dissolved, and Kalina rolled over and lifted both her hands to clasp Anusia's. Eagerly. "How kind, how very, very kind you are, sister dear."

At two o'clock the jangle of the doorbell roused her from an uneasy, drugged sleep. There was a murmur of voices below, and in moments Wanda was peering into Kalina's face.

"It's Libby Hughes, Madame."

"Make my excuses, and tell Miss Hughes another time." The pale face of Mrs. Kewalski flitted through Kalina's muddled brain. Libby had promised to take her to the young mother today. "And oh, Wanda," she added, "please give Miss Hughes one of Dunia's extra blankets, one of the thick, woolly ones. Tell her it's for little Hania."

When she woke the next morning, the Murav home had been turned into a fortress. Two sleek black Dobermans were put in the charge of the gardener, and two armed, helmeted policemen paced back and forth, forth and back, on the sidewalk fronting the long iron fence. Stefan had left orders that no one was to leave the house for any reason, and groceries were delivered by the market boy. The cook grumbled at the nuisance. A telephone was installed in the bedroom to supplement the instrument already in the library.

Stefan came and went as usual, his pistols at his belt, but he was plainly worried. "It's too quiet," he rumbled. "Riots, fires, strikes, we can handle, but not this damn nothing."

"The calm before the storm," Anusia commented.

Preoccupied with her own half-sick condition, Kalina tried to ignore the tense situation. The nausea continuing, she kept to her bed and received Dunia and Wanda several times each day. She had read in the *Manual for Motherhood* that a woman with child must not expose herself to unpleasant events or conversation.

Ninny that she was, what on earth could she possibly do about it anyway?

Libby kept her informed of events. Under Stefan's direction, the Carnegie Steel Works became an armed camp. Fifty extra guards were hired and trained to shoot to kill any and all intruders. Searchlights were mounted on newly erected platforms. A heavy, wooden fence topped by three strands of barbed wire went up almost overnight on both the alley and the river sides of the mill.

In the Homestead saloons, the men joked about "Fort Murav," many welcoming, however, the fifteen cents an hour for hammering nails and sawing wood. Some even left their mill jobs to train as guards. The riot that had ended in poor Kewalski's death was buried in yesterday's news.

Or so it seemed.

What Stefan Murav didn't tell his women was that every man who had been arrested that fateful night had been fired for all time, that more layoffs were promised, that company spies had infiltrated the workers, and that boatloads of cheap immigrant labor were even then unloading in New York, Philadelphia, and Baltimore.

Chapter Seven

Braemar Cottage, June 1902

Mercifully, time and nature had its way, and the long, cruel winter loosened its stranglehold on the city of three rivers. On a fresh morning in the first week of June, Kalina woke in her third-floor bedroom with a fresh happy feeling. She lay supine, luxuriating in that joyous sense of well-being with which childbearing women are often blessed. Her dark eyes swept lazily over the large, square room. A shaft of yellow sun shone through a crack at one side of the heavy damask that covered the tall window, warming the cold marble top of the massive walnut bureau on the opposite wall. Still in shadow were the flowered wallpaper and the curved writing desk, on which her letters, her slim gold pen, and a stack of the romantic novels, to which she had become addicted, lay in careless disarray.

She stretched and sat up in bed, flinging back her tousled hair with one slender hand, then bringing it down to clasp the other across her swollen belly. The wife of Stefan Murav was in her eighth month of a difficult pregnancy and had spent a good part of the new year of 1902 in bed.

A soft knock at the door was followed by the immediate entrance of a bright-faced Wanda. "Good morning, Madame," she called out in her sweetly accented voice, her pretty face lighting up in a contagious smile.

An answering smile crossed Kalina's face as the maid walked to the window and slid the curtains along the brass rod with a whoosh. She had become inordinately fond of the young Polish-American girl, finding in her a strength and gentleness she remembered from her mother Hania, although the maid was barely twenty. In her crisp white-and-gray-striped uniform and stiffly starched snowy apron, with a ruffled cap over her glossy braided hair, Wanda enhanced the already happy day.

"Time to be up and get dressed for the picnic." With strong arms Wanda lifted the heavy ewer from its basin on the mahogany washstand. "I'll fetch some lovely hot water for your morning wash."

The girl gone, Kalina rose awkwardly, her two hands holding the lower part of her silk-clad body tightly to support her unborn child. Cautiously, she descended the little ladder. A fat, saucy robin hopped about on the sill outside the window, cocking his head in a comically brazen manner at her through the glass. The bird family nesting in the maple tree that shaded this side of the house had been her sole company during the last difficult months when she had seen no one on a regular basis but Wanda, Dunia, and Anusia.

It was astonishing how Anusia had changed, she reflected, as she flicked the window with her finger, causing the bird to fly up to a nearby branch. Somehow, the bird reminded her of Anusia, whose somber voice had given way to a cheerful chirp. The nunlike aspect had vanished, she seemed younger somehow as she popped in several times a day to make sure her brother's young wife lacked for nothing.

The robin returned and fixed her with a beady eye, impatiently awaiting his daily ration of crumbs from Kalina's breakfast tray. "Your belly is as round and firm as mine," she laughed, throwing open the window and causing him to fly off once more, somewhat indignantly, to a leafy branch. Kalina sniffed. The air was balmy, smelling of roses and only slightly of the ever-present soot from the mills across the river.

Turning to the desk, she picked up a letter from Libby, written in her exquisite hand on delicately perfumed creamy paper. She hadn't seen her friend for two whole months, not since early March, long before Easter. A frown creased Kalina's smooth brow. When Alec Hardie, the young Scottish doctor Stefan had engaged to care for his wife, ordered her to bed to save the child, she had looked forward with eagerness to long visits, long talks, from her new best friend.

But curiously, the superintendent's daughter, who had been so solicitous after the dreadful night at the Carnegies' when Stefan had brutally murdered John Kewalski, had called but three times at the Murav house on Rutherford Drive. Her letters were more frequent however.

"Young women of Miss Hughes' breeding must surely feel uncomfortable in the presence of a woman in your delicate condition," Anusia had offered with a tiny blush.

Kalina bent to the letter, reading every line, searching for hidden meanings. "My settlement house work absorbs me completely . . ." She ruffled the thick paper impatiently. Not a word about the romantic interest the girl had hinted at before Christmas. "The workers are in such dire straits, so many layoffs—"

Annoyance clouding her earlier joy, Kalina threw the letter down on the blotter and stood wrapped in thought, ignoring the renewed chatter of the birds. Talk of the mill was not what she wanted from Libby. She got enough of that from Murav during his infrequent visits to her bedroom.

"The men are getting mean," he had reported. "They demand a ten-hour day, more safety rules at the furnaces, higher pay all round." His big laugh had boomed out as though it were all a joke, but his face remained grim. "Fat chance. They're a passel of anarchists." Talk of a strike did not frighten the new Big Boss of the Carnegie Works.

Nothing frightened Stefan Murav, Kalina had decided. He was certainly not afraid of hellfire in the hereafter, often boasting of how he single-handedly had quashed the pre-Christmas riot with a couple of well-aimed shots.

Kalina's feelings toward her husband remained in the dormant, paralyzing state which that fateful night had engendered. The *Manual for Motherhood* advised sternly that a tranquil mind was of the most importance. And so Kalina strove to drive the dreadful scene from her thoughts.

But at least, thank the dear Virgin, Stefan willingly gave up his conjugal rights when Dr. Hardie suggested such a course. In fact, he had taken to sleeping in a small bedroom on the second floor, near the maid's room and Dunia's nursery, confessing to his wife with a grin that sleeping in the same bed with her "like brother and sister" would be a torture beyond imagining.

Many nights, however, he spent at his club, an exclusive male establishment on the north bank of the Allegheny River, far across town. Often too he traveled to New York or Chicago or the nation's capital on steel business. Stefan Murav, soon to be the new Big Boss of the Carnegie Works, was much in demand in places where the destiny of America's industrial might were decided.

Wanda reentered with the water and fresh towels over her arm, bringing with her through the open door a horrendous racket from belowstairs.

Kalina tensed. Dunia was throwing another temper tantrum, an almost daily occurrence, it seemed. "What is it this time?" she sighed.

"Our little tomboy refuses to let Susanna and Anusia dress her for the journey to the train station." Wanda helped her mistress doff her robe and then whipped up a fragrant, sudsy mixture in the flowered porcelain basin. "You know how strong-willed our little Dunia has become of late."

"Her mother was like that," Kalina said. "Always the rebel, ever the quick temper." Her heart caught at thoughts of Zuska.

But she couldn't help thinking as she bathed and put on silky underthings, preparing to don the poinceau mauve silk traveling dress that the dressmaker had cunningly altered to fit her expanding figure, that it was as much

151

Anusia's stern ways as the child's temper that inspired the daily outbursts. Since Kalina's confinement, the older woman had, with some help from Wanda's young sister Susanna as nursery maid, taken over complete charge of the little girl, releasing Wanda for Kalina's exclusive and personal use. To her credit, Anusia had eagerly welcomed Zuska's bastard child into the family. Dunia was, after all, of Kalina's blood, a circumstance that both Anusia and her brother valued. Eventually, if the mother could not be found, he would consult his lawyers about adoption procedures, Stefan had promised.

The din continued, Dunia's shrill screams resembling more a soul in purgatory than a privileged adopted daughter of Stefan Murav. How could a person maintain a tranquil mind as the *Manual* advised in the face of such an uproar?

She whipped around to face Wanda, who was on the ladder straightening out the high bed. "Has Anusia touched the child?"

"No, Madame," came the quick response. "Not since that last time she struck the little one and you got so upset." The maid giggled. "Mr. Murav set her straight, right back on her heels if I do say it myself." She climbed down the ladder and took up the mauve frock from the armoire. "Don't worry about that little one, Madame, she's a match for the old—" Catching yourself, she added, "for Miss Anusia Murav."

"Of course," Kalina murmured. In her heart she found herself yearning for her mother. Hania should be here, now, in America, with her daughter and grandniece. Hania could handle Dunia and high and mighty Anusia as well. Without seeming imperious or authoritative, Hania Olkonsky had the rare ability of making others behave in a civilized manner.

But Hania was not here. Her mother might never come to America. Instead, she had written that she no longer lived at Pan Mikolai's manor but in a cottage in an outlying village. "He's a Cossack, but he has married me in church." Kalina concluded that her mother was perfectly happy where she was.

Fully dressed, her black hair brushed to a sheen and coiled neatly in a fashionable chignon caught with an emerald and diamond pin, Kalina studied her image in the armoire mirror. Her pregnancy had imparted a charming fullness to the cameolike features; her wide mouth was soft and pink, and her cheeks had taken on a rosy hue. The scrawny immigrant girl from Jaslo was now a woman born.

"You must eat for two," Anusia had said, instructing the cook to prepare rich puddings and desserts for the *enceinte* young matron. Only by dint of stubborn refusal had Kalina managed to avoid the unsightly and uncomfortable bloating suffered by so many.

Wanda fastened pendant diamond earrings on the ears of her mistress. "You hardly show at all, Madame," she said in a tone of mild surprise. "But then you tall ones carry well."

In the foyer, a sulky, tear-stained Dunia awaited, costumed like a china doll in starchy white furbelows and ruffles. As Kalina, supported by Wanda, descended the stairs, the child's wails broke out afresh, and, running from the nursemaid, she clutched at her mama's cashmere traveling cloak.

Kalina threw a withering glance at Anusia, just then emerging from the rear of the house. She was dressed in her customary drab-brown merino. She addressed the woman sharply. "The white ruffled look is hardly suitable for the train. There is so much soot and grime." She grimaced, patting the child's head under the beribboned bonnet. "She will be most uncomfortable."

It was perfectly clear why there had been such a ruckus. Dunia favored at all times simple, roomy cotton and linen frocks, which gave her growing muscles room to play and dance about.

"As a child is dressed, so will she behave," responded Anusia to Kalina's remark. "In simpler garb, she would be inclined to frolic around the railway coach at her usual antics." The thin lips disappeared into a hard line. "She will humiliate us before the steward and the passengers."

Cupping the child's face, Kalina lifted it up. Her heart caught. She was the image of Hania. Soft, chestnut-brown eyes brimmed with tears. "When we get to Mr. Carnegie's farm, darling, Susanna will put on one of your play frocks. Whichever one you choose."

"Can I ride the pony and chase the geese?"

"Of course, darling, as much as you want," Kalina smiled down at the now eager face.

Mollified, Dunia took Susanna's hand. "We're going to a real farm just like the one my mama grew up on."

Kalina sighed. If only she were not too ill to care for the child as she would like. Dunia was never permitted to venture outside the iron-fenced garden. Kalina's suggestion to Anusia that she be taken to a local park or the zoo where animals and rolling grassy slopes would provide a refreshing change was met with shocked eyes and raised brows.

Their destination this warm, June day was far from the simple barnyard farm in Poland however. They had been invited, along with a large group of other important guests, to spend a long weekend at Braemar Cottage, the Carnegie summer retreat high up in the Allegheny Mountains. Fifty miles east of the city, it would be a welcome relief from the oppressive heat and grime of Pittsburgh.

It was hardly a picnic, either, as one ordinarily thinks of those affairs. Stefan had persuaded Kalina's doctor that her presence at the gathering was not only desirable but vital. The occasion would mark the fabulous Scotsman's final retirement from business and bring together munitions tycoons from many European nations to view for the first time, the new cannon-proof armorplate for battleships.

"You will be sitting in on history, my dear," he had told his wife.

Stefan had easily managed an invitation for the young Dr. Hardie, assuring him the prospect of many future clients among the rich and famous guests, and the doctor had gladly consented to Kalina's leaving her long imprisonment.

Still in his twenties, the young practitioner was freshly arrived from Scotland, where he had studied at the University of Edinburgh. "He is well versed in the most modern techniques of childbirth," Stefan averred.

The expectant mother would be carried into the carriage, onto and off the train, and wherever else she needed to be by the stalwart young man himself. He would be in constant attendance, watching for any untoward sign of early labor. A circumstance that pleased not only her mistress but the maid Wanda, who had taken an instant and painfully obvious liking to the doctor. He was not only handsome but blessed with a delightful Scottish burr.

Thanks to Anusia's promptly falling asleep, which she did the moment the train got underway, Kalina was able to calm the excitable Dunia and the hours passed swiftly and pleasantly. Woman and child lounged side by side on a wide, velvet couch, Kalina reciting sidewalk rhymes remembered from her days on Mulberry Street.

"One, two, buckle my shoe, three, four, close the door." Dunia's childish laughter filled the coach. It was going to be fine, Kalina told herself, wondering why there had been such need for her to lie abed so long. She looked forward with great anticipation to the outing. Those inveterate party-goers Lillian Russell and Jim Brady would be there along with many of the society folk she had not seen since December.

But best of all, Libby was coming. Her letter had made certain of that. At the station the Murav party was ushered into two colorful and well-padded pony carts, and, as they were driven up through the thick, pine-scented forest, little wings of happiness beat inside Kalina's heart.

She and Libby would have that long delayed heart-to-heart, woman-to-woman talk. At long last Kalina would learn from her friend the name of her secret beloved.

The following afternoon, Stefan Murav lowered his wife to the thickly padded wicker lounge chair and, taking the silky wool throw from a servant, tucked it securely around

155

and under her legs. He leaned his broad-shouldered form over to kiss her on the brow. "You are not to move, my dearest," he said with mock sternness.

Then he was gone to a meadow in the far reaches of the vast estate where in the next few days the testing of his new battleship armorplate would take place and where he had spent all waking hours of the past week preparing for the affair. He called the new alloy "his," with a sense of propriety as though he himself had developed it. In truth, though, the strong metal was the product of years of work and research throughout the many small mills that had been gobbled up by the Carnegie Empire.

Diplomats and industrialists from many foreign countries would be observing the tests. If they were sufficiently impressed, they would buy. U.S. Steel would be, in Stefan's words, "in clover."

The day was warm, and Kalina welcomed the deep shade of the giant beech under which she sat, feeling, she mused, like the queen Stefan promised she would be one day. Murav had chosen her costume for the day — pearly white satin trimmed with gold loops at shoulder and wrist, diamonds at her neck and ears, an ice-green emerald tiara in her hair.

"I'll feel overdressed," she had protested.

"You will be on display," he had replied curtly. Then, "I've asked little from you these past months."

In her gold and satin, she reminded herself of the ancient queens of Poland whose portraits hung on Pan Mikolai's manor walls, but she no longer brooded over her husband's mad pretensions to royalty. She must accept it as one accepts a deformity or chronic disease in a member of one's family. What will come, will come. Her children were her future.

"Madame, you quite take my breath away. May I sketch you?" The voice was softly accented and belonged to a young man in a French beret and flowing white shirt, open at the neck. A lad behind him, in identical costume, carried an easel, a palette, and a folding chair.

Kalina smiled at the engaging picture. Itinerant artists

were *de rigueur* at social gatherings and were much favored by the ladies over the brash newspaper photographers, who were apt to catch one in an unflattering pose.

"Oh, I don't think so," she replied. "I must keep my blanket around me."

He bowed deeply. "Your husband sent me."

The covering could remain, he assured her. Mr. Murav had requested a head-and-shoulder pose done in pastel watercolors.

As he sketched with swift, sure strokes, Kalina fixed her dark eyes on a nearby grassy slope where a group of children, mostly girls, were jumping rope. They chanted an old rhyme. "Cinderella, dressed in yellow, gone to town to buy an umbrella, on the way she met a fellow, how many kisses did she get, one, two, three . . ."

Their thin, high voices fell sweetly on the pleasant air. A deliriously happy Dunia squatted on the ground, playing jacks with little Margaret Carnegie, sole issue of the Scotsman's late marriage. She was a quiet child of the same age, who had a blessedly calming effect on the more high-spirited Murav heiress. Kalina took pleasure in pointing out to her sister-in-law that, like Dunia, Margaret was not attired in dainty ruffles but in a simple, unbelted frock of ordinary grenadine. Zuska's child, born in a mining shack, had never seemed happier. Kalina resolved to speak to her husband about purchasing a country place.

Wanda hovered close, along with a most attentive Alec, while Anusia happily removed to join a group of older women engaged in a lively game of whist set up on folding tables under a wide-branching chestnut. On another grassy expanse croquet players moved about, the ladies in their varicolored summer frocks appearing like a garden of animated flowers in a painting by Millet.

The artist, whose name he said was simply Andre, completed his sketch and moved on, promising to return next day with the finished portrait. Kalina leaned her head on the padded back of her chair and closed her eyes. Croquet mallets clicked, the children sang softly, the women at their cards chattered in a birdlike way. A marvelous tranquility lay over everything, and Kalina lay in a golden dream of happiness.

If only Libby would arrive. The Hughes heiress was driving from the city in her brand-new automobile, so Louise Carnegie reported. "And not alone," she had added, with a matronly giggle and a roll of the eyes.

Max O'Hara.

Kalina jerked awake. The once-beloved name echoed clear and strong, falling on the air like a bugle call. She must have been dreaming. But it was no dream, for it came again, this time spoken in a loud, sharp voice from the ladies under the chestnut. "His name is Max O'Hara, and I have it on the most reliable of sources—her own maid to my maid—that she actually means to marry him."

Audible gasps were heard, followed by a babble, as several others joined in the talk. "An Irishman . . . handsome as the devil, shoulders like a stevedore . . . she taught him to read and write . . . Millard Hughes is certain the man has great potential for leadership . . . young, not yet twenty, while Libby is closer to thirty than she will admit . . ."

Nervous laughter. "An old maid like Libby Hughes can hardly afford to be particular . . ."

Then Anusia's familiar sarcastic tone. "When one is rich, *any* man can be bought."

Max! And Libby!

Kalina's heart was pulsing in her ears, a thick knot of agony lodged in her throat. Be tranquil, a part of her brain cried out. The name was common, Pittsburgh was filled with Irishmen, there must be a dozen Max O'Haras. But as she clung to the chair arms with a kind of desperate frenzy, she knew with a sinking feeling that the secret lover, the man her friend had kept hidden all these months was no other than the man whom she, Kalina, had loved and lost.

But if he were here, so close, romancing her best friend, surely he would have called . . .

Suddenly there was no more time for speculation, neither of dreams nor of reality, for the chugging sound of a motorcar stopped the chatter of the whist players. All heads turned to watch as a brilliant, cherry-red automobile with a shiny, black roof and gleaming, silvery wheels, emerged in a cloud of dust from the dirt road not fifty feet from where they sat.

Kalina stared, mesmerized. Two goggled figures sat in the high, leather front seat. The noisy machine emitted an acrid smell of gasoline that befouled the pure, mountain air. The motor stopped, an expectant quiet fell on the waiting guests, the man behind the steering rod leaped down and ran round to encircle the waist of his companion, lifting her carefully to the ground. A mass of vibrant, carroty hair sprang up from his head as though it would lift off the jaunty touring cap and send it spinning through the air.

Shrieking, the children gathered round to examine the marvelous machine. Coolly, with complete aplomb, Max O'Hara pushed up his goggles, swept off his cap, and with deeply freckled hands ran his fingers through his hair. His brown eyes swept the crowd, coming to rest on the reclining figure in the lounge chair.

Even at a distance, the clear shock in his eyes was plain to Kalina. Clearly, he had not known that she was here, in Pittsburgh, wife to his boss Stefan Murav. All the blood in her body rushed in a dark, hot tide to her heart as the bucolic scene beneath the tree dissolved. The dream replaced the reality. She was back in a New York cellar, sipping hot soup and brandy, gazing into a pair of laughing brown eyes, staring into what she thought would be her future.

"Kalina, Kalina, darling, are you asleep with your eyes open?"

It was Libby, gently shaking her shoulder, bending to lay a cool kiss on her cheek. "Come on, dear, wake up. There's someone I want you to meet."

Kalina thought, those lips have kissed the lips of Max O'Hara. Quickly collecting herself, she said brightly, "How smart you look, Libby." The young woman was attired in a cornflower-blue touring suit that hugged her slim figure like a glove. A crisp straw cartwheel sat firmly on her golden hair, held down by a frothy chiffon scarf.

But she would have been just as beautiful and radiant if she had been wearing sackcloth and ashes. Kalina could not tear her eyes from the dazzled look in her friend's blue eyes as Libby turned to the approaching Max. His brown eyes, which had been so open moments before, were now veiled.

"So this is the famous Kalina Murav," he exclaimed, taking Kalina's proffered hand. "Libby has been keeping secrets from me, I fear. I only learned of your existence as we drove up from the city this very day."

Words came from Kalina's mouth, but they might have been so much gibberish. Relief flooded her, leaving her weak. Max made it obvious that he would keep the secret that only two others shared—herself and Murav. Perhaps, she hoped, Stefan would be so absorbed in his cannons and armorplate that he could not even discover Max's presence at the picnic.

Curiously, as though she peered through a camera lens, she noted every detail of his costume. The ragged street urchin was gone, no more stolen garments. A fashionable, buttonless white shirt peeked from beneath a cashmere jacket of the most delicate fawn. The narrow silk tie was crimson, rivaling the automobile in brilliance. A slim, gold arrow slashed across the tie. It had a tiny flawless ruby at its tip.

Any man can be bought.

After what seemed an interminable time and much to Kalina's relief, the happy couple departed to change their dusty garments and refresh themselves. "We drove up from the Altoona station," Libby explained. "You see, the vehicle was shipped from New York by train, but Max couldn't wait until it arrived in Pittsburgh." She threw an adoring glance at her companion, linking his arm in hers. "I do believe if the roads were fit for automobiles, he would want to drive it the whole fifty miles home."

The sun, which had burned so cheerily through the day, had slipped behind a cloud. Kalina felt a sudden chill and sent for Alec Hardie to carry her inside.

Her hope that Stefan was not aware of the man who had taken his wife's virginity had become part of their exclusive social set was dashed scarcely an hour later. Kalina stood, dressed for dinner, on a small balcony outside their spacious room. The sun was orange behind the mountains, birds called sweetly from the trees. There was a glimpse of blue lake in the distance.

The door slammed, and she heard her husband's voice behind her, dismissing Wanda. Then he was upon her. "I understand you've met that guttersnipe of a thief who is now Libby Hughes' fancy man."

His strong arms encircled her in a hurting pressure. "Your lovesick friend may choose to throw herself at swine, but I must warn you, my dear wife, that, if you by any sign or word betray your previous knowledge of this man, the jig will be up for Max O'Hara." He lifted the thick chignon from her neck, burying his face in the warm flesh beneath. "You are more desirable than ever," he murmured thickly, in a typical change of mood that never failed to surprise her. "You are mine, all mine." He moaned, softly. "Hurry and expel this child, else I will go mad."

In his way, Stefan adored her, Kalina realized. She sighed compassionately. "You are no more anxious than I," she said. Then, she added, "My womb has been unusually quiet all day. I think my time is near." As he pressed her buttocks to his bulging manhood, she said calmly, "Max O'Hara is nothing to me. Our brief encounter was more one of convenience than of passion. I was a mere child."

The lie was needed. He could tear Max's life to smithereens, making it impossible for him to ever rise in the steel business. They moved to the door, hand in hand. "I understand they are affianced," Kalina said in a light tone.

"Humph. Many a slip 'twixt cup and lip as the saying goes. I don't think that Hughes will allow the marriage. He's simply letting his daughter have a little fun before he kicks the scoundrel clear to hell and back."

After supper there was to be an entertainment followed by dancing on the wide, wraparound veranda. Gaily colored paper lanterns hung in the trees and across the vast stretches of lawn. The musicians were already tuning up their instruments on an improvised platform. The guests themselves, however, were expected to perform regardless of degree of talent. Like the sketch artist earlier, the practice was a feature of all affairs in higher social circles.

As expected, Stefan and Millard Hughes retired to the library to smoke Havana cigars and talk of battleships with the important foreign guests. The Scottish doctor had been called to attend an ailing guest, so Kalina was carried into one of several opulently furnished sitting rooms by the corpulent Jim Brady, who left her then to join Diamond Li'l. The two would enact a scene from *Lady Teazle*, which had been one of the actress's most beloved roles.

· The program was varied, if uneven in quality. Louise Carnegie rendered Scottish ballads on a grand piano, and there were the inevitable bagpipes, this time accompanied by a troupe of twirling dancers in bright tartan kilts. With great self-control Kalina drove from her thoughts memories of that dreadful night when, to the sound of pipes, a young husband and father had been murdered.

Despite her delicate condition, the young Mrs. Murav was expected to contribute to the merriment. The years of lessons with Aunt Litka had given her a repertory of declamations and speeches from classical works, so with delight she recited, from her chair, the impassioned speech of Shakespeare's Portia, in which she pleads for mercy for a despised Shylock.

"The quality of mercy is not strained, it droppeth as a gentle rain from heaven upon the earth beneath."

She was met with thunderous acclaim, Lillian Russell rushing forward with a hug. "Such a marvelously throaty voice, my dear. If ever you tire of your Cossack, you would surely bowl them over in the theater."

A single act remained. It was to be a tableau, a living rendering of a painting or a scene from literature. The lights were darkened for a few long moments, then brought up again to reveal a charming scene that had been hidden from view in a curtained corner. A cunning balcony, a few trees, a strumming guitar, and two costumed figures. A rippling sigh swept the spectators. The performers were Libby Hughes and her paramour Max O'Hara playing at Romeo and Juliet.

The flaming red hair was cloaked by a long, flowing, coal-black wig. Libby's blond hair hung free, cascading over the wrought-iron railing. One white hand was extended to grasp that of her ardent lover. Since it was a tableau, no word would be spoken, but none was indeed. The crowded sitting room grew quiet, feeling the presence of a great passion on the stage.

I am happy for them, Kalina told herself, but a tiny shadow, as from a bird that flies across one's line of vision, passed over her heart. The curtains closed, and in the ensuing applause and confusion, she rose from her chair and walked swiftly to the door, unnoticed. Reaching the veranda, she darted past the musicians and onto the lantern-lit lawn. In her white satin she must have seemed a fleeing ghost to them. She reached a clump of trees and melted into thick darkness, stopping at last to embrace a wide-girthed, gnarled trunk. Kalina yearned for tears, but none would come. As if sensing her need, a night bird began to sing, trilling as though its heart would burst.

"Damn few birds in Homestead can sing like that."

Max O'Hara spoke in the distinctive street accents of New York, which all of Libby's drilling had failed to erase. Kalina turned to face him. Moonlight filtered through a break in the trees. He had not removed the tight breeches and satin weskit of the tragic Romeo. She tried to speak, but her tongue clung to the roof of her mouth.

"How are you, Kalina?" He pressed both hands to the tree, imprisoning her in the cage of his arms.

"You've changed," she said, finding a voice that seemed to belong to somebody else. She flicked her eyes over his resplendent figure, coming to rest on a gleaming silver ring bulging from the third finger of his left hand. "Damn few outfits like that in those trunks you had in that cigar factory cellar," she added, mockingly.

"So have you." He was the same cocky Max. He wore his new finery with an easy flair. Then, as now, she felt no scorn for his "taking" ways. He was Max, he was a man who took what he wanted.

She lowered her gaze modestly, trying to arrange her face into a matronly pose. "I am no longer the silly girl you knew. I am a woman, complete with husband, child, a household to manage."

"Which is quite an establishment, I am told. A three-story affair on Rutherford Drive."

Her head came up. "Have you seen it?"

He shook his head so vigorously a lock of unruly hair tumbled onto his brow. Libby has not quite made a dandy of him, she thought, amused, clenching her hand into a fist to keep from reaching up to smooth the lock into place. The well-groomed man of 1902 applied heavy doses of hair oil to achieve an almost lacquered effect.

"We've both become somebody else," she said with a little shrug. "There was an old philosopher who said that life is like a river, always flowing. You can never step into the same place twice."

"Heraclitus."

"What?" Her brow wrinkled in amazement. "Is this the fellow who never heard of Cinderella? Now it's Greek philosophers, no less."

"I've learned a lot since then."

"That's the story of America, I guess. Did you ever think, as we lay in that smelly boxcar, that in a year or so you would be lounging in the palatial home of your idol Andy Carnegie?" She laughed, spontaneously. She had forgotten how easy it was to talk with Max, how the jokes and banter always poured out like syrup from an upended jug. Talking with Stefan and Anusia was such an uphill battle, like plowing through mud with your boots on.

The bantering tone disappeared, however, and he grew serious. "Believe me, Kalina Olkonsky, we've been in the same city — just across the Monongahela from each other in fact — and I've known your best friend Libby since last fall. But I never knew you had even left Shenandoah." He shook his head again, causing the red brush to fall into his eyes. "I swear." He flashed an impish grin. "Cross my heart and hope to die."

But he didn't cross his heart; his arms remained like iron bars on both sides of Kalina. And from the cat-that-ate-the-canary look of him, dying was the last thing he wanted to do, she reflected.

"I've thought of you often, wondering," she said, suddenly feeling the longed-for tears behind her eyes. She swallowed hard, determined to keep from showing him how much she cared that he had deserted her. "I should have listened to Zuska. She said you wouldn't come back."

"How is Zuska, by the way?" he asked, offering no apology for not returning to the mining shack where he had stranded her. His tone was casual, he might have been inquiring after her dog or her ailing maiden aunt.

"I don't know. She left, too, soon after you, leaving me with Dunia."

"Oh, Christ, kid, I didn't know."

There was a sudden spangled burst of polka music from the bandstand. They were both silent, thinking, as the music flowed around them, enfolding them in a cocoon of memory. Neither spoke of what was in their hearts—the indisputable fact never to be changed by any will of God or man—that each was pledged to another, that Max and Kalina were lost to each forever.

The music stopped, they heard the sound of people clapping. From far below in the town, church bells tolled the hour. Silently, Kalina counted, praying between the knells as she always did. "Midnight," she said, shivering a little. "I must go in."

The band began the lilting strains of "After the Ball Is Over." It was always the last tune of the evening.

The satin-clad arms of Romeo dropped from the tree, but Max remained quite still, his muscular form blocking her way. Did she imagine it or did he sway toward her? Did his arms swing upward ever so slightly as if wanting to embrace her?

But, no, he moved aside at last, bowing deeply in courtly fashion, one freckled hand splayed across the skin-tight breeches. "Let me escort you through the woods, Red Riding Hood," he said, laughing. Smiling despite her thumping heart, Kalina hooked her hand in the crook of his proffered arm. As they stepped back onto the lighted lawn, Kalina sprinted, heedless of her pendulous belly, back toward the veranda.

Long after she had been swallowed up in the house, Max remained fixed, all mirth gone, gazing after her like a navigator at the helm of a ship that has been lost at sea. Only when the high, clear voice of Libby Hughes called from the steps of the veranda — "Max, are you out there?" — did he begin to walk toward the house.

But, unlike Kalina's, his steps were slow and unhurried. He walked like a man who has nowhere special to go and is not especially anxious to get there.

Chapter Eight

They started shooting off the cannons at dawn. Kalina stirred but did not waken fully, burrowing deeper into the cave of silken sheets. Must be a mountain storm, she thought, yesterday's sky at sunset had been red. The old rhyme ran through her head. "Red sky at morning, shepherd's warning, red sky at night, shepherd's delight."

But that wasn't right. A red night sky should have brought a fair day. She slept again, unaware that Stefan had risen, moved about the room quietly dressing, and left to join his cannons and armorplate in the meadow.

"Wide-bore guns from Krupp in Germany will shoot cannon balls at the new armorplate." That was what her husband had muttered last night as they crawled, both numb with exhaustion from the long day, into their respective sides of the massive four-poster in their guestroom. "Be warned, my dear. The shooting will go on all day tomorrow," he had added, "Louise Carnegie has ordered special music and games to distract the female guests and children from the noise."

But now, hours later, Wanda was drawing the curtains to flood the room with golden sunshine. She then walked to the bed where an attractive breakfast tray lay on Stefan's empty side. Kalina sat up, yawning. "Goodness, how long will they keep that up?" Despite Stefan's warning, she hadn't really believed that the racket would be so loud. Could it possibly go on all day?

"Cannon balls cost money, don't they?" she asked

Wanda somewhat petulantly.

"Andrew Carnegie has lots of money for cannon balls and anything else he wants to spend it on," came the cryptic reply. Wanda was none too fond of the Scotsman or any of the big bosses. Her father and brothers worked fourteen hours each day for money that would probably not buy a single bullet, let alone a cannon ball.

Then, mindful of her mistress's delicate condition, she changed her tone and added lightly, "Until the men get their fill of the fun." Lifting the silver cover from a plate of scrambled eggs and tiny, succulent sausages, she giggled. "The place is full of men in uniforms, blue, red, every color of the rainbow."

Kalina took the cup of hot, dark tea from the maid, grimacing as she raised it to her lips. Dr. Hardie felt strongly that the rich, dark coffee she loved was injurious to her unborn child. "You may go out there if you wish, Wanda, to watch the gunplay," she said teasingly. "I can manage without you. There's Anusia, and of course young Dr. Alec to minister to my every whim."

"I'm not one of those silly girls who loses her head at the sight of a uniform!" she replied stiffly.

"You prefer the medical variety of male, I gather."

Wanda heaved a sigh, pretending to be annoyed at her mistress's teasing, but Kalina noted the quick heightening of color on the girl's cheeks at the mention of Alec's name. She wondered just how much the Polish-American girl knew about men. Her full figure, fresh face, and sparkling eyes must surely have attracted many before the Scottish doctor happened along.

"Speaking of doctors, yours wants to visit you when you've finished your breakfast." Then, the maid was gone, leaving Kalina to her thoughts. She felt unusually weary; every bone and muscle seemed to ache. Three more weeks until her time. How could she bear it?

Wanda soon returned with the physician, banishing her pensive mood. Gathering the pregnant woman's pink silk robe discreetly to the sides, the maid stood aside as Alec pressed the stethoscope to the bared abdomen. Amazing,

Kalina thought, that a length of tubing could transmit a tiny heartbeat to the outside world. She stared fixedly at the balcony outside the window, waiting for the doctor to finish his examination. A bird hopped about on the railing, she wondered how her robin family back home was faring without her. The doctor stood up, and Wanda replaced the silk.

"Well, doctor, is the baby's heart steady?" She grinned as she posed the question she asked him every time he listened to the heartbeat. "Is it a boy or girl? If it's a girl, you might as well tell her to go back to Heaven. Stefan will be furious —"

Kalina stopped. She was babbling.

There was no immediate answer, no answering laugh, as Dr. Hardie took an unusually long time at folding up his instrument, replacing it in his bag, and washing up at the basin.

"The child is quiet," he said calmly, returning to the bed, "but the heart is strong." Smiling, he reached out to touch her wrist. "The mother's pulse is also strong, though a mite too rapid. You must avoid any undue excitement today."

"How can one be tranquil with those cannons booming?" It was almost a wail such as Dunia might have produced. Not for the first time Kalina wondered why Stefan had been so insistent that she come to this affair. The foreign dignitaries he had wanted her to meet had so far been invisible — to her at least.

She was in a querulous mood, seemingly unable to control her irritation with the doctor's extraordinary caution. "In Poland, women work in the fields until their pains come upon them. The old ones always said it was better that way, that the child would simply slip out."

Old Anya's voice echoed in her ears, *Keep on your feet, it comes more quickly then.*

She did not miss the raised brow and swift sidelong glance that passed between the doctor and her maid.

Within the hour Kalina was dressed and seated in her lounge chair alongside a pretty little duck pond where her normally happy mood was restored somewhat by the sight

169

of Dunia and her little playmates. A dish of rosy strawberries was at her elbow on a little white table. The place was almost deserted, Anusia and many of the older women having joined the men in the meadow where the booming continued unabated. Kalina's head throbbed, and a solicitous Wanda had laid a cool, wet cloth across her eyes and brow.

The diverting music Louise Carnegie had promised drummed from the bandstand, but it only served to intensify the oppressive atmosphere. Later, after luncheon, there would be moving pictures in one of the sitting rooms. "New York in a Blizzard" was to be the featured film. Kalina wondered idly if the cameras had gone to Mulberry Street to film their snow. It had been snowing when she and Max had run through the streets to Pennsylvania Station.

Max! He and his lovely Libby were not in sight. They were probably at the meadow with the others. She would have a day's reprieve from the agony of seeing them together again. But there would be dinner tonight and afterward a social affair of some kind. She hoped they would not appear; as lovers they might want to go off somewhere together—

"Darling Kalina, have you a megrim?" The sound of Libby's voice immediately dashed her hopes as two magnificent horses trotted from a nearby trail onto the green. Kalina lifted the cloth to gaze into her friend's anxious face. Libby added, "I suffer much from headaches myself. There is a mixture I use which is most effective."

"Please," Kalina murmured, "it is nothing. My physician feels that covering my eyes will encourage tranquil thoughts." She smiled. "But the sight of you is all the remedy I need."

Indeed, Libby was a joy to the eyes this fresh morning. She was striking in a smoke-hued riding outfit, featuring the new and daring split skirt that enabled women who chose to do so to ride astride. What Max wore, she could not have said for she kept her eyes studiously fixed on Libby.

An especially loud noise from the meadow caused Kalina to flinch. She brought both hands up to her ears.

Libby frowned, clucking her tongue with disapproval. "Why must they keep testing that armorplate?" She turned to Max. "Do you think there will be a war soon?"

"Dunno," Max said in a curiously abstracted tone. "But if it comes, United States Steel will be ready to sell whatever it takes to all and sundry."

"To both sides?" Kalina sat up, astonished at his implication. Her eyes flew to his, unguarded.

"Of course," was the cool reply. "That's only good business. Bullets and battleships work just as well with the enemy as with friends." His tone was mocking, but his eyes were troubled.

Libby interrupted. "Please, Max, no more talk of war. Our little mother must not dwell on such horrors."

Just then Wanda came to say that Dr. Hardie had been summoned to tend an ailing guest who had the vapors. "It's that Mrs. Phillips. You remember, the fat one."

Kalina nodded, shaking her head in puzzlement. Like many of her social set, the woman had more money than good sense and was monstrously obese. Accretions of flesh encircled her arms like ivory bracelets.

She waved a dismissing hand. "I'm fine, Wanda, you may follow him. Perhaps you can render some assistance." She smiled as the maid ran off toward the house. A woman of Mrs. Phillips' wealth and obvious poor health would be a solid addition to the young doctor's budding practice. Stefan had agreed that the physician could serve any guest who needed medical attention.

Wanda had no sooner left than the nursemaid Susanna ran up to complain that Dunia had waded into the edge of the pond. "I couldn't catch her, she's that fast," she cried, close to tears for fear of being scolded.

"Don't fret, girl. Just take off her wet shoes and stockings. Let her run barefoot on the grass with the others." Kalina leaned back again. She would discipline the child later in private.

With a cheery wave, Libby and Max remounted to

resume their morning ride, Kalina watching as they moved into the trees. Susanna walked to a sunny spot a few yards from the pond to set Dunia's little shoes to dry, and after making sure that Dunia was at a safe distance from the water, Kalina leaned back once more to invoke the prescribed tranquil mood.

The events that followed were to remain a blur in Kalina's mind forever. She was never able to say which came first — her sense of impending disaster, Susanna's shriek, the frightened quacking of the ducks, or the ominous sound of splashing in the water. There was a single heartrending "Mama," and then she was in the icy water. She did not remember leaping from her chair or the dish of strawberries tumbling to the ground.

She found herself on the shore, sprawled on the grass. Libby bent over her, tucking her woolen riding cloak around her friend's wet, shivering form.

Max O'Hara was splashing from the water with Dunia in his arms. "She's OK," he yelled. "More scared than hurt."

He handed the child to the waiting Susanna. Then scooping up Kalina, he walked with rapid strides toward the house. Kalina felt the thunder of his heart as her face pressed into his pulsing neck.

Libby ran for Dr. Hardie and Wanda. Servants quickly directed Max to the Murav bedroom, and, as he laid Kalina down on the silken comforter, he leaned close to whisper hoarsely, "Kalina, my darling little Polack, if anything ever happened to you—"

His voice choked in his throat, and, with a groan, he laid his head on her chest, but not before she had glimpsed the palpable longing in his eyes. Instinctively, her arms reached up to encircle his body.

They remained in their wordless embrace until a commotion at the door caused Max to lift his head up. He was not swift enough to prevent Libby from seeing him in Kalina's arms. With a strangled cry, she fled from the room, the hard leather heels of her riding boots rapping sharply along the polished wood corridor.

To Kalina the sound was more ominous than the cannon

that continued to boom from the meadow.

Max tore out of the room, and there was no more time to think of Libby and Max or anything at all, as a wrenching pain tore through Kalina's lower body. She rose up with a shriek of terror.

"Remove her wet clothes," the doctor barked, and as Wanda set to work, Max reappeared at the door. "Is she all right, Doc?"

"Yes. Now please leave us." Grim-faced, the physician set about calming his patient.

Max lingered at the open door, his fingers running distractedly through his red hair. "She must not suffer, Doc. Do you have chloroform?"

Dr. Alec Hardie's kindly, stolid face darkened with quick anger and not a little measure of astonishment at the Irishman's concern for a woman he had just met. "Everything will be done, Mr. O'Hara," he said testily. "Mr. Murav has spared no expense to ensure that his wife will not suffer needlessly."

"Please." Wanda was pushing Max out the door. "Please hurry and notify her husband that my mistress is in labor."

The midday sun was hot when Max and Libby left the bridle path to seek out a pleasant place where a little brook chattered noisily over rocks. Libby sat down on a stump, brushing off the fringy yellow blossoms of a tall shrub that grew at the water's edge. Drawing off her hat, she reached out to pluck the white flower from a May apple whose umbrella-shaped leaves covered the ground.

The ride from the meadow had been charged with silence, and Max approached his sweetheart with trepidation. He would brazen out any suspicions that might have been aroused by the scene in Kalina's bedroom.

"Those are also known as mandrakes," he commented. "They are reputed to have aphrodisiac powers. One of the many things you taught me, my sweet." Squatting behind the stump, he drew her to him.

"Don't do that." She bolted up with such force that he

173

sprawled backward. She stared into the brook, tearing the petals from the blossom and throwing them into the water. The current bore them swiftly out of sight.

"Libby, dearest, what is it? Have I done something?"

She whipped round, her pretty face white with anger. "I will ask the questions, sir, and you will answer. What is going on between you and Kalina Murav?"

"Why, nothing." He came erect and vigorously brushed off twigs and leaves. "Before yesterday I had never set eyes on the woman."

"Liar!" Her shout caused a bird to clatter shrilly. "I may be a foolish old maid but I am not a fool. I suspected it yesterday when we arrived, but now it's perfectly clear to me, and everyone else, that you and my best friend not only know each other but have been intimate."

The jig is up, Max thought and immediately felt within himself a kind of peace. At this moment he knew, with a burst of illumination that issued like a beacon from the burning sun above, that the dream was over. He had known it for months but could not admit, even to himself, that it would never work. The vague discontent that had plagued him throughout the spring was now dissolved. The chains were off; no longer must he agonize. He would have to break it off with his goddess.

Max O'Hara of Pittsburgh had gambled with the person who had been Max O'Hara of New York and lost. The silver ring on his finger caught the sun, and he wanted to rip it off. For the merest fleeting moment, he regretted the loss of the cherry-red automobile.

He would tell her soon. But not now. Not with that glazed look of agony in the sky-blue eyes. Not with the sun so bright, the birds so damn cheerful, and Libby herself with that desperate unasked question in her eyes: Tell me it isn't so.

"You're right. We knew each other in New York." The lovers stood face to face on either side of the stump as he told her briefly, quietly, about his friendship with Kalina. He spared only the details of the encounters in the boxcar. She must never know that he had taken Kalina's virginity as he had also taken hers. The fact that both women had been more than willing did little to dull the knife edge of his guilt.

"She was a little snot-nosed kid, her aunt was dying, she was half-starved, and, to top it all, the coppers were after her. What could I do? I took her in, fed her, buried her aunt, and saw that she got to the mining town where her cousin Zuska lived."

"Then you left her?" Libby asked, coming around the stump. "Immediately?"

He nodded. "The very next day." Sweeping off his hat, he threw it into the May apples, and, stretching out his arms, he embraced her. She shook with weeping, and her voice was muffled as she spoke. "How could you not know that she was here in Pittsburgh, wife to your own boss, Stefan Murav?"

"Simple. Since the day we met in the library of your house, we've both been living in a paradise of love. You canceled your social engagements, I never had any to worry about." He laughed with relief that the break-up was put off for a while at least. "We shut out the whole world, as lovers do, spinning a cocoon around ourselves. You never mentioned the name of any friends and certainly not that of Kalina Murav."

She lifted her tear-stained face for his kiss. "Oh, Max darling, you speak such precious truth. You are the whole world to me. Nothing must come between us. If you should leave me, I would surely die."

A full six weeks after the day upon which Kalina gave birth to a stillborn son, she sat in the cozy inglenook of Louise Carnegie's little sitting room in Braemar Cottage. Though nearly mid-July, the weather had been unseasonably cold, and the maid had laid a fire in the grate. As she sipped her third cup of breakfast coffee, Kalina leaned her head on the cushiony back of the built-in settee, inhaling the piney fragrance of burning logs. If only she could bottle it and take it back to Pittsburgh, whose air was more likely to smell of coal smoke than of fresh, green forests.

It was a pleasant room. The dark wainscoting was offset by the rich tapestry-patterned wallpaper. The opaque light of the electrolier set into the arabesque ceiling cast a soft light on golden walnut upholstered in bright pink-and-green cretonne. An Aubusson covered the floor and rich velvet hangings framed the single window through which Kalina glimpsed an ashen sky. Thunder rumbled from the distant hills. The day promised to be stormy, but she had resisted all of Louise's pleas to postpone her return to Pittsburgh.

She would leave this beautiful place with real sorrow. Many happy hours had been spent in this very room, chatting with her hostess over informal lunches and after-dinner conversation while her husband had lingered with his business colleagues over cigars and brandy in the dining room. Feminine visitors had been rare.

"How pretty you look! All packed, dear?" Louise Carnegie stood in the open door, a book in one hand. She was a tall, handsome woman in her late thirties, much younger than her husband and possessed with a quiet dignity and natural kindness that had been a godsend to the gravely ill Kalina. Together with a trained nurse, the wealthy woman herself had tended to her every need.

Louise walked to the settee, and Kalina lifted a cheek for her kiss. She sat down beside Kalina. "Your dressmaker is most clever to fashion garments in your absence."

"Mrs. Raymond knows my figure as if it were her own. I have only to consult the latest fashion books and send along instructions."

After weeks in bed, followed by more weeks lounging around in robe and slippers, it was invigorating to be fully dressed in fashionable attire, her hair done up in a coronet of braids. The gown she had chosen for her journey home was a smart sailor dress of rich blue with a wide, snowy collar and decorated buttons marching down the front. A perky nautical hat completed the effect.

She glanced at the book in her companion's hand. "Nothing like a good book on a rainy day. What is it?"

Like herself, Louise was an omnivorous reader, her taste, however, running to the more serious.

"It's for you, my friend. A new novel I ordered for you from New York."

Kalina exclaimed with delight. "Oh, you are too kind." As she took the thick volume, she covered the older woman's hand with hers, pressing it fervently. "But for you and your unswerving devotion, I would surely be in Heaven at this very moment looking down on the loved ones I left behind me."

"Nonsense. It was your own healthy young body — you are hardly more than a child — and your own strong will to live that saved you in the end." Embarrassed, Louise tucked a nonexistent strand of hair into her neat bun. Kalina's eyes misted with tears. Andrew Carnegie's wife was always exquisitely coiffed, and despite her husband's legendary wealth, attired in simple garments. This morning she wore a crisp, white linen frock shot with tiny purple violets. A fold of fresh cambric softened the line of neck and throat.

Kalina ran her finger over the illustration embossed in silver on the red buckram cover of the book. It outlined the tall figure of a man in frock coat and stovepipe hat. "Abraham Lincoln," she said, reverently. She looked up. "It was he who freed the slaves."

"He did indeed," Louise said, filling a Limoges cup with coffee from the silver pot. She sipped the hot brew, and then continued. "*The Crisis* is written by the very talented Winston Churchill and describes events in our Civil War. A terrible time. So many died. I was scarcely born —" She stopped. "But you must read it for yourself." Then, dimpling, "Have you overcome your addiction to romantic novels?"

Kalina laughed, reddening. "No. I must confess I still enjoy them, but I feel the need for more serious reading. Most especially I need to learn more about my adopted country. Stefan sent some books by train, but they are so dry and scholarly."

Both women flinched as a loud clap of thunder shook

the house. Rain torrented down outside. "Oh, my," Louise exclaimed, "I really think you should tarry another day."

"No, I am quite determined. Stefan is most impatient for my return. And Dunia, I fear, might well have forgotten her dear mama." She cast an anxious glance at the streaming window. "Unless you feel the horses will suffer in the downpour."

"Not our nags," chuckled the other. "They can trot down our mountain blindfolded, I swear. And the buggy is closed up tight, so that you need not fear a drenching." She excused herself to summon the trap.

When she had left, Kalina leaned her head on the back of the settee, moodily stroking the book. Home. It would not be the same. Nothing would be the same again, ever. The life she had known in the big house on Rutherford Drive was gone. Wanda and Susanna had been dismissed by an almost apoplectic Stefan, who had blamed the sisters for the whole affair. If they had attended their duty, Dunia would not have entered the pond, and Kalina would not have plunged in after her. And so it went.

But it was the young physician who had borne the brunt of Stefan's rage. There had been no placating him. Despite the testimony of the specialist summoned from New York and who had arrived by special railroad express the following day and had told the stricken Murav, "You should get down on your knees and thank that young physician for his skill in saving your wife. As for the child, it would not have lived under any circumstance. Your wife's entering the water merely precipitated her labor. It did not kill the foetus."

The babe had been strangled by the umbilical cord, which wrapped around its tiny neck. The specialist also had told Stefan Murav that any attempt to bear another child would mean the death of his wife.

But Murav had been beyond reason. "You'll never practice in this country again," he roared at Alec Hardie. "If you even try, I'll track you down like a dog and have your life." To the astonishment of all save Kalina, who had known her husband was capable of irrational fits of temper, he had whipped from his vest pocket the sharp little knife given him by his father long ago and had thrust it into the face of the exhausted young Scot.

Sensible to the steel magnate's power and influence, Alec Hardie was now in Canada along with Wanda, whom he had married in a hasty civil ceremony in Pittsburgh. Susanna had gone home to her family in Homestead.

As for Libby—Kalina closed her eyes against the surge of pain within her. The woman who had been her best and only real friend since Zuska left was also gone from her life. Millard Hughes' maiden daughter adored Max. That much was obvious to all who saw her. The look of anguish on Libby's face when she had glimpsed her beloved embracing her best friend would remain with Kalina till her dying day.

What was more, if further proof was needed, there had been the evidence of Kalina's own love for the Irishman. In her delirium she had called his name over and over and over.

"You called for him, all heard you, the Carnegies' maid, the doctor—" So the tearful Wanda had told her mistress before she fled with her Alec.

For a time Kalina was oblivious to all but the soft crackling of the logs and the rapping of rain on the tall window. Suddenly she became aware of men's voices in the library on the other side of the wall. Carnegie had been at breakfast in the dining room with a number of male guests.

She tensed. Gradually words and sentences emerged from the babble. Everyone seemed to be talking at once. They were discussing, in heated tones, the recent demands of the steelworkers for more pay and a shorter working day.

"We want eight, we won't wait" was the rallying cry of the rebellious workers. On his single visit to Braemar Cottage since her confinement, Stefan had gone on about it. "They'll have their damned union over my dead body," he had sworn.

"A strike is coming, mark my words." That was Millard

179

Hughes' slow, cultured tones.

"More guards, that's the answer. It worked in '92. It'll work again."

"We have got to nip this union thing in the bud. Forewarned is forearmed. How about setting young O'Hara to mingle with the workers, spy a little?"

"Libby's young man?" Hughes again.

There was a silence as if someone had signaled for order. Then, in Carnegie's thick, self-righteous brogue, she heard, "Too much money and leisure ruins good workers. I myself started as a mere bobbin boy in a shirt factory on the Allegheny—"

At that moment, Louise reentered the sitting room. She grimaced, rolling her dark eyes toward the library. "Why do men think that the louder they talk, the more sense they make?"

Both women joined in friendly laughter. Then they walked rapidly into the corridor, past the tumult in the library toward the foyer, where, donning her voluminous rain cloak, Kalina kissed Louise good-bye and hurried out to the trap.

Halfway down the mountain, the driving rain relented, and by the time Kalina reached the Altoona station, a brave sun had broken through the clouds. She entered the private car, sat down in the plush seat, and opened her brand-new book. After a few moments, she closed it again and, reaching out to draw the curtains, fixed her dark eyes on the rain-washed Pennsylvania landscape.

Everything—trees, houses, distant hills—was fresh and green. Kalina Olkonsky Murav smiled with her heart as well as her face. She was going home. She was young and rich and filled with hope for the future.

Chapter Nine

The September night was warm and pulsing as Max O'Hara left the Libby Furnace, walking slowly through the gritty yard and out the gates. He doffed his cap and waggled his hand to the guard high up in the tower but got no answering wave. There was a time, before he became Libby Hughes' fancy man, when the man would have slid up his window with a cheery, "How's it goin', Max?"

But no more. Few of the men spoke to him except in essential matters of their work. The big Irishman was no longer one of them; he was one of the despised management. For the past few months Millard Hughes had been moving him about in various positions of authority. "You've got to learn all aspects of making steel," he had said. "Heater, roller, melter, even puddler. Start at the bottom, work up."

Libby didn't like it. "Father never did all those nasty jobs," she complained. "He's just testing you, hoping you'll give up and go back to the ranks."

The superintendent was far from happy about his daughter's entanglement with Max.

Max had not seen Libby for a week, the work Hughes demanded from his protégé consuming not the usual twelve, but fourteen to twenty hours per day. His hand dived into the pocket of his grimy work pants, rattling the note she had sent by her maid Helena. "I must see you. At once."

181

In his mind's eye Max saw her at the little writing desk in the sunny library, dipping her pen in the silver ink bottle, snatching a piece of her scented paper, scribbling furiously. Maybe her tongue would be between her teeth. The lovely face would certainly be set in the unattractive grim lines she had taken on these past months. Their relationship had deteriorated steadily since that day in the woods at Braemar Cottage, the day she had seen him with his head on Kalina's breast, almost weeping with anxiety for a woman he scarcely knew. Or so he had claimed. Libby Hughes, his angelic goddess, the woman who had dazzled him into forgetting who he really was, had let jealousy turn her into a shrew.

His resolution to break it off with her had come to nothing. Not for lack of purpose, but because he had been anxious to learn as much about the big bosses' plans for strikebreaking as he could before casting his lot once more with the workers. But, as if sensing Max's duplicity or perhaps in the hope that the romance between the young man and his daughter would come to a welcome and natural end, the superintendent had not invited him to sit in on policy meetings. Max had not been given a key to the locked file cabinet, and, whenever he entered Hughes' office for consultation, scattered papers on the desk had been hurriedly covered up by his boss.

Max started up the hill to the Leskos', his shoulders slumped, his steps slow and labored. He had made a rotten mess of things, all right, he reflected glumly. A woman passed him in the dark, he doffed his cap, but she stared straight ahead, pulling her long shawl close around her thin shoulders as if shrinking from him. His heart sank. Would the people of Homestead, who had once treated him as one of their own, who had thought him a grand guy, ever trust him again?

It was damn lonely. He missed Gus like the very devil. His one-time friend was working at Lucy Furnace, and when he bumped into him at the saloon or on the street, the jolly Dutchie cut him dead.

Max stopped at the crest to gaze down, as he always did,

at the vista of mill and river below. From within a house a gramophone moaned, "My sweetheart's the man in the moon." The sky was hot; acrid fumes filled the night air, invading his nostrils. Production was at fever pitch; orders for the new armorplate were rolling in from all over the world. Predictably, accidents were also up as the foremen spurred the men on to higher and higher quotas, demanding longer and longer hours at the furnaces.

A train hooted, then passed by along the river. Was it just last summer that he had stood in this very spot and thought of sending for Kalina? A snort escaped him. He had thought her pining for him in Shenandoah. Little did he know that she had bettered herself, far exceeding anything he could have dreamed for her.

"Wait for me," he had begged her. "One day I'll be rich." What a joke on him!

But like all his ambitions for wealth and power in the mill, all thoughts of sweet Kalina must be buried. But not forgotten. No, never that. For the love that had sprung up between him and the girl from Mulberry Street was the everlasting kind. No matter how many women he would possess—and knowing his own appetites, he knew he could be no damn priest or monk—Max realized that he would take that love with him to his grave.

The train disappeared around the Monongahela bend, hooting again as it passed the ferry. For two cents he would hop the next freight for New York. Or better still, Detroit or California. Far away. Anywhere.

But seconds later, he pushed open the splintery door of Stan Lesko's little company house. Though past midnight, Elena was at the blazing coal stove, stirring garments in the big copper boiler. Steam filled the kitchen. The man of the house sat at the table, his black-stockinged stumps cradling a whiskey bottle. As Max entered, Stan looked up. "Well, how's the big boss tonight?" He started to his feet.

"Shut up," called his wife without turning. "Don't start that stuff. And let up on the drink before you pass out and I have to cart you upstairs again." She whipped around, brandishing her long wooden stick. "Must you shame me before outsiders?"

Outsiders! Max grimaced, as he walked past Stan to set his lunch bucket on the sink. That was how this family now regarded him. No more camaraderie, no more washing up in the kitchen after work. The girl Mary brought him water in a pitcher to his room along with a tray of food. Elena had hinted strongly that he should move to "better" quarters, but when Max offered her twice the money, she had relented.

Upstairs in his gabled cell of a bedroom he now occupied by himself, Max ignored the greasy plate of potatoes and meat at the foot of his bed and upended his own whiskey flask to his lips. From below came the sound of angry, squabbling voices. Philadelphia gangsters had moved in on the pushcart business, and Stan had been elbowed out into the cold. It was the last straw and the crippled man simply gave up on life.

Max drank far into the night, long after the Leskos had banked the stove and gone to bed. The loss of their love was a raw and living pain. Well, what did he think? That he could straddle two worlds like some ancient Colossus, who spread himself so wide whole ships sailed between his legs?

No, he thought as he tumbled into his wrinkled sheets. He felt more like that Atlas fellow, who carried the whole world on his goddamn back.

It was full daylight when Max awakened. His mouth was full of cotton and the inside of his head felt like a blast furnace. Grabbing the empty whiskey bottle, he pelted down the wooden stairs. The house was empty, the kids in school, Elena delivering laundry, and Stan most likely at Koster's Millgate saloon for an early nip.

In the back yard, which was shared by three other company houses, he filled the bottle with cold water from the iron spigot and drank it in a gulp. Then, ducking his head under the stream, he wet his thatch of hair. Twisting round and round, he let the cool water dribble on his face, shoulders, chest and back, and into his wide open mouth, swallowing until his stomach was full.

After a long time, he straightened up and shook himself like a dog, and smoothing his hair back into place with his fingers, he started off toward Kensington Road and the house of Millard Hughes.

"Been swimming?" the maid Helena inquired with a sidelong glance as she opened the door to his rap. She giggled, her black eyes merry. "Or maybe you just fell into the old Monongahela."

"Neither." He chucked her playfully under the chin, resisting the impulse to kiss her on her rosy lips. She was one of two in this town who still greeted him with a smile, Mary Lesko being the other. For a time last fall, before she realized that the elegant Miss Hughes had herself actually fallen head over heels for the big Irishman, the Croatian immigrant girl had made a transparent play for Max's affections.

He followed her into the library, and she ran upstairs to fetch her mistress. Standing by the window with the billowy curtains, Max studied the familiar petunia bed. The once-pretty flowers had gone to seed, the white blossoms mostly gone, the lush green foliage yellowed and sere.

"Max, dearest, what a pleasant surprise!"

He turned. Libby stood in the doorway, somewhat in disarray. She wore a much-wrinkled white linen frock, which even to his masculine eyes appeared badly in need of laundering.

"Libby—"

He got no further, for she was upon him, her arms tight around his neck, lifting her face for his kiss. Taken aback, he did not at first respond. With surprising strength in one so frail, she pressed his wet head with her hand, forcing her mouth to his.

Her lips were hot. He pulled back, not without effort. "Are you ill? You seem to have a fever."

"I'm fine, now that you're here." She cupped his face, holding so tightly that her sharp-nailed fingers dug into his cheeks.

"Libby, we've got to talk." Max felt as though he had just been thrown into a dungeon. The sound of a cell door clanging echoed inside his head. Almost absently, he noted that her pompadour of golden hair, normally smoothly arranged, was falling about her face. The long metal pins stuck out here and there.

The pret-ty young girr-rl is my sis-ter, he remembered. How elegant, how perfect, how very precious she had been, standing like a porcelain figurine at the front of that dingy Settlement House classroom.

Despite his recent drenching, Max felt the sweat streaming down over his ribcage and between his thighs. *Damn!* If she was his sister, he would have killed any man who said what he was about to say.

He licked his lips and then plunged into it. "Libby, it's all over. I can't marry you. I thought I could, but I can't. I still love you in a funny kind of way, but marriage is not for us."

The torrent of words came to a halt as the blue eyes widened, then narrowed, and the thin face became white, then red. For the first time he noticed the deep, purple shadows under her eyes, the faint trace of wrinkles around the edges of her lips.

She screamed, a bloodcurdling noise that brought a frightened Helena to the still open door. "Miss?"

"Get out of here," Libby yelled at the girl.

Clearing his throat, Max began to speak. "No, you're wrong, dead wrong—"

"Don't lie to me. You and that Polish slut have been at it ever since New York. Being married means nothing to her kind apparently." She pushed her face into his once more, hissing like a snake. "That dead child was yours, wasn't it? Her maid said its hair was red."

Now it was his turn to go white. "You're imagining things, woman. The child was bald. Alec Hardie told me himself before he left for Canada."

"So-o-o, you were interested enough to discuss it with the doctor, were you?" Her voice was soft and slithering;

186

her eyes took on a vacant look.

She's going mad, he thought with sudden panic. He had known some like her in Gotham Court, men and women both, upon whom life had dumped more than its share of woe.

But he could not weaken. He dare not. It was his life or hers. And Max O'Hara had grown up in the city jungle, where only the fittest survive.

He must be like Galahad, whose strength was the strength of ten because his heart was pure.

A pure heart knows only truth.

"You're right," he said, quietly. "I love Kalina, I always have and always will. But I cannot have her for she belongs to another."

"You're mine, you're mine, she'll never have you." She hurled herself upon him once again, her fingers scrabbling at his face, her shrieks and sobs intermingling in a kind of horrible keening like women at a wake.

Max tried to reason desperately. "It would never work, Libby dear. Within a month, you'd hate me. I'm not cut out to be a manager. Your father knows it. He also knows that no matter how much you try to educate me, I'll still be Max O'Hara, street kid from New York, until the day I die."

With a kind of madness akin to Libby's within him, Max plunged toward the door, dragging the clinging woman along with him. "Helena," he yelled.

Immediately the maid was there; she had obviously been listening in the corridor. Her sweet, pretty face was grim. "She gets like this," she muttered. "It's not your fault."

Between the two of them, they got the distraught woman upstairs and into bed. "Now go quickly. It's best that way," advised Helena. "I'll give her a powder."

The blast of the noon whistle from Lucy Furnace, accompanied by the more melodious Angelus bell from St. Michael's Catholic Church, fell on Max's ears like a choir of angels as he ran back down River Road a few minutes

187

after the Hughes' front door slammed behind him. He was free. Libby would be fine, he told himself. She had Helena and her father to care for her. The rich always do fine. It was best this way. She will realize too that a clean break is best.

The guard was startled as the sweating redhead rushed through the gates. "I thought you were on the six o'clock trick—"

But Max heard nothing but the wonderful crashing sounds of the mill. How he loved the thunder of falling iron plates, the hoarse cough of engines, the earsplitting clang, the shriek of ladles swinging wildly in the air. It was better than a damn merry-go-round.

"Hal-oo-oo-o!"

The familiar warning shout rang through the vast echoing shed, and big burly men darted out of the way, seeming to Max like dancers in some infernal ballet.

He stopped to watch as an upended ladle spilled its liquid gold into an ingot trough and a fountain of sparks rose and fell like a shower of stars.

It was the mouth of hell, so some said, but to the man who had just come home from a faraway place, it was heaven.

Hughes was in his office, his gray head bent over his eternal papers. He looked up, annoyed. A deep frown creased his smooth brow. "How many times must I tell you not to barge in without knocking?" His lip curled in distaste. "And if you're going to be a manager, you can't come into the mill looking like that." His blue eyes, so much like his daughter's, narrowed. "Have you been drinking? Your clothes look slept in."

"They have." Max grinned.

It took less than a minute to say what he had come to say. "My prayers have been answered," the man said when he had finished. Then, more heatedly, "Now get out of my office, out of town, and out of my life."

Max turned serious. "Your days or ordering me about are over, Boss Hughes," he said, his own voice low and deadly. "You'll be seeing more of me than you think.

What's more, what you see and hear won't be much to your liking. Or your buddies Carnegie and Murav either."

There was only a momentary compunction as he pawned the gold arrow tiepin that had been Libby's Christmas gift to him. Max held the callous indifference of one born poor toward finery that has outlived its purpose.

At Koster's Millgate saloon, he found not only the already drunk Stan Lesko but Gus Koval as well, who was quite sober, in fact, morose. The big Dutchie sat alone at the long bar, his booted feet on the long brass rail. He was drinking beer.

"Ho, Gus," Max shouted, sliding onto the neighboring stool. "I'm back."

His old mate turned, pale-blue eyes stared into brown. A long time. Max waited, knowing that no words were needed between the two of them. The whole goddamn story was surely in his eyes, as plain as the nose on his freckled face.

Gus Koval must have liked what he saw, for he drained his schooner and slid it along the bar. "Ho, Koster, another draft." His big hand slapped Max on the shoulder. "And a couple for my friend."

More men came in, lunch buckets rattled, the mouth-watering aroma of garlic, onion, and baloney filled the place. The bloodied welts on Max's cheeks were duly, if silently, noted. Men who could not read or even speak "the English" managed, with native acumen, to put two and two together and come up with four. Or maybe five, Max reflected ruefully.

Libby Hughes' fancy man had come a cropper. By tonight the whole story would be all over town. Homestead wives, daughters, sisters worked in the big houses on the hill. The grapevine of servant gossip would serve as well as any newfangled telephone to spread the delicious gossip.

The talk boomed out in several languages, but it revolved around a single subject. Conditions at the mill. The arrogance of the big bosses. The desperate need for a strong and effective union. A union with a wallop.

Maybe now they would have it. Their Max was back.

While Max and Gus lingered at Koster's, hoisting schooners and talking of old times and new plans, Kalina Murav stood in the long reception line at Buffalo's Temple of Music, awaiting her turn to shake the hand of President William McKinley.

Nervously, she twirled the ivory handle of her folded parasol. The day had been hot, the sun quite glaring for September, and, but for her utter weariness, she would have relished the comparative cool of the high-walled building.

It was her first trip away from home since her long illness following her disastrous confinement, and she gloried in the change and, incidentally, in the fact that the ridiculous and awkward bustle was going out of style. She and Stefan had left Pittsburgh the week before and had spent a few days in New York before proceeding to the Buffalo Pan-American trade fair and exposition. Her husband was much interested in the new machinery, but Kalina was taken with the artistic displays, especially the heroic sculptures of St. Gaudens and others.

She ran a finger under the high tight collar that threatened to choke off her very breath. How fervently she wished the fashions would change. Some women she had seen in New York had actually been uncorseted. Shamelessly. The new freedom diminished the prescribed hourglass effect, but oh, what bliss, she thought, to let your natural figure fall where it may.

While Stefan conferred with J.P. Morgan and others in Carnegie's New York townhouse, she had attended matinees and even evening theater performances with the other wives. The young, ethereal Ethel Barrymore had moved her deeply in Ibsen's *A Doll's House*. The disturbing story of a woman who, feeling that her life was closing about her, had left husband and family to make her way alone had moved her deeply.

I too sometimes think that life has somehow passed me by. The errant thought came unbidden as she stared at her husband's broad back. He turned to whisper, "We're almost there. Stop that nervous twirling. It's unseemly."

She pressed her lips together to keep back a sharp retort. Why is a husband allowed to scold a wife with impunity, but she is thought a shrew if she gives it back to him in kind?

A man with a bandage on his right hand now stood before the president. Suddenly the air was rent with an explosion like a firecracker, followed quickly by another. Bedlam erupted; people shouted and scurried about. The bandage had concealed a revolver.

"The president has been shot! Stay here!" With an air of importance Murav elbowed through the press of bodies, bystanders moving aside as they always did for the tall, fierce man with the imperious manner.

After a time he was back, plainly relieved. "It's a shallow wound in the abdomen. An operation is needed, but the doctor says he will recover."

Drawing a handkerchief from his pocket, he passed it over his eyes and chin. "Whew! That was a close one! If McKinley dies, Roosevelt will become president, which would be rotten for business right now. We've got this big merger in the works, and he'd be quick to have us up on antitrust charges."

He grabbed his wife's hand and half-ran to the door. "Pray there's no infection."

Kalina prayed, as her husband had commanded, but for vastly different reasons than he had imagined. She feared greatly for the president. Far more patients died from the damages of the surgery than from their wounds.

Despite her prayers and the prayers of the nation, infection *did* develop, and exactly one week later the country's twenty-fifth president died of gangrene. Teddy Roosevelt hurried down from atop a mountain in the Adirondacks to be sworn into office.

Kalina was to remember the exact moment the news arrived because her finger was directly on Vienna at the time. The family were in the back parlor—herself, Anusia, Dunia, and Stefan—enjoying a rare evening of domestic quiet. They had brought back from the exposition a cunning world globe, equipped with a clock device that told one what time it was, precisely, in any part of the world. Though she was yet too young to read the time, Dunia was intrigued by the myriad little countries, each with its own distinctive color—red, blue, pink, yellow—and Kalina had been spinning from one place to the other for the child's pleasure and enlightenment.

Anusia was at her knitting, an art at which she was quite adept; the frock Dunia wore and the shawl across Kalina's shoulders were both products of her busy needles. Stefan's sister sat as usual in a straight-backed chair, feet solidly on the carpet, her sallow face set in grim, unsmiling lines as she bent to her work.

Her brother, on the other hand, reclined in his favorite rocking chair, reading the *Pittsburgh Post*.

From time to time, he would snort and read a line or two, sometimes a longish item dealing with the local or national scene. Stefan had been tense and nervous since they had returned from Buffalo. News of the president's condition was not what had been hoped at first. When Stefan Murav was nervous, he rocked vigorously, causing the chair to move forward.

"Stefan, really!"

Kalina giggled as she saw the rocking chair butt up against Anusia's chair. With a little shamefaced grin of his own, Stefan rose up, picked up the rocker, moved it back into place by the little piano, from where he would resume his rhythmic journey.

Kalina smiled. She was happy. Considering her failure to fulfill her duty as a wife and produce an heir, considering that she had called out for Max in her delirium, relations between her and her husband had not been as she had feared. There had been but a single mention of Max.

On the first night of her return home, they had undressed and prepared for bed. Stefan had tossed aside the nightgown the maid had left on the bed and drew her to him, naked. "One warning, wife. If you ever try to see that Irishman or take up with him in any way, it'll mean not only his death but yours as well."

He had reached out to the bureau top and touched his father's little dagger, which he placed there each night before sleep. Kalina felt little fear of him, though she was perfectly ready to believe he meant what he said. To the boy who had scarcely known his parents, the knife was a talisman, a thing that meant power over anyone who got in his way.

Their nights in the big bed were not, however, as in the early days when her cries of passion had filled the night. Now she felt little pleasure in the act.

The *Manual for Motherhood* had noted, ". . . the best wives and mothers know little or nothing of sexual pleasure. Love of home and children are their natural passions."

Perhaps they knew best, the omniscient authors of the informative little book. She glanced around the pleasant little room with its soft tints, its many electric lights, its scenic prints on the walls. Knowing her distaste for gloom and clutter, Stefan had had the room redecorated while she had been recuperating at the Carnegies'.

This—being together as a family—was her joy.

Dunia's shrill young voice and laughter, the click of Anusia's bone needles, Stefan's steady rocking, the distant sound of singing from the kitchen as the new maid washed up.

If only her darling Zuska were here within the family circle! Or living nearby with a family of her own. What times they would have visiting back and forth. More and more of late Kalina's errant cousin occupied her thoughts. Litka's daughter might well be dead, she thought with sudden terror.

But to think of Zuska dead, to even imagine that vital spirit quenched forever was akin to thinking of the sun and moon as gone from the sky.

If Kalina thought of Max at all, it was in that fleeting moment before she fell asleep at night when thoughts are vagrant. But even then, she schooled herself. Whatever they meant to each other at this time in their lives, neither she nor Max were free to indulge those feelings.

But Kalina's idyll was soon to end. A knock at the door would set in motion a long chain of events so intricately woven into her life that they would not only tear her from the country she loved but from those nearest and dearest to her as well.

She had been regaling a rapt Dunia with stories of Vienna and waltzes and music and the glitter of kings and queens. "One day we will travel to this marvelous city," she said. "It's called the City of Dreams."

Such a trip might well come to pass, for Stefan had been talking more and more of removing his business operations to Europe once these labor troubles were taken care of. Only tonight at dinner he had declared, "If that cowboy takes over this country, pack your bags."

In a pedantic tone that seemed to imply that the information was news to Kalina, Anusia had just said, "Vienna is the capital of the Hapsburg Empire," when the loud bang of the front knocker brought them all up short. The latest in a series of new maids, an orphan girl named Laura whom Anusia had engaged during Kalina's stay at Braemar Cottage, fetched the ominous envelope on a tray to her master. There was a single whoop from Stefan as from an animal who has just been shot.

"My God, that damn cowboy has made it to the White House! That anarchist Czolgosz has done us in."

Chapter Ten

Pittsburgh, October 1902

"Ma'am, I would like to give me notice."

The maid Laura entered the dining room where Kalina was going over the week's menus with Anusia.

Anusia's head came up from the writing pad, her pencil in the air. "Nonsense, girl. Now get to your dusting."

Laura fixed her brown gaze on the woman, then with a swift, defiant motion, drew her gray-striped coverall apron over her red curls. Bunching the thick cotton garment into a ball, she threw it into a corner. "No more dusting for me, Miss Murav, nor washin' dishes either. I've got me a real nice position at a milliner's." Stepping up to the table, she put both hands on the blue linen daytime cloth. "Three bucks a week and all nights off and Sundays."

Furious, Anusia rose up, knocking her chair to the floor. "Why you ungrateful little whelp. I took you from the orphan home, out of the goodness of my heart. But I should have known better than to employ a filthy Irish slut—"

Kalina broke in. "Anusia, that's enough. Now please leave us. You may have hired Laura in my absence, but I am still the mistress in this house." She had discovered that her sister-in-law responded best to a firm, authoritative tone. Subservience certainly did not work.

The woman flounced out, and Kalina questioned the maid. She had not been oblivious to the frequent and often

195

noisy rows between Anusia and the orphan girl — loud disagreements over dust balls under the furniture, her refusal to wear a tight-fitting cap over the flame-red hair, Anusia's objections to the girl's loud singing while she worked. And many more that were seemingly without cause.

The two were like oil and water, Kalina had decided. Laura's announcement was hardly a surprise.

The girl had not only courage but ambition. The nuns had taught her fine sewing, she said, and she anticipated a career in the millinery business. "Maybe a shop of me own one day," she boasted.

"Why not?" Kalina smiled at her. Her heart did a double turn as she gazed into the fresh, young face. She could be Max O'Hara's sister, she thought, with that outrageous hair fairly springing from her head, those marvelous eyes, those freckles. Max had ambitions too, though far surpassing Laura's.

"Dunia will miss you," she said.

Laura's face fell. "And I'll miss her, she's a dear little thing." Her face brightened. "But I know a girl who you could hire to take my place. Not as a slavey, like Miss Murav tried to make me, but as a nursemaid."

Following Susanna's departure after the debacle at Braemar Cottage, there had been no nursemaid for Dunia. In the months since her return, she had not sought one out, but now she felt the need to pursue interests outside the home — her social work, the weekly soirees at Lillian Russell's, a matinée now and then.

As for evening entertainment, Stefan had little time for that now; he was completely absorbed in labor problems at the mill and was rarely home before midnight.

Laura's friend was a girl named Mary Lesko. She lived in Homestead, she was a hard worker, reliable and clean, could read and write like a "swell," though she was not so keen on sewing and dusting and cleaning up. So said Laura.

A wide grin made the freckles dance. "But one thing that might displease Miss Murav. She likes to sing, almost more

196

than I do. We met in the chorus at the Settlement House."

"I like singing too." Kalina laughed so loudly it brought a still frowning Anusia to the door. "And Dunia simply adores it. She can warble like a nightingale if she likes."

After dismissing the girl with a week's wages and a reference, Kalina set out for Homestead on the trolley. She had more sense than to invade the workers' domain with her chauffeur and brand-new electric motorcar. The workers' town across the river was in an ugly mood. Anything could happen to a "swell" who drove around in high style, lording it over the men.

She wore a simple dove-gray frock of tucked linen and perched a smart, stylish French beret on her pompadour. Like her frock, the hat was plain with no feathers or elaborate decorations — only a red grosgrain around the brim and down the back.

She had declined Anusia's suggestion that she don babushka and apron so as to appear like a worker's wife or sister. The October day was fair, if windy, and she hoped it wouldn't rain, for in her haste she had forgotten her umbrella.

As the trolley crossed the bridge and the horses turned to go up the long street fronting the mill, Kalina fingered the paper in the pocket of her frock. She carried no handbag or roomy reticule because of possible thieves but had wrapped some money in a handkerchief and tucked it up her close-fitting sleeve.

Anusia had been highly disapproving. "You'll be robbed, raped, maybe murdered. Someone's bound to recognize you. Your photograph's been in the papers."

"I want to see the kind of home the girl comes from," Kalina replied calmly. "I'm not going into deepest Africa. These people are, after all, Stefan's employees."

She failed to add that if this Mary Lesko came to the house to apply for the job, Anusia might well scare her off. She and Anusia had struck an agreement. Kalina would tend to Dunia's nursemaid, and Anusia would manage the household servants — the cook, the cleaning and wash-up girls, the gardeners, and any occasional help as needed.

She would also personally do the marketing, an occupation that Kalina knew the woman took great pride in.

While she had no intention of permitting Stefan's sister to usurp her own role as mistress, Kalina was sensible to Anusia's need to be busy. Without the press of many duties, the old maid would be even lonelier and more unhappy than she already was.

As she started up steep River Road, Kalina was not prepared for what she saw. Although it was Thursday—a workday—the street swarmed with people, not only the women and children she had expected but men as well. Stefan's reports of laying off men for strike activity had not been exaggerated. They filled the open doorways of the tiny company houses, whose dingy, unpainted fronts lined both sides of the street. Their loud talk emanated from the inevitable saloon on almost every corner. They sat on the wooden sidewalks, blocking her path. They split ranks, readily enough, to let her pass. No one accosted her. All were polite, if reserved. No one spoke to her.

Anusia had been right. All knew who she was. Whispers followed her. "That's the Cossack's wife, the Polack. What's she doing here in Hunkytown?"

An effigy of a man hung from a gas street lantern. The swinging figure was dressed in a black suit and stuffed with straw and manure obviously scraped from a stable floor. It had a thick black mustache made of horsehair and a sign that read "Cossack Murav."

Uniformed policemen mingled with the crowd, walking casually up and down the street swinging their wooden clubs. Kalina wondered how many of the men dressed as workers were plain-clothes detectives from the Pinkerton agency. Stefan had told her they had been hired to spy on the workers.

She reached the crest and turned onto Seventh as Laura had instructed. "Is this the Leskos?" she inquired of a woman staring at her from a doorway. Like most of the women, she was dressed in an apron and a long, black cotton frock. A colorful babushka hid every scrap of her hair. Her arms were crossed on her chest, and she seemed dispirited. Most of the women Kalina had seen in Homestead had that listless, vacant, almost hopeless look about them.

"Nah. Over there." She pointed across the street. "With all the furniture in front."

As Kalina crossed the narrow, cobblestoned street, a woman emerged from the house carrying a wooden chair under each arm. She drew near and stifled a startled gasp. The woman's face was haggard, with that kind of deathly pallor that marks a long, debilitating illness.

"Mrs. Lesko?" she asked.

The woman put down the chairs and glanced up. The eyes that stared at Kalina were blue and frightened. "Yes, I'm Elena Lesko. What do you want of me?" She drew back. "Are you from the sheriff? We're getting out today."

Before Kalina could reply, a cart came round the bend at Seventh, its iron wheels clattering on the rough stones. Two young boys, ten or twelve or so, ran along the sides while a tall girl of fourteen pushed.

"What took you so long?" Elena Lesko called to them. Her eyes flew to the sky. "Looks like rain, we've got to hurry."

"Sorry, Mother," said the girl. "There's such a crowd in the street we had trouble getting through."

"You must be Mary." Kalina walked up to the girl as she maneuvered the cart close to the open front door. "Laura O'Hagan says you are seeking employment as a nursemaid."

The girl's eyes lightened. Like her mother's they were a deep, lovely blue, reminding Kalina of a mountain lake. But unlike her mother, Mary's face was fresh and alive with the vibrancy of youth and good health.

Mary's hand went to her mouth, and she cast a stricken glance at her soiled frock and the ragged sweater that was slung across her shoulders. "Oh, my goodness, are you Mrs. Murav?"

Kalina smiled. "Yes, I am."

At that point, the mother interrupted them. Sweeping a hand toward her sons, who were gaping from the door, she yelled, "Get inside and load the cart with dishes and pots. Now scat." Then, turning to Kalina, she said in a milder tone, "Come inside, Mrs. Murav. The Leskos' furniture may be in the street, but we don't talk business where the world can listen in." She looked pointedly to the woman across the street, who had left her doorway for the sidewalk.

There was no table in the kitchen, Elena explaining that it had been moved to the new place yesterday, Elena said. "Jake Hruska loaned us his coal wagon—" She stopped abruptly and then said, "But then you're not interested in our troubles." A wan smile tugged at her pale lips.

Kalina said nothing to that and silently accepted the cup of steaming coffee from the woman. The cast-iron stove was part of the house and would remain. It was burning fiercely, filling the room with heat. The coffee was rich and strong, and Kalina drained the cup. She would need it. It was clear that, as Murav's wife, Polack or not, she was the enemy.

The two women stood facing each other in the near-empty room. The boys made a great clatter with the pots and dishes, and Mary sat on the floor, her hands clasped nervously in her lap. The adolescent girl had a very pretty, softly contoured face, with the promise of the kind of beauty that comes with the years.

Elena Lesko pursed her lips. "I don't know as I want my daughter working in the Cossack's house. He's a mean one and would shoot a man as soon as look at him."

Kalina flushed at the reference to last winter's murder of Kewalski but said only, "The household is strictly my domain, Mrs. Lesko. My husband does not meddle with the servants just as I do not concern myself with his dealings with the workers."

The scarfed head came up sharply. "Well, you should, Madam," she said indignantly. "It's Stefan Murav who's putting us out of the house we've lived in since Mary here was born. Seems to me it's a wife's job to know what her old man is up to."

"Oh. I'm sorry. I didn't know—"

The girl stood up. "Men who aren't working in the mill have to get out of the company houses so's other men, new ones, can move in." As she spoke, she drew her long, thick braids up on top of her head, tying them loosely together in a knot. Kalina wondered how this one would take to wearing starched, white caps, and determined at that moment that the nursemaid could go about bareheaded. As did Dunia and herself. Putting hats on servants when indoors suddenly seemed to her a ridiculous custom.

Mary ran up to her mother and encircled the thin waist with her arms. She looked pleadingly into Elena's tired face. "Please, Mother, may I? Laura says that Mrs. Murav is the sweetest, kindest person in the world. It's only that old one you've got to watch out for—"

The mother looked shocked. "That's enough, girl!" Embarrassed, she addressed Kalina. "Awful how these silly girls do chatter." She managed a faint smile that was a bit warmer than the last.

"I don't mind. I'm pleased to hear such a good report of myself." Seeing the woman's hesitation, Kalina pressed her advantage. "It's three a week and board," she said quickly, impulsively raising the wage by a dollar. "The food is plentiful and we have a lovely garden."

"I just bet you do." The hostility returned but only for a moment. "It *is* one less mouth to feed," she said, her hand on the knotted braids.

Mary's face brightened, then clouded. "But what will you do without me for the heavy work? You know you can't lift or carry any more."

Elena glanced at the boys, who, having finished their loading, stood waiting. "Those two are big enough to do anything."

"And no heavy cleaning nor scrubbing." She simply had to have this girl, Kalina thought. So sweet and fresh and so solicitous of her mother. Perfect for Dunia.

A tall man, very drunk, lurched into the house. Mrs. Lesko pushed Mary out the door. "Go help the boys."

Stan Lesko peered at Kalina with bloodshot eyes. "Well, if it ain't O'Hara's doxy." He took a step toward Kalina,

201

who shrank back against the wall. "If you're looking for Max, he ain't here. He's down at the church, settin' things up for the big union meeting Saturday."

With a quick motion, Elena lifted the ladle from a bucket by the stove and unceremoniously dumped water on her husband's head. "Now, you leave the lady alone. And let's not have any more dirty gossip."

Unperturbed by the drenching, Stan shook his head and wiped his face with his sleeve while his wife handed him a cup of coffee. Her gaunt face was beet red. "Stan's not himself," she said to Kalina. "It's all this talk of a strike and trouble coming that's got him going."

Kalina's heart was thudding in her chest. O'Hara's doxy. What did it mean? Was it all over Homestead that she and Max had once been sweethearts? And what on earth did Max have to do with unions? He was training to be a manager.

The children left again with the cart, and Elena Lasko took Kalina into the bedroom. "You seem to be a good sort, Mrs. Murav, so I feel you should know that Max has left Libby Hughes. It's all over between them," she said, "and our Max is back where he belongs. He's just the shot in the arm the men need."

"Max is good at that," Kalina replied. "He practically saved my life back in New York."

Elena took her hand and pressed it between her own. "Whatever you are, Murav's wife or fine lady, you are the woman Max really loves. He told us all about you when he first came to live with us." Her eyes softened. "We all felt bad when it didn't work out. You married Murav; he got messed up with Miss Hughes."

A few minutes later, Kalina left the Leskos to their moving, with a promise that Mary would report for work on the next day bright and early. As she started back down the hill, she raked the sky for St. Michael's steeple and, making her way toward it through the twisting lanes and alleys, stood a long moment watching the men go in and out of the brick sanctuary. No sign of a tall redhead. If she saw him, what would she say? That she was glad he was back with the workers?

Or that she was glad he had broken it off with Libby?

She might warn him, *My husband says one day you'll wake up dead.*

Must she betray her husband to save the man she loved?

The next morning it took Dunia all of ten seconds — just long enough to take a good, long look — to fall headlong in love with her new nursemaid. She had missed Susanna sorely. As Kalina had foreseen, Mary disdained to wear the confining cap politely but happily donned the print frock and snowy apron the laundress provided. She had pitifully few garments of her own. Anusia notwithstanding, the sound of her warbling filled the house. Mary possessed a rich, soaring contralto and seemed to have a vast quantity of both folk and popular songs in her repertoire. There was no need for a gramophone to entertain Dunia.

Despite Kalina's discreet questioning, however, Mary declined to talk about Max and Libby. "Mama says I'm not to gossip," she said primly. "You'll have to get your information elsewhere."

"Elsewhere" proved to be the Settlement House where Kalina took over the English language classes formerly taught by Libby. Nobody seemed to know what had happened to Miss Hughes. "She went out of town," said one. "She's ill," said another.

Her anxiety increasing, Kalina resolved to find out the truth. Going up to the Hughes house was out of the question, there might be any ugly scene with Libby or her father. As it happened, the girls' chorus also met on Tuesday nights. The Hughes' maid Helena was part of the group as was Wanda's sister Susanna, and Laura. Perhaps their mothers had not forbidden them to gossip, Kalina hoped.

The first Tuesday after she had visited the Leskos, Kalina approached the three girls as they left the building arm in arm. They were more than eager to talk, especially Helena, who was deeply troubled by her mistress's condition and expressed the hope that Mrs. Murav could help the woman who had been her friend.

"I am still her friend and much concerned about her welfare," Kalina said. "Please tell me where she is."

"After Mr. O'Hara broke it off with her and quit his manager job, Mr. Hughes sent her away. Nobody knows where. Maybe a sanatorium or hospital. She's pretty sick. The doctor said she had a nervous breakdown."

Kalina could not control her sudden weeping. Tears ran down her cheeks. Images scudded across her mind. Was it possible that just a year ago she had hidden in Lillian Russell's lavatory, and an exquisite girl in apple green with satiny apple blossoms caught in her moonlight hair took up a pair of scissors and snipped away with glee at a dreadful purple dress?

"I was one of many who aspired to be Mrs. Stefan Murav," Libby had said. Now she had failed once again in love.

Respectfully, the girls waited for Kalina to regain control of herself. Boldly, as though aware that the usually dignified wife of the big boss was just a few years older than herself, Laura pressed her red head close to Kalina's ear and whispered, "It's all over town that she's—well, you know what I mean?"

Kalina blanched. The girl's meaning was clear. When a young woman disappeared for a time, no matter what excuse was offered, it was taken for granted that she was what was euphemistically referred to as being "in trouble."

"Oh, no, never that," she replied quickly. "Max—Mr. O'Hara—is not a man to desert a woman if that were the case. He's"—she searched for words—"the kindest, most honorable person I've ever known."

They stood under the gas lantern, and Kalina caught the sly exchange of glances. There was a small silence. Finally, Helena said, "Mr. O'Hara *is* everything you say, Madame. And I don't for a minute believe the gossip. My mistress is sweet and gracious, but she has been pampered by her father. She's the apple of his eye. Now that she can't have what she most wants in the world, she's throwing her little tantrum."

Another silence, when Kalina replied, so softly the girls had to lean close to hear. "Wealth and position often bring more unhappiness than joy."

It was November before Kalina saw Max again. Stefan had been gone for weeks in Washington for consultations with the new president. True to his promise to break up the trusts, Roosevelt was wielding what the press called a "big stick," Big steel, big oil, big coal—all felt the blows.

Husband and wife had attended but a single social event that fall. Jim Brady threw a sumptuous banquet at the Schenley Hotel to honor the English actress Lily Langtry, who was touring the country. It was a spectacle such as Kalina had never seen. Champagne flowed like water, and rare orchids and hothouse roses filled the rooms. Long tables groaned with rich foods. As the guests walked up the red carpet under the marquee, onlookers crowded on both sides. Many were beggars—some of them small children, who ran up with upturned hats or baskets.

The little pinched faces haunted Kalina. With Mary Lesko in charge of Dunia and the rest of the household running as smoothly as clockwork, thanks to a vigilant Anusia, Kalina found herself free to indulge her penchant for social work. The Settlement House classes took two evenings a week, but there were still the long afternoons to fill.

She continued to attend Lillian Russell's soirees, however. The actress was deeply involved in charitable works. "Why don't you adopt a slum family or two or three?" she advised Kalina. "It's very rewarding. You determine their needs, bring them food, clothing, even supply medical care when needed. Try not to give them cash outright. It's not good form." Her magnificent eyes swept over the assembly of fashionably dressed women. "They become your friends—true ones—a refreshing change from the people one is forced to cultivate."

Promptly, Kalina adopted not only the Kewalskis, to

whom she had been sending Dunia's garments, but the Leskos and a family called Mielchek, with whom Mary's parents shared a house. Anna Mielchek's husband had been immolated in the firepot at Lucy Furnace the previous year, an accident for which Anna had received the grand sum of seventy-five dollars. Little did Kalina know that the death money had come from Max and had been painfully saved up to bring her from Shenandoah.

They all lived in Cesspool Alley, the Leskos and Mielcheks at Number Seven, Mrs. John Kewalski next door at Number Nine. The unsavory name for the street came not from its unsanitary state—the women kept it swept and clean—but from the presence of the sewage system at one end.

One cold, rainy day Kalina set out for Homestead with a basket on each arm. They were filled with bolts of cloth purchased by Anusia during those first months of Kalina's arrival in Pittsburgh. The fabrics were sturdy, but the colors were dark and dismal to Kalina's eyes. The three mothers were ecstatic. "With all that black smoke pouring out of the mill, we'd be forever scrubbing if we wore bright things like you, Ma'am," exclaimed Anna Mielchek.

The wife of Stefan Murav became a familiar figure in the streets of the mill town. Her tall, erect carriage and the unique mingling of dignity and honesty about this young woman of eighteen told these immigrants, who had known nobility in the "old country," that here went a genuine aristocrat. The great dark eyes, strongly marked brows, and sculptured mouth softened a face that on another might have seemed proud and imperious.

Though well past the time when she must go home to her own dinner with Dunia and Anusia, Kalina lingered in the cozy kitchen, glancing occasionally out at the driving rain. She longed to bring Zuska's child here one day. Unlike Rutherford Drive, Cesspool Alley never lacked for little playmates.

Big lumps of coal hissed and crackled in the stove; it was one commodity that was plentiful and cheap. Bread was baking in the oven, and she would be given a crusty loaf to take home, wrapped in a tea towel. A seemingly bottomless coffeepot simmered, its blue enameled surface black with smoke. Lina Kewalski pumped industriously at a sewing machine, running up pants from Anusia's cloth for her three little boys. Little Hania, whom Kalina had held that day of the Libby Furnace blowing-in, toddled around the room. Neighbors and small children walked in and out the narrow door. Nobody bothered to knock; all were welcome.

She soon discovered that the hostile stares of the women she had seen on her first excursion to the workers' town were a facade meant for the outsider. Times were hard and bound to get harder, but the women were undaunted.

Each time she came here, the Lady Bountiful from across the river where the houses were big and cold and hid behind tall, thick hedges and spiked iron fences, where dogs and uniformed guards paced up and down the sidewalks, found it increasingly difficult to leave. It all brought a pang of nostalgia to her heart. This is how it had been in Jaslo, in the kitchen of Pan Mikolai's manor. I may be Pan Mikolai's daughter, she reflected wryly, but I am a peasant at heart.

She had put on her cloak, preparing to leave, when one of the Lesko sons burst through the door. "Dad's in a big fight down at the river. Max says you better come right away."

Elena ran out into the downpour, her boy chasing after her. Kalina stood transfixed. Max was at the river. She had not seen him since that summer night in the mountains when she had fled in her satin dress to weep among the trees.

Hurriedly making her excuses, she departed—but not to the homeward-bound trolley. As if possessed of a will of their own, her feet turned toward the Monongahela, where she melted into the throng of women watching from the railroad tracks along the wharf. She learned quickly that the immediate cause of the trouble was a boatload of fresh immigrants that had just unloaded from a river barge.

It was a pitched battle. The men ran about like cursing,

screaming lunatics, beating the bewildered newcomers with stockings filled with iron scraps, with billy clubs, shillelaghs, baseball bats, walking canes, sticks — anything that might inflict a telling blow. There were no guns; the men of Homestead were not killers.

The new immigrants were driven back into the river, their heads bobbing as they struggled to reach the other side. The water was shallow at this point, and there was little danger they would drown. The barge from which they had just disembarked was already out of sight.

Elena and her son were lost in the melee. Kalina grabbed the black sleeve of a priest, one of many who moved among the rioters in a vain attempt at restoring order. The Leskos were in a shed adjacent to the mill, he said, pointing. Heedless of the danger, she ran toward it, skirting the edges of the rioters. Her hand was on the knob when suddenly the door opened from inside and she found herself staring into Max O'Hara's freckled countenance.

"Kalina!"

"Max!"

They spoke at once. Neither moved. They seemed rooted to the spot, gazing into each other's eyes. Neither was conscious of the pouring rain. Max's red curls were plastered to his head, his torn shirt clung to his muscled torso, the tight-fitting workpants were smeared with blood. Water poured in a stream from Kalina's silk-lined hood onto her face, seeping under the collar of her cloak.

A sound of scuffling and loud voices from inside the shed broke their seeming trance. "Stan," she said, "Is he hurt?"

"He's OK, mostly shaken up." Grasping her by both arms, Max pushed her roughly inside. "Now get in there and don't come out till I come and get you."

The door slammed behind her, and she turned to find Elena bending over a cot on which her husband lay as if dead with a cloth across his forehead. "He's only stunned," Elena said quickly, noting Kalina's concern. She lifted the cloth to reveal a large purplish bump. "Max says to let him sleep awhile before taking him home. He's coming back to help me."

Kalina sat down on a three-legged stool, stunned herself at seeing Max. Her heart was racing so that she could not speak. The tiny place was stifling; a fire was roaring in a little stove. A wooden table was littered with cigar butts and dirty coffee cups and crusts of sandwiches. The shed was used by the guards on their breaks.

Gradually it grew quieter outside on the wharf. Elena pushed the window open and leaned out. Max O'Hara's New York voice was heard, belaboring the men, urging them to go home. "This is no way to behave. You're no better than the company cops."

Kalina was lost in feeling. Her whole body was alive. She knew now the depths of her desire for this man. He was her first and only love, and so he would remain.

Elena closed the window. "The men are dispersing. There's a strike meeting tomorrow night at St. Michael's." She shook her head, laughing almost hysterically with relief. "Your Irishman may be a loser with women, but he's a natural born leader. The management's loss is our gain, thank God."

By the time Max returned, the hard rain had let up, and a milky sun filled the little window.

His big form filled the doorway. "You better go back across the river, Mrs. Murav," he said coldly. "It's not safe for the likes of you." The brown eyes, which had been so warm when they had met at the door, were now cool and frosty. "You may enjoy playing Lady Bountiful in Homestead, but the town's full of strangers, steelworkers from other towns for instance, who might mistake you for a company spy."

He bent over Stan, who was sitting up, groaning, and holding his head in his hands. "I can't answer for my men, either. They don't take to swells."

Max put both hands in Stan's armpits, and the two men walked outside, Elena following. "You best do what he says, Kalina," advised the woman.

Stung by Max's coldness, Kalina chased after them. Was Max her enemy now? Must she lose him as well as Libby?

A wagon pulled up with Hruska Coal printed on the side. She would not be put off like this. She may be Stefan Murav's wife, but she was still Kalina Olkonsky and she had a right to know what was on the man's mind.

Stan and Elena climbed into the wagon bed. Max opened the cab door, but before he could get inside, Kalina clutched his sleeve. "Where's Libby? I've got to know."

The hostility in the brown eyes flickered for the merest moment, yielding to a kind of pain. Little lights came and went in his eyes. She had not remembered that they were such a deep, lush brown, the same, burnished hue of the carpet in their little sitting room. But then, they had been together for such a little time—hardly more than a week at most.

Finally, he spoke. "I don't know, Kalina. Cross my heart." The wide mouth twitched as if trying to break into a smile. He climbed up into the wagon, picked up the reins. "A man—or woman—does what he must. You should know that, Mrs. Stefan Murav."

But as she stood uncertainly on the sooty gravel by the shed, he turned and yelled, "Ask Lillian Russell."

Next evening, Kalina sat at her writing desk staring out her bedroom window. The hard rain of yesterday had left the city washed and clean, and a brisk wind had arisen. Even the smoke and grit seemed to have gone elsewhere, at least temporarily. But the firelit sky across the river assured her that United States Steel, Carnegie Works was still very much alive.

The telephone call to Diamond Li'l had revealed that Libby Hughes was at Andrew Carnegie's summer place. "She has the best of care. Dear Louise has fetched a nerve specialist from New York." The actress was reassuring.

But Kalina was troubled. She must see Libby, she must see for herself. The wastebasket at her feet overflowed with crumpled-up, discarded note paper. In the hour since dinner, she had made many aborted attempts at putting down in writing what she wanted to say to the woman she dearly loved despite all that had happened.

"There is nothing between me and Max. His leaving you has nothing to do with me. I do not love Max, nor he me. Please get well, I want to help. May I see you?"

No. It was all bad. Best to take the actress's advice and leave it alone. Time will heal; it always does.

Besides, was it the entire truth? Max's look down by the river when they ran into each other at the shed had betrayed the bald truth. He loved her still. And Kalina knew with every fiber of her being that she was still in love with Max.

Hearing quick steps in the corridor, she turned to see Mary Lesko at the open door. Her face was sober, and Kalina thought again how pretty the girl was and how beautiful she would be in a few years. "Is Dunia fussing again about going to bed?" she asked, sighing. The little girl was in the process of "testing" her new nursemaid.

"No, Ma'am," replied Mary quickly. "She's fast asleep. She played so hard in the park today—" Her head turned toward the corridor. "Helena is here, she wants to see you."

"Helena!" Kalina rose from her chair. "Is it about Libby—Miss Hughes?"

"No, Ma'am. It's—"

The Hughes' maid pushed past Mary into the room. She was obviously in great distress; her hands were tearing a handkerchief to shreds, and her black eyes were wide and frightened. "Oh, Ma'am, it's simply awful. Maybe I shouldn't tell you. I feel like a Benedict Arnold." Tears spilled out of her brimming eyes. "A servant is supposed to be trustworthy. I may never get another job again."

"You told me about your mistress being sick," Kalina said calmly. "It was exactly the right thing to do. Now, what is this new trouble?"

"It's Max," burst in Mary, unable to contain herself a moment longer. "They're going to assassinate him tonight at the meeting."

Kalina felt the blood draining from her body. Her heart seemed to freeze. A voice within cried out, *Stay calm*.

The sound of Helena's weeping filled the room while

Mary's face began to work as if she too would burst into tears. "Stop that, Helena, and get hold of yourself. Tell me how you know and, more important, *what* you know, exactly."

Again Mary spoke for her friend. "She overheard the bosses talking in the Hughes' library. They've brought in a sharpshooter who's supposed to mingle with the crowd and pick off Mr. O'Hara while he's on the platform."

"What?" Kalina bolted up, knocking over the chair. "Surely you heard wrong. Exactly who were the men in the library?" At least Stefan was not mixed up in this, she thought with fleeting relief; he had not yet returned from Washington.

Helena found her tongue at last. "It was Mr. Hughes and Mr. Frick and—" She clouded up again but recovered quickly. "Your husband was there too. He was the one who sent for the assassin." She hiccuped. "He fetched him back from Washington with him on the train."

Chapter Eleven

Telling Anusia that there was an emergency in Homestead concerning one of her adopted families, Kalina bade the Murav chauffeur Andrew drive her and Helena across the iron bridge. She dismissed him before they entered the town itself. "It's too dangerous for you here," she told the man. "Go back and await my telephone call. There's an instrument in the saloon." She pointed to Koster's on the corner by the mill gate.

The chauffer's plain face was filled with concern. "Mr. Murav will be furious—" he began, but Kalina all but pushed him into the motorcar. "My husband is in Washington, Andrew. Now, do as I tell you."

Surely Stefan could not be so mad as to have Max shot in cold blood in front of the workers. But so many things about him were mad—his absurd ambition to be king of Poland, for instance.

She hurried Helena through the gas-lit streets. The wind had freshened, and a veritable gale sent street litter flying into their faces. Clothes drying on backyard lines flapped and snapped like firecrackers. Or gunshots, Kalina thought, fighting the sickness in her stomach.

"Hurry, Helena, we must reach the church before—" Kalina could not utter the horrible thought.

Panting, the girl replied, "The speeches begin at eight. She glanced up at the Carnegie Library tower. "It's only just past seven."

"Thank God for that much."

The crowd around St. Michael's Church stretched a block in all directions. Like New Year's Eve at Trinity, Kalina thought with a pang, and with fresh resolve to save the man who had saved her then, she pushed her way up to the very entrance, calling in a loud voice, "I'm a nurse. There's a man in the church who needs medical attention."

It worked like magic, the servant girl beside her giving a half-hysterical giggle at the stratagem, which Kalina had conceived in a moment of inspiration upon leaving the house. In truth, in her flowing black cloak and black hood completely covering her chignoned hair and most of her face, she looked every inch the part. In her hand she carried a black Gladstone, a spare that Stefan kept in the motorcar.

Max was quickly found, sitting at a table in the choir rehearsal room. The cigar smoke was so thick that Kalina choked and backed out the door. "I must see you, Max."

With a face like thunder, he took her into a smaller room, which was filled with priestly vestments hanging on wall hooks. "I told you to stay away from Homestead," he said between clenched teeth. "Now get out of here. Quick." He grabbed her by the elbows, but she clung tightly to the back of a chair.

"Max, you've got to listen." She told her story in a few words. "The big bosses are out to kill you, Max. Tonight."

"They wouldn't dare," he exploded. Even after Helena had testified to the terrible truth of it, he registered disbelief. "Not even a devil of a Cossack like Murav would desecrate a house of God by committing murder within its sanctuary." Opening the door, he peered out into the church. "Already packed, and more out on the street. Nobody who isn't known can possibly get past the guards. And no weapons are allowed."

"Oh, Max, the guards can't know everyone," she pleaded. "In this mob, the killer could easily slip in. please, *please* leave. Ask someone else to deliver your speech. Surely you have your thoughts written down."

A dry laugh. "A smart leader puts nothing down on paper that can later be used against him."

Not all her pleading could dissuade him from conducting the strike meeting as planned, so an hour later Kalina stood with Helena against the wall as close to the podium as she could get and waited for the program to begin. Half under her breath, she mumbled all the Polish prayers she had learned at her mother's knee, directing her gaze to a tall, stained-glass window with a picture of a guardian angel, wings and arms outstretched protectively over two small children crossing a precarious-looking bridge.

Helena slipped rosary beads through her fingers as did most of the other women, who stood three deep in the side aisles. The pews were filled with men, for tonight a strike vote would be taken. Not all were for stopping work, for with no money coming in and no nest egg, starvation was a real threat. The last attempt at facing down the company in '92 had come to tragedy. Men, and women too, were killed in the rioting. Children sickened, and some died from hunger.

The most bitter of all was that Andrew Carnegie had stood firm on his rights to own them body and soul. The embryonic union was seemingly smashed forever as though a giant fist had come down on it from above.

From time to time, she glanced at the arched entrance to the sanctuary. Men still poured in, but the guards let them pass with only a cursory glance. Kalina strained for a sight of a tall, dark man with a thick mustache. It would be just like Stefan to take on the assassin's job himself. He loved to kill and he was a crack shot.

At last the speeches began. Three men from other towns got up and urged everyone to vote for a strike. The message was simple and direct: Profits are enormous, the robber barons get richer while the steelworkers get poorer every year. It was time for a showdown.

"We want eight. We won't wait!" The shout lifted to the vaulted dome, which was filled with flying angels and fleecy clouds. The very statues appeared to tremble at the unseemly noise within a sacred place.

An eight-hour day, thought Kalina. It seemed little enough. A man should have some time with his family.

Why was Stefan so intractable? He was a family man himself. She sighed. Commerce and business were deep mysteries to her. One day she would study the whole business thoroughly. Men liked to think that such things escaped women's understanding.

The men in the pews grew quiet as Max O'Hara walked to the podium, which had been set up on the platform before the altar. Behind him on folding chairs sat several parish priests, and immediately behind Max his best pal Gus Koval, sat, his big body hunched over tensely.

A palpable tension hovered over the crowd. Kalina felt it press against her face and body like a blanket. It was obvious that the plot to kill their leader was no secret. Heads turned, furtively scanning those behind, beside, in front. The place was stifling; a priest opened several of the windows with a long, hooked pole.

Max had uttered but a sentence or two when a woman's scream rent the air. "There's a gunman in the window." A split second before two shots rang out, Gus Koval leaped into the air, headfirst like a diver in a swimming pool, knocking Max down to the tiled floor. All hell broke loose. The sanctuary became a sea of flailing boots and shouts as men ran for the back of the church to hunt for the gunman.

The window through which the assassin had aimed was the one where the guardian angel hovered.

When Kalina got to the podium, Max was bending over a bleeding Gus, whose chunky arms were outspread like a child's in sleep. An ugly, gaping wound had torn off his right cheek, and already the blue eyes glazed in death.

A priest was mumbling prayers over the dying man, dipping his fingers into holy oil, touching brow, mouth, eyes. *"In nomine Patris, et Filii, et Spiriti Sancti."* The age-old prayers for the dying.

"Requiescat in pace," Kalina murmured. Rest in eternal peace, dear Gus. Crossing herself piously, Kalina stood a moment in silent prayer.

Max had fallen on Gus's chest, his shoulders trembling with his weeping. His work shirt and pants were red with blood. It took four men to drag Max away from his dying pal. "You've got to hide. O'Hara. Gus is with God," they urged him.

Outside the church a full-blown riot was in progress. Uniformed cops tumbled out of patrol wagons and plunged into the mob with clubs and whistles. The women, who moments before had been praying in the church, attacked the police and company guards with folded umbrellas, sharpened sticks, hat pins—anything that came to hand. Gunshots were heard from both sides. Pinewood flares cast an eerie light on the scene.

Edging her way along the building to keep from being crushed, Kalina searched frantically for the men who had taken Max. He had been wounded in the shoulder and was bleeding profusely. He might die, she thought wildly, if no doctor is summoned.

An equally frantic Elena Lesko was on the corner, holding tightly to her two sons. "Got to get these kids out of here, no telling who they might shoot." She choked on a sob. "One of the Mielchek kids got hit with a club, went clean out of his head for awhile." She pointed up the hill. "They've taken Max to Hruska's junkyard. But he can't stay there long." Her eyes were anxious. "Come home with me, Kalina, before you get yourself hurt. Hruska's wife is a practical nurse and will take good care of Max."

"No, no. I must go to him. Do you understand?"

Someone had set a patrol wagon afire, and the quick flames lit up Kalina's anguished face. After a long moment, Elena said, "Yes, I think I do. I was in love like that myself once."

Kalina started at a run up the hill, but at the next corner she halted as a man walked toward her from an alley. Something about his bearing reminded her of Stefan. Terrified, she froze for an instant, then quickened her pace, running like the wind, picking up her long skirts with her hands. Midway in the next block, she turned round, but the man had vanished. She forced herself to be calm. What would the big boss be doing in the middle of the riot? If he were recognized, he would himself be murdered.

Stan Lesko stood guard at Hruska's fenced-in establishment at the very top of River Road. "Stay," he yelled at two watchdogs who leaped up at sight of Kalina. Then he said to her, "He's OK, Go on in, but don't stay long."

She headed for the lighted window of a shed set into the scrubby hillside. Inside, Max lay on a cot, his face white from the loss of blood. Mrs. Hruska, a tall, capable woman with a shawl on her head, bent over him, winding a bandage tightly around his upper arm. She glanced up as Kalina entered, and her face darkened. "The man don't need no more trouble than he's got, Missus. Go on home where you belong."

The woman backed away, putting her scissors and bandage roll into a covered basket. Max struggled up and sat on the edge of the cot. There was nobody else in the shed. He said briefly, "Leave us, Mama Hruska, if you please. I'll be fine, thanks to you."

"That herb poultice should stop the bleeding, but send for me if its starts up again." With a last venomous look at Kalina, the woman went out the door.

Kalina rushed to Max's side, falling on her knees by the cot. "Did she get the bullet out?" Anxiously, she placed her hand on the bandaged arm.

Laughing shakily, he shook his head. "The bullet skittered off. It's probably lodged in the altar." Then, he said brokenly, "Gus took the first one full force in the chest." His brown eyes bored into Kalina's and the suffering there was a sword in her heart. His face was swollen from earlier tears. "I was an ass not to listen to what you and Helena told me about the plot to kill me. Now the best friend I ever had is dead because of my muleheadedness."

At last the tears she herself had been holding back burst from her eyes. Tears of grief for Gus, tears of joy at seeing Max alive and well. She laid her head on his knees, his hands came together on her shoulders, warm and strong. After a while he said, "Now you must go, Kalina, before Murav sends his cops to fetch you." He rose, drawing her up with him. They embraced, and he turned her head for his kiss.

The lovers stood a long time, close and silent. "I'm not leaving you tonight," she said, her lips against his neck. "Whatever comes, I want this little piece of time for us."

Convulsively, his arms tightened round her. "It's madness, dear. Murav will kill both of us." He lifted her chin to gaze into her eyes. "My life is worth little, but you—" He groaned aloud. "God knows I want you like the devil, but we can't risk it."

They kissed again, clinging as though these truly were their last minutes on earth. Finally, Kalina said, with a force of passion that both amazed and frightened her, "I have a premonition that after tonight I may never see you again." She shivered as a blast of wind shook the little wooden building. "Terrible things are going to happen, just what I can't say. There is a destiny that molds our fates, and I feel inside myself that this night belongs to us. Take me, Max, as you took me in that smelly boxcar so long ago. I want to feel your body in mine, so that no matter what comes, even death for both of us, we will have had that much."

Unexpectedly, he grinned. "Still the same little passionate Polack. When you were a little girl and came down to the stables by the river, you used to ask for an apple just as passionately." He tried to laugh, but it came out in a kind of half-sob. "Like you absolutely had to have it, or you would simply die."

She smiled, too, through her tears. Gus was dead, she and Max might both be killed tomorrow by Stefan or one of his minions. Life was here, in this rude shed, calling out to them in a voice that could not be denied. All thoughts of home and family and duty fled from Kalina's heart. For too many months she had been tortured by images of Max in Libby's arms. Now she would assuage her longing.

Their hiding place was easily reached. Deep within the hillside towering over the junkyard lay an abandoned coal mine, the entrance to which was hidden by a pile of rusty wagon wheels, broken-up furniture, and trash of other sorts that Hruska collected and sold for scrap. Leading her by the hand through the littered yard, Max came to an old vendor's cart which he lifted easily and tossed aside. He bade Kalina to follow closely behind him as he crawled into the hole, calling out to Stan to get someone to help him replace the camouflage. "It'll be some time before Murav thinks of looking in a mine for us. The hillside is combed with them, and this one's been worked out since way back in the eighties."

Scurrying footsteps were heard behind them, and the rumble of the cart against the hill. Men were arguing in low voices. Kalina caught the sound of her name. What did they think of her, she wondered, wriggling on the ground and following a hunted man like a slut? She had read somewhere that in some countries it was the custom to provide a condemned man with a woman the night before he was executed.

As if to reinforce her thought, Stan's voice rang out. "Let 'em go. It may be his last night in this world."

That was the last she heard as they were swallowed up in the winding tunnel of the mine. The interior was surprisingly fresh and airy with none of the sulphurous odor of the mill. Kalina felt that she had suddenly been dropped into the countryside. Max explained that the mine was close to the surface and that the rock shale was threaded with cracks. Soon they could stand up in a space bigger than a room, where the moonlight was so bright from a hole high up in the vaulted ceiling that she could see plainly several cots, a table, and some chairs.

Almost reverently, he drew her to him, loosened the tie of her cloak, and pushed back the confining hood. He spread it out on one of the cots and opened up his arms. She fell into them, and they sank together as one. Max gathered the ends of the voluminous cloak around them like a cocoon, and the lovers lay quiet and supine, side by side, for a long time without speaking.

They removed their shoes; they dared not undress, for despite his assurance that a mine was the last place her husband would look for them, the fear of discovery was ever present. At last, warmed by the fur-lined cloak and the rising desire within their young bodies, their hands

220

reached under garments to find and explore each other and delight in the touch of lips and fingers. Opening her shirtwaist, Kalina guided his callused fingertips to her nipples, then her lips. Lifting up her long skirt, she opened her thighs and wrapped her long stockinged legs around his hips, her own hands kneading his hard buttocks, glorying in the demanding thrust of his swollen manhood against the softness of her female mound.

So they became adventurers, time halting obligingly in its course as it has done for lovers since time began. They moved slowly, savoring each moment of exquisite pleasure. They were acting out a dream. There could be no tomorrow for them. Max must flee for his life; she must return to her appointed role as wife and mother.

Their frenzied coupling bore little relation to the hasty interlude in the boxcar so long ago. They were little more than children then; any suffering they had known in their short lives was now eclipsed by the events of the past year. He had loved another woman and driven her to near madness. She had borne a dead child to a man she now despised. Max and Kalina held within themselves the pain of knowing that their clutchings at security and happiness had served but to destroy themselves.

Most tragic of all, in their heart of hearts, the lovers felt the chill winds of a kind of spiritual death. Their bodies would go through the motions of living, eating, sleeping as bodies must and, the flesh being what it is, each might even couple with another.

But nothing would ever be the same.

Sated, they slept until the blast of the whistle from the mill woke them to the gray morning. "This is not the end for us, darling Kalina," Max vowed as they kissed goodbye. He flashed the old cocky grin. "Cross my heart."

"But do not hope to die," she said softly.

Stan was still on guard, asleep on a pile of junk, a ragged coat thrown over his skinny frame, the stockinged stumps of arms covering his face. Grim-faced, he escorted Kalina downhill and put her on the trolley for home.

When she got there, Anusia awaited her. Like an avenging angel, she stood at the wrought-iron gate, arms crossed on her skinny chest. Hate sparked from her eyes, bringing an unwonted luster to their depths. "You slut," she snarled. "How dare you come back to this house? You don't deserve to breathe the same air as decent people." Pursing her thin lips together, she spat at Kalina's feet.

One of the uniformed men who guarded the Murav residence, rounded the corner on his rounds. As he drew near, Anusia hissed. "Leave us." The man scuttled away, having no wish to tangle with the old one, whose fury he had already tasted in an earlier confrontation.

"Sister, have you taken leave of your senses?" exclaimed Kalina. "Let me pass. I am weary from tending the wounded at the riot —" Without warning, the enraged woman lifted her hand and struck Kalina hard across the face. "Everyone, from the filthiest worker to the high and mighty people you call your friends, knows where you spent the night. You have brought humiliation and disgrace to our noble family." She snorted. "To think my noble brother, descendant of kings, would think to start a dynasty from your polluted womb!"

Her eyes smarting from the blow, Kalina drew back. In her present state, Anusia might well kill her. Stefan had given the woman a revolver, after the troubles in the fall. The guard was out of sight and would certainly not walk back this way until Anusia left the gate.

Trying not to panic, Kalina cast her eyes up and down the street. A thick mist lay over the city; the houses were nebulous hulks. From across the street she heard a door slam as a maid came out to pick up the can of milk that had been delivered in the predawn. Anusia had just begun to speak again — "Go back to your paramour. Maybe he will feed and clothe you" — when to her immense relief, Kalina heard the chugging noise of a motorcar coming down the street. Whoever it was, she would run out and scream for help.

It was Stefan, with Andrew at the wheel, coming home from his long night at St. Michael's riot. The vehicle pulled into the driveway, and rushing past Anusia, Kalina ran up to her husband as he leaped onto the macadam. Whatever his mood, despite her infidelity, he surely would not keep her standing in the street like a beggar, for all the world to see her shame.

To her astonishment, he threw his big arms around her and drew her close, kissing her roundly on the lips. "You have salvaged what otherwise might have been a disastrous night, my pet." He said no more, but ordering Anusia away from her post — "Sister, stop acting the idiot" — the three of them went into the house.

Baffled at his good humor, Kalina followed her husband into the house through the now wide-open gate. Why did her infidelity please him so much? For surely he knew. She had expected rage, even physical abuse, anything but the bubbling merriment in his amber eyes.

Anusia fled to her bedroom, and Stefan shouted to the cook that he wished a huge breakfast of steak and eggs. After a hasty bath, Kalina changed into a flowered, linen morning dress, and sat across from her husband in the dining room, picking at a dish of fruit and nibbling at toast and jam. She drank cup after cup of strong, black coffee. From above came small noises as Dunia and Mary began their day.

But she was fearful in every pore. Something was wrong. Perhaps he hadn't heard about her night with Max. If he had, he surely would not have kissed her. And what did he mean by "you salvaged a disastrous night"?

Anusia had said that "everyone" knew. Obviously, she had been seen running into Hruska's junkyard. The town was full of company spies disguised as workers, who would fly at once to tell the bosses where Max was hiding.

Max! With trembling hands she laid the bit of toast on her china plate as a prayer filled her heart. Had he gotten away? The police would charge him, along with many others, with inciting a riot. Was his capture, or his death, the reason for Stefan's good humor?

She found out soon enough when her husband swallowed the last juicy bite of steak and rang the bell for Jean, the maid, to clear the table. As Kalina rose to leave, he came around the table and led her none too gently into the little sitting room. She sank down in a chair while he remained standing, tall and enormous. It was the familiar teacher-pupil relationship he preferred for their serious conversations, one that had begun on their honeymoon when he had lectured her at length about the relationship of steelmaking to war.

The sensuous lips parted in a smile, and his powerful fingers stroked the thick brown mustache, smoothing out the ends into points. "First, I must tell you that the gunman at the church window was my idea." A kind of giggle escaped him.

He's mad, really mad, she thought, but the thought no longer frightened her.

Striding to the tall window, he yanked the curtain aside and gazed into the street. A pale sun shone upon this little room where they often gathered after dinner for a cozy family evening. Kalina placed her hand on the cunning clockwork globe, which she had spun one night for Dunia—the memorable night that McKinley died—talking gaily of the wonderful places they would journey to.

He turned, his darkly handsome faced wreathed in smiles. It struck her again how much he looked like the Cossacks who used to ride into her village. Surely he must be one of the wild, untamed horsemen of the steppes who serve only themselves and the czar of Russia in time of war. His passion for war was the most Cossack thing about him, she reflected now. After that first time in the train on their honeymoon, he had said nothing about his ancestry. One day she would trace his family tree; perhaps his bloodlines were not as noble as Anusia liked to think.

"I hired an assassin who was also a steeplejack," he said proudly. "We put a rope around him and dropped him over the side of the church."

"Clever," she murmured.

"Not so clever as my second plan," he said. "When Gus Koval took the shot designed for O'Hara, my first thought was to go after you." Leaving the window, he stood behind her chair, dropping both hands until they squeezed her breasts, hard, but Kalina declined to please him by crying out. Removing his hands, he walked around the chair to face her and cupped her chin in his hands, twisting her head up so that their eyes were close. "I saw you on the street as you ran like a whore after your wounded lover. I could have shot you like the bitch you are and left you there to die."

She spoke through clenched teeth. "So it *was* you! I despise you, Murav."

"Good. That's how I want you to feel."

"I will never lie in your arms again."

"That is not for you to say yea or nay. You forget, dear wife, that I know your capacity for passion. I did not kill you because my need to keep you alive overcame my righteous wrath as a cuckolded husband."

Releasing her again, he walked to the little desk, picked up a stack of books, and thrust them into her lap. "From this moment until we sail for Europe in the spring, you will read and study. These books are just a start."

She gazed down at the top volume. *History of Europe.* The others had similar titles. They were all concerned with politics and commerce. There was one slim volume on protocol and diplomacy.

Unbelievingly, she flipped through the pages, staring with unseeing eyes at page after page of dense printing. Stefan ranted on; though insensible to most of his high-flown language, Kalina caught the gist of his tirade. She was being groomed to be his consort, eventually to be queen of Poland. Her beauty and accomplishments would be renowned in every capital in the world. She would be his helpmate in the coming critical years before the great-world-encircling war that would change the face of the globe. She knew the script by heart.

"You see, Kalina Olkonsky Murav, issue of Pan Mikolai, whose line like mine goes back to ancient Polish kings, I have grand plans for you. Grander than you can possibly imagine at this moment. Your foolish escapade with that Irishman won't stand in my way." He flicked his hand into the air as if brushing off a fly. "Whether you wish it or not, you will become an instrument of history." His dark eyes narrowed, eyes that had once persuaded her to an enslaving passion. "I will make you dance and sing like a puppet. And there isn't a damn thing you can do about it."

Gripping the wicker chair arms with all her might, Kalina rose up, tumbling the heavy books to the carpet. "You're mad as a hatter, Murav. What if I decline the honor of being crowned queen of Poland? What if I do not choose to be your dog on a leash?" She faced him squarely. "I'll run away with Dunia."

Every trace of mocking laughter left his face, and he gripped her shoulders so hard that this time she could not stifle her cry of pain. "I won't strap you to the bedpost." He drew her close, his hot breath blowing over her face like a desert wind. "Go if you like, but you'll never see your precious Dunia again." His eyes narrowed into slits. "Never. Do you comprehend?"

"She's not yours to keep! She's mine. Zuska left her with me!"

Snorting with contempt, he took his hands from her shoulders and flung them wide. "The adoption papers are ready. Her mother's signature can be forged. No judge in the world will give a child to a wife who is unfit."

The blood froze in her veins. He had played the ultimate card in his hellish game. No freedom, however sweet, was worth a child's life. And leaving Dunia in Stefan and Anusia's care would mean a kind of death for her cousin's child. She was not yet four, still pliable; left in the care of the mad brother and sister, Dunia would surely grow up as twisted as they.

Stefan Murav had her trapped. He was the master puppeteer and she the hapless figure on a string.

A week passed quietly enough. Things settled down around the house. Murav went to the mill each morning, came home each night to a sumptuous dinner, after which the family gathered in the little sitting room as before. Kalina read her history books, Dunia played with her dolls, Stefan read his papers. The violence of the riot, Kalina's night with Max, Stefan's disclosure of his fiendish design for her life—all might have happened in a nightmare.

Kalina felt she had died and gone to another world that was neither heaven nor hell, but some kind of purgatory in between.

Anusia, cowed by her brother's command to act like a decent woman and forget her hatred of her brother's wife for the good of the family and the brilliant future he foresaw, sat in her wooden chair, knitting furiously, heaving great sighs, and casting evil glances at Kalina. From time to time she was heard to mutter loud enough for all to hear, "Vengeance is mine, saith the Lord."

The seething woman had also taken to leaving scraps of paper around the house with other telling Biblical selections concerning the fate of harlots and unfaithful women.

None of it troubled Kalina so much, however, as her concern for Max. He had escaped the network of police and all of Murav's hired guards. But exactly where he was, nobody knew for sure. Mary Lesko returned from her afternoon off to relate what she had heard in Homestead. "He's safe, that much Daddy knows, but he won't tell anyone where he is. Not even Mother."

Each night Kalina prayed for the missing Max. The company, drumming up a charge that he had killed a guard at the riot, had ordered him shot on sight. The death grip that United States Steel had on the town was so tight that not even the county sheriff dared to defy it. Union leaders went underground.

The morning of December first, the unbearable suspense came to an end in a way that engraved itself in her memory for always. She had awakened to fresh snow, the first of the season, and the wonderful sound of Dunia's shrill laughter coming from the yard. "Whoo-whoo-whoo!" She and Mary were playing at Indians again, their favorite game. Stefan had departed early for the mill after a night of the violent kind of love-making he had subjected her to all week.

She had just reached for her wrapper to cover her nakedness when the door burst open and Anusia strode to

227

the middle of the room. As usual, every hair on the woman's head was in place, the tight braids in a bun on top. Her white shirtwaist and black skirt were freshly ironed and spotless. She assumed her avenging-agent pose, but instead of a trumpet or a brand of fire, her skinny hands clutched a newspaper. She snapped it open with a bang. "Don't cover your nakedness from me, whore of Babylon. I know you for what you are."

Then to Kalina's growing horror and disbelief and to the sounds of glee coming from the snowy yard, Anusia showed her the crimson headline. The letters were inches high and stretched clear across the page.

"Foul Murder in Stately Home."

Anusia read. "Disguised as a guard, hunted labor leader Max O'Hara entered the home of his former sweetheart and shot her dead in cold blood. The daughter of Superintendent Hughes was reportedly with child, and it is thought that the cowardly deed was committed to hide the killer's seduction of the young woman. Money in large bills was scattered on the floor. Police think that the murderer had demanded money for his escape from town. The shot was fired from Libby Hughes' own pistol. The room showed signs of a struggle.

" 'My daughter tried valiantly to defend herself,' said Millard Hughes. The coroner's men had to tear the body from his arms."

Kalina froze, as her blood seemed to flow together and drain from some invisible hole in her body. It wasn't real; she was in a fever, in the midst of a delirium.

But nothing could shut out the hellish sound of Anusia's voice. She droned on and on interminably. Max O'Hara was in jail, charged with murder, first degree. The case was airtight. The grief-stricken father had come in a split second too late and had himself taken the smoking gun from the murderer's hands.

The trial would be swift. An angry Allegheny County judge had promised "to push everything else off the docket." There was talk of using the new electric chair for the execution. The fiendish device had been used with great success in New York.

Nearly transported with elation, Anusia climbed the bed ladder and thrust the paper at Kalina. "Here's your picture, harlot. Now all will know you for a filthy piece of garbage." A deep laugh boomed out from her thin chest. It was the first time Kalina had ever heard the woman laugh outright.

"Now my brother will think again of who he makes queen of Poland." Her eyes grew wilder. "Only I deserve that great honor." Anusia started to sing, a strange kind of song in a language Kalina had never heard. It was certainly not Polish, which she and Stefan claimed to be their native tongue.

The story of the night Kalina Murav had spent with Max was told in exquisite detail. But with embellishments. She was accused of being a company spy, of drawing the unsuspecting O'Hara into a clandestine relationship for the purpose of betraying him to her husband. While pretending to be Lady Bountiful to poor Homestead families, Kalina Murav reported on union activities to the big boss. So said the press.

"Lies, all lies," she screamed into Anusia's laughing face. "How can they tell such monstrous lies?"

But in her heart Kalina knew the answer. Like so many other business concerns in Pittsburgh, the tabloid was owned outright by Stefan Murav or the steel company he ran as his personal kingdom. More than anything else, Stefan wanted to blacken her name with the workers so that none would help her.

Long after her spiteful sister-in-law had tripped out of the room and gone singing downstairs to her bedroom, Kalina lay in a stupor. Gradually she felt the easing of the iron band around her heart, and her blood resumed its normal flow. Max was alive. That he was completely innocent of murder, she knew with the same certainty that she knew that it was snowing like mad outside and that snow was blowing through her open window into the room.

It was all a frame-up as they used to say on Mulberry

Street when someone was caught with stolen goods unwittingly bought from a fence. The truth would come out; a just God would not permit an innocent man to die.

But beneath her bravado, a disturbing thought knifed into Kalina's consciousness. Murav's hand was in this. And Murav never loses.

Chapter Twelve

Helena knew the truth about the death of Libby Hughes, but the girl had been intimidated into silence. Distraught, the Hughes maid had sought out Mary Lesko after chorus rehearsal at the Settlement House. "I must talk to somebody," she had wept. "Or I really will go out of my head."

The two girls sat with Kalina in her little sitting room, having crept quietly into the house through the servants' entrance. Anusia had retired for the night; Stefan was still at the mill. Fearing for her life if she remained at her place of employment, Helena had moved back home.

"Mr. Hughes and Mr. Murav said that if I told anybody what I saw the night Miss Hughes was shot, they'd see that I never worked again, anywhere," she told Kalina. "My mother says they could even have me declared an imbecile and put me in an institution for the rest of my life."

"They might even kill you, the way they did Gus Koval," shivered Mary. "They struck him down like a dog."

Her friend's sobs broke out afresh, and handing her a clean handkerchief, Kalina scolded the nursemaid. "Stop scaring Helena with such nonsense. Of course they're not going to shoot her. Everyone would know immediately that they were trying to keep the whole truth from coming out."

But within herself, Kalina knew that her husband, and perhaps Libby's father too, might be perfectly capable of arranging an "accident" for the girl.

The story was brief and tragic. Concerned about his former sweetheart's health, Max had come out of hiding, and gained entrance to her house by disguising himself as a

231

cop who had been sent to check out a reported prowler in the vicinity.

"He got a uniform easily enough," broke in Mary. "The cops are his friends. Actually, Mr. O'Hara is well liked by everyone in Homestead." Her pretty blue eyes shot fire. "Absolutely nobody I know thinks he killed Miss Hughes."

Kalina's heart soared. What joy to hear from the girl's lips what she herself had not dared to hope. As if reading the unspoken question in her mind, the nursemaid rushed on, "And nobody is fooled for a minute by the terrible gossip that you were a company spy."

With many interruptions for fresh handkerchiefs, Helena related the events of the tragic night. Libby had demanded that they elope, saying that they could take a ship to Europe and live in some foreign place where her father would never find them and where Max would be free from the company's assassins.

"I've never seen her so wild as she was that night," said the maid. "When she came into the library and saw him there, she rang for coffee, and, when I brought it in, they were going at it, just like the last time when he broke it off."

"And the gun?" prompted Kalina. "Why did he let her get hold of the weapon?"

"She went to the desk to pull out the money she had saved to help them elope. But Mr. O'Hara said he didn't want her money. She threw the money up into the air, and it came down all over the place. Seeing her in a state like the last time when he broke it off with her, he yelled to me to come. I did, and he started to walk out of the room."

Convulsed with grief, the girl could not go on. Mary wrapped her arms around her friend, letting her sob against her shoulder. "I know the rest," she said. "The gun was in the same drawer with the cash, and when Mr. O'Hara turned his back, she told him that, if he walked out the door, she'd shoot herself."

"And what did he say to that?" asked Kalina.

Helena sniffed. "He said, 'Now, Libby' in a soft way, trying to calm her down. But he came back into the room."

232

But not even Max O'Hara who had run from many a copper on the streets of New York was swift enough to stay the fatal bullet. He tore the gun from the crazed Libby, but she had already pulled the trigger. They fell together, and the weapon spun out, but not before the unfortunate man had covered it with incriminating fingerprints. At that point, Millard Hughes had entered the house.

Early next morning, Helena was put on a train for Chicago to stay with an aunt until the "thing blows over." So reported Mary to a much relieved Kalina. The newspapers, especially the lurid tabloids, continued to make capital on the scandal. The Olkonsky family history was unearthed and spelled out in full panoply for all to read. Kalina was astonished to discover, among other outlandish journalistic fabrications, that in her veins flowed the blood of medieval Polish kings, that Aunt Litka had been a society matron in New York, that Zuska was now performing as an actress on the New York stage.

Anusia snorted. "Imagine anyone believing such trash." The woman was beside herself that such high-flown lineage had been attributed to Kalina although Stefan had often hinted at such a thing. She turned her attention to the elaborate accounts of the manner of electrocution. She was fond of waking up Kalina as she did that first morning with a carefully selected passage.

"Wires are attached to the crown of the prisoner's head and the calf of one leg. Then the victim is strapped in—"

"He hasn't come to trial. For all you know he will never be convicted," Kalina said wearily. She refused to expend any more emotion on the woman.

But she was thankful that the yellow press had not bothered to uncover the real facts about herself. If they had, she thought with a chuckle, she might herself be sought by the New York cops for burglarizing old man Lenz's butcher shop. Dunia was too young to read, and anyone who mattered knew the truth.

If only the truth about Libby's murder were so easily

sloughed from her troubled mind. With the sole witness silenced, he was lost. Every scrap of evidence was against him. Escape from prison was his only chance.

All of Homestead knew it too, and rumors flew that a prison break was being arranged. The swift but reliable wireless telephone of gossip from house to house on the sooty hill above the furnaces reported that, even if he *had* shot his one-time mistress, the workers would do their damnedest to set him free.

Despite her nursemaid's assurance that she was not hated in the town for being a company spy, Kalina dared not resume her social work. The nervous hours of waiting for word of Max were passed with Dunia, who at four was at the age when she must begin to learn her numbers and letters. Until a suitable tutor could be found, Kalina would take on that job herself.

She relied on Mary to bring her news from her parents and others on her afternoon off, and it was with a happiness she had not known since their night together that she heard that Max O'Hara, who had not yet come to trial, had escaped from the grim stone-walled penitentiary on the Allegheny River.

It had been laughably simple to accomplish. One read such things in thrilling novels all the time. Alexander Dumas' Count of Monte Cristo had fled his dungeon by slipping into a burlap sack meant as a burial shroud for a dead prisoner. Max had bribed a guard to slip him into a coffin containing a corpse about to be delivered to a mortuary. Once outside, he lifted the lid, and before the horse-drawn vehicle could gather speed, jumped out the back. "Right in the Allegheny River," Mary giggled. "The driver heard the splash but never suspected that his dead man had come back to life."

The guard who had taken the bribe was summarily dismissed. Murav and Hughes demanded that he be tried as accessory after the crime, but the police, wearied perhaps by the whole affair and not entirely in sympathy with the giant steel company and its stranglehold on life in Pittsburgh and environs, refused to hold the man for prosecution. "All men are vulnerable where money is concerned," a spokesman told the press. The guard, a man named Voichek, became a local hero.

The atmosphere in the house on Rutherford Drive changed dramatically but not for the better. Anusia stopped her vicious and monotonous reading aloud from the papers, but her unwonted cheerfulness vanished like the sunshine before a storm. No longer could she taunt her defenseless sister-in-law with gruesome images of an electrocuted lover. Her high-pitched singing ceased.

But, alarmingly, the old woman vented her spleen on the hapless Dunia. Several days after Max's escape, Kalina found them squabbling right outside her bedroom where she was engrossed in the household accounts. It was Mary's Sunday afternoon at home, and the child had been sliding up and down the corridor, which had just been waxed and rubbed to a high polish.

There was the unmistakable sound of a hand hitting a tender cheek, and when Kalina rushed out, she found the child on Anusia's knee, her frock over her head, stockings and undergarments around her ankles. The enraged Anusia was striking the little bare buttocks with the flat of her hand.

Like a virago, Kalina sprang at the woman, knocking her down with such force that she slid along the slippery floor and tumbled halfway down the stairs. At that moment, Mary returned and took the sobbing Dunia to her room, where she was soon quieted.

Not trusting herself near Anusia, Kalina quickly dispatched Jean the kitchen maid to see to the older woman. When the girl reported that Miss Murav seemed perfectly able to walk and refused to have a physician called, Kalina felt her obligation done. Anusia had tumbled a mere three steps before grasping the banister.

Her mind was eased, but there was no quick relief from her anger. For the sake of his digestion, Stefan had long ago forbidden any quarreling or reports of trouble at the dinner table. Anusia ordered a tray to be taken to her room and did not come down. Kalina was forced to wait until her husband had eaten and had his after-dinner cigar and brandy before confronting him with the outrage perpetrated on a helpless child by his sister.

The confrontation took place in Anusia's gloomy bedroom where the window curtains were never opened. The clutter of dark, heavy furniture and the single, flickering gaslight at her bedside added to the oppressive atmosphere. Her room had been wired for electricity like the rest of the house, but she stubbornly refused to give up the gas, maintaining that the softer light was easier on her eyes.

She sat upright in bed, a mass of pillows behind her head. Kalina noted with dismay the ugly purplish bruise on her brow. A white bandage was wound tightly around her wrist.

"Thanks to this slut you married," she fumed as they entered the room, "I may never walk again. Modesty prevents me from showing you the bruises on my legs." Her plain nunlike face took on a look of extreme suffering. "Your wife left me sprawled unconscious on the stairs. I might have been dead, for all she seemed to care."

"Unconscious, you say?" Stefan raised his brows. "How did you get to your bedroom from the stairs then?" A smile tugging at his lips, he walked to the window and pulling the heavy curtains aside, peered into the murky night. "Looks as though it will rain all night," he said, in a tone that suggested complete indifference to his sister's fate.

"The maid came running and almost carried me downstairs and helped me into bed."

Kalina gasped. "She's lying, Stefan. It was I who sent Jean to see to Anusia. She reported to me that there were no broken bones, only a few minor bruises." Kalina glared at her sister-in-law, tightening her lips in a vain attempt to suppress her outrage. "I called you through the door and offered to telephone the doctor to examine you."

Turning to Stefan, she exclaimed, "Your sister got out of bed and slid the bolt when I knocked."

Dropping the curtain, Stefan whipped round, his dark eyes sparking irritation. "Damn it all, you two sound like a couple of cats on a backyard fence. I've got more troubles than I need right now without the two of you piling more on me." He fixed a baleful gaze on Kalina. "Thanks to your lover skipping off from prison, I've got egg on my face before the workers. Have you any idea how his outsmarting us will work against the company in any labor negotiations?"

She stiffened. "I had nothing to do with Max's escape."

Anusia broke in, obviously more concerned with her own suffering, real or imagined, than the celebrated O'Hara affair. "Stefan, I demand satisfaction. This woman, whom you were fool enough to marry, must be punished for what she did to me."

"Punished?" The beleaguered man barked and then burst out in a dry laugh. "Shall I have her flogged at high noon in the town square? Or maybe put her in the stocks like the Puritans of old?" The thick, dark brows shot up, the sensuous lips parted in a broad smile. "Maybe you'd also like an 'A' for adultery branded on her chest, as the Puritans did."

Then, he seemed to collapse, his shoulders sagging beneath the English wool jacket. He drew a hand across his brow. It was a gesture of fatigue, and, startled, Kalina found herself inexplicably filled with compassion for this man who had seemed till now equal to any disaster. Whatever he had tried to do to Max, however mad his ambitions, and despite the fact that he had killed one man outright and another by fiat, she saw a man before her who seemed driven by forces over which he had little power.

At the same time, she felt a surge of triumph that a man like Max O'Hara, whose own heart was as big as the world itself, had brought Stefan Murav to this vulnerable state.

But her softened feelings were short-lived, for in the next breath, he exploded. "Work it out, you two. As for Dunia, Anusia is free to discipline the child when she sees a need. A spanking never hurt anyone. I had plenty of them."

With that, he left the room, slamming the door behind him. Moments later, storming back to her own room,

237

Kalina heard the echoing slam of the front door as he left for the mill and the interminable strike negotiations.

The situation between herself and Anusia was clearly intolerable. Given free rein, the unstable woman might well injure Dunia seriously. A severe blow on the head of a child had been known to cause imbecility or even death. Wearily, she climbed fully clothed into the high bed, but, restless, got up again and walked downstairs to her little sitting room.

The house was quiet at last; even the cook and housemaid had retired for the night, their labors over. She turned on the electric light, sat down in her favorite chair, and gazed morosely at the landscapes on the wall. How she longed to be in some quiet country place, away from this life that had become a kind of hell for her and Zuska's child.

Zuska! Dammit, where was the girl? The old resentment surged within Kalina. How she longed for the cousin who was really more a sister, for they shared a common father. Irrepressible, adventurous, forever bold and undaunted, Zuska would make short work of Anusia. Zuska was a Valkyrie, one of those mythic warriors of old, who would happily do battle with the sour one upstairs. In any war of wits and cunning with Stefan's sister, Zuska Olkonsky would triumph.

She chuckled, imagining the confrontation. Idly, she spun the globe on its wooden stand beside the chair. Like a rainbow, the myriad colored lands whirled before her eyes. Pick one, her brain commanded, and flee there with your little girl. Zuska would do it without a second thought.

Her finger stopped the globe at Poland. Her letters to her mother had remained unanswered. What was wrong? Was Hania dead? Her heart swelled with yearning for her mother. Hania was wise and knowing; she could guide her erring daughter at this troubled time. But her mother was not here. Nobody was here to help her. Like Zuska, she must be adventurous and brave. She must act. She was a woman fighting for survival. She was a lioness protecting her cub and must use tooth and claw and anything else that came to hand.

Bolting from the chair, Kalina paced the room, then darted feverishly to the tall window to gaze out at the gas-lit street. A uniformed guard stopped at the fence, alarmed perhaps by the slit of light from the house. Dropping the curtain, Kalina went up to bed, but it was a long time before sleep arrived to calm her racing heart.

Next morning, she was up at dawn and at the desk poring over her accounts. Flight — to anywhere — required money. Careful planning might extract a few hundred dollars here and there, but it would take months, during which time Dunia would be in constant peril from the obviously mad Anusia.

Where to pare expenses? She had ordered a dress from Worth in Paris for Lillian Russell's grand Christmas ball. Perhaps she could cancel it. Turning, she swept over the open armoire stuffed with gowns, many of which she had worn only once.

Suddenly, struck by an idea so simple it left her breath-less, Kalina ran to the armoire and began to tear the garments from their hangers one by one, dropping them in a heap on the floor. Her frocks — her Paris originals — even the creations run up on her sewing machine by the clever Mrs. Raymond had cost thousands and would bring half the amount if sold.

Her hand reached for the telephone, a remark once made by Lillian Russell coming to mind. "My dear, I never appear in the same dress twice. I sell them, one by one, recouping a measure of my loses."

But as quickly as she had picked it up, Kalina replaced the earpiece on its hook. Lillian would want to know why she needed money, and even the four-times-married Mrs. Moore might look askance at Kalina's intended purpose of leaving her husband and running God knows where with her child. Besides, the loquacious woman might, in an unthinking moment of conversation, spill the secret.

As with so many problems in high society, the below-stairs servant network proved to be the elixir. The gregari-ous Mary Lesko readily supplied the name of the maid who tended the actress's boudoir. "She's a girl named Martha," Mary said. "I went to school with her."

Helpful Martha, Kalina thought with glee, just like her namesake in the Bible. Within a day, the names and locations of several outlets for used garments were on Kalina's desk. With the intuition of her sex, Mary Lesko did not need to be told why her mistress wanted to sell her expensive ball gowns. "You're running off," she exclaimed, clapping her hands in excitement. Then, more pensively "Take me with you. I'm dying to get out of Homestead."

The relationship between Kalina and Dunia's nursemaid had become something more than the usual mistress-servant affair. The Homestead girl was exceptionally mature for fourteen, having been the oldest in the family, and to Kalina, who was not yet eighteen, she seemed more friend than servant.

Kalina became a coiled spring as she appraised her gowns, one by one, with a critical eye. At Stefan's insistence, she had kept careful accounts and was able to determine the cost of each. Gauzy silks, furry velvets, cloudy chiffons, rich moires. All were lavishly embroidered in brilliant hues and trimmed with yards and yards of creamy Belgian lace. Her hand fell on the sable coat Stefan had purchased for her birthday in that first extravagant year when he had seemed determined to make her the clotheshorse of Pittsburgh.

No, she thought, that was risky. It was an exclusive design and could be easily traced. Neither did she dare to sell her jewelry though the diamonds and rubies and emeralds would surely bring many times the money as the gowns. No one would think twice about buying a discarded frock, but jewels and furs would be suspect as stolen goods.

Like a child who has just invented a brand-new game, Kalina set about carrying out her plan. Mary offered to sell the garments for her, but the titillation of doing it herself intrigued Kalina. If she were truly to strike out on her own, she herself must walk the streets of the big city, her ball gowns on her arm.

Stefan was no longer concerned about her seeing Max, figuring the man was surely in China by this time, so two days later, on a blizzardy morning and completely unchallenged by the watchful Anusia, Kalina boarded the trolley for Pittsburgh. Mary had been instructed to guard Dunia with her life, if need be, from Anusia.

Three transfers and at least four river bridges later, she alighted in Allegheny, the neighboring town across the river of the same name. No one on the horse-drawn cars took notice of her for she seemed to be a worker, dressed as she was in the garb of a servant girl. Mary had been helpful in that too. A woolly scarf protected her head against the falling snow; a long, shabby coat reached to her ankles. Locked within her covered wicker basket lay the gold-thread dress that she had worn at the breaking-in of Libby Furnace. She would take special delight in ridding herself of the frock in which she had seen John Kewalski shot down in cold blood.

The house that answered to the number she had memorized lay atop a hill so steep Kalina stopped twice to catch her breath. It could be a manor house in Poland, she thought, sitting so regally behind tall trees and thick hedges. The snow blanketed the ground by now, and a yardman was shoveling a path from the sidewalk to the house. At her question, he pointed a gloved hand toward the servants' entrance.

Mary had coached her carefully on what to say. "Please, I am looking for work as a domestic. I can scrub, clean windows, sew. The nuns taught me." Despite the danger of her enterprise, Kalina's heart was high with excitement. Her blood sang. She could be Red Riding Hood plunging into the woods on her way to her grandmother, a basket of goodies on her arm.

The woman who answered the knocker looked more like an aging, painted china doll than a loving grandmother, however, as she stood in the open door in a filmy peignoir and a face so slathered with lip rouge and blue eye cream that it was hard to tell just how old she was. "You the new skivvy?" she asked. "The agency sure worked fast." Sharp blue eyes raked Kalina's shabby figure. "Tall, though.

That's good. Most girls can't reach the tops of things."

The woman led the way down a stone passage into a basement kitchen set into the hillside high above the river. A gleaming copper boiler loomed over a massive, combination coal-and-gas range that took up an entire wall. An iron sink featured two copper spigots, one for hot, one for cold.

A rich household, Kalina mused. They might buy not only the gold dress but all the rest as well. She wondered about the painted woman. Could she be the mistress of the place?

"Here, have some coffee. You look worn out. Sit down, love." The woman filled a schooner-size mug with the hot brew and set it on the wooden table in front of Kalina. Gratefully, she drank, suddenly remembering that she had quite forgotten to eat breakfast.

The painted woman went to a door that led to a back staircase and yelled. "Come and get it, gals."

A very fat woman in a dirty white apron emerged from a pantry and, hurriedly pulling two trays of fresh hot rolls from the enormous oven, slammed them down on a side table and began to slather thick icing on them with a spatula.

"Christ, you almost burned 'em," yelled the painted woman. She turned to Kalina, quietly drinking her coffee on a wooden chair. "You cook, too?"

Kalina nodded. "Some." A gramophone sounded from upstairs. "Daisy, Daisy, give me your answer true . . ."

The clatter of heels on the wooden steps was followed by what could only be described as an avalanche of beautiful but sleepy-looking women. As they tumbled into the kitchen and took places around the table, Kalina gazed at one after another. All wore rouge and eye color that had obviously been on their faces through the night. The chatter was deafening; all tried to talk at once.

Some smiled at Kalina. "The new skivvy? Looks OK to me. Intelligent, nice eyes, not like the last one who couldn't tell a dust mop from a boa constrictor." A dark-haired beauty sitting next to her picked up her hand. "Hmm. Kinda soft and white for a skivvy." Heavily lacquered blue eyes narrowed. "This your first job?"

Kalina nodded, fear suddenly thickening in her throat. Maybe one of them had seen her photograph in the papers during the hubbub over Libby's murder and would recognize her. But a broad smile spread the painted lips and the woman said. "Don't worry. We all got to start somewhere." She laughed, biting into a thickly iced roll. "You're a looker. Maybe you can move upstairs pretty quick."

There was a rush of footsteps on the stairs and a striking blonde woman fairly plunged into the kitchen. Her peignoir hung open halfway down her curvaceous body, revealing two lush breasts, the dark nipples of which made little points in the filmy blue chiffon.

"That's our Zuska, late as always," the cook mumbled angrily. "I told you whores that I won't serve meals at any old time you please."

Kalina's head shot up. She peered with astonished eyes at the face of the latecomer. Despite the heavy coat of rouge and streaks of face powder, she recognized her longlost cousin. Zuska's abundant hair streamed like a golden river over her shoulders and down her back to the firm, round buttocks she remembered so fondly. The two girls had slept together, like spoons curved side by side in a drawer, ever since they were babies. Kalina knew her cousin's rounded curves as well as she knew her own.

Zuska caught Kalina's eye and as her own recognition dawned, screamed so loud the cook dropped the pot of coffee on the floor with a bang and a shriek of her own.

What followed was, in the words of the cook who spent her days off at the cinema, better than any scene she had witnessed downtown at Mr. Harris's Nickelodeon. The humble servant girl, who turned out to be a rich muckymuck from across the river, was engulfed in the arms of the whore of the top fancy house in Allegheny, who had been telling them for the past year that she was the daughter of some damn nobleman in Poland.

A torrent of tears and numberless cups of coffee later, Kalina drew out her golden dress. "I came to sell it." She told her cousin of her plans to run off with Dunia.

"No," said Zuska firmly. "Running off is no solution. Take it from one who's learned from bitter experience." Suddenly she was convulsed with a fit of coughing and lifted the hem of her peignoir to cover her wide-open mouth, revealing thereby a considerable expanse of rosy flesh.

Shameless as ever, Kalina reflected, but a twinge of fear struck at her heart. Aunt Litka had died from the galloping consumption. Could Zuska have inherited her mother's feeble lungs? She waited until the coughing had ceased and then impulsively hugged her cousin, squeezing so hard that Zuska yelled in mock pain. "From now on we'll never be separated. I'll see that you get the best of care," Kalina vowed.

The woman whom she had thought as strong and dauntless as a Valkyrie seemed at this moment to be as weak as a kitten found on a winter doorstep. Kalina had become the strong one. It was she, when all was said and done, who had married wealth, who had a husband who valued her, kept her in expensive gowns, and was determined to cherish her as his wife, regardless of infidelity.

Kalina's heart contracted as she speculated on how Zuska had ended up in such a place. For now it was plain as day that Mary Lesko had sent her to a whorehouse.

All were in tears at the joyful reunion, and Madame, the one who had answered the door, insisted that the cousins be driven back to the Murav home in a closed motorcar by the house chauffeur. They were pulling out of the snowy drive when Kalina spied the iron sign, which had earlier been covered with snow. The yardman had brushed it off to disclose the brass lettering, *Phoenix Club*. She stifled an exclamation. Could this house be the private masculine establishment that Stefan frequented, where he played cards and gambled at tables in the basement with other tired businessmen?

She glanced at Zuska reclining happily on the seat beside her and admiring the gold-thread gown that she had taken from its basket. In a kind of ecstasy she pressed it to her face as if to devour it, her blue eyes limpid. Could Stefan have stroked those sculptured cheeks, kissed that painted mouth? Could her husband and her cousin, whom she loved so dearly, have frolicked in sexual abandon in one of those upstairs rooms?

The thought did not trouble her. She had never imagined that a man of her husband's Cossack-like virility had done without female solace during her long illness and even longer pregnancy. It was a situation a wife was forced to tolerate.

Kalina's mental questions were answered that very night when Stefan walked into the dining room where Zuska was already seated at the table. A child could have seen that her husband and cousin not only had previous knowledge of each other but were strongly attracted to each other. The first startled recognition in Stefan's eyes turned at once to a kind of mirth as he exclaimed, "Welcome to our home, Cousin Zuska Olkonsky." Bending over the back of her chair, he lowered his head and kissed her on the creamy brow. Quickly, Zuska curved her arms up to encircle his neck, drawing his face to hers.

She kissed him directly on the lips. Anusia frowned and coughed behind her napkin, but Kalina burst out in a spontaneous laugh. It was better than a stage play, one of those drawing-room comedies where the actors are constantly kissing and embracing and calling each other "darling."

Stefan beamed. His face was flushed as he sat down at the head of the table and began to carve the roast. "My dear wife's cousin is more beautiful even than her tales led me to believe. And to be reunited with your daughter must be bliss for you." His face clouded. "The adoption can of course be reversed if you wish." He held the carving knife in the air, awaiting her response, Kalina held her breath. It was clear that he feared Zuska's reaction to the adoption.

Given his wife's barrenness, Dunia meant the world to Stefan. He had declared his intention to make her his heir.

"By no means must you give up Dunia," caroled Zuska. "We are one big happy family. If anything should happen to me"—she put a white hand over her mouth and coughed obligingly—"I would rest easy in my grave knowing that my dear little girl is well provided for."

She faced Kalina. "I do not think it wise to tell the child that I am her real mama. She has quite forgotten me, I'm sure." At Kalina's gasp of protest, Zuska held up her hand. "No, don't protest. I know what I am doing." A racking cough interrupted her, and she picked up her water glass. When she put it down, Kalina saw flecks of blood on her cousin's lips.

"It would be tragic for Dunia to lose me twice," Zuska said flatly, without emotion, and wiped her mouth carefully with the napkin.

Murav did not go back to the mill that night, working instead at his desk in the library. There was a davenport in there where he often fell asleep, leaving Kalina alone in the big bed until dawn, when he came up to bathe and dress for the day. The sky was still dark through the open window when she woke to the sound of a closing door. The familiar squeak told her that the door belonged to the guest bedroom where Zuska had been installed. Moments later, Stefan entered the room, and, as in the dining room, Kalina needed no further evidence than the look on his face to know that he had not slept on the davenport in the library.

The situation in the Murav household in the ensuing months was not exactly a *ménage à trois* for Stefan never came to his wife. No attempt was made on the part of the illicit lovers to hide their flagrant affair. Kalina was astonished at the ease with which she accepted the arrangement. Zuska had always taken what she wanted, even from her cousin.

Most surprising of all was Anusia's reaction. The woman fairly swelled with pleased satisfaction and a kind of pride. "It is a king's prerogative to have both wife and mistress with none to fault him," she announced.

Amused, Kalina wondered what place in the royal household Zuska would assume when they all took over the throne of Poland. Kalina went into gales of laughter, alone in her bed, imagining Anusia as Dowager Princess, all decked out in ermine tails and satin with a golden crown upon her dark head.

Dunia accepted the newcomer as an aunt who had been traveling in the West. Mother and daughter got along famously, for there was hardly a soul alive who could resist the carefree Zuska. How self-sacrificing, Kalina thought, to deny your own child out of love for her welfare. But within herself she suspected that it was not her possible death from consumption that had inspired Zuska's decision, but the probability—perhaps the certainty—of once again "running off" to freedom.

Ironically, Kalina Murav was more content than she had been since Max had disappeared. She was relieved of Stefan's strenuous love-making, and she was free once more to indulge her passion for social work. Her families—Mielcheks, Leskos and Kewalskis—welcomed her back with open arms. They had never believed the gossip that she was a company spy.

Elena Lesko proved to have a moderate case of consumption, and Kalina happily sold the hated gold dress to the Madame of the Phoenix Club, and with the money dispatched Mary's ailing mother to a sanatorium in Arizona.

When in April Zuska began to thicken at the waist and blatantly announced that she was pregnant, Anusia was wild with joy. "At last we will have the son you failed to provide," she chortled to Kalina. Her cousin had accompanied the Muravs to several of Lillian Russell's parties, and it was a simple matter to attribute the child to a young man who had paid ardent attention to the lovely blond Olkonsky.

He was an out-of-work actor named Donald Hill and readily accepted Stefan's generous offer of money to acknowledge the child and entrain immediately for Cincinnati where Stefan had arranged for a job for him in a music hall.

If anyone in town suspected the truth, none dared spread such vile gossip. Stefan Murav was still the big boss of the Carnegie Works, and even the highest in Pittsburgh society trod cautiously around the powerful and much-feared man.

On a brilliant day in September, after a mere two hours of labor and without a drop of chloroform, Zuska gave birth to a healthy baby boy. She did it well and beautifully; Aunt Litka would be proud, Kalina reflected. The child was a miniature of his father, the resemblance so startling that an artist could have fashioned the babe on order. Great, dark-brown eyes had a spark about them just hours after birth, and the firmly drawn, strong mouth closed voraciously on Stefan's finger, much to the father's delight. They were forced to take a comb to the brush of dark hair.

Which is precisely what an ecstatic Kalina did, the moment the infant was washed and swaddled by the midwife. But first she had to fairly snatch the babe from Anusia's outstretched arms. "Mary and I will be nursemaid to little Stefan," she declared. Then, softening, "But of course as he grows, there will be much that you can do for his welfare."

Privately she resolved that her husband's sister could not be trusted with the child any more than she could with Dunia.

The Murav heir became the hub around which the wheel of the Murav household revolved. He was a bright and cheerful infant with none of the colic and digestive upsets common to newborns. Stefan stayed home every night to hold the child, cradling him to his starched shirt in the sitting-room rocking chair. To the amazement of the women, who never had heard of such a thing, the big man gave his son his bedtime bottle of milk.

The blooming mother was the only fly in the ointment. To the indignation of all, Zuska refused to nurse her babe, insisting that Kalina bind her overflowing breasts with flannels to stop the milk. The child did not take to cow's milk, so a wet nurse was obtained to provide mother's milk for a month or two.

Her cousin's concern for her figure and the inconvenience of nursing Kalina could understand, but when the new mother showed no interest in the truly adorable Stefi, she became alarmed. "It's unnatural," she scolded.

Zuska gazed at the angry Kalina from inside the armoire. In her underslip, she had been flicking through Kalina's gowns, trying on one after the other. The blue eyes flashed. "Bearing a child does not make me a mother. A cat can do as much. I left Dunia—" She whipped around, realizing the implication of her remark. "What I mean is, I love him, I love both my children, but I don't have the knack of being a mother to them."

She came to the chaise where Kalina sat engulfed in the tossed-out gowns and threw her arms about her, hugging her fiercely. "You should be glad that I leave that part of it to you. After all, you can't have—"

She fled back to the armoire. "Christ, I can't talk without putting my foot in my mouth. Forgive me, darling." Then, petulantly, "Hey, where's that fabulous gold dress you brought to the Phoenix Club?"

"I sold it," Kalina said tonelessly. "But you can wear any of the others."

"Drat, I was wild about that one." Dragging out a sapphire velvet creation trimmed with ermine at the sleeves and hem, she slid it over her head. Kalina reached up to do the buttons at the back.

"Beautiful," she murmured. "It looks better on you than it does on me." She ran her finger along her cousin's waistline. "You'll slim down. Been only a month since your confinement."

"Yeah. Once I get away from all this rich food."

Kalina sat down again among the frocks. "Please, Zuska, don't run off again. Your health is bad, and, though your cough is somewhat better, it might just come back. Your children really need you. I need you." Tears sprang to her eyes as she thought of life without Zuska. "I can't bear to lose you again, and I promised to take care of you that day I found you at that fancy house."

"I can take care of myself," replied Zuska, twirling round and round before the armoire mirror. She picked up the ermine hem and danced around the room, humming a waltz tune. Then, putting words to her melody, she sang out, "You've got your husband, darling. He doesn't love me, only wants my body and my child. If I stayed, I'm still a fifth wheel, and, before you know it, I'm out in the cold again."

She was right, Kalina reflected miserably. Stefan had already bought steamer tickets for their Atlantic crossing in the spring. The envelope on his desk contained four vouchers—two for adults, two for children. There was none for Zuska, none for Anusia.

The thought of Anusia and Zuska together, alone in this big house, was too comical to contemplate.

A week later, when she returned from an afternoon of visiting in Homestead, Kalina found an outsize note pinned to her pillow, penned in Zuska's elaborate handwriting, so carefully learned from Litka.

I took the cash from your desk and a couple of gowns. Donald is waiting for me in Cincinnati—I know him better than you think—and will take me out West where the air is clean. The Pittsburgh soot is hell on my lungs. Love you, dear. Will write.

Anusia reported that Andrew had driven "Stefi's mother" to the train. "She took two of your best reptile Gladstones and probably half the silver."

The silver was intact, but Kalina's armoire was not as full as it had been. She smiled through her tears. She was certain that the restless daughter of Aunt Litka would be far happier in the brilliant gowns than she had ever been.

Kalina put the note into her drawer to join the postal card Zuska had sent years before from Shenandoah. With a joyous laugh, all tears gone, she raced downstairs to the nursery. Stefi was sound asleep, but she lifted him from his blankets and pressed the warm little body against her own.

Zuska had taken little but had given much.

Part Two
Europe

All the world's a stage,
And all the men and women merely players:
They have their exits and their entrances;
And one man in his time plays many parts.

— William Shakespeare

Chapter Thirteen

Vienna, New Year's Eve, 1913

There were letters from America!

The footman brought the message on an encrusted salver and stood at attention in his wintry livery of midnight velvet and gold as Kalina read the folded note. A rosy tinge brightened the porcelain smoothness of her face, and she glanced over her shoulder where Mary Lesko stood at the half-open door. Since leaving America in 1903, the steelworker's daughter from Homestead, Pennsylvania, had blossomed with an élan and enthusiasm that entranced everyone at the Austrian court. At twenty-two, in her dual role as Stefi's nursemaid and Kalina's personal companion, she had become indispensable to Kalina.

Following Kalina's glance, Franz Josef, Emperor of Austria and absolute monarch over half of Europe, set his ivory pawn back on the chessboard with a sigh. He lifted a veined hand, and a second footman, hovering at his elbow, poured an ounce of golden brandy into a snifter and held it to the old man's lips while Franz Josef sipped. The footman set the snifter back on the tray and handed him a smoking Havana from the crystal salver on the table.

The emperor took a long, luxurious puff. "Come in, girl. Don't hide behind the door like a pesky Serbian spy."

They sat in the firelit card room of the Hofburg, the winter palace of the Hapsburgs, and from whose sprawling eminence the legendary family had governed the vast Austro-Hungarian Empire for half a dozen centuries. The emperor raised his voice, for a spirited clamor emanated from an anteroom where seven-year-old Stefi Murav played at blindman's bluff with other children of the palace and their nannies.

Tripping in, Mary curtsied gracefully before the monarch, her voluminous crimson skirt brushing the richly figured carpet as she pressed her lips to the man's beringed finger. He beamed and taking her slender hand in his, drew her to her feet, exclaiming, "How bewitching you look, my dear."

"She's come directly from the Opera House where she is performing in *Carmen*," offered Kalina. The emperor fixed his clear blue eyes on the embroidered bodice that covered Mary's swelling bosom.

"I'm only a cigarette girl, Your Highness." Mary blushed. "But one day I mean to be a prima donna and sing the title role of the alluring Carmen herself." Stan and Elena Lesko's oldest child had more than amply fulfilled her early promise as a singer. To please Kalina, the emperor had used his influence to get the girl into the exclusive State Opera School.

"You will, you will! I decree it!" The old man burst into a hearty laugh, the movement causing the phalanx of bejeweled medals on his brocade jacket to dance and catch the light from the chandelier hanging from the frescoed ceiling.

Kalina admired the old man enormously. Though his health was failing and the reins of power fast slipping from his hands, he appeared each day before the people. It was a symbolic attempt to hold together the remnants of a floundering empire, about which ominous clouds of destruction were already gathering.

His life as a man had been marked with tragedy — a

much-loved wife and empress felled by an assassin's knife, his eldest son and heir apparent dead by his own hand at Mayerling, a second son gone mad. Franz Josef loved youth with the passion of the very old, and most especially he adored Kalina Murav, the beautiful, witty American woman who played chess with him each afternoon in the quiet pre-dinner hour in the imperial apartments.

Mary stepped back to stand beside the footman. "Must you go?" the old man demanded sharply of Kalina. "Our hour has scarce begun."

"Forgive me, Your Highness, but I must dress for the masque tonight." Her voice was soft but firm.

"Plenty of time." He knit his thick Hapsburg brows. "We do not appear until nine at the Opera Ball."

"Letters have arrived, and I am anxious to read them." She smiled and touched his hand across the table, not wishing to offend. She felt no fear, having learned that his autocratic manner cloaked a tender and compassionate spirit, at least where she was concerned. In their years of travel on the European continent, she and Stefan had stopped frequently and for extended periods at the beautiful and historic city on the Danube. Kalina had developed a warm relationship with the eighty-year-old man. Despite his majestic ways, he had become the father and the grandfather she had never known, Pan Mikolai taking no interests in his progeny. There were many in Vienna, though, who looked upon the curious intimacy of the young Frau Murav and Franz Josef as something more than that.

Both her husband and the monarch were pleased with the gossip, Franz Josef because of the flattering tribute to his virility and Stefan for his usual reasons — overweening ambition and the inordinate desire to be connected in any way, no matter how trivial, with every crowned or uncrowned head of importance in Europe.

The look the emperor cast upon her now was not altogether fatherly, she thought. Knowing his fondness for elegance, she dressed to please him. He was, after all, still very much the man. This afternoon she wore an emerald China silk robe in the fashionable midcalf length. A long-sleeved cloak of green silk taffeta covered her bare shoulders, for like all palaces, the sprawling royal residence was filled with icy drafts.

With mock petulance, he upended the chessboard, sending kings and queens and knights tumbling to the carpet. As if, mused Kalina, they were part of some ancient gigantic Hapsburg battle. "There's an end to it, then," he pouted. "We were stalemated in any case. Go then to your precious letters. I will join the children. I trust that the little ones do not have letters that they prefer to their sovereign."

"Most of them can't even read," cajoled Kalina. The old man favored her with a blown kiss before disappearing into the anteroom to join the game. Eagerly, she took Mary by the hand and left the card room for the upstairs suite that the Muravs always occupied when at the Austrian court.

Bustling around the exquisite bedroom, which had belonged to the dead Empress Elisabeth, was a bright, young Croatian girl named Agnes, who had been given to Kalina to help her and Mary with the care of Stefi and anything else the Murav ménage might require during their stay. Her eyes were blue and merry, her hair long and blond, and her demeanor ever cheerful. She reminded Kalina of her dear, wandering Zuska.

Mary picked up the letters from the escritoire and handed them to her mistress. "There are three, Madame. One from Dunia, one from your sister-in-law, and the last from my mother." She took a rumpled envelope from her bosom. "I got one too."

Kalina sat down in the Louis Philippe chair before the desk. "And how is your family?"

"Fine. Mama has not had a recurrence of her tuberculosis and the boys are both melters in the mill, bringing home twenty a week and more." Her eyes brimmed with tears of

Zebra

HOME SUBSCRIPTION SERVICE, INC.

Your FREE
Book Offer
Card

☐ YES! please rush me my Free Zebra Historical Romance novel along with my 4 new Zebra Historical Romances to preview. You will bill only $3.50 each; a total of $14.00 (a $15.80 value—I save $1.80) with *no* shipping or handling charge. I understand that I may look these over *Free* for 10 days and return them if I'm not satisfied and owe nothing. Otherwise send me 4 new novels to preview each month as soon as they are published at the same low price. I can always return a shipment and I can cancel this subscription at any time. There is no minimum number of books to purchase. In any event the Free book is mine to keep regardless.

Name _____

(Please Print)

Address _____ Apt. No _____

City _____ State _____ Zip _____

Signature _____

(if under 18, parent or guardian must sign)

Terms, offer and price subject to change.

1 86

PRINTED IN U.S.A.

happiness. "Knowing they're all right, even with Papa dead in that awful street accident, I can go on with my voice lessons here—" She hesitated. "Providing you still think you can do without my services."

Extending both hands to clasp the girl's, Kalina exclaimed with feeling. "We agreed that you should stay on when we return to Paris and pursue your operatic career. Professor Streng assures us that strong contralto voices like yours are rare and that you are sorely needed in the State Opera."

Impulsively, Mary threw her arms around the older woman. "Mama would have died if you hadn't sent her to Arizona." Then, drawing back and reddening, she added, "Forgive me, I sometimes forget—"

Kalina hugged her in turn. "I am your friend always and your equal in every way but in the eyes of the world."

Mary left to prepare for a performance at one of the myriad New Year's Eve balls that marked the opening of *Faschung*. As might be expected of a city given always and unashamedly to excess, the Viennese opened their pre-Lenten Mardi Gras festivities at least two months ahead of the customary Ash Wednesday opening.

While Agnes drew her bath and selected undergarments to be worn under madame's costume for the Grand Ball, Kalina gazed at the letters in her hand. Which one first? She could not repress the tiny pang of disappointment that none of them was covered with Max O'Hara's schoolboy scrawl. Even if he was alive, and she dared not think otherwise, and even if he knew her whereabouts, she knew he would not be so foolhardy as to attempt contacting her so directly.

But, oh, how fervently she wished it!

Grief over the lover, who like both Zuska and herself in many ways, had become a wanderer on the earth, was real and constant. Murav had put a price on Max's head, posting ten thousand dollars with the county sheriff for his capture. But there had been no word of him, no clues to where he might be. As far as Homestead was concerned, Max O'Hara had dropped off the edge of the earth.

The letter from Elena Lesko conveyed much the same message as Mary's. "We miss you. When are you coming home? The Mielcheks kids are OK, Anna kind of poorly. Johnny Kewalski is fourteen and going to high school. Imagine! But he is very bright, wants to be a doctor. The trust fund you set up for him will make it all come true."

"I miss you too," Kalina murmured, kissing the thin envelope before placing it with the stack of others in a jeweled leather box. The nightmarish night when Stefan had shot Johnny's father on the steps of the Carnegie mansion flashed briefly into her mind.

Both sides of Anusia's letter were closely packed with her crabbed handwriting.

> Dear Sister,
> Since Stefan is probably in some outlandish place peddling his armaments, I write directly to you. The autumn has been severe. The chestnut tree in the back garden fell on the roof, and I had to summon a man to replace the shingles. I took in a cat who showed up on my doorstep half-starved and who repaid my kindness by giving birth to ten more of her kind . . .

There were pages more of the same household and weather reports, but Kalina saved it for a more leisurely moment. Nothing momentous ever happened to Stefan's sister. Despite strong and persistent hints on her part, Stefan steadfastly declined to issue an invitation to her to join them on their travels.

"She is a troublemaker," he told Kalina. "What's more, her dowdy, unpleasing appearance detracts from the regal impression I wish to make." Distressingly, Murav continued to nourish his fantasy of becoming monarch of Poland, after the war he predicted. "All we need, my dear

258

is an incident," he said. In the past she had taken his fantasy lightly; it seemed harmless enough on the surface. But, in a man of her husband's well-known tenacity, such a fixed idea could become dangerous, if not life-threatening, to both himself and his family. What if he should actually go to Poland and declare himself king? The Poles did not take kindly to usurpers and were even now chafing under the iron fist of Austrian rule in the south and German rule in the north. Like the Serbians, they were in a constant ferment of rebellion.

That Stefan's reasons for not including his spinster sister in the family circle abroad were only excuses for a much deeper, more significant problem between the two, Kalina often suspected. In the years since their marriage, the love that her husband once held for his older sister seemed to have vanished completely.

Kalina's feelings toward the woman who had made her early married life miserable were mixed. Whatever Anusia's transgressions in the past, she was grateful at least to her for forwarding Zuska's rare postal cards. Enclosed with the letter were two from California. One featured a hacienda surrounded by orange trees, the other was a photograph of Zuska in a slinky, fringed dress reaching barely to her knees with a feathered wide-brimmed hat on her shining hair.

> I'm in the Follies here. Donald is looking into motion pictures. A man from New York is building a studio in California. Soon you won't be the only rich and famous one in the Olkonsky family. I am well, not much of a cough, only at night. How is Dunia? Please don't tell her the truth. Love, always. Your loving cousin.

But Dunia had known the truth about her parentage ever since she learned how babies were made. Two years ago, at ten, the girl had challenged Kalina. "You were too young to be my mother. When I was born, you were only fourteen." They had been sitting on a bench in the park surrounding the French school where Dunia had just matriculated, Stefan thinking it high time she stopped being a tomboy and got the training a crown princess would need.

"Zuska is my mother, isn't she? Just like Stefi. Aunt Anusia told me you can't have any babies." Dunia had faced her defiantly and then said quickly, "Shall I call you Aunt Kalina?" The soft, brown eyes were guarded.

"Whatever you like, darling," Kalina had replied, her heart near stopped with grief. "But may I remind you that, while I did not give birth to you, I am your mother in every other sense. My husband adopted you, so legally there is no problem. Love and affection—all the things that go into being a mother—I endeavor always to provide."

"Why did Aunt Zuska give me away?" The child seemed more bewildered than suffering. "Did she hate me so much?"

Dunia was close to tears, and Kalina gathered her close. "Hate you? No, dear, she loved you very, very much. That's why she left you with me. Your mother felt that she could not do the things for you that I and Daddy could. She was very poor. My own mother sent me off to America from Poland to live with Aunt Litka so that I could become a fine lady. I was ten, exactly your age."

Dunia wriggled out of Kalina's arms, and stared a long time at a squirrel running up and down a tree. "I think I'll call you Mama Kalina," she said quietly.

Kalina's heart ached for the girl. After sixteen years her own anguished longing for her mother was as sharp as it had been at ten. The terrible fact that Zuska had deserted her child—not once, but twice—seemed not to dampen Dunia's longing and professed love for her "real" mother. That she continued to love the woman who had raised her as her own Kalina never doubted for a moment.

Now as she unfolded Dunia's letter, she prayed that the constancy of her own love would secure the girl against the storms of life.

260

Dear Mama Kalina,

I hate this place. I am so homesick for you and Daddy and Stefi that I cry myself to sleep every night. I have a new friend named Lini. She is Swiss, and her real name is Adeline. She calls me "Merry" because it sounds like "American." Her parents have invited me to their estate in Switzerland for the spring holiday.

I got my period. It was just like you said, not much. Thank you for telling me about it. Some of the girls wake up bleeding and think they are going to die. They call it "the curse."

Love and kisses to all,
from your daughter Dunia.

P.S. I cut my hair in a frizzy bang. Lini says it's very "moderne."

Agnes was at her elbow. "It is late, Madame. Your bath is cooling."

"Coming." She turned to face the girl. Merry. The word also fit the little maid. "Where are your parents?" she asked Agnes, climbing into the high tub and sinking into the fragrant sudsy water.

"In Croatia, Madame." A cloud passed over the light-blue eyes. "But times are hard. There is no work for me there."

Kalina sighed in sympathy. "Vienna is filled with young women who must leave their loved ones to find work."

The maid's face darkened. "Not all of them are to be trusted, Madame. You must beware especially of those from Serbia. They are all plotting to overthrow the emperor."

Agnes departed to fetch a supper tray, for there would be no dinner at the palace tonight, appetites being saved for the magnificent New Year's Eve buffet at midnight. When

Agnes returned with the tray, her smile was back. Seeing it, Kalina's brooding over Dunia lifted. The young are so resilient, a quality that Dunia had in abundance. Zuska may have deprived her daughter of many things, but she had given her the most precious gift of all—a happy spirit.

Dunia's sweet face—half child, half woman—skittered through her mind as in a kaleidoscope. Last week on Dunia's Christmas holiday, they had walked the streets of Vienna, eating hot, roasted chestnuts from a sack, laughing at the antics of the organ grinder's monkey, riding on the Prater ferris wheel—doing all the things one was expected to do in gay Vienna. How ecstatic the girl had been when she had been chosen by the emperor to help distribute gifts to the children of the palace. She had stood beneath the giant Christmas fir in the Rittersaal, her rounded breasts straining at the blue organdy frock.

All were enchanted with her. All remarked on her vivacity. Kalina sang as she dressed for the ball. Dunia would be fine. She was an Olkonsky.

Bathed and dressed for the ball, Kalina stood before the mirror, while an admiring Agnes expostulated. "But it is so amazing, Madame! You look exactly like the picture in the history book!"

"Um-m, I must say I surprise myself," Kalina replied. "If it weren't for your wonderful brown lotion though, I would be more paleface than Indian despite my black hair."

"Going to the masque as Pocahontas was your inspiration, Madame, not mine. You will surely win the grand prize."

Dispassionately, Kalina appraised herself in the mirror. Tall, reed slim, but sufficient bosom to intrigue. "Stylish," a proud Stefan declared. Unlike most of the matrons in the international set, whose curves were more hourglass than reedlike, Mrs. Murav wore the new straight-line fashions with aplomb. The stark Indian costume was perfect for her.

"At last year's ball there were ten Marie Antoinettes,

thirty Napoleons, and countless shepherdesses, each with a flowered staff," she remarked to Agnes. "One of them even fetched along a real sheep."

"And he left his own little prize right on the polished dance floor." Agnes doubled up with laughter.

With a "Happy New Year, Madame," Agnes left for the servants' ball downstairs. The emperor had sent word that he required a half-hour to complete his toilette, so Kalina sat by the window, nibbling at some cheese and fruit, listening to the growing revelry in the frosted streets, and gazing at the lights on the Ringstrasse, the famed chestnut-lined thoroughfare that encircled the inner city. She wondered which of the myriad uniforms from the crazy quilt of countries in his empire Franz Josef would don for tonight's gala. Polish, Bulgarian, Rumanian, Serbian . . . ?

So many little countries, the very ones that she had pointed out to Dunia so long ago on the little globe, were part of the vast Austro-Hungarian collection of subjugated peoples. Like all conquered peoples ever since time began, they were in constant ferment. Franz Josef's armies were spread far and wide from Poland in the north to Rumania in the east. But like every tyrant before him—Alexander, Caesar, Napoleon—the Austrian emperor was fast losing hold of his domain.

Serbia, which had lost its independence just two years before, was the sharpest thorn in Franz Josef's flesh. A fierce mountain people, the Serbs had infiltrated Vienna and were conspiring to achieve independence and waiting for the right moment to strike.

Andreas Kara was a Serb!

Kalina's thoughts turned to the young nobleman who held the coveted title of Master of the Horse at the famed Royal Spanish Riding Academy. When the monarch was closeted with his ministers and could not entertain her, she was wont to visit the academy within the Hofburg to watch Andreas on his white stallion, moving with the other handsomely attired horsemen in the incredibly intricate

263

quadrilles and studied drills, which visitors came from all over the world to view.

"One day the Serbs will be free," Andreas often told her as they sat over coffee in a nearby café. He had shrugged and lifted his cap to reveal the thatch of bright-red hair. "But now is not the time." His mild words were belied however by the dark rebellious passion in the brown eyes so much like her dear lost Max.

As her friendship with Andreas grew, Kalina had found herself wondering if she dared to love again. Even if she could bring herself to be once again unfaithful to Stefan, a liaison with a Serb was to court trouble.

Franz Josef warned her. "The city is infested with anarchists posing as shopkeepers, policemen, even horsemen in the Spanish Riding School. Trust no one."

Her eye fell upon the portrait of the slain Empress Elisabeth on the opposite wall. The emperor's voice had been low and grave. "Nobody is free from anarchists. My own dear sweet one took a knife in her breast. Your photograph is in every paper; it is even sold in shops and souvenir bazaars. You cannot go unrecognized. You know what they call your husband?"

"The Merchant of Death," she had answered, shivering at the dreadful soubriquet.

Andreas had also warned her. "How can you love such a devil as Murav? He is a mad dog. He sells death to all, pits nation against nation, and plots like a Machiavelli. He tells England that Germany wants war; to the Kaiser he says that Franz Josef is growling at the borders."

"He is my husband. We made a bargain." That the bargain involved her children went without saying. Nor did she tell the charming Serbian that if she were caught betraying her husband, she would never see Dunia and Stefi again.

Andreas wanted her, and God knew she was hungry for a man. She yearned for Andreas as she had yearned for Max, with every fiber of her body. She and Stefan shared a bed, but there was no love in their infrequent couplings. Rarely did he come to bed before she slept; his evenings were spent poring over his charts and maps, moving little magnets about, marking in his bold block letters how many ships, how many guns, how many soldiers each nation possessed. He had become fabulously wealthy, even beyond his wildest imaginings. Though feared by every head of state, he was welcomed everywhere; no one dared to turn him away.

For Stefan Murav knew their secrets. When and if war came, the Cossack from America would be the stage director who moved the players about in the European drama. His wife was but one of the actors, enacting the role he had given her that morning in Pittsburgh when she had come from her lover's arms.

As Agnes had predicted, Pocahontas garnered the grand prize for the most original costume at the Grand Ball. Kalina was forced to share it, however, with a dashing Hiawatha, who in the person of Master Horseman Andreas Kara, had slapped a black wig over his carrot top.

"Someone told you how I would be dressed," she pouted, as he swept her into the first waltz of the evening. "It was supposed to be a secret."

"Nothing's secret in Vienna," he said darkly.

Then all talk of secrets and anything else went out of their minds as they held each other close. Kalina surrendered to the delicious feel of arms that were strong and muscled, to the touch of hands that could subdue a stallion but that on her back and bare arms were marvelously gentle.

"Come to me tomorrow," he crooned into her ear. "An hour or two. I am on fire. There's a little hospital beyond the Vienna woods; the head nurse is my cousin. No one will wonder that the gracious Mrs. Murav is visiting the sick."

"I will bring flowers and a basket," she murmured back, amazed at the ease with which she entered into the age-old game of mutual seduction. For it could be no more than the joyous meeting of bodies, male and female. Kalina had no intention of surrendering her heart.

Next afternoon as she dressed for her rendezvous, Agnes burst into the suite. Her bright Croatian face was stricken. "Andreas has been arrested as a spy!"

Trust no one, Kalina thought. How close she had come to risking not only her reputation but her life!

That afternoon over the chessboard the emperor remarked, "That Kara with whom you were so taken has been shot. He was the leader of the infamous Black Hand who were plotting against my life. We've been watching him for months."

"The Black Hand?" inquired Kalina with a forced casualness. She moved her king to within striking distance of his queen, praying he would not notice her trembling hand or hear her pounding heart.

But the man whose iron fist ruled the rebellious Serbians was too absorbed in his own wrath to take note of the agitation of his partner. "It's an underground group that has plagued us for years," he said. "Now that their leader is dead, I'm sure this mad idea of Serbian independence will come to a quick and merciful end."

Archduke Franz Ferdinand went to Serbia, not because he wanted to but because Franz Josef, who was both sovereign and uncle to the young man, had hinted strongly that it was the expedient thing to do. The weather was unseasonably warm, and the corpulent heir apparent to the Austrian Empire suffered greatly from the heat. Franz Ferdinand was not the emperor's favorite nephew but though he no longer knew why, he had made the archduke his heir. His own beloved son Rudolf had now long been dead.

The dialogue the week before at the Imperial Palace had been short and to the point.

"There is much unrest in Serbia. My spies report an assassination plot," said Ferdinand.

The emperor replied, snorting through his beard, "Every Serbian comes out of the womb screaming 'Death to the Emperor!' In school they teach them how to make assassination plots. Go and face them with the courage expected of a Hapsburg. Besides, I shot their rebel leader, that damned Andreas, and *my* spies report that they've not found anyone strong enough to replace him."

So on a sweltering Sunday morning, June 28, 1914, after a week of watching military maneuvers in various parts of Serbia and its neighbor, Bosnia, the archduke started for the Bosnian capital, a thriving trading center called Sarajevo. As their motorcade moved slowly through the teeming streets his disposition improved. Cheering subjects lined the narrow streets, and little girls in white dresses ran up with flowers for Sophie, the archduke's wife and the mother of his two sons and a daughter.

The heir apparent was glad that he had come. It was, as the old man had said, a good rehearsal for kingship.

Behind him, in the third car back, rode Stefan Murav with his own wife, the famous beauty, Kalina Olkonsky. They had been invited, at the emperor's suggestion that Murav was a man to cultivate, to be in the royal retinue during the historic tour. Besides, Sophie adored Kalina; the American was one of the few women the shy wife of Franz Ferdinand could be at ease with. The night before, despite warnings from both husbands that the morrow would be tiring, the two had stayed up late chattering about America.

Like the archduke, Kalina had not been enthusiastic about the journey. "It's so hot, and Stefi has a pesky summer cold. Go without us, Stefan. Besides, it's very dangerous now in those little Balkan countries. There are anarchists everywhere."

"It's vital that I be seen with the old man's heir," her husband had replied. "He represents the most powerful political organization in Europe. I've got to cultivate him for the future."

Murav's amber eyes lit up as if a candle burned inside, and Kalina sighed. Whatever excuses he invented to enter Serbian territory with the heir apparent, she knew it was the thrill of danger that persuaded him the most.

As his wife, Kalina was expected to share that danger.

But she was glad at least that she could leave the sniffling Stefi back at the hotel with the archduke's three little ones. Three Serbian girls, specially chosen for the honor, had promised to take excellent care of them. When the parents had left, they were all involved in a quiet game of snip-snap-snorum, a card game from America that the little Murav had learned from his nurse, Mary Lesko.

The archduke's open car reached a bridge over the Miljacka, turned right, and headed up Franz Josef Street, where hundreds more, ostensibly adoring subjects waited. The sweating archduke turned his head and smiled at his wife, who was just then stifling a yawn with her white-gloved hand. He fingered his black handlebar mustache, smoothing the damp hairs into place, and glanced down at his bemedaled tunic to make sure that each decoration was firmly in place.

As the motorcade made its turn, a young man of eighteen, who, it turned out, was a brand-new member of the anarchist Black Hand, emerged from a coffeehouse on the corner. One could also get a glass of fiery *slivovotz* inside, and, from his flushed face, it was plain that the boy had done just that.

The two people who Gavrilo Princip hated most in all the world sat in all their majesty, not ten feet away. As calmly as if he were reaching for one of his Turkish cigarettes, Gavrilo Princip pulled a pistol from his pocket and fired.

The first shot hit Franz Ferdinand in the chest, cun-

268

ningly finding its way through a gap in the medals. The second hit the yawning Sophie in her rounded belly. For a long agonizing moment, the royal couple sat erect. Then, as the car skidded to a stop, both lurched, Sophie collapsing on her husband while he remained upright, staring glassy-eyed at the widening red stain on his snow-white tunic. Blood frothed from the corners of his mouth.

The crowd fell upon the youthful assassin, and police came from every corner. The Muravs leaped from their own auto and reached the dying Hapsburg couple in time to hear the archduke mutter, "Sophie, Sophie, don't die. Live for our children."

But of course the obedient wife was incapable of obeying, and, within minutes of her husband, she too was dead. It became Kalina's sad duty to inform their children when she returned to the hotel.

"We must hasten back to Vienna," she told her husband. "The emperor will be overcome with grief. He will need the solace of dear and trusted friends."

Stefan shook his head. "No. The city will be in a ferment. Not even the Hapsburg's head is safe right now." Striding to the window, he pushed aside the curtain. "Best to get out of here immediately, too. That's an unruly mob down there, and there are riots everywhere. The police can't handle it."

She looked up from the bed where she was throwing things into suitcases. "But surely we are safe. We are not Hapsburgs after all."

He came to her then, and his tone was fearful. "As my wife, you are suspect by many who don't approve of my sales of arms to Austria. Others loyal to the emperor connect you with Andreas Kara—" Her eyes flew up, startled. "Oh, I know all about that peccadillo, but I know that you remained the good and faithful wife."

The royal children were hustled into a closed auto for a quick departure from the country. Stefan, considering auto transport too dangerous with all the roads cutting through

269

the open plains, took his wife and son to the railroad station and put them on a train for Paris. There, they would book passage to America on the first steamer crossing the Atlantic. "I don't want you mixed up in a European war," he said, but it was his own heir apparent, Stefi, on whom he cast his anxious gaze.

Half the people of Sarajevo apparently shared the same intention to flee. The coaches were jammed with all sorts—soldiers and sailors who had never marched in the parade, farmers and other vendors carting wares that they had not sold to the crowds, well-dressed tourists who had come just for the fun.

Stefan thrust mother and son into a third-class coach where the passengers stood closely packed like herrings in a jar. To ensure that she was not recognized, Kalina wore a voluminous peasant dress and babushka from one of the hotel maids. Stefi appeared every inch the country boy, with leather knee pants and wooden clogs on his feet. A quick rumpling of the black curls and a smear of dirt on his face and bare arms transformed him with little difficulty.

"A bit uncomfortable in there," Stefan grimaced, as she boarded, "but you'll have an hour between trains where you can change." From Vienna they would entrain for Paris by a first-class compartment.

As the train began to move, Stefan stood on tiptoe to shout at Kalina's face in the window. "This means war, you realize. Those two shots will be heard round the world." The gleam was back in his eyes, and his smile was exultant. "I'm off for Vienna by limousine. Got to make sure the old man doesn't soften up and forgive the Serbians."

Watching his tall, dark shape diminishing on the platform as the train began to move, Kalina thought, *He's had his incident*. For Stefan there had never been any doubt that a world war would happen. It was simply a matter of time and a particular incendiary act, such as an assassination, to light the waiting tinder.

It was two o'clock in the afternoon, a searing wind was blowing from the mountains, and though she was sweating profusely beneath the heavy homespun, Kalina felt a chill cut through her bones. She turned to her son, who was shuffling a deck of cards, and slung an arm about his slight shoulder, drawing him close. He looked up, smiling, his dark eyes untroubled by the all the disguises and playing games.

"Want to play snip-snap?" he said.

"Sure, darling. You deal."

Chapter Fourteen

Southern Poland, 1914

"Prosit!"

Manfred von Richthofen, heir to vast baronial holdings in Silesia, hoisted his stein and drank. His three companions joined him. The game was to see who would be the first to slip under the long refectory table or maybe to rush out, hand over mouth, to the woods behind the hostelry.

The four youths were on a summer walking tour through the Carpathian Mountains, whose spiny ridges cut a meandering border between southern Poland and Slovakia and tapered off into southern Russia. It was Saturday, the first of August, 1914, and the youths had stopped at a beautiful watering place near the Polish village of Jaslo to rendezvous with four young women who were coming up from Italy.

At twenty-eight, the American Max Dressler was the oldest, Manfred being but eighteen, his brother Lothar a few years younger. The fourth, an old man they had picked up on the trail, boasted a hale and hearty sixty.

They had been gorging on thick black bread and Russian oysters, reputed to possess aphrodisiac properties. Or so the old man asserted. He never gave his name, and nobody asked since all knew the cardinal rule of the road, "Don't ask questions."

The rule did not apply to close friends, however, and now between drinks, Manfred pointed his finger at the red-headed American. "Who do you know in Jaslo?"

Max started, and a slow flush crept into his deeply freckled face. He was no more adept at hiding his feelings than he had been twelve years ago when he had left Pittsburgh. At least not in matters of the heart.

"Nobody. How could I? This is my first trip to Poland."

"Hmm. If that's true, then it's one of the few places in the world you've not visited at one time in your life."

To cover his embarrassment, Max picked up an empty oyster shell from the litter on the table and threw it at a dartboard hanging on the opposite wall. It hit dead center.

"Ho," yelled young Lothar from the far end of the table. "You're a crack shot, Yank. They could use you in the army."

"America's not at war," responded Max, tossing a second oyster shell playfully at the lad and hitting him square on his Prussian nose.

Suddenly turning green, Lothar put his hand to his mouth and with a whimper sprinted out the door. The old man hooted and followed him. "I'll see to the lad, Baron. I've had enough to drink, anyway." He winked broadly and made a lewd gesture with his hand toward his groin. "Got to rest up for the ladies tonight."

For awhile the room was quiet except for the clink of dishes in the adjoining kitchen. The waitress entered, and on seeing the two men at the long refectory table, exclaimed, "Pardon. I thought you'd left."

Max smiled up at her. She was tall and slim and dark-haired, with sloe black eyes that reminded him of someone he once knew. He wished fervently that he could bed with the girl tonight instead of the aristocratic blond Kundry, Manfred's distant cousin. The smile she gave him and the way she wriggled her ass when she walked back into the kitchen told him that she shared his wish.

"Come on, friend. Play fair," Manfred exploded in his precise, educated German. In these parts, Max had learned, one could tell a gentleman from a peasant not so much by his dress as by his speech. Though he was called Baron by the locals, the softly handsome, fair-haired youth who faced him wore a rumpled homespun shirt, lederhosen, and Tyrolean hat with feather. Like himself, like everyone who trekked through the mountains.

Manfred pressed on. "When you heard us say that Jaslo was down there in the valley, you got as nervous as a doe at rutting time." He lowered his slanted gray eyes and kicked Max's shin under the table. "If you don't tell me your secret, I'll make up something for the others."

The American winced. Manfred's penchant for storytelling was renowned and justly feared. God knew what he would invent. By week's end, Max's hypothetical, romantic exploits in the Polish village at the foot of the mountain would be legend in these parts.

"Seems to me I do all the talking when we're together," he said mildly. "I should charge an entertainment fee."

"That's because you've got the most to tell. You're the one who's been around the world a couple times; you've had the women, every age, every color, every shape. You've raised horses in Argentine; you've mined gold in South Africa. All I've ever done is grow up in Silesia on a farm and go to school and learn to hunt and fish and shoot wild boars. Pretty useless stuff compared to you."

"You're not useless, pal." Max spoke in English, which Manfred understood but did not speak. It was easier to express deep feelings in one's native tongue. "You're a friend, a rare commodity in anyone's life."

He reached across the table to clasp the hand of this man who by ordinary standards should have been the last person in the world to become Max O'Hara's friend. The Prussian had been born with the proverbial silver spoon in his mouth, and he was the idol of a wealthy landed family whose ancestors had driven the Huns from northern Europe. Max O'Hara had been a rent baby abandoned by his parents. He had lied and thieved to survive.

Tears came to the German's eyes at the heartfelt words. Max liked the way European men wept unashamedly. Not

like in America, where a man had to get roaring drunk
before he let you see into his soul. "You're the best friend I
ever had," he said huskily. Even Gus Koval had not been
like this to him. There were many things which the Dutchie
had not understood about the man who had toiled beside
him at the blast furnace and who drank with him at
Koster's bar — his thirst for knowledge, his risking his neck
the time he went to the Hughes' house to see Libby and was
caught with a smoking gun in his hand.

With Manfred von Richthofen Max felt the kind of
intellectual intimacy he might have had in marriage with
Kalina.

Their hands separated abruptly as if each felt the burden
of emotion too much to bear. Despite his love for the
youth, there were some things that Max could not share
with this man whom he had met in a Berlin café eight
months ago on New Year's Eve. How the clear eyes would
darken if he heard that he was drinking with an accused
murderer. Surely the hand that was so warm in his would
stiffen and fly to his mouth as he stared with astonishment
if told that the man who lay beside him under Carpathian
skies had a price on his head. Would this young baron
want to know that the man who called himself an American could never go home again, that he must roam the
world and never set foot on his own native soil?

"Okay, as you say in America," Manfred chuckled,
drumming his long, tapering fingers on the rough table.
"Now tell your best friend in all the world the name of the
girl you knew who lives in our tiny Jaslo." His thin, well-
marked brows came together. "She's not a Cossack, is she?
The damned barbarian horsemen keep pouring over the
Russian border and setting up households in Poland
though the country is officially under Austrian rule."

Max shook his head, laughing inwardly at the idea of
Kalina as a Cossack girl, replete with high fur cap and
saber clinking at her belt. "She no longer lives there," he
said. "She emigrated to America when she was ten."

"Oho! Right on target! So what's her name? I know a
good many of the families in these parts. In fact, they are

275

our vassals in a manner of speaking since my family has title to the land around here. Everyone pays us rent."

"Kalina." The name burst from Max's lips before he could think to stop it. He rolled it round his tongue, then repeated, "Kalina." How glorious to say the name that his ear never heard, even from his own lips. In dreams sometimes he thought he heard an echo of it. Kalina, Kalina, Kalina.

Manfred brightened. "Now we're getting somewhere." Banging his stein on the wooden table, he shouted to the kitchen. "Schatzi, more beer!"

Returning, the girl took both steins to a barrel in the corner and drew the beer. She set the foaming vessels on the table and boldly placed a hand on Max's shoulder. Annoyed, he shrugged it off, and without returning her seductive glance, raised his stein and drank. Thoughts of Kalina had driven out his fleeting lust. While his friend's eyes were closed tight above the stein, Manfred bolted impishly from the bench and dived for Max's rucksack, piled with his own just outside the door.

"What the—" Max muttered, plunging after him. But he was too late to prevent his friend from opening the canvas sack, pulling out a photograph in a silver frame, and holding it aloft.

Manfred whooped. "Something tells me that the grand lady in this picture, that you gaze at now and then when you think no one is looking, is the same little Polish girl who came from Jaslo."

A kind of rage boiled within the American. He was on the Prussian with a roar, tackling him to the ground. The photograph fell on the rocks, and the two men struggled for it, rolling around and around like schoolboys on a playing field. Manfred won and, scrambling to his feet, turned it over and read the printing on the back. *Mrs. Stefan Murav, famous Socialite and Beauty.*

He frowned. "But this is the wife of the devil they call The Merchant of Death, the one who peddles his guns and battleships and submarines to every country in Europe and Asia." He whistled. "You don't mean to tell me—" Von

Richthofen's eyes widened in amazement.

Max snatched back the photograph. "Don't be an ass. Photographs like this are sold all over Europe. Mrs. Murav is one of those called 'professional beauties,' women whose pictures appear as advertisements for photographers. People collect them like postage stamps."

"Uh huh. Now lie some more and tell me that you don't have a crush on her, that you don't gaze at her face like some rosary-toting old lady staring at the Virgin Mary."

A sudden buzzing as from a giant hornet caused them both to gaze up at the sky where an airplane was just emerging from a cloud bank. Silently, the two men watched, their heated talk forgotten, as the winged vehicle dipped toward them until it was so close they saw the goggled head of the pilot. Seeing them, the man waved from the open cockpit, a broad smile on his face. Gracefully, he dipped his wings in greeting, and then, with a singing of motors, the airplane flew up again.

"My God, to soar like a bird," Max breathed. He had seen many flying machines in his European travels, most of them over Germany.

"An Albatross," said Manfred with authority. "It's only for scouting and reconnaissance. We're developing other models with more speed and maneuverability to be used as fighters."

The airplane vanished behind the next peak, and the two men headed for the hostelry. The disputed photograph was seemingly forgotten as Max slipped it quietly back into his rucksack.

"Future wars will be fought in the skies," said Manfred. Then, striking his leather thigh with his fist, he growled, "Damn, if only I weren't stuck in the goddamn cavalry!"

"Wonder what it's doing here," Max murmured absently, "Is little Jaslo at war?"

Upstairs, the women waited for them. Kundry lunged at Max and boxed him playfully on the ears. "You scum, I've been here for hours while you drink with Manfred." A lusty glint brightened her blue eyes. "You know what too much beer can do to a man's desire."

"Not mine," Max said shortly, slapping her firm ass sharply. The woman was already in a kind of thin cotton nightdress, and his hand told him that she wore nothing underneath. With Kalina's photograph safely back in its little hiding place, his blood began to warm with anticipation of the night ahead in bed with the luscious and very willing cousin of his best friend. At thirty, Kundry was vastly experienced in the arts of erotica, and sex with her was a hedonistic exercise, more strenuous than Max sometimes liked. But tonight she would tire him out, and maybe tomorrow when they passed through Jaslo, he wouldn't make a fool of himself in front of Manfred by looking sheepish or making stupid inquiries.

They all slept together in one large airy room on military cots. Despite the squeals and giggles of Lothar and his girl tussling not five feet away, and somewhat abetted by the old man's unabashed roars as he climaxed time after time, Max thoroughly enjoyed himself. From Manfred came no sound, he and his mate had apparently fallen asleep without making love. But during the night, Max heard his friend raise his voice. "Ho, cousin, you know all the swells in Europe. What Mrs. Murav's Christian name? You know, the woman who sits on old Franz Josef's lap and tickles his you-know-what."

"Oh, that one," replied Kundry sleepily from Max's shoulder. "Kalina. She's Polish, said to come from some village near here actually."

Max groaned. His secret love was secret no more.

At dawn the waitress Schatzi burst into the room. Her face was white, her sloe eyes brilliant with excitement. "It's war with Russia. The Baron is to report to his regiment at once."

The German troops would rendezvous at Ostrava midway on the northern Bohemian border before proceeding west to march into France where the front would be established on the border. Manfred's face fairly glowed with anticipation as he, Max, and Lothar mounted the horses they had swiftly commandeered from the hostel landlord. Their old companion had already resumed his walking tour alone, but headed south, declaring, "I've had my wars."

"The Fatherland is now at war with Russia and *La Belle France*. Tomorrow Great Britain will join them as our enemy. Shortly, everyone else will fall into place on either side. In days, the European continent will be mobilizing." Manfred spoke from atop his horse, his tone that of a commander addressing his troops.

To Max his friend seemed like a young Napoleon setting out on his first war, but, laughing mirthlessly, he remarked, "Sounds like two gangs of kids lining up on either side of an alley."

The Prussian stared icily at the American. "War is a serious business with us Europeans. We do not joke about it." Angrily, he dug his spurs into the mare's flanks and sped away, but they had not gone a hundred yards when he slowed down so that the American could catch up. They then cantered side by side down the mountain toward the village. Manfred's tone was light as he said, "Now you'll get to see that notorious Jaslo where your goddess came from. Believe me, pal, it's not much. For a little peasant girl, she did well for herself, I must say."

"Anything can happen in America," grumbled Max, already regretting his decision to accompany his friend to Ostrava. Wishing to be with Manfred for these last days before the battle began he had ignored Kundry's pleas to go south with her to Switzerland. "As far away from this war business as possible," she said. Manfred's unexpected reaction to his gibe about the war being kids' play left a chill in his bones. Had he and his new best friend come to a parting of the ways? They themselves talked little of war although there was talk about it wherever they stopped.

It was high noon when they reached the village. For a long time there was no sound but the pounding of hoofs on the shale that formed the lower foothills. As they rode, other horsemen joined them, and, when they pushed into Jaslo's rutted road, there were fifteen. All but Max were cavalrymen answering the call to arms.

The baron, who as the only officer in the group, had assumed leadership, raised a hand, and they dismounted before a church. A black-robed priest answered Manfred's knock. The youth clicked his heels together.

"Are you the priest here?"

The young man touched his Roman collar with a faint smile. "Father Gomulka, at your service."

"War has been declared, and I have the pleasant duty to inform you that we are now taking over the village from the Russians."

The indifference on the pale, clerical face said plainly that the announcement was hardly news. Ever since the priest was born and for centuries before that, Germans, Austrians, Russians, and others whose racial strains were not so clear had paraded through his little village at will. In and out, in and out. It was monotonous.

If one were to go by the books, southern Poland was the private property of the Hapsburgs in Vienna. But no one—most assuredly not the free-wheeling Cossacks—paid any attention to that. Most of the villagers couldn't even read. If a vote were taken, thought Father Gomulka on those rare occasions when he thought about it, the handsome and virile Cossacks from across the Russian border would win hands down—especially if the women had anything to say about it.

Now this autocratic squirt of a Prussian was telling the holy priest that *he* was taking over. *C'est la vie!* Father Gomulka pointed to a thatched house across the street. "There's beer and bread and cheese over there. The Cossack regiment stole all our meat and animals when they evacuated across the border two nights ago."

One of the riders cursed. "Damn, I was looking for a skirmish at least." He grinned. "To warm us up for the big stuff, you know."

It started to rain as they ate. It was a hard, ferocious rain, the kind that promised to last the rest of the day. One of the nuns who were serving them scurried in with a fresh armful of crusty peasant loaves and goat cheese and remarked — a bit casually, Max thought — "There is talk that the Cossacks have returned with reinforcements from across the border."

Immediately, as if on cue, a noise came from outside. "The Cossacks are coming! The Cossacks are coming!"

Kalina had told Max about the feared Cossacks. They raped maidens, speared infants, and cut old men in half. "And that's only the beginning," she had said, shivering at the memory.

With more trepidation than he cared to admit to anyone, Max went out the door with Manfred and the others, expecting to see a battalion of Lucifers sprouting horns and toting pitchforks, but instead saw a group of mounted men facing the church, with bushy black beards, fierce expressions, large fur hats, and evil-looking ammunition belts around their rainbow-colored shirts. Across each saddle rested a carbine. They were so still, they might have stepped out of an ancient tapestry.

The Germans had nothing but small arms and none of them was in uniform.

Two men walked toward Manfred. One was the priest, the other a tall man with a long, scraggly gray beard, who appeared to be some kind of leader. He was not a Cossack, it turned out, but Pan Mikolai, the local squire, who spoke for the people of the village.

The priest acted as interpreter, speaking in German, which all understood apparently. "The Cossacks say they do not want to fight because they are many and you are few, and you are not in uniform." He smiled wanly. "They are very proud."

Manfred von Richthofen had been schooled to know when retreat is the best defense. So without a word, the Germans mounted and left the village. It was Sunday, but no church bells rang, nobody was in the street, and all the houses they passed were heavily curtained. Not a face appeared at the little windows. Except for a dog barking now and then, the village seemed deserted.

"Scared to death," remarked Lothar. "I imagine they prefer the Cossacks to us. They've had them on their backs for fifty years." Lothar was fresh from school and knew his history. Manfred's brother was also a student of philosophy. "One prefers the devil he knows to the one he doesn't."

Max took a long, thoughtful look at the dismal landscape. The hidden villagers had missed a battle today, but he would bet his last nickel that they would have a lot more before the war was much older. Kalina was well out of it. So that was the Pan Mikolai who had fathered both her and Zuska. He could believe it. Tall, straight, virile, with enough black hair to fill a mattress.

But as they reached the rail terminal, he felt a pang of regret that he had not gone up to the man and said, "Hi, I love your daughter." He doubled up with laughter at the idea, and his friend, the baron, was certain that the American was suffering from a bad case of the jitters over the near battle with the Cossacks.

"My God, it's a party," Max exclaimed, as they reined in their horses on the platform. "Better than the Fourth of July back home in Homestead."

Beside him, Manfred chuckled. "War is—what is your American word? Oh, yes, *fun*! A shot in the arm, a welcome relief from the tedium of everyday existence." He pointed to a group of girls in native costume dancing to the music of an oomph-pah-pah band, made up mostly of trumpets and drums. "Women claim they hate war, yet they are the first to celebrate its coming."

An admiring group of men surrounded the ring of dancers, and from time to time, an ardent youth reached into the circle to grab a maid and twirl her round and round to their own private dance, kissing her roundly at each turn.

In fact, a great deal of kissing and embracing was going on, not only between young couples but also between mothers and sons, fathers and daughters. Even fathers and sons were unashamedly entwined. It was difficult to tell, though, which of the men were going to war and which were staying, for even very old men were in uniform. Most wore the drab gray-green or field gray of the German army, but here and there something gayer caught his eyes.

"What's the rank of that graybeard over there, the one who's leading the band," asked Max. "I've never seen such a get-up outside a circus."

"Saxon Hussar," replied Lothar. "Frogged blue jacket, silver buttons, spiked helmet with silver eagle on brim. All of the military men in this area are in our Imperial Army."

Some peasant women, also in holiday attire, ran up and pressed rounds of bread and cheese and strings of dried fish upon them. Max drew back, uncertain, but Manfred said, "Take it. There'll be no food on the train."

Max was puzzled. "I thought we were in Poland. Why should these people be so happy about a German war?"

"The Poles are all part of greater Deutschland," Manfred said crisply. "Many of them have intermarried with the German landholders." Curving an arm upward, he shouted to the men on horse to follow him, a signal to Max that no further dialogue was needed on the question.

Finding the coaches too crowded and already malodorous from sweating bodies and lack of sanitary facilities, the von Richthofen brothers, together with Max and a few others, repaired to the boxcar where they had stabled their horses. Both air and straw were clean, the smell of horses pleasant, and they could sprawl to their heart's content. Whiskey bottles appeared immediately and soon a different kind of party from the one they had left commenced.

They traveled through the night, sleeping off and on. At intervals the train was sidetracked as munition trains went by. Max stared with amazement at the strings of flatcars piled with cannons, tanks, and wooden cartons that were obviously guns and ammunition. There was even an airplane, one of those new Fokkers with a Maltese cross painted on the long cigar-shaped body. More recruits were picked up at sleepy little towns. At one point a group of boys looking no more than sixteen clambered on the roof,

283

the train being full. "We're a whole class from the academy at Cracow," they said with pride. "We all signed up the minute we heard about the war."

At dawn, Max rose from a fitful sleep to gaze out on the spectacular vista of forested mountains, silvery lakes, and meandering rivers. He had wakened several times in the night to walk to the open door and watch the sparks from the locomotive swirl like golden stars into the heavens or to stroke a restless horse. The straw, the horses, the manure — all brought back poignant memories of Kalina. Sixteen, naive, eager for life, offering herself to him. *I want it too, Max.*

The whistle hooted mournfully as the train passed through a tunnel, echoing Max's heavy mood. But within minutes there was no time for brooding, for they were at Ostrava, and Manfred left the train, along with Lothar and most of the soldiers.

They stood on the platform, shaking hands, wanting to embrace but too embarrassed to do so in front of strangers. "This is not good-bye, but *Auf Wiedersehen*," said Manfred. "We will meet again, sooner than you think. It'll all be over by Christmas."

"You bet," broke in Lothar, who liked to talk American. "Don't go wandering off to Argentina or Africa or somewhere on the other side of the world. Come to our estate at Silesia for the holidays."

Although the train was half-empty now that the military were gone, Max remained in the boxcar. He gave the ticket conductor a sum of money sufficient enough to ensure that the railroad dicks wouldn't trouble him. More horses were boarded to join Max's mare from the hostelry at Jaslo. He had named her Bonny for one he had loved in his stableboy days on Mulberry Street. Frequently, his car was shifted to another train, and more than once it sat on a sideline for a day or so. He didn't mind; he was in no hurry. The food he had gotten from the women at Jaslo ran out, but there was plenty more in the countryside. He kept his money in his boots. A thief would have to kill him first.

He continued to travel west, deciding that he would end

his journey in Paris. There he would consider whether to take ship or stay in the city on the Seine until the war reached it, if it did. Kalina was much in his mind. Where was she now? Surely not in Vienna where there must be fighting? Perhaps with the Austrian emperor at his summer palace or in a hunting lodge away from the scene of battle.

The rucksack that held her picture was his pillow. Maybe that was how she got into his head, he reflected, amused at his vagary. Elena Lesko, who was given to premonitions and second sight, once told him that one thinks hard about a person or event when they are close at hand.

But surely, Mrs. Stefan Murav was not in Belgium, for that was where Max finally left the boxcar. After three weeks it had become a kind of home to him.

The scene at the Charleroi station could only be described as bedlam. There was no festival atmosphere as at Jaslo and at most of the depots in Germany where their trains had been met with bands and singing and waving flags and girls with flowers for the soldiers.

Here a kind of frenzied confusion reigned as people fought tooth and nail to board the northbound train. Most were women, old men, and children, all toting canvas sacks and sometimes small domestic animals. The officials were kept wildly busy pushing them back, for within minutes of its arrival, every car bulged with passengers.

The war had come to little Belgium. A brief conversation with a vendor, from whom he bought some wine, informed him that the little country north of France, which Max had assumed was neutral in this alley-cat European fight, had been invaded by the German army. "The Germans have nothing against us," said the man in a patois Max could easily understand. "It's the quickest way to get to Paris with an army."

Max took his bottle into the town. It was plain that the peaceful Belgians had not taken kindly to the Kaiser's troops using their little country as a highway. He might meet up with von Richthofen a lot sooner than either of them had imagined. Certainly long before Christmas.

It was Sunday, and black-garbed women poured into a church that had been partly blasted away. The bells in the steeple rang out cheerily as if they were in some damn cathedral in the middle of New York or Paris.

To the Kaiser's enormous surprise and great chagrin, the Belgians had put up a fierce fight, making their stand at the town of Mons some forty kilometers to the north and west. The battle had been savage, and the historic town was now a shambles.

"Big guns, sixteen inches across. Bombs dropped from airplanes," a woman among the mob on the road told Max, as she ran alongside a cart loaded with furniture and two scared-looking kids. The refugees were a pitiful sight; some had bandages on their head or arm, and some limped along on crutches or were carried in goat carts or dog wagons. Max was one of the few on horses, the Germans having taken the rest.

The sides of the road and the surrounding fields were littered with German dead. Flies formed a thick, black cloud over the bloated corpses in the field gray of the German army. Scavenger birds screeched overhead. The populace had buried their own dead, which was comprised not only of Belgian but of British and French soldiers as well.

Max struck out on the lesser roads, heading for Mons. At least the battle there was over. The region held rich deposits of coal and iron, steel mills lined the rivers and canals. Smoke poured from tall stacks, and the sky was orange with flame. Even the acrid smell was the same as back home, and the close-packed houses—those that were still intact or didn't have gaping shellholes in the side—were encrusted with soot.

But life went on, as it must. At sunset it started to rain and he stopped at a house where a woman and small boy were digging in a square of garden. He leaned against the wooden fence. Maybe they would put him up for the night. He still had plenty of cash in his boots—good French currency—having converted his Polish zlotys somewhere in Germany.

"Bon soir, Madame."

Dropping her hoe, the woman shrieked and grabbing the boy's hand, ran into the house. Did he look like a German? Max wondered with irritation. Sighing, he turned and advanced up the road toward a cluster of lights. He had gone but a few yards when he turned and saw a young girl at his back. She was tall and slim-hipped, with sweet breasts poking under a white but very dirty smock that reached halfway down her calves. He cursed softly under his breath. In the few hours since he had been in this war-ravaged place, he had been approached by four women who offered their bodies in exchange for money to get on a train.

He had given them money but refused the merchandise. This one was still a child. It was enough to wring your heart dry.

"Yes, what is it?" he said in English, hoping to scare her off with a foreign language.

She replied in perfect, charmingly accented English. "Sir, I perceive by your dress that you are not a German soldier, and I—"

"I am not a soldier of any kind," he broke in, "but you should be more cautious. A uniform is easily discarded." She put her hand to her mouth and started biting her nails. Moving close, he snatched that hand as well as the other and held them in his own. "I am an American."

She started but did not remove her hands. It was apparent that she felt strengthened by the touch of his warm masculine flesh.

"Begging your pardon, I know a German when I see one. There's a certain way of walking—" She attempted a smile, but suddenly tears began to stream from her eyes. They were lovely eyes, a rich blue-black. Something about her reminded him of Kalina in New York on New Year's Eve long ago. Her eyes had been like that, the color of dead-ripe blackberries. Heavy, black hair straggled untidily over the girl's thin shoulders, which reinforced the image. He longed to touch it but feared that she might take the gesture amiss. He stared at the fine, thin bones of her face through flesh that was so pale and translucent, she seemed made of china.

But immediately the thought proved false, for a rosy flush suffused her face, and squeezing his hands, she cried out passionately, "Please come with me. A flying machine has come down in our wood, and the pilot has vanished. I am so afraid—"

The black eyes filled with fear, and Max did not need to be told what it was that she feared. The flying machine was German of course; he doubted the British had their men in the air at this early stage in the war.

Her name was Sidonie and her grandfather was a viscount. They were the last of their family, her parents having died long ago in an epidemic. They walked rapidly through a swampy field and then up a steep, vine-covered hill and into a small wood where, to his immense relief, Max saw that the airplane was not German. Manfred had told them that all the kaiser's machines had Maltese crosses on them. Painted on this one's flank and tail was a circle in red, white, and blue. Except for a fabric wing crumpled like so much paper against a tree, the craft was hardly damaged. A machine gun thrust its long nose through the propellers, and when Max poked his head inside the cockpit, he saw a basket with what looked like little bombs in it. A tiny Union Jack was stuck in a window casing. There was also a tiny painted legend on the board beneath the window, *Kill the Hun.*

Laughing boisterously, he backed out and turning, threw his arms about the fearful girl, giving her a hug. "You can stop chewing your nails, to begin with."

Releasing her, he said, "It's British. Now we must find the pilot. He has obviously gone into hiding and may be wounded."

"First, I must go home and tell *grand-père*," she said. "He is ill and will be anxious about me." She paused. "I have not told him of the airplane. He thinks I am buying medicine in the town."

Max followed her to a very large house on the other side of the wood. It sat tall and imposing atop a rocky outcrop

288

and had towers and spires in the medieval style. One side had several gaping holes in it from exploding shells. As they climbed a flight of stone steps toward the place, he whistled. "You live in a castle, girl. Are you a princess then?"

"It is our home, a château as they call it in France. But we are not rich, as you may be thinking." She sighed. "Long ago our family owned all of the land as far as one can see, but now —" She stopped abruptly. "But I am sure that you have heard enough sad stories during your stay in Charleroi."

Inside, they found their missing pilot. He sat in a cavernous room at the end of a series of rooms, one gloomier than the other, there being no light but a few tallow candles stuck here and there in sconces. "Our electricity has been cut," explained the girl.

As they entered, the Englishman picked up a revolver from a little table at his side and rising, pointed it at Max. "Relax, Englishman," grinned Max. "I am not a Heinie."

Sidonie rushed to a massive bed where a skeletal figure lay almost smothered in blankets. The room was icy cold. "He is American, Father, and very kind."

"All Americans are kind," the old man muttered. "They have never known war." The pilot put down his gun with an explosive breath of relief. To Max's surprise, he was not dressed in the khaki of the British army but in a deep blue. On his collar was a silver insignia that read RFC.

"Jimmy Nelson, RFC," he grinned. "That means Royal Flying Corps. And your name, my friend? And what the blazes are you doing here in the middle of the war?"

Max grinned and took the Englishman's hand. "Max O'Hara, New York born and bred." He had always liked the English. Unlike with the Germans, one was not forced to stand on ceremony. "My reasons for being in Belgium with German shells whistling over my head are deep and devious and would take more time than we have right now to tell." He pursed his lips, squinting at the blue uniform. "We've got to get you out of here. You'll be taken for a Heinie officer."

"Righto. The viscount and I were just discussing the matter. He has some clothes in trunks somewhere, and we were waiting for his daughter to return and render assistance."

From the bed came a racking cough. Sidonie bent over her father but turned her eyes on the Englishman. "The Germans are gone from here. They are moving south toward Paris. You are in no immediate danger. Before I find new garments for you, I must go for the medicine for his cough."

The old man sat up and put two skeletal hands on his daughter's shoulders. "No, no," he said in French. "I am dying and your money must be saved for food."

Tiredly, Sidonie slumped in a chair beside the bed. The task of caring for her grandfather had obviously exhausted her. Max walked to the bed and lifted the girl in his arms. "I'm taking you to your own bed, Sidonie, but before you sleep, point us to some food."

Childlike, she cuddled against him. Like Kalina in that cigar-factory cellar, he thought, as he laid her down in an adjoining room. Jimmy followed them, and then the two men went to the kitchen where they found little enough to eat — some moldy cheese, a few crusts, and some apples in a basket. There was plenty of wine in the cellar though, and carrying their food upstairs to the bedrooms, they sat down by the old man's bed.

During the long night, their tongues loosened by the wine, the two men talked, spinning out their life stories as new friends are wont to do. Feeling that unlike Manfred, this easygoing Englishman would understand, Max told him sketchily the tragic circumstances that had made him an exile. It was good to tell someone. Tomorrow both of them might well be dead, victims of a bullet from an airplane, or they might step on an unexploded shell lying innocently in a field.

From time to time, the old man woke, asked for water, and then slept again. Max touched the parchmentlike brow. "He's got a devil of a fever."

Sidonie slept like the dead, however, as if the knowledge

that two valiant knights were at her side gave her the peace she sorely needed. Max and Jimmy looked in on her, both noting the bitten nails, the bones sticking through her sweet, young body.

"We must take them with us when we go," said Jimmy. "The Huns will be back to set up an occupation government."

Max nodded. "She needs a woman's care."

But with the dawn they saw that any departure would have to wait. The sick man's face was bright and hot; his frail body was scalding to the touch. With help from the men, Sidonie wrapped him in wet sheets. But nothing availed, neither wet sheets, nor hot steam from a kettle, nor the herbs Sidonie brewed on the ancient stove. For days the fever raged, and he shrieked in his delirium. Most of his ravings concerned the family silver and jewels that he had buried in the wood behind the château before the German juggernaut arrived.

"It was raining hard and very cold that day," sobbed Sidonie. "He caught a congestion in the lungs. He was always a stubborn, old man."

Viscount de Chambre, the last of a noble line, died on Friday morning, five days after Max had come to Charleroi. They buried him in the family cemetery behind the house, just off the wood where his treasure lay.

"One day you'll return for your inheritance," Max assured the grieving Sidonie. "The war will last a year at most."

Jimmy found some black peasant pants and a shirt to replace his telltale uniform. Max, on Sidonie's advice, stuck some cloth between his shoulder blades to give himself the look of a hunchback. All three wore wide-brimmed peasant hats. Then men and girl struck out across the border into France, turned east, skirted the Argonne Forest, followed the beautiful river called the Marne. "There's a place I've heard of," said Jimmy Nelson, "in Champagne province. A kind of refuge and hospital combined, run by a rich American woman. We can leave Sidonie there. I'll try to get back home to my outfit."

"Count me in on any water travel," said Max. "War is not exactly what I had in mind when I started my European tour."

They laughed and headed toward the refuge somewhere between Compiègne and Château-Thierry in the French province of Champagne.

Chapter Fifteen

Champagne, France, 1914

On the first of October, exactly two months into the great European war, Max and his companions Sidonie and Jimmy Nelson entered the *Villa d'Este*.

"The directress will see you presently." A dour-faced Frenchwoman in nurse's white glanced up from a desk fronting the door. There was a red cross on her apron and nunlike head covering, matching the *rouge croix* on the roof of the villa. The villa itself sprawled halfway up a limestone bluff that overlooked a pretty river in Champagne some fifty kilometers from Paris.

Nodding, Max slid down to the tiled floor, leaning gratefully against the rough fieldstone wall. He reached inside his shirt to pull out the hunchback wadding. Jimmy slid down to join him while Sidonie remained standing, gazing nervously out the arched window at a copse of trees. A group of children in black smocks and coats were jumping about on the green. "Walnuts," she said, absently. "*Grand-père* used to grow them for export."

A smile flitted across the nurse's features as she gazed at the girl. "There's a pretty vineyard up the slope and some orchards, mostly apples and peaches." There was no reply from Sidonie, nor did she turn around. The nurse persisted. "Sit down, girl. You look exhausted." But Sidonie stood statuelike at the window, chewing her nails with a frightening intensity.

Max spoke up. "She doesn't mean to be rude, nurse, but she's in a bad way." He looked anxiously at Sidonie's back. From the moment they buried her beloved grandfather and left Belgium, she had deteriorated rapidly in mind as well as in body, withdrawing from her companions and from reality. Now she seemed unable to comprehend where she was.

The nurse bent to her papers but continued speaking. "The war has come with a vengeance to our lovely Champagne province. But for the sign of mercy on our roof, we'd not be sitting here in relative peace and quiet."

As if to contradict her statement, there came a sudden echo of distant booming. "Even the beastly Huns can't bring themselves to bomb a hospital." She paused as if thinking. "Not yet."

She glanced at Sidonie, and her blue eyes softened with pity. "We get them every day like that. Worse. Don't worry. She'll be fine. Madame Olkonsky is a miracle worker."

They were in a kind of spacious, vaulted foyer that fairly hummed with activity. White-garbed women sat at desks, talking into telephones or scribbling on papers. Max saw several wooden contraptions that appeared to be folding gauze mechanically as two women watched on either side. Five sat in a row before a long table, knitting socks at another device. The women were all ages and chattered in low tones in several languages.

"I say, look there. That machine's winding bandages by electricity," marveled Jimmy. "I guess all I've heard about American efficiency is true."

"Yep," responded Max. He closed his eyes, which still burned from the residue of gunpowder smoke that had lain thick in the last wood they had gone through. The trees had been half-blasted away, and the place was full of barbed wire and trenches. In that same wood Max's horse Bonny had caught a fatal chunk of shrapnel in her flank. The journey had taken twice as long as they had figured — more than a month — for they found themselves smack in the middle of the fighting, Germans on one side, British and French on the other. A fierce struggle was being waged for the provinces watered by the Marne. At several points they had narrowly missed being shot to pieces when the big guns had started blasting away and they had to duck for cover. Even the crazy airplanes dipped down to see if they were worth hurling a bomb at or maybe knocking about with their damn machine guns.

He must have dozed off for when he woke up with a jerk, he heard a woman say in French, which while a great deal smoother than his own, had a distinct American flavor, "Mam'selle Gaillard, have those new ration books arrived from Paris? Without coupons our people cannot buy meat and milk for their children."

"This afternoon, Madame Olkonsky," replied the nurse in her rapid, slurring French. "They promised on a stack of Bibles." She sighed and smiled again. "We French have not the efficiency of the Americans, but we are trying. You must be patient."

The one called "Madame," who was obviously the directress for whom they waited, was tall and slender, but Max and Jimmy could not see her face, for her back was toward them. Like the rest, she was all in white, a shoulder-length veil falling to her shoulders, completely hiding every trace of hair.

"Yes, of course. Forgive me. I will try harder to curb my American-style impatience." That the difference in their national traits was no hindrance to their relationship was obvious from the worshipful look on the face of the Frenchwoman. Walking quickly to Sidonie, the American took the girl by both shoulders, swinging her around to face the room. "You are newly arrived, they tell me, and seek shelter. What is your name, my dear?"

For a long moment the frozen Sidonie stared at the kind and beautiful face. Then collapsing with a sob, she fell into the woman's embrace. Max looked up, and the woman stared back from over the heaving shoulders of the girl. Suddenly, the name that Mam'selle Gaillard had uttered earlier registered in his tired brain—Olkonsky! As he saw startled recognition lighten the black eyes of the tall woman and gazed stupidly into the most beautiful face in the whole world, he knew that the marvelous directress of the Red Cross villa was his very own Kalina.

Swiftly, he rose and moved toward her as in a dream. "So you're the fabulously rich American lady who's the talk of the countryside." It wasn't at all the tender words he wanted to say, but all sensible thought had left him. The woman who was famous throughout northern France for the astonishing executive ability with which she had almost overnight converted her luxurious *Villa d'Este* into a hospital with all modern conveniences and who was never without the right words to say to the sick, the wounded, or the merely hysterical was struck dumb. Like a schoolgirl she gaped at the tall American with the incredible amount of freckles on his face and arms.

Woodenly, Max took a few more steps toward her. Grinning nervously, he threw up his hands in a gesture of great surprise. "But perhaps you have forgotten me, Madame Olkonsky. It's been so long since we last met." His voice was tight and superficially polite as if they were sitting across the table at a swank dinner party.

Sidonie moved out of Kalina's arms and sat down in a chair. Mam'selle Gaillard offered her a spotless, white handkerchief, and the girl blew her nose with such force that the quick honking broke the tension.

Kalina found her tongue. "Max," she breathed, in English. "I thought you dead."

The statement was far from the truth, for she had never, even in moments of near despair, allowed herself to think with such finality. But it was the kind of thing one said when greeting a person who has not been heard from for twelve long years.

Except for the clatter of the machinery, the busy room had grown quiet, the women ceasing their talk to listen. A story was in the offing, and a romantic one at that if one could judge from the looks the handsome stranger and their directress were exchanging. Becoming aware of the silence, Kalina blushed and said, "Come to my apartment. Please." Then, as if noticing him for the first time, she addressed the Englishman. "And you too, sir." She reached out to raise the now quiet Sidonie from the chair and quickly, in the manner of one who has just remembered an urgent appointment, walked through the foyer with a firm, strong stride, glancing neither to right nor left.

Not so the two men. They smiled on both sides at the boldly staring women. Jimmy winked, and Max said "Hi," nervously raising a hand to wave at one and all. An air of merriment pervaded, the arrival of two, good-looking, young men being a welcome relief from the tedium of hospital routine. By the time Kalina had led them through the first hospital ward, both men were in high spirits. Max felt as if he had just died and gone to heaven.

Several large rooms were filled with cots upon which lay sick and wounded. At the bedsides sat more white-clad women — some of them very old, others barely out of childhood — reading, chatting, or changing bandages. Gramophones, playing dance tunes, were here and there. The *Villa d'Este* had all the little comforts so essential to getting well but so seldom found in hospitals.

"She must have half the women in France working for her," mumbled Jimmy.

"Safest place to be when shells are flying through the air looking for a target," Max replied. "That red cross on the roof is better than a suit of armor."

Faded tapestries, obviously very ancient, covered the stone walls. The arched windows were curtained with heavy damask in gold or scarlet. Lintels above the doors sported elegant crests in bronze or gold. The *Villa d'Este* had been built by the great Emperor Charlemagne some twelve hundred years before, Kalina explained, as she led them across a pretty flagged courtyard and into a smaller wing of the rambling structure.

"Every owner since then has expanded the building, adding his own peculiar touches to the architecture," she continued. Her accent was a delightful fusion of Polish, English, and French, and Max thought it was the sweetest, most melodious sound in all the world.

The office of the directress was spartan, the furniture

having been moved out of a cozy sitting room to make way for file cabinets, high stools, a few straight chairs, and a long, scarred wooden table piled high with papers and ration books. A brisk fire burned in the grate, however, and Kalina set the trembling Sidonie down in front of it.

"I am very cold-blooded myself," she said kindly. "I must have a fire even in the midst of summer."

"Maybe you suffered from lack of warmth in your childhood," Max remarked, the bleak Mulberry Street room flashing across his mind. Kalina shot him a swift glance, telling him without words that the tenement room where Aunt Litka had died was also in her mind. But quickly she tore her eyes from his and turned from him with a detached expression. To a disinterested bystander, they might have been two old friends, who had perhaps gone to school together or shared a common but distant ancestor.

Max gazed at her hungrily, but Kalina, schooled in the diplomatic circles of Europe, remained the efficient directress.

The matter of the Englishman was taken care of first. Speaking rapidly into a kind of tube that transmitted messages to other parts of the hospital, Kalina ordered fresh clothing and traveling supplies for the downed pilot, enough to get him to his airfield on the Normandy coast. Within minutes Max's new friend took his leave, promising to look him up when the "bloody war" was over.

Sidonie was handed over to a pretty, young woman, who entered with a burst of energy. She took one look at Max and shrieked, "Max O'Hara, do my eyes deceive me or are you a ghost?"

It was Mary Lesko, who had left a promising opera career in Vienna to help her former mistress in war-relief work. "Oh, Max! Max! You're not dead after all!" she exclaimed, covering him with kisses.

"Reports of my death are, I am happy to say, very premature," he laughed, stifling a growing hysteria.

The first wild greetings over, the two sat down to talk, but Kalina broke in impatiently. "Sidonie must be given a bed and put into it right away. I could call another aide, but Mary is so good with cases of shock such as Sidonie exhibits."

"Sure, Kalina"—the two had been on first-name basis for some years—"but there's something I have to tell Max." She giggled. "You too. Just wait till you hear—"

"Enough," responded Kalina with a tolerant smile as she hustled Mary and Sidonie with both hands. "Whatever your great news is, it'll be all the more wonderful for the waiting."

Mary's bright face fell. "Okay, you're right as always. Bye, Max." She rolled her blue eyes and winked at him. "By the merest luck, do you have any cigarettes?"

He guffawed. "I was hoping to cop some from you, kid."

When she had gone, Max inquired huskily. "And pray, Madame Directress, where do I sleep? Do you have a pretty girl in white to hold my hand and sing me to sleep?"

"I'll hold your hand, but as for the singing—" Kalina opened an inner door and led him into a spacious bedroom that looked through a bank of windows onto a pretty courtyard. "It's very private here. It was once our top guest quarters. England's King Edward slept here and the kaiser—" She stopped, unable to maintain the bantering tone with which she had hoped to stave off the inevitable flood of emotion.

With an explosive groan, Max bounded toward her and drew her close. They stood locked together without kissing for long minutes, her face against his neck, his mouth against the stiff white veil. When he could speak, he muttered, "Am I invited then to sleep with the ghosts of kings?"

Nibbling on his ear, she answered, "No. You are being taken prisoner." Her voice was shaky. "My royal prisoner, my very special, very own King Max."

Kalina having urgent duties that could not wait even for newly crowned kings, Max spent the afternoon touring the *Villa d'Este*. The severely maimed were not brought here nor those whose death was near. In fact, there were few soldiers in the beds, the patients being, in the main, women, children, the crippled, the old—all who had been caught in shellfire or forced to leave gutted homes with everything they owned destroyed. The field hospitals and aid stations that received the freshly wounded soldiers lay some kilometers away.

"When the battles started, Madame Olkonsky drove an ambulance right onto the battlefield," Mam'selle Gaillard informed him. "But the authorities stopped it." The nurse also told him that he could call her Lily, explaining with a blush that their directress preferred the more informal American way of address. "After hours, we all call her Madame," she added.

"Call me Max," he responded, grinning wickedly at the old maid. The cocky Irish-American was an immediate sensation in a place where men, especially young men, were as rare as hen's teeth.

Kalina refused to end her workday before the sun set. "We must carry on as usual," she told him. Then—with an impish glint in her black eyes—"November nights are long and made for love."

Darkness came at last. After a supper of bread and wine and sausage, Max sprawled on the massive bed that kings had slept in. He tossed about, seeking a comfortable spot. The mattress was thin and lumpy. Maybe old Charlemagne himself had used it, he thought wryly, wondering why the rich Mrs. Murav had not replaced it with a plump feathery creation. The room was pleasant enough with low, dark furniture, soft with the patina of age. The view was unsurpassed. The little courtyard was thick with trees and vines on trellises while a skylight in the ceiling showed a square of starry sky.

Idly, he wondered what Mary Lesko was so hellbent on telling him. Probably news from Homestead. Maybe the steelworkers finally got their eight-hour day. He hadn't kept up on the labor movement, newspapers from America not being an everyday article in the places he had called home these past years.

He sighed. Despite his great happiness at finding his beloved Kalina well and still in love with him as much as he was with her, he felt an overwhelming sadness at the thought of Stan and Elena Lesko. They had been like family to him, the family he had never had back in New York.

When Kalina came, she had to waken him. "Hmm," she dimpled. "My swain is not as ardent as I had hoped."

"Been on the road a long time," he mumbled. "Twelve years this month." He shut his eyes and pulled her down to lay atop his stretched-out form. "But I don't want to think of that awful time when I was facing the electric chair."

"Think about nothing but *amour*," she whispered, pressing against him in erotic little movements. Max lay still, letting the almost forgotten desire bloom in his veins. But his lover was impatient. Bolting up, she slid off the bed and tossed the white veil from her head. She began to undo the line of buttons on her long, white uniform. Her fingers shook and she cursed in her sweet, ladylike way.

With a whoop, Max was upon her. "Hey, that's my job."

His own big fingers were small improvement, and they ended by undoing only half the slippery buttons, enough to allow Kalina to step out of the stiff cotton. Shoes and stockings were quickly disposed of, and she stood before him in a kind of satiny chemise through which her nipples and the enticing triangle between her thighs showed darkly.

"You have no brassiere," he burst out, "and where's the almighty corset?"

"I got rid of the corset years ago and as for the brassiere"—a wave of scarlet enveloped her face and neck—"I took off the thing this afternoon"—her eyes grew brilliant with desire—"because I could not bear it any longer."

"Bear what?" He pressed her to him, so that the bulge between his legs thrust into the satin where it caressed her mound. "Say it, darling."

Shamelessly she clung to him while wave after wave of desire convulsed her. "I want you, Max, so very much."

It was almost exactly what she had said at sixteen when they had first coupled in the boxcar out of New York, but the resemblance between the two events ended there. The

301

frightened, inexperienced virgin of 1900 was gone, and in her place was a mature and sensuous woman. The Kalina of 1914 had known married love with Stefan Murav, who was adept at bringing a woman to ecstasy.

Feverishly, she undressed her lover and within seconds thrust him back down upon the bed, rolling round and round with glee.

"Charlemagne slept here," she said, giggling, "but not on this mattress of course."

"Can't say that I blame him," he replied. "It's filled with rocks."

Then there was an end to talk.

Later, she was to tell him that she had given the feather mattress that belonged between the hard-oak bedposts to the old women's ward because old bones needed comfort more than hers. But now there was no time for that, as two love-starved people strained for each other, rolling about and tossing on the lumpy mattress as though they were roped together.

So many times in her lonely, heartsick nights Kalina had imagined the joyous reunion with her first sweetheart, the only man she ever truly loved. In her feverish nighttime fantasies they floated together on a cloud, their faces grave and stiff with longing. At the joining of their love-starved bodies, the angels would sing, stars would fall, the heavens themselves would explode.

None of this celestial nonsense happened, but their love-making was more joyous than in her wildest dreams. They cried, they moaned, they shrieked, but most of all they laughed, these two who had not thought to meet again on this earth. Nothing was sacred. Arms, legs, buttocks, breasts, the delicious spaces between, were fair game for biting and caressing. They gasped, they reached, they strained. Yearning had never been so painful, so unenduringly sweet.

And when he plunged his swollen manhood into her warm sweet mound, she shivered with a kind of swooning delight that no story she had ever read could even begin to make real. When at last he shouted with his own release and her own fulfillment came with a kind of shivering, beating, swooning excitement, she knew that anything she had ever experienced with Stefan was mere child's play. The feel of Max within her pulsing body was to Kalina like nothing she had ever encountered before. She was on fire, she was freezing cold, she trembled as one in the throes of fever. Her insides exploded while a kind of paralyzing warmth pervaded every bone, every muscle, every nerve.

The pins fell out of her hair, and almost savagely, Max took the heavy mass in his hands and covered their bodies as with a blanket. They cried out as one, each oblivious to the other's shrieks. For long moments their straining, poking, stroking continued unabated. Incredibly, the desire that had been so hot and searing that nothing on earth, they thought, could possibly assuage it gradually diminished, and the lovers were at peace. Nature took its course, the demons within were quieted, and Max and Kalina lay sated, side by side, not touching. The heat of their love-making surrounded them as a hot desert wind.

The countries that were their bodies had been rediscovered and explored. Claims were staked afresh. Both felt that never in their lives could they give themselves to any other. It was unthinkable.

Drenched with lovers' sweat, they lay side by side staring at the ceiling where painted cherubic angels floated, blowing with puffed-out cheeks at their tiny trumpets as though the world had not just seen the cataclysmic struggle by which two human beings go about making love. The cold, October rain drummed on the courtyard flags, the distant throb of gunfire and the occasional yellow flare of rockets from both sides of the battlefront were grim reminders that those two lovers were taking their pleasure in the midst of war.

The breakfast bell sounded throughout the villa, but there was no sign of the directress in the staff refectory. At the long tables, knowing smiles, sly glances, and lifted brows appeared. It was no secret where the handsome

303

American had slept. Love had come to their beloved Kalina Olkonsky. That she had a husband — somewhere — and a very rich one too, all were fully aware.

"But this is *La Belle France*, not stodgy old England or stiff-necked America," more than one was heard to remark. "Every true Frenchman loves *amour*."

In the days that followed, it became clear that the beautiful American lady was madly in love with the handsome red-headed American who had shown up on her doorstep from out of nowhere. She went about her duties wrapped in a kind of glow that made everyone in the sprawling place feel happy just to look at her.

"Ah, *languissante d'amour*, she is lovesick," crooned the Frenchwomen. Most of them had someone at the front — husband, sweetheart, lover, son, brother — many had lost these precious ones. They wished her joy. Take love while you can, where you can, with whom you can. That was the philosophy in the midst of the hell their beautiful country had become.

"She's been sprinkled with stardust," sighed Mary Lesko as she sat at coffee in her curtained alcove with a group of women known as the "American contingent." They were ten, mostly women who had been caught at the outbreak of hostilities while traveling in Europe and who feared the terror from German torpedoes on the high seas more than they feared the shelling a few kilometers away.

Among the group was Wanda Hardie, who had been living for the past two years with her Alec in Paris, where he was studying under heart specialists at the famed Sorbonne. When the war came, Alec volunteered his skills to the French army while his wife signed up with the Red Cross. By the sheerest coincidence, she was sent to *Villa d'Este*, where the woman whose maid she had been in Pittsburgh was in charge.

"Fortunes of war," commented Max when he finally met with Wanda and Mary Lesko in Kalina's office two days after his arrival. Both girls had blossomed. A qualified nurse, Wanda had been supremely happy in Canada with her Alec. Mary's womanly curves and radiant face fair took his breath away.

They all embraced, Max weeping happily along with the women. He held Mary at arm's length. "What happened to the skinny snot-nosed kid who used to wake me up with coffee every morning in that stuffy little room?" Hastily pulling a handkerchief from his pocket, he blew his nose. "Damn, but I miss the old days. You and your parents and your kid brothers—"

"We felt that way about you too, Max," she said. "No matter what happened afterward—the mess with the strike and the murder of Libby Hughes. We never for a minute thought you did it."

Kalina had been shuffling papers on her desk while the others enjoyed their happy reunion. Now, looking up, she said, "Mary, what is this big news you have to tell us?" Her eyes widened in fear. "Is it your mother? Have her lungs gone bad again?"

"No, she's fine. Thanks to you, Kalina." She turned to Max. "This wonderful lady sent her to a sanatorium."

"We're not here to talk about me," said Kalina tersely. "Out with it, girl." Her brows contracted. "Are you in love? Engaged? Do you want to return to Vienna to your music studies?" She dimpled. "Have you been offered a leading role?"

Mary was in the grip of a fit of giggles that threatened to turn into hysteria, but presently she composed herself and drew a rumpled envelope from her apron pocket. She waved it at Max. "This is from Helena. You remember her?"

"Sure. The girl who could have freed me with her testimony but was hounded out of town by Hughes and Murav."

"Well, she will now. Testify, I mean. In fact, she *has*! Millard Hughes is dead, and Murav"—she shot a glance at Kalina—"well, wherever he is, Stefan Murav is no longer in the United States, and besides, he was not exactly an eyewitness."

Kalina's face was like the sun. She gave a little strangled cry and rose up in her chair. "Darling, you are free," she shouted at Max. "With both your chief accusers gone, no jury will convict you. Oh, you must sail for America immediately and demand a hearing."

Mary thrust the letter at Max, who scanned the contents swiftly. "She says no trial is needed, that since I escaped from jail before I was indicted, and with the chief eyewitness Hughes dead —" He gazed at Kalina, and his face was stricken. "I could have come home three years ago when Libby's father died." It was a cry of agony.

Heedless of the others, Kalina rushed into his arms. After a moment, she turned on Mary. "You wicked girl! How long have you known about this?"

Mary pursed her lips. "Only about a month. Helena didn't want you to know until she was certain. She's been living in California with her husband and five children, and when she came home for a visit, it all came about. Seems the judge called her in and talked to her about the old charge."

"Helena always wanted a large family," broke in Wanda in an effort to lighten the atmosphere.

There was never any question of Max's sailing for America now. "Even if I cared to risk being torpedoed into kingdom come by the German subs, I don't want to leave you a single moment," he told Kalina.

Mary pursed her lips and impatiently took the letter from Max's hands. "You don't have to go home right now, anyway. Helena dictated her testimony to a court stenographer and it's all there in the files."

Max turned to Kalina, seemingly bewildered. "I'm free! I'm free, do you understand?"

But freedom was not the word to describe the young man whose life had just been given back to him by a few sentences in a letter from America. Ironically, he was caught in a web of love, he was imprisoned with his beloved Kalina in a paradise that needed no walls or vigilant angel to protect its borders.

In daylight they were apart, Kalina working her miracles with shell-shocked and evacuated civilians while Max found many uses for his man's strength and mechanical skills. At night, blind with fatigue, the lovers sank into the lumpy bed in Charlemagne's old love nest. Often, it seemed that nerves and bones and flesh could not evoke a single spark of passion, and they slept, entwined. But in the night, the moon filled the skylight, waking them, they moved together and began the ancient, mindless ritual of love-making.

"What if Stefan comes?" asked Max one time.

"He won't," she replied. "And if he does, my sentries will inform me in time for you to hide."

He frowned. "I will do battle with the scoundrel. I will be your knight in shining armor."

She laughed. "His wife's chastity is probably the last thing on his mind right now. His last letter was full of his plans to travel to Poland to lay the groundwork for his new government there in his native land."

Max let out an astonished bellow. "You mean your husband actually means all that baloney about having himself crowned king of Poland? The man's stark, raving mad." He drew her close. "I hope someone takes a potshot at him or he falls in front of a German tank."

Shocked, Kalina wriggled out of his arms. "Max! He is after all the father of my children. Even if Zuska gave birth to them, they are just as dear as if they had come out of my own womb."

He looked abject. "Sorry I got so violent. But I go crazy when I think that you're still married to him." He sat up as if inspired. "You're known here as Olkonsky. Maybe we could get married without anyone knowing you're the wife of the detested Murav."

"Silly, but thanks for asking."

They also talked of quieter matters. Max spun tales of the places he had been, of the people he had met, of the work he was forced to do to survive. "I worked coal mines in Wales, gold mines in South Africa, rustled cattle in the Argentine, even did a stretch in an English steel mill." The best times were spent, he said, on the water. "I crewed freighters to China, worked fish trawlers on the Mediterranean and even steamships crossing the Atlantic."

"You could have come home," she exclaimed, "and gone way out West or up to Alaska. You changed your name. No one would have known." Her black eyes regarded him soberly. "Sometimes I think that you were actually enjoying yourself, being foot-loose and fancy-free. A married man can't go to all those exotic places or do all those interesting things."

Max flopped over on his back, staring at the angels. "You may be right. If you had only been free—" He chewed his lip. "Once I got to wandering, I couldn't stop. It was as though I thought the farther from America and you I got, the easier it would all become."

Kalina talked about her travels with Stefan. "We were wanderers too, in a high-society kind of way. I find it amazing how the very rich scuttle frantically from place to place seeking the happiness their money cannot bring." She wept for her children in the south of France, her tears dampening his chest. "I miss them sorely," she said, "but when the Germans began their offensive in August, the nuns at Dunia's school evacuated the pupils to Auvergne and offered to take Stefi too. I felt it was the best thing. The kaiser's navy was sinking ships right and left, and crossing the Atlantic was too dangerous at the time."

Sometimes they lay comfortably side by side staring at the faded angels floating in their clouds, thinking of the country they had left behind, wondering when and if they would ever see their America again. "When I was sixteen, I searched for the real America," she said, "but now I know it's nearer than I ever thought. Right here in my heart."

On a blustery day in March, 1915, three months after it had begun, their paradise came to an explosive end. Red Cross International sent word that the *Villa d'Este* must close its doors and evacuate to the south.

As far as you can get, but leave at once. The Huns are bombing everything, your red cross on the roof will no longer protect you. They are using poison gas.

The enemy had severed the telephone lines, so the message was brought by courier in the person of a neighboring farmer too old for combat, a weathered, little man named Dupont. "I'm getting out by boat," he said, "me and my whole family. Traveling by land is impossible, what with trenches everywhere, and the Boche are even bombing the trains."

"Bastards," grunted Max. His eyes flew to the sky. For the past week airplanes had been circling overhead like buzzards waiting for the kill. There had even been a small "dogfight," or sky battle, between the Allied flyers and the Germans. Good thing Manfred was in the cavalry, he thought. Max couldn't imagine his hiking pal putting his hand in a basket and dropping a bomb on innocent women and children. But, though his heart said "no," his head said "yes." Von Richthofen had been trained as a soldier, and soldiers, especially those born in Prussia, did not disobey an order, no matter how barbarous it seemed.

The bombardment was getting uncomfortably close. One of the barns behind the Villa was set afire by a bursting shell, the fire destroying a great quantity of flour and other foodstuffs. A school suffered a direct hit and five children were brought in for burial.

Weeks before, back in February, Max had urged Kalina to evacuate, but she held on stubbornly. "The battle's been close before," she said lightly. "The Allies and the Germans go back and forth like a seesaw."

But the command from headquarters could not be ignored. Monsieur Dupont offered help in gathering boats—barges, fishing smacks, pleasure craft, even a houseboat that had been beached on a sandbar but was still seaworthy. In ordinary times, the rivers of France were busy thoroughfares, and thousands of people lived and died and raised their families on the water.

"I myself was once a boatman, a *batelier*," he said proudly. "I brought vegetables and milk to Paris each day. I know the waters like my own farm."

By nightfall other boatmen appeared as if summoned by a genie, each with a seaworthy vessel, mostly flat-bottomed barges. It was decided that they would head for Paris, and follow the Seine to Chatillon where a château had been made available.

Airplanes did not fly in the dark, so Kalina and her staff labored through the night, bundling up the children and older patients in blankets and settling them in the boats so that they were tightly packed like so many sausages. Each was given a canteen and a bundle of bread and cheese. Dupont assured them that in Paris they could get more supplies. The French capital was not yet under siege, but the battle was getting uncomfortably close.

The country of France was blessed with a marvelously intricate network of canals that connected one river with another, and with Dupont in the lead, the evacuees slipped out of the *Villa d'Este* tributary and onto a narrow stream scarcely wider than a ditch. The men who were able stood upright and casting experienced eyes about for hidden rocks and debris, pushed the barges with long poles through the shallow waters. There were in addition many intricately constructed weirs and locks to negotiate. Max, bringing up the rear, piloted the ancient houseboat with Kalina at his side.

"Heigh, ho, the sailor boy," he joked as he took the wheel. "I'm back on the rolling seas."

They had been poling about an hour. The inky sky was fading, and a milky sun poked through the clouds. Kalina sighed with relief and prayed that it wouldn't rain. So many of the vessels were open to the weather. But, thank the Holy Virgin, they were clear of the worst of the battle zone, which lay to the east beyond the Marne.

Suddenly a noise like hell torn asunder shattered the dawn, and a fierce bombardment began to the north in the region of Verdun. The very air trembled as if a giant god had taken hold of the earth and was shaking it in anger. The sky turned red and orange and purple and white.

Kalina looked up and gasped. "It's like a gigantic blast furnace."

Max took a hand from the wheel and drew her close. "Don't look up or back, just straight ahead. The shells won't come this far."

His words became etched forever in her brain for in the next instant the wheel was wrenched from his hands, the houseboat flew into the air, and Kalina found herself flying helplessly after it. The sun, exploding into a thousand pieces, disappeared. The world turned dark.

She woke up on her back on the floor of a farmhouse kitchen. Anxious faces hovered over her. Sidonie, Mary, Wanda. Kalina opened her eyes and swiftly closed them against the knifelike pain in her head.

She heard Mary say, "She's okay," and begin to weep.

An exploding shell had hit the canal directly behind the houseboat. Those who had not been struck by flying shrapnel or drowned in the waters had sought shelter in the empty houses along the banks. Most of the occupants had already fled. Kalina had been fished out of the water as had everyone else on the houseboat, but there was no sign of Max.

"The boatmen thrust their poles into every inch of the canal bottom," sobbed Mary, "but there was nothing."

"The poor devil was thrown clear like you, Madame," opined Monsieur Dupont. "He may be out of his mind or hurt. He's probably wandering around on the other side, right into the trenches."

No one had to be told what the Boche swine did with the hapless civilians caught behind the lines. They were shot as spies with no questions asked.

Chapter Sixteen

Southern France, June, 1915

"Kalina is out of her mind. I've seen it a hundred times on the battlefield." Dr. Hardie ran his fingers distractedly through his sandy thatch. "We call it shellshock although it can happen also to those who have not been actually hit."

His wife Wanda stood anxiously at his side, and the Scottish physician, who had tended to Kalina when she had given birth to her stillborn son, turned to his wife. "The appearance of her eyes indicates that there is some concussion too. But with time and care and her own strong spirit, she'll recover."

The young doctor had been in Paris studying diseases of the mind when the war broke out. As refugees poured in from the north, both he and his nurse-wife had volunteered their services for Red Cross work. He was assigned to base hospitals at the front while Wanda was sent to *Villa d'Este*.

Concerned for the welfare of his wife in besieged Champagne and suffering himself from extreme fatigue and a nasty shrapnel wound in the hip that had refused to heal properly, he left his post and set out to join her in Champagne. He had arrived at the hospital minutes after the motley evacuation fleet left the dock.

"Why did you wait so long to leave," he said crossly to Wanda. "The fighting was not ten kilometers away."

Shrugging, she cast an affectionate glance at Kalina,

who sat hunched in a chair, her hands clasped in her lap, her black eyes fixed on nothing. She wore a simple home-spun frock in unrelieved black that had been left behind by the former occupants of the house when they fled to the south.

She seemed like a child who had to sit in a corner as punishment. Wanda tucked a ragged shawl around Kalina's shoulders. "As you say, she possesses a strong spirit that refuses to admit defeat until it is almost upon her."

The battle drawing ever closer from the north and east, it was urgent that they resume their flight, and since Kalina's physical injuries were slight—a bump on the head, a scratch here and there—a new vessel was acquired to replace the lost houseboat. With Alec at the wheel, they turned south once more. Alec had painted a new name on the hull. "Let's call it *The Max*," he said. "If O'Hara is alive and searching for us, an unusual name on the boat might help."

They could not wait for Max to appear, though Alec assured them that he was probably wandering somewhere along the Marne and maybe had shellshock himself.

The château promised by the Red Cross was in the region of Tours, a distance of two weeks' journey or more by canal. But, at the doctor's suggestion, they headed instead directly for the mountains of Auvergne, still deeper to the south and further east. "That's where the Murav children are being cared for," said Alec. "A reunion with Stefi and Dunia could do miracles to hasten their mother's recovery."

Wanda Hardie and Mary Lesko, together with the French girl Sidonie, whose own experience with emotional shock was still fresh in her mind, spelled each other in caring for their directress. A fourth, a Belgian whose husband and child had perished at Mons, volunteered to help. Stately and blond with a Venus-like figure, the young woman, whose name was Clara, had a kind of sunny glow about her person that appealed to Kalina.

As they skirted past Paris and moved onto the pretty little streams and canals flowing from the broader Seine, the ailing Madame Olkonsky, now addressed as Madame Murav, was heard to call ever more frequently for Clara. In her delusion, Kalina imagined the Belgian to be Zuska or sometimes Libby. Both of these lost loved ones had possessed the same golden aura that Clara exuded.

"She's living in the past," said a worried Wanda.

"Excellent, excellent," replied her husband. "At least she has roused from her earlier dormant state. Her mind is no longer static. Gradually, she will move on to the present, I promise."

When Mary or Wanda tended her, Kalina imagined them as Aunt Litka or someone called Hania, whom Mary said was her mother in Poland. She conducted long conversations with all the lost loved ones, who marched through her fevered brain as warmly alive as they had been so long ago.

It was April, and, as the refugees moved toward warmer climes, the trees along the banks turned a frothy green. The smell of peach, apricot, and plum blossoms wafted over the rolling countryside, and children were seen frolicking before neat, stone houses.

The first of June was hot and cloudy with dark rainclouds overhead, but the smell of roses filled the Auvergne. Alec edged *The Max*'s prow into a tributary that came down from the mountain village beyond which lay the convent of the Sisters of Charity who operated Dunia's school.

Except for occasional ramblings and periods of brooding silence, Kalina was herself again, much of her delusion having vanished. She asked for Stefi and Dunia and when told she would see them within hours, danced around the deck like a girl.

She never mentioned Max's name; him alone she had blocked out of her mind.

"As far as she is concerned, the romantic interlude with her lover at *Villa d'Este* never happened," said Alec. "For her, Max O'Hara never returned from his self-imposed exile after his escape from prison."

When the evacuees left the boat at sunset, Kalina glanced at the name on the hull, remarking, "Max. What an odd name for a boat! They're always named for girls, aren't they?" She drew her dark brows together. "I once knew a Max. He was an Irishman."

They hired a goat cart to take them to the convent where Dunia and Stefi had been living since the previous July when Kalina had fled from Sarajevo and decided against taking them to America. Nestled atop a stark volcanic peak overlooking a historic walled town, turreted and surrounded by a dried-up moat, the convent was a castle-like fortress built by Richard the Lion-Heart on his way home to England from a crusade. Its architecture was strongly reminiscent of *Villa d'Este*, and, as they approached, Kalina stood a long time gazing at the place. Alec held his breath, hoping the sight would trigger her memory, but she said only, "France has so many ancient structures. In America, everything is new."

With its slits of windows, its cold, damp stone walls and floors, the interior was forbidding. When the Mother Superior came into the gloomy, vaulted, reception-room chamber, she proved to be no more cheerful than her surroundings. She flicked cold blue eyes at Kalina, who still wore her peasant black, and exclaimed in an incredulous tone, "*You* are Madame Stefan Murav?"

Alec stepped forward to speak, but Kalina waved him back. "We have fled the war in the north, Mother Celeste, and I have come to fetch my children." Her own tone was polite but tinged with hauteur.

The nun pursed her lips. "I trust you have brought some money to settle your account. We have heard nothing from your husband for many months."

"It will be taken care of in due course. Now, may I see Dunia and Stefi?" Kalina flushed with irritation but seemed fully in command, her languor of the past month dissipating in favor of her customary efficiency.

When the children were brought in, twelve-year-old Stefi stood immobilized, staring at Kalina as if at a ghost.

"Mama," he began and moved toward her stiffly. He bit his lips, fighting unmanly tears. Kalina held out her arms. "Stefi, come here."

Weeping like a baby, the gangly boy hurled himself against Kalina with such force she would have fallen to the rough stones had not Wanda pushed a heavy wooden chair beneath her.

"Oh, Mama, I thought you were dead," the boy sobbed, his head in her lap. Kalina's own tears flowed freely, but she said cheerfully. "As you can see, darling, I am very much alive."

Dunia stood aside, some distance from Kalina. "That's what the old bitch Celeste told us," she said, her pretty face sulky. She said that the Red Cross had telephoned to report that *Villa d'Este* had been bombed and was nothing but rubble and that everyone inside the hospital was dead."

Shaking her head from side to side, Kalina murmured, "I'm so sorry, Dunia, that you have suffered from a false report. The Villa must have been hit shortly after we evacuated. Nobody was inside, I assure you."

Dunia was wearing a baggy knee-length dress in a bilious purple color that reminded Kalina of the dress that had brought her so much grief as a bride in Pittsburgh. She extended a hand toward Dunia. "Dunia, darling, come here. I've missed you so."

Woodenly, the girl approached and bent to kiss her adoptive mother on the cheek. Drawing back quickly, she wailed, "Please take us out of here. I'll die if I have to stay in this dungeon a minute longer. Everybody hates me and"—she tugged at the high collar of her frock—"they make me dress like a child."

"You are certainly no child," broke in Alec, smiling at the girl. "You are very pretty, Dunia, like your mother."

Dunia snapped, "She is not my mother. She's my aunt. My real mother is in America. Aunt Anusia writes that she's a famous actress in California."

Ignoring the gibe about their relationship, Kalina inquired softly, "When did you last hear from Aunt Anusia?"

Drawing a rumpled letter from her pocket, the girl

handed it to Kalina. "There's a letter for you too in the envelope. Aunt Anusia said I was not to open it but to send it along to you or give it to you if you should come for a visit. She didn't have your address."

"I'll read it presently, but first we must have some supper and make some plans. I can assure you, Dunia, that we will leave this place in the morning. You may pack your trunks."

Dunia snorted. "This rag is all I have, Mama Kalina. We had to leave our clothing in Paris."

Kalina sighed with relief. She was still Mama Kalina to Zuska's obviously unhappy daughter. Mary Lesko raised her brows as if to say that the girl lacked the manners to be expected in one educated in a convent, but Kalina threw her a sidelong glance. Handing the tearful Stefi to his former nursemaid, she took Dunia by the hand. "We are going to Switzerland, darling, and you can shop to your heart's desire."

Despite her cheery tone, her mother's heart was heavy. Dunia's brown eyes had a lackluster look about them, her skin was sallow, and her abundant chestnut hair had apparently not been washed for weeks. Her rude behavior troubled Kalina not at all. Memories of herself at sixteen were sharp and clear. She had blown hot and cold in her feelings toward Aunt Litka, sometimes loving her dutifully, sometimes rebellious at the unending knee-pants work. Often she had spoken in the heartless tones with which Dunia was now addressing her.

As for Stefi, he was much too thin, even for a fast-growing adolescent. His nose was running, and he had a nasty cough. His mother and her mother before her had been born with weak lungs. Kalina took his hand again and breathed a fervent prayer that the boy would be spared the curse of tuberculosis.

Supper in the bleak refectory consisted of hard bread, cheese, and watered-down wine. Delicately, trying to be unobtrusive, Kalina picked bits of mold from the cheese.

"Old Celeste says mold is good for you," said Dunia nastily. The girl appeared to be half-starved and picked crumbs from her plate with a wetted finger just as she used to do when a baby.

"Please, darling, don't speak of the Mother Superior in that disrespectful way," admonished Kalina mildly. But she was truly distressed at the miserable food and privately sympathized with the children.

Later, as she sat on a cot in a curtained alcove, she glanced up to see Dr. Hardie just returning from a walk around the grounds. His kindly face was grim. "The moat is filled with garbage and as for the kitchens —" He threw up his hands. "What on earth do they do with the money the parents send? All of the children are suffering from malnutrition." He gazed somberly out the slash of window into the moonless night. "Mother Celeste complains that there is no food in the town because everything is sent to the armies."

"She is probably telling the truth," muttered Kalina, reluctant to think that pious folk could also be avaricious. "I am so grateful to you, Alec, for bringing me here instead of to Tours as planned." She bowed her head, covered her face with her hands, and groaned in self-recrimination, "How blithely I gave my precious little ones into the hands of strangers. I've been living in a fool's paradise. I've seen children fresh from invaded areas who were healthier than Dunia and Stefi."

Kalina had lost her cash when she had been pitched into the canal, but Alec had letters of credit that more than satisfied the unpaid bills. Maddeningly, in the morning as they were preparing to board the goat cart that had brought them up the mountain, a violent thunderstorm delayed their departure. Even if they wanted to brave the pouring rain, the roads, so Mother Celeste assured them, would be impassable for days.

The waiting was made tolerable for the children by the constant attention of the young women — Mary, Sidonie, and Wanda. Taking an immediate and passionate liking to Sidonie, Dunia allowed a rare smile to brighten her dour expression. The sunny Clara, who had been so instrumental in bringing Kalina out of her shock, had tearfully left them at the foot of the mountain. A sister lived on a farm a mere ten kilometers downriver.

On Sunday morning, the sun being out at last, the visitors made ready to leave again. As they came out of the chapel after Mass, a young nun approached Kalina and informed her that a man who said he was her husband awaited her in the reception room.

Stefan! Here? Such a thing was impossible. His last letter had come from somewhere on the Black Sea where he had gone to ensure that his shiploads of armaments and supplies that he had sold to the Turks did not fall into the wrong hands. "There's a fierce battle being waged for Constantinople," he had written. "I'll be here in the eastern sector until it's settled." The letter had come a few days before they had evacuated.

The large reception chamber was dark, the narrow windows never catching the sun even on the hottest day. Stefan stood with his back to her, gazing at a wall tapestry on which a battle was being waged between ancient opponents. His hands were clasped behind his back, and a wide-brimmed straw hat was pulled down low over his head.

Abruptly, he turned and walked swiftly toward her, his nailed boots hitting the stones with sharp, metallic sounds. "Where the hell have you been?" was his angry greeting. "I've been chasing after you for weeks. They said you went by boat, but you must have traveled on every backwater in the whole damned country."

She didn't answer at first but put her arms around his neck and kissed him fully on the lips. The love she had had for her husband as a bride was gone, but she cared for him as a human being and the father of her children. "I've been wild with anxiety for you, Stefan," she exclaimed. "Must you hurl yourself into the midst of battle? Surely, you have people working for you who—"

He pushed her from him. "Where are the children? I want to see them." He might have been speaking to a stranger.

When the children ran in, Dunia favored her father with the hugs and kisses she continued to withhold from Kalina,

319

but Stefi clung to Kalina's skirts, fearful of this man he had scarcely seen since he was a toddler. In the past, during the infrequent times when the father was with the family, he seldom bothered to make himself acquainted with his son. Pretty little Dunia had received much more attention from the busy Mr. Murav.

Though Murav was obviously exhausted from his journey, he insisted that they all depart for the foot of the mountain as soon as possible. Kalina was puzzled about his appearance. Her husband had always been well-groomed in the extreme, the luxuriant handlebar mustache and beard unfailingly trimmed and glistening with scented oil. He commissioned his suits from the best tailors and was almost annoyingly fastidious about his personal toilet. It was not uncommon, in the house on Rutherford Drive, to hear shouts and wails emanating from the basement where he was berating some unfortunate laundry maid for failing to produce the proper stiffness in his shirts.

Why the ragged attire now? He looked like a beggar. As they climbed into the goat carts to proceed down the steep mountain road, Kalina gazed almost unbelievingly at Stefan Murav. Besides the straw hat that had several holes in the crown and brim, he was garbed in a woolen suit that not only looked as though it had been scrounged from a rag barrel but smelled to high heaven. She was reminded of the clothing taken from the dead during the battle in Champagne. His boots were caked with mud, and the fingernails, which he had buffed and polished each night before retiring, were encrusted with dirt.

Her own black dress, though plain, was clean. She would purchase more suitable clothing in the very next sizable town.

"Stefan," she said lightly, deciding to approach the matter with humor. "Are you perhaps in disguise? What happened to your clothes?"

He glanced up from a letter he had pulled from his pocket. His mouth widened in a smile, but there was little mirth in the amber eyes. "They're after me, all of them."

"Who, dear husband?" The scheme at Sarajevo after the

320

archduke's assassination came to mind. *You are in danger. Anarchists are out there, waiting to shoot you.*

"Anarchists of course," he snapped, returning to his letter. "They are determined to eliminate all the crowned heads of Europe. The heirs as well are in danger."

"But Stefan—" She stopped, remembering his delusion about becoming the king of Poland. In the seat behind her, Alec leaned forward to touch her on the shoulder. She turned to see him mouth silently, "Humor him for now."

"Zuska is very ill. Dying. She's in Pittsburgh with Anusia."

Stefan's startling announcement thrust all else from Kalina's mind, even her concern for his sanity. "Zuska ill and at home with Anusia? Your sister has not written to me about it."

Swiftly, she pulled from her own deep pocket the letter Dunia had given her on the day of their arrival. She had delayed in reading it since Anusia's missives were usually of a depressing nature and never said anything that could not bear waiting.

Dear Kalina,
Your cousin is with me. She is dying of the consumption and the doctors don't give her much time. Why did you not come when I wrote Stefan about it . . .

Impatiently, Stefan thrust his letter at his wife, knocking her own from her hand. To her dismay she saw that it was postmarked in January. Six months! Surely Zuska was already dead.

Stefan erupted in a nasty laugh. "Probably wants to make a deathbed confession of all her sins."

Grateful that Dunia and Stefi were in the second cart with the Hardies and could not hear the conversation, Kalina spoke no more until they reached the tiny railroad station in the town. Then she said, "I must go to Zuska. She deserves to have someone of her own blood at her side when she dies."

321.

"Nonsense," snorted Stefan, standing at the ticket window where he was dickering in a loud voice with the stationmaster about tickets out of France. "We are going to Poland — all of us. Time we assumed our rightful positions in the government. The war is going badly for the Russians there. General Pilsudski of the Polish nationals has summoned me to pull things together."

He's fantasizing, thought Kalina, stricken.

Though Dunia was only inches shorter than he, Stefan picked her up like a little girl and whirled her around the platform in his arms. "You are going to be a princess, my pretty. How would you like that? There'll be balls and receptions and suitors by the mile."

Wailing, the frightened girl wrenched free and ran to Kalina, who stood open-mouthed, an anxious Alec at her side. "He's really mad," the doctor whispered. "We should get him to the hospital. It may be severe shellshock." He squeezed Kalina's hand reassuringly. "He was near the battle, you say?"

She nodded but was more concerned at the moment with the near-hysterical Dunia. "Of course we're not going to Poland," she scolded the girl. "Stop that caterwauling. We're all taking the train for Switzerland to our house on Lake Geneva."

Dunia raised a tearful face. "Oh, Mama Kalina, may I go stay with my friend Lini? When the rest of us were taken to the Auvergne, she went home to Switzerland. She invited me, and Stefi too, to come and stay as long as we want while you were working for the Red Cross, but old Celeste wouldn't let us go because she had no permission from you."

Reaching into a string bag that held her collection of letters and toilet articles, the girl triumphantly pulled out a much wrinkled envelope.

A feeling of relief and joy filled Kalina's heart as she read the warm words from Frau Winkler, Lini's mother. "Your children are more than welcome. Switzerland is strictly neutral and well out of the path of the dreadful war. Lini is wild to have you."

322

It was a good solution. With a free conscience she could take the ship for America to see Zuska. The letter said that a number of evacuees were also at the villa on the slopes of a pretty lake close to Geneva. She cast an anguished glance at Dunia and Stefi. Could she bear to part with them again after so short a time together? Especially now when Dunia was beginning to smile again and show affection for her Mama Kalina? The girl had bitterly resented being left with the nuns.

She could. She must. The young must serve the old. Though at thirty-three it was ludicrous to think of Zuska as old. Zuska would never be old. She would die in youth, forever beautiful in memory.

There was a whole lifetime ahead for Kalina and her children. For her cousin, there was only now. Pray God she was still alive.

Dunia's radiant face confirmed the wisdom of her decision. The hug she gave her Mama Kalina was hard and tight and long. "Oh, Mama Kalina, I'll be so happy with Lini. I know I will. Switzerland is a wonderful place to live."

As for Stefi, his ready tears soon dried up when assured that there would be horses to ride and lots of male companionship for him. The adolescent boy had suffered much embarrassment and loneliness as the only boy at the convent.

While Stefan drank wine in the station café, seemingly oblivious of his family on the platform making plans, it was decided quickly that Alec, Wanda, and Sidonie would accompany the children to Switzerland by train. Mary, anxious to return to her operatic career in Vienna, would continue her journey to the Austrian capital after a few days rest with the Winklers.

There was the problem of Stefan. "I cannot leave you with him in this irrational state," Alec protested. "He must come with us, by force if necessary. There is a clinic in Geneva that has worked marvels in cases like this." He cast anxious eyes toward the train. "We must hurry though."

Kalina gazed through the open door of the café at the

323

miserable, ragged figure hunched over a table, his hands clutching a carafe of red wine. "No," she said slowly. "Not only is he irrational and likely to cause a commotion on the train, but he is rapidly getting drunk. He is my husband. I can manage him." Her confident words did not match the uncertainty she felt within, but it was imperative that the children be removed from the spectacle of their father in his present state. They must remember him as he had been and, God and the Virgin willing, would be again.

The train pulled into the station. There was no time for further argument for it would depart in five minutes. With forced gaiety Kalina bade her beloved children farewell. If Dunia speculated on why her Mama Kalina felt it necessary to go across the U-boat-infested ocean to visit her Aunt Anusia and Zuska in America, she said nothing. Years before when she had discovered her true parentage, her avowals of affection for her natural mother had been passionate and frequent, but now Zuska's name was hardly ever on her lips. When told that Zuska was gravely ill, she cast down her brown eyes and said merely, "Get the best doctors for her, Mama Kalina." She did not ask to accompany Kalina on the voyage, for which Kalina was truly grateful for she most certainly would have had to refuse.

A rowdy group of hikers had gotten off the train and were now in the café. When Kalina entered, they looked up and whistled. "Ho, here's a pretty baggage!" One burly youth slung an arm around her waist and roughly pulled her into his arms. Drunkenly, Murav rose up and fell upon the ardent young man. "Unhand my wife, you swine!"

The café erupted into laughter and delighted shouts. "Fight! Fight! Fight! Let's see what the old cock can do."

The barman took a wooden club from the wall and swung it round and round his head. "Out, all of you. I'll have no brawls in here. Out, all of you, or I'll call the police."

The youth who had accosted Kalina felled Murav with a punch. Kalina ran to her husband and attempted to lift him up but, shaking her off, he yelled, "I am the king of Poland, you scum, and you'll all be tried for treason." He

324

pulled his father's tiny dagger from his trousers pocket. "I'll cut the throat of anyone who dares befoul my wife."

An uproar ensued, and people from the platform crowded in the doorway to watch with glee. What sport on a dull morning in Auvergne! The stationmaster pushed through the crowd and took Kalina by the arm. "Please, Madame, remove yourself and your husband, or I cannot guarantee his safety."

Terrified that Stefan might start swinging wildly about with the dagger, Kalina, together with the stationmaster, got Stefan out the door. He had never been a weak man, but his madness seemed to give him extra strength. He flailed about in desperation, like a wild animal who has been caged for a long time.

"My husband has been in the battle," she panted to the stationmaster.

He nodded with compassion in his eyes. "I've seen many like him. There is a clinic in Clermont-Ferrand, a half-day's journey by train. Take him there."

Once outside, the crazed Stefan became suddenly quiet. Casting grateful eyes on the stationmaster, who was short but strong and stocky, Kalina panted, "I am so grateful for your help, sir, I could not have handled him alone."

The man pursed his lips, shaking his head doubtfully. "He is calm now, Madame, but I fear he may become agitated before you reach the hospital. People in his condition are unpredictable. I cannot leave the station, but perhaps I can get someone else to help you." He scanned the platform. "Ah, there's a lad. I'll send him to fetch my son who lives nearby. He is a tall, strong young man."

Putting two fingers to his lips, he emitted a piercing whistle, which fetched a small boy who had been skating up and down the long wooden platform. The child, who appeared to be about ten, skated rapidly toward them. As he attempted to stop, he extended both hands to steady himself and fell against Stefan, who roared. Since Kalina and the stationmaster were still holding his arms tightly, he kicked the child away with such force that he fell down, wailing.

Releasing his hold on Stefan, the stationmaster helped the lad to his feet. At that moment a horse-drawn jitney drew up, and Kalina hailed the driver. The volatile Stefan was quiet once more, though breathing heavily, and Kalina turned to shout back at the stationmaster, who was still soothing the boy.

"I think it best, sir, that we be alone. Strangers seem to upset my husband unduly."

"Just hold onto him," the man replied. "He may try to escape."

The lad skated off again, seemingly unhurt, and, approaching the trap, the stationmaster addressed the driver. "Take Madame to the hotel, and keep an eye on her husband. He is ill." He turned to Kalina. "It is less than a kilometer into the town."

The driver turned round and fixed Stefan with a wary eye. "We could tie him up. There is some strong rope in the box on the roof that I use to fasten luggage."

Kalina stiffened. "No, that would surely undo him completely. He cannot endure any kind of restraint. Please, gentlemen, he is quiet now. I am confident we can manage to get him to the hotel." But under her breath, she muttered a quick prayer to the Virgin.

Meekly, Stefan climbed into the vehicle and sat down on the leather seat. Kalina joined him. He took her hand like a child and laid it in his lap. Thereupon, he leaned his head back and closed his eyes.

Kalina observed him for a moment or two. Deciding that he was dozing, she leaned back herself. He would be fine, and, if he started up again, the driver could stop and help to restrain him. Like many of his kind, the man had large muscles in his arms and shoulders from years of handling teams of horses.

Stefan twitched, his whole body jerking as in a spasm. He clutched her hand more tightly but did not open his eyes. He was dreaming, she thought, reliving some terrible secret nightmare of war.

The heart within her was heavy with anxiety. She was torn. Zuska lay dying in America, but Stefan needed her desperately here in Europe. It was obvious that she was the only one who could help him now. He was her husband, and her first loyalty lay with him.

In sickness and in health, till death us do part.

She must get him into the hospital and stay at his side until his sanity returned. Alec Hardie had said that familiar faces of loved ones were the best medicine for one in emotional shock.

As soon as the doctors thought it safe, they would sail together for America. Perhaps a male nurse could accompany them. Just as loving care and the sight of familiar faces had restored her mental health, so too might Stefan be healed by the sight of Anusia and Pittsburgh and the mill where he had been so happy as the big boss.

The horses galloped along the cobbled main street of the town, which was known simply as Castle after the fortress atop the mountain. Few people were about, it being Sunday, and those of the population who were not in church were probably sleeping or off to the countryside for an outing. The shops were boarded up. Beside her, Stefan continued to sleep. His hat had fallen over his brow; his filthy hands had become limp, releasing hers, and hung loosely between his knees.

He will be fine, she told herself again. She had suffered herself from a similar, though less violent irrational episode. Stefan Murav was a Cossack; he was invincible.

For a blessed moment, she closed her own eyes.

"There is the hotel," the driver called out. "The two-story building on the right."

Kalina glanced up and saw a frame-and-stucco structure with shuttered windows and a red-tiled roof standing amid an attractive park with trees. Behind it the forested mountain loomed.

The jitney slowed as they approached the hotel, and suddenly Stefan opened his eyes.

"We are at the hotel," Kalina said gently, taking his hand once more. "It looks cool inside, and we will order some tea and luncheon—"

With a violent movement, he jerked away and, catlike,

reared up and, leaping out of the speeding vehicle, landed feet first on the cobbles. With another catlike bound, he vanished into a copse of trees beside the hotel. The startled driver shouted and tugged at the reins, but the horses, shying at the commotion, broke into a gallop. They were well past the town before the animals were brought under control, and by the time they drove back to the place where Stefan had made his escape, he was nowhere to be found.

"He's scrambled up the mountain," commented the driver. "Folks get lost up there. You may never find him." He spat on the cobbles. "If he loses his footing—"

But Kalina wasn't listening. Picking up her long skirts, she was running through the park and toward the mountain behind. A few of the hotel guests sat at round café tables under wide-branching trees sipping coffee, and as she ran past, she shouted, "Please help me. My husband is very ill and has run up the mountain."

The lone man in the group rose up immediately and sprinted after Kalina, who had reached the foot of the mountain.

"We saw him running past," the young man said, "but we thought him engaging in early morning exercise."

Kalina stared with frustration at the forbidding volcanic peak. What was not sheer rock bluff was densely forested. The helpful young man directed her to a place where a path had been trodden into the dense growth by hikers. She followed him up the steep, narrow track for half an hour by her watch. Finally, exhausted, dusty, and hot, she stopped for breath.

The young man shook his head. "He would not probably stick to the path, Madame." He gestured to the thick growth on both sides. "He may be anywhere—"

Discouraged and close to tears, Kalina trudged back to the hotel along with the helpful young man.

The policeman who arrived shortly was not encouraging but promised to organize a search party immediately.

Kalina settled into the hotel, which was not as cool as it appeared to be. Each day the police sent out men to search the densely forested mountain. To compound the difficulty, the volcanic mount was pocketed with caves that wound torturously deep into the rock.

"I cannot risk the lives of my men by sending them into the caves," the police chief informed her.

The helpful young man and other guests with whom she conversed at dinner and in the park tried to reassure her with tales of lost hikers who had subsisted for weeks and months on the mountain. Small game was abundant, they said, and berries and roots.

He had his dagger, she thought, and could kill a rabbit or squirrel. He had told her once that he and Anusia had run off from an orphanage and had survived in a forest for almost a month, eating off the land.

Despite its barren appearance, the young man assured her also that many streams threaded their way through the rock.

Two weeks later, there being no sign of the missing Murav, the police suggested she cease her vigil. They would care for Stefan if he were found. But they also hinted strongly that they could not devote any more time and men to the search.

Kalina sadly boarded a train for Marseilles where she had booked passage for America. Their small French ship would be escorted across the ocean by a convoy of combined military and civilian craft. A vicious wolf pack of German submarines was ravaging the northern routes. The sinking of the *Lusitania* in May with a great loss of innocent lives was but the latest in a series of torpedo attacks.

A few days out into the voyage, Kalina leaned on the ship's rail, gazing miserably into the dark waters. She continued to agonize over Stefan. Was he dead on the mountain? Had he run off again to meet the battle? The police would continue to search, they had assured her. Should she have struck out herself, blindly? He was probably headed for Poland. "No, Madame," the police had warned. "You cannot think of going to Poland. The entire country is a battlefield, the bloodiest in the war till now, with the Turks and Russians going at it hammer and tongs. They say there's even poison gas."

Searching through Europe, she could die too and for what? For a madman who had thrust home and family aside for a grandiose delusion of power?

Zuska needed her in Pittsburgh. She had fulfilled her obligation to Stefan as much, at least, as was in her power to do so.

"Are you unwell again, Madame Murav?" A tall young Belgian with a thatch of red hair heartbreakingly like her dear Max approached. "Have those medicines I provided not helped the seasickness?" Crippled in the war, he was emigrating to America to start a new life with a sister in Milwaukee.

"Some," she murmured. "You are so kind to inquire. But it's mostly in the mornings that my stomach decides to be uncooperative. I have never been a good sailor." She glanced up at the starry night sky. "We are halfway to Baltimore, are we not? I can endure."

The young doctor gave a nervous cough before he said, "Forgive me, Madame, but your symptoms lead me to think that perhaps you are with child." He smiled. "Such a thing would make your misery more endurable, would it not?"

"Pregnant?" she blurted out. "But that is impossible. My husband and I —" Blushing furiously, she turned from him to stare at the waters once again. "No, it is not that. I have been that way before and it's nothing like."

But even as the words were uttered, a wrenching nausea gripped her stomach, and she leaned far out to retch into the water. "Careful, Madame, lest you topple over —"

Fearful for her safety, the man grasped her shoulders and drew her back against his chest. His steadying arms went about her, and for a few minutes she rested there while the spasm passed.

The feel of the man was wonderful and warm. Kalina closed her eyes and leaned against his masculine hardness. Her arms went up around his neck, and she breathed, "Max. Oh, Max!"

"I only wish I were this Max you sigh for," was the

murmuring response.

The sound of the voice, which was not at all like Max's New York accent, brought Kalina out of her trance. Her eyes flew to the ones that now gazed at her with concern. The moon came out, and, for a moment, the face of the stranger became the face of Max O'Hara.

With the sudden brilliance of a lightning stroke, the months with Max at *Villa d'Este* — months that had been submerged when she had lost her memory — flashed into her memory.

Her heart thudded, and her body warmed, as the images surfaced with photographic clarity. The big bed, the angels on the ceiling, the leafy courtyard.

They had made love each day in Charlemagne's love nest while the battle raged beyond the ridge.

And then Max had been blown to bits.

She had survived, only to mourn her lover forever.

With a cry of anguish, she wrenched free. "I beg your pardon, sir. I did not mean to be so bold."

Clapping her hand over her mouth in dismay, Kalina flew along the deck toward her cabin. She was listed on the passenger list as Mrs. Stefan Murav. Unwittingly, by speaking the name of a lover, she had made herself a fool in the doctor's eyes. Or worse — an unfaithful wife.

Happily, however, her dismay was short-lived, for as the days passed and she became convinced of doctor's diagnosis, Kalina was filled with joy.

She was carrying Max's child.

Chapter Seventeen

The night before the ship docked at Baltimore, Kalina
saw a falling star. Standing on the rail she watched the
milky trail as it curved gracefully down to earth, sinking at
last into the ocean. She recalled the superstitious legend
that, each time a star died, a soul went into heaven to take
its place. "Please, dear Virgin," she prayed. "Let it not be
Zuska. Not yet."

But her cousin was still among the living, she discovered
to her great joy when she entered the house on Rutherford
Drive three days later. Zuska was comfortably ensconced
on the daybed in the little downstairs sitting room where
the family used to gather after dinner. She was propped up
on pillows and Kalina was reminded of Zuska's mother,
Litka, as she lay dying in the Mulberry Street tenement
fifteen years before.

But the daughter was nothing like the mother had been.
In place of the rumpled nightgown and plethora of blankets with perhaps a ruffly night bonnet on her head to keep
off drafts, Kalina was surprised to see the patient clad in a
gaily flowered silk peignoir. The blond hair flowed in loose
rippling waves over her shoulders and around her arms like
a golden cloak.

There was also a complete absence of the medicinal
smell that makes sickrooms so unpleasant. Instead, the
pleasant little room with the flowery wallpaper fairly

332

reeked of gardenias. Two huge crystal vases filled with the pungent, white exotic flowers stood, one on either side of the open door.

"Why, you faker! You don't look sick at all!" exclaimed Kalina, astonished and deliriously happy at how well her cousin looked. "You're not even properly in bed." During the long motorcar ride from the railroad station, she had chanted over and over in her mind: Don't weep, be cheerful, whatever comes.

But now, at sight of the clear blue eyes and of the dearly remembered face as beautiful and bright as it had ever been, Kalina could not restrain her happy tears. Flinging herself upon the coverlet and burying her face in the soft, yielding breast like a baby, she sobbed uncontrollably.

"Hey," yelled Zuska after a time, her own voice husky. "You're getting my peignoir all wet, kiddo. The old harridan will have a catfit." She grimaced. "She does all the laundry herself and complains every minute."

As if summoned like a genie at the sound of her name, Anusia walked into the room, tall and silent. Without so much as a nod in Kalina's direction, she picked up an ivory-handled brush from the bedside table and applied it vigorously to the tangles in Zuska's spread-out hair. The maid had let Kalina into the house, and now, as she saw Anusia for the first time in many years, she was so startled at the woman's changed appearance that she couldn't find her tongue to greet her.

It was disturbing, almost eerie. Much as Stefan had undergone a transformation for the worse, so had his sister. The skinny Anusia of 1903 was buried in rolls of fat, the once-bony face had become a pudgy mass of flesh, in which the dark eyes were like raisins in a bread pudding. The ugly sallowness was gone, and, despite the obesity, she seemed, curiously, to be healthier than before. Almost blooming, somewhat like an overblown flower in summer.

"You look well, Anusia," Kalina finally managed to blurt out. "It's been a long time."

"No fault of mine," replied the other brusquely. The

raspy voice had not changed, mused Kalina. It was still the same sour thing it had always been.

With quick, practiced fingers, Anusia rolled the shining coils of yellow hair atop Zuska's head and secured them with long, pearl-tipped pins. "Ouch, you bitch," yelled Zuska. "I lose enough blood from my lungs without your taking it right out of my head." Although the tears she had not shed at the sight of Kalina now glistened in her eyes, her tone was bantering and affectionate.

Anusia's face remained impassive at the profanity. She had undoubtedly become accustomed to Zuska's vulgar turns of speech, which were vastly different from what she had learned at her mother's knee. But Kalina's heart lurched at the mention of blood. "Are you hemorrhaging, darling?"

She spoke to Zuska but cast her eyes upon Anusia, who drew her lips together in a line and, peering from above Zuska's pile of hair, shook her head back and forth in a signal that the matter was not to be discussed.

With a curt, "Don't tire your cousin," Anusia left the room, Kalina noting that she did not move with the catlike agility of old. Waiting until the echo of heavy footsteps died away, she burst out, "Zuska, how can you be so nasty to the woman? After all, she is taking care of you like a trained nurse, and what's more she isn't a blood relative. You should get down on your knees every night and thank God and your lucky stars for Anusia Murav."

A bubbling laugh from the sick woman brought a faint color to the pale cheeks. "If I got down on my knees, you silly, I'd collapse all over the floor and stay there until Anusia came to pick me up."

Kalina smiled. "I didn't mean it literally."

Then, Zuska went on softly. "We get along, me and the old gal." She slanted a sly glance at Kalina sitting in the chair. "A lot better than you two ever did, from what I hear. Anusia and I are as different as night and day, but in a funny way we understand each other. We're two of a kind, I think. If I were as mealy-mouthed as you are, she would treat me like she does you." She chuckled again, drawing Kalina into laughter with her once more. "Tit for tat, you've got to give her exactly what she dishes out."

Suddenly, Zuska was convulsed by a fit of violent coughing and, reaching for a folded cloth on the table, held it to her mouth. Helplessly, Kalina waited for the coughing to subside. Zuska, drained, removed the cloth and sank down weakly on the pillow.

The cloth was drenched with blood. Bits of red stained the corners of Zuska's mouth, and, gently, with heavy heart, Kalina wiped the full lips clean with her own handkerchief. She could not bring herself to touch the bloody cloth.

For a long time Kalina stood gazing down at her cousin, who seemed to have fallen asleep. Her face was flushed as from a fever. Kalina was filled with apprehension. Everything she had ever heard or read about tuberculosis scurried through her head. Toward the end there is a false appearance of health; the cheeks are rosy, and the patient may show unwonted high spirits. Hemorrhages are frequent.

Zuska not awakening, Kalina rose after some minutes and started to tiptoe out of the room when her cousin suddenly raised herself. "Come back later, darling. We'll have a nice long talk." A radiant smile illuminated her face. "Just like the old days, huh, kid?"

Sinking back again, she closed her eyes. "And say, kid, be nice to Anusia, if only for me. The gal is real gold underneath all that blubber. She never asked me for a cent and pays for everything—my special foods, lots of milk and custards"—she waved languidly at the gardenias—"Even orders fresh flowers twice a week, whatever kind I want."

It was on the tip of her tongue to mention that it was not actually her own money Anusia was spending so freely, but reproving herself inwardly for such mean thoughts, Kalina left the room silently.

Anusia was in the basement kitchen, sitting at the long, wooden cutting table on which was spread a large quantity of food. As Kalina entered, she did not look up or speak but continued eating with the same grim intensity with which she had brushed Zuska's hair. Kalina's eyes flitted with astonishment over a half-eaten leg of lamb on a platter, a large brown crock of baked custard, which Kalina recalled as enough to serve the entire family, several fruit pies, a crusty loaf of bread, and a pan of fragrant cinnamon rolls.

A blue-enameled coffeepot simmered on the gas range. Filling one of the heavy crockery cups on the sink, Kalina moved to the lone window to gaze out into the garden. It was late July, and the climbing roses on the back fence should be in their fully glory. She remembered the brilliant display with nostalgia. But the curtains were tightly drawn and, except for a low-burning kerosene lamp on the drainboard, the long, cavernous room was dark. Anusia maintained her aversion to electricity, she mused.

With her free hand, Kalina flicked the curtain to one side and tugged at the sash. "Don't do that," Anusia barked, just as she had that first day when Kalina had come as a bride and impulsively turned on the lamp in the gloomy front parlor.

"I just thought to look out into the garden," Kalina stammered. "The roses are so lovely this time of summer."

"Don't bother. I haven't kept up the garden. Everything is dead."

Anusia lumbered to the stove for coffee. "I keep a very small staff these days, nobody but the girl who let you in." She sat down again to resume her meal. Just then the hall clock chimed eleven, and Kalina wondered if Anusia were at a late breakfast or an early luncheon.

Uncertain as to how to begin a conversation with a person she hadn't seen for twelve years, especially a person with whom she had never been exactly on the best of terms, Kalina leaned against the sink, taking small sips of coffee.

336

Should she embrace Anusia as she had Max and Zuska? Should she talk about the children? Zuska's condition would have to be discussed, complete with doctor's reports and so on.

But, fearing the worst, she wanted to postpone that until she got some rest. The matter of Stefan was more immediate, however, and undoubtedly, Anusia would ask questions about her brother. Frantically, Kalina mentally rehearsed all the lies she would be forced to tell. She could hardly tell her that her baby brother, for whom she had sacrificed so much and loved more than anyone else in all the world, had tipped over into insanity and was wandering all over war-torn Europe proclaiming himself king of Poland.

Anusia scooped up the last bit of pie from her plate and flicked a finger at the window. "The smoke out there is so thick and acrid, nothing can survive. Trees, flowers, little children drop like flies, their lungs black with it. The curtains and windows must be closed day and night to keep out the poisonous air. A body can hardly breathe. When I go to market I put a cloth around my nose and mouth so as not to inhale the fumes."

It was a long speech, and Anusia seemed to collapse as if from exhaustion.

"I noticed as I came from the station that the air is very thick," Kalina agreed, happy that the talk had started on neutral ground. "The mills are going full blast, I imagine, with making steel for weapons to send to Europe. There must be work for anyone who wants it."

"Humph," snorted Anusia. "At least there's been an end to the monotonous demands for an eight-hour day."

Sitting down opposite her sister-in-law, Kalina regarded the viands on the table, trying to whip up an appetite. Eating together might serve to break the ice. Anusia took up a carving knife and cut a slice of rosy lamb from the haunch and placed it on a small plate. She shoved it across the table. "Here, eat. You look half-starved."

Kalina smiled her thanks and bit into the meat. "I'm

337

afraid my shipboard appetite was nonexistent." What had Zuska said? Real gold under the blubber. "Delicious. My compliments to your cook."

"Fired her too, along with the gardeners. None of them worth a hill of beans."

Standing up abruptly, Anusia came round the table and rudely thrust her hand at Kalina's abdomen. "How many months along?"

Thrown completely off-guard, Kalina stammered, "Three months." Then—"But I didn't think it showed as yet." Red-faced, she smoothed out her blue skirt, which was pleated from the waist and with which she had hoped to conceal her condition during what she thought would be a very brief stay in Pittsburgh. "Stefan does not know. He has so many other problems with his work—"

"Stop it. I'm no fool." Her voice was sharp. Turning, she walked to the door and opened it to admit a large black-and-white cat, who padded to the stove and dipped its head in a dish of finely chopped meat. Obviously the one Anusia had written about in her letter and who had blessed her with ten offspring.

"There now, you naughty kitty. Where have you been for two whole days? Mama missed you terribly." With gentle strokes, the spinster caressed the animal's arching back, her unpleasant voice mysteriously losing its familiar rasp.

Kalina marveled. The woman had always detested animals. She must be terribly lonely, she reflected with a pang, rattling around in this big house with but one servant to keep her company. Her own adored brother had abandoned her, refusing to have her with him in Europe. So she was compelled to reign alone in a dark house in an even darker, smoke-clouded Pittsburgh. Suddenly, it all came together in Kalina's mind. The lonely old maid had formed an almost fanatic attachment to the cat as well as to the dying Zuska. Beneath the gruff manner, she did, in truth, hide a heart of gold, one filled with a great capacity for love and compassion. But a heart that opened only with a key supplied by Anusia alone.

338

She was as blunt as ever. Hoping to stave off talk of her pregnancy, Kalina inquired about Zuska. "When do you think she can resume her normal life?"

"Never," was the terse reply. "Your cousin is dying. Two weeks, maybe three." She looked up, and any kindness in her heart was well cloaked with hostility. "I trust, Madame, that you can spare us that much time before you return to your dissipated life in Europe."

Kalina stiffened but held her tongue. "I will remain with my dear cousin as long as she needs me."

Anusia's next remark banished the hope that she would not pursue the pregnancy discussion that had been interrupted by the entrance of the cat, which now sat purring on Anusia's lap. "If you try to tell me that the baby is Stefan's, don't bother. I have a letter from him, dated in March, in which he says he hadn't seen you for six months, ever since the outbreak of war in September."

"We were together early in April," Kalina replied calmly. "Stefan came to Auvergne to visit the children shortly after he wrote that letter, I imagine. By chance I happened to arrive at the convent the day before he showed up to take them to Switzerland." She had no intention of allowing Max's child to be born illegitimate. Stefan had adopted Dunia who had been born to an itinerant peddler, and she was certain he would not disown any child from the body of his wife. In his present state, he might not even remember exactly what month he came to the convent.

The lies were necessary to protect an unborn child from the world's contempt.

"Liar." Like a rifle shot, the word dropped into the dark, stifling room and hung between the two women. For a long moment, the only sound was the swish of a carpet sweeper from above where the maid went about her morning chores.

Sudden, unreasoning rage tore through Kalina, and feeling that her lungs would burst if she did not get some air, she shoved back her chair and made for the door. She must escape those probing eyes before she herself blurted

339

out the truth, if only in defiance.

But Anusia had the last word as usual. "It's Max O'Hara's bastard, I know all about how he showed up from the dead at *Villa d'Este*." She cackled like a hen who had just laid a prize egg. "Thought I wouldn't find out, didn't you? Well, Helena's still visiting her mother in Homestead and got a letter from Mary Lesko. Soon's your belly starts to bulge, everyone in town will know that you're still the whore you always were."

Desperately, Kalina held her hands to her ears in a futile effort to drown out the hateful voice, but it followed her up the stairs. "At least your cousin is honest about her harlotry. What's more, if you want my opinion, she's a hundred times the woman you are. At least she's borne a living child."

Reaching her third-floor bedroom, Kalina flung herself across the room and, yanking aside the damask curtains, unlocked the window and pushed it up as far as it would go. Any air, no matter how polluted, was preferable to the air inside this hateful house.

Later, as she rested in the high bed where she had lain with Stefan in passionate married love and suffered through her first hard pregnancy, she found herself not unhappy that the sister-in-law she knew of old had not changed an iota in her feelings toward her brother's wife. Anusia had been kind and caring during the pregnancy, but, when the child emerged stillborn, had reverted to her true nature.

Curiously, Kalina was relieved. The old Anusia was a known quantity. She could deal with it. Zuska had uncovered a quite different Anusia.

Just before she slept, Kalina wondered idly what version of Anusia would surface after Zuska died. And more troubling still, how would the spinster react when she learned—as she must—that her adored brother had lost his mind?

It was dark when Kalina awoke to a violent thunderstorm that shook the big house and almost drowned out the noise of the mill. The heavy curtains blew in and out of the open window, smacking heavily against the sill. They must be drenched, she thought in panic as she jumped out of bed without the benefit of the little ladder. Even the carpet was wet under her bare feet.

Anusia will be furious. As she reached up and curled her fingers around the sash, she stopped, mesmerized by the brilliant sky across the river over Homestead. The clamor of the steel mill battled with the rolling thunder, and a roaring pillar of fire shot suddenly out of a smokestack.

Catching her breath at the splendor of it, Kalina thought about the times she had stood here, like this, thinking of Max over there in the fire. How he had loved the mill! Wrapped in thought, she stood at the open window, heedless of the rain and the flapping damask, until, realizing that she was getting soaked, she shut the window with a bang. Quickly, she peeled off her wet clothing and hastily donned a cheerful linen robe figured with violets and roses. She must endeavor to be as gay and cheerful as Zuska tried to be.

On impulse, she unpinned her chignon, and let her black hair flow loosely over her back and shoulders. It might serve to remind Zuska of a happier time when they were both children and ran about with hair as unburdened as their hearts.

As she bent to lace her shoes, she impishly slipped them off again. In Jaslo, they had run barefoot through the long, hot summers.

She found Zuska half-reclining on the daybed, a knitted afghan flung over her sheer peignoir. Waves of heat emanated from a small mica-fronted gas burner. Anusia was sitting on a chair beside the bed and spooning hot soup into Zuska's mouth.

"How are you feeling, dear?" Kalina hurried to the bed. The roses that had colored her cousin's cheeks in the morning were gone, and the blue eyes were no longer clear and shining.

"She's had another hemorrhage," Zuska grunted. "Don't make her talk."

"Is there no medicine? What does the doctor prescribe?" Swiveling, Kalina's eyes swept the room. No sign of bottles or pills.

"Doctors! Fools, all of them!" Anusia snapped. "They take your money and give you nothing in return but contagion from their other patients." From the table she picked up a cup, at the bottom of which Kalina saw a mat of wet tealike leaves. "I prepare my own herbal mixture to help her sleep."

Fleeting thoughts of Aunt Litka and Mrs. Cipriani's soothing herbs passed through Kalina's mind.

Impatiently, Zuska pushed the spoon away. "I'm full," she said with petulance. She smiled wanly at Kalina. "It's always worse at night. Don't look so tragic."

Grumpily, Anusia gathered up her tray and left the room. "Don't excite her," she called from the corridor. "Excitement brings on the coughing."

When she had gone, Zuska waved a languid hand. "Sit down, darling. Talk to me."

Seating herself in the chair vacated by Anusia, Kalina took the limp hand between her own and began to talk. For an hour or more she played Scheherazade, describing exotic places she had been, the people she had met, the great events she had witnessed. She did not talk about the war.

Zuska brightened when she heard about her cousin's intimate friendship with the Emperor Franz Josef, puckering her full lips and whistling in admiration, a fondly remembered childhood habit that brought a lump to Kalina's throat.

"When we were kids, the name Hapsburg was next only to God," Zuska breathed in awe.

Stefi's photograph which Kalina produced from her reticule brought no maternal response. "Looks like Murav," she commented laconically. "The same fierce eyes and nose."

"But he is nothing like," said Kalina lightly. "Your son is artistically inclined and is possessed of a meeker spirit than his father."

Dunia's picture evoked more interest. "So my little girl is sweet sixteen," she marveled, gazing long and hard at the photograph Kalina produced. "Pretty, but dark like you and your mother Hania. That's good. Blondes have the worst of it. Look at Libby Hughes, murdered in her own library."

Ignoring the reference to Libby, Kalina said coolly, "A bit of the Italian vivacity about her too, I think. From her father."

Zuska bristled and snatched her hand away. "I'll thank you never to mention that man to me again. Some things are best forgotten."

"Yes, darling. We'll talk only of pleasant things." In the following days, no matter how Kalina pressed, Zuska steadfastly refused to disclose more than a brief glimpse into her life between the time she left Mulberry Street and when Kalina found her at the whorehouse.

Kalina was eager to hear of the motion picture industry in Hollywood, but there too her cousin was unaccountably taciturn. Obviously, the glowing comments on the picture postal cards had not reflected the true situation. Donald Hill, the man whom she had gone to Cincinnati to meet after Stefi's birth, was never mentioned.

"You know me, kid," her cousin muttered. "Don't cry over spilled milk."

Eventually, the fevered head on the pillow turned to the wall, and Zuska seemed to sleep. Softly, Kalina rose and gazed a long time at the still figure, noting how sweetly the lashes curved on the pale cheeks. Like a child.

As she padded toward the door, however, Zuska turned and spoke in a loud voice. "Let's talk about Stefan."

Frowning, Kalina returned to sit on the edge of the bed, thinking swiftly of what to relate concerning her husband's present state. She never could lie while looking into

Zuska's eyes.

Zuska motioned that she wanted to sit up, and, after plumping up the mass of pillows and stuffing them behind her back, Kalina said brightly, "So what about Stefan? I never thought you really cared for him."

"I didn't. I wanted to tell you that. We were never more than bed partners, each of us taking our pleasure." She grinned, and, for the first time that night, her blue eyes sparkled. "He was the most virile lover I ever had, a real Cossack. You're lucky, little cousin."

"I do not love him," said Kalina. "I married him for security and what I thought at the time was love. He was unfaithful to me many times."

"As you were to him with that Irishman," was the tart response. "Don't throw stones if you live in a glass house, darling."

Kalina reddened but smiled sheepishly at the gibe. "I married in haste and repent now in leisure."

Zuska cocked an eye at Kalina's voluminous robe. "I can't tell from your belly, but that glow on your face tells me that you're with child. Is it Stefan's or Max's?"

"I haven't seen Max for twelve years," Kalina began, but, unable to lie to the probing blue eyes, she said simply, "Yes, it is."

"Hmm." Digging underneath the blankets, Zuska fished out a slim volume bound in flowered cloth. "Tell me. How is it with someone you really love? Is it the way they tell in the romances?"

"Why, that's one of mine!" Kalina chuckled. "When I think of the hours I spent poring over those romances!"

"I can see why. Pretty good reading." Zuska flipped to a page which bore the marks of having been read and reread many times. "He took her in his arms and held her close, and she wanted it to never end. The sweetness was almost unbearable. If he should leave her, she would surely die."

Moving to the little globe, Kalina whirled it round and round on its axis. "Max is out there somewhere in this vast turning world. If I never see him again, my love will remain." When she turned to face her cousin, her sloe-berry eyes brimmed with tears. "I have always been a little jealous of you, Zuska—your golden looks, your cheerful disposition, the way you charm everyone you meet. But it saddens me to think that the one thing above all else in life that makes it all worthwhile you have never known."

"I know. Love!" An anguished cry came from the bed. "I go to my grave without ever knowing the true love of a good man."

"I love you, darling. Please don't talk about dying." Kalina threw herself upon the bed and clasped the fragile form to her breast.

As Anusia had predicted on Kalina's arrival, Zuska grew weaker with each day. Uncanny as it seemed, she had held onto the frail threads of her life until her cousin appeared to be with her at the end.

"Happens all the time," said Anusia. "Now you're here, she'll go in peace." The plump face remained impassive, and, were it not for a slight trembling in the woman's voice and the way she rose abruptly from the breakfast table to leave the room, Kalina might have thought her uncaring.

One evening during the second week of Kalina's visit, Anusia did not appear with Zuska's supper tray. She was almost painfully punctual in her habits, and, when a half-hour passed and still no sign of her, Zuska expressed concern.

"Do you suppose she's sick?" Her face showed alarm. "With all that fat, she could have a stroke or a heart attack and we wouldn't know—" Anxiously, she cast eyes upward to the ceiling. "Her room is directly above. I don't hear any movement."

Kalina sought out the maid, who informed her that "Miss Murav has not gone to market. Here is her basket." She pointed to the wicker basket on its hook in the kitchen. "I believe she has retired to her room for the night." She grinned slyly. "She sometimes falls asleep after one of her enormous meals," offered the girl in the insolent manner she assumed with Kalina. But she "got along" with Anusia for much the same reasons as did the impudent Zuska.

Genuinely frightened now, Kalina walked upstairs and down the long, dark hallway to Anusia's room. Recalling the dark, musty place, she did not relish entering. There was no answer to her repeated knocking, so she turned the knob, very gently, in the event the woman really was sleeping, and pushed the door half open.

At first she saw nothing, for the curtains were tightly drawn and there was no lamp burning. Then, as her eyes became accustomed to the gloom, she saw Anusia crouched like an animal on hands and knees, her ear pressed to the floorboards at a place where the corner of the carpet had been drawn aside. She did not rise as Kalina entered and, in fact, seemed oblivious to the world.

"Anusia!" Kalina exclaimed. "What on earth are you doing down there?" She rushed over to bend over the woman. "Are you all right? We thought you were ill."

The woman reared up with a roar. "How dare you enter my bedroom uninvited! Get out of here at once." She struggled to get to her feet, leaning for support on a little table at her side but instead knocking the table over. A little drawer slid out, spilling its contents on the carpet. Anusia tumbled after it, but fell on her back, her arms flung out, her legs beneath the heavy black skirt she habitually wore bent in an unnatural position. For a stunned moment, she stared at the ceiling.

Alarmed, Kalina sprang to her side. "Are you hurt, Anusia? Let me help you." Quickly, she stepped behind the prone, spread-eagled figure and placed both hands in her armpits, but, with a violent twisting movement, Anusia flung herself over and flung herself on top of the bric-a-brac that had been in the drawer.

Her eyes were slits and her voice like iron gratings as she said, "Now leave, whore, before I take this gun and shoot you." Frantically, she scrambled among the contents of the drawer for the little revolver she kept there.

346

Swiftly, before Anusia saw it, Kalina reached under the bed to retrieve the gun. She hurled it out the still-open door. Then, while the enraged woman struggled to her feet, Kalina darted to a window and drew the heavy curtain aside. She turned back to Anusia, who had managed to get into the rocking chair. "Now, what is this all about? If you persist in carrying on like this, you'll surely have an apoplexy."

The early evening sun streamed from the window, clearly outlining the place where a tiny hole had been gouged out between two of the soft pine boards with a sharp knife. She turned on the woman, mingled shock and indignation in her voice. "You've been spying on us, listening to everything Zuska and I say."

Suddenly, as distinct as if she were right beside them, Zuska's voice rang out clearly from the sitting room directly below. "Hey, you two, what's all the ruckus?" Her voice was clear as a bell.

Kalina stooped and shouted through the little hole. "Did you know she is listening to our conversations?"

"Oh, sure, but what's the difference. She gets little enough pleasure out of life. Titillates her, I guess."

Rising up, Kalina stood, arms akimbo, glaring down at Anusia. The woman had heard her admit that the baby belonged to Max. While she had been talking to Zuska, Anusia had apparently slid back to the floor and frantically gathered up the odds and ends there.

Now she sat on the floor, her back against the bed. The long skirt was around her knees and in the triangle formed by her black-stockinged legs lay the spilled contents of the drawer.

Seeming oblivious to Kalina's accusing words, Anusia rocked back and forth, staring fixedly at a picture in her hands, an eerie, bone-chilling noise emanating from her mouth.

She's hysterical, Kalina thought, and, bending swiftly, she slapped the mesmerized woman smartly across the cheek. With a startled cry of pain, Anusia gazed upward

347

and then promptly burst into a paroxysm of weeping.

"Stefan, Stefan," she gasped between sobs. "Why are you so cruel to me? I'm the only one who truly loves you."

Taking the picture from the crazed woman's limp hands, Kalina saw that it was an old-time copperplate daguerreotype of a little boy of five or so in a garden. That bushy hair and fierce expression could belong to nobody in the world but Stefan Murav. Physically, the likeness to young Stefi was remarkable, except that the force of the father's dynamic personality seemed almost to leap out at her from the cold metal.

Recovering from her first fit of weeping, Anusia reached up and snatched the plate from Kalina. She returned to devouring it with her eyes. "He was such a clever little fellow," she said in a dreamlike voice. "So bright, so quick." She squinted up at Kalina. "And so terribly beautiful it took your breath away."

Stunned at the abrupt change of mood, Kalina sank to the windowseat, listening with mingled astonishment and compassion to the woman whose brother had left her to rot alone in a dark, old house in a smoky city while he lived in plush hotels and dined with titled heads of Europe.

To Anusia, Stefan Murav was a god. "Did you know that Stefan's eyes glow in the dark like amber? In ancient Egypt the king was considered as a god. Stefan is like that. All the knowledge in the world is gathered in his magnificent eyes." Lifting the plate to her lips, she kissed it. "Sometimes I think he looks like Jesus."

The voice that, except for a very short time in their lives together, was always cold as ice to Kalina, fell like rose petals into the musty room. Not for the first time did Kalina conjecture that Anusia was not really Stefan's sister but perhaps his mother, having borne him out of wedlock when a young girl. She professed to being fifty-five to Stefan's forty-eight, but, with that ageless kind of face, no one could rightly tell.

"His mother was a whore," Anusia continued. "She deserved to be plunged into the ocean. She was traveling with a man not her husband, who called himself a count. We never knew our father. My uncle was taking me to America to be a slavey to him and his ten children." She heaved a great sigh. "So I decided to run away."

The sentences were strung together in the unconnected manner in which a child might tell a story. She fell silent, then, and, with pounding heart, Kalina waited for the confusing tale to continue. Mother, father, uncle, count? Perhaps she and Stefan had different mothers and the same father. Dare she question? She burned with curiosity, but pressing Anusia when she was so distraught might serve to bring the confession to a halt. Kalina had long suspected that the story Stefan had told her on their honeymoon about his family history had been concocted. All that nonsense about his father being a Polish officer, and himself being descended from a line of kings she had taken as delusions of grandeur. Too fantastic to be credible.

Anusia flitted her dark eyes upward once again. They glistened with a kind of childlike fervor. "Stefan is in trouble. He needs me. I always know when he needs me." She pressed the picture to her heart.

"Yes, Anusia, your intuition is right," Kalina began. "Stefan is ill, very ill." Whatever she was to Murav, the suffering woman deserved to know the true state of affairs.

"I know," snapped Anusia. "He writes to me constantly." Triumphantly, she extracted a letter from beneath the neckline of her shirtwaist. "I keep it in my breast. It came last week. He's in Poland, near Warsaw."

Kalina's heart leaped. Stefan must have regained his senses. A wild thought struck her. Perhaps his irrational behavior at Auvergne was all pretense.

But why? What nefarious purpose would feigned madness serve? Surely, such posturing could not help in his aspirations to kingship!

Lumbering to her feet, Anusia stepped to the window and, leaning past Kalina on the windowseat, pulled the curtains together with a jingle of the brass rings. Unexpectedly, she rapped her fist sharply on the top of Kalina's head. "Now get out of here, young woman, before I call the police." The rose petals had departed from her voice, and the look she cast upon her sister-in-law was that of a hostile stranger.

Moments later, downstairs in the sitting room, Kalina sat on the daybed, flicking her eyes anxiously to the ceiling and hoping that Anusia had not returned to her listening post on the floorboards.

Leaning over her cousin, she whispered, "Did you hear all that nonsense? She's as nutty as her brother—" She frowned, her black eyes showing her own bewilderment. "What do you think?"

Zuska broke out into delighted laughter and an impish look brightened her wan features. "I have given this matter a lot of thought, dear cousin, and what I think is this: The real honest-to-God truth about the true relationship between the man you married in Pottsville, Pennsylvania, in a kind of a hurry, not because you loved him but so that you would be rich and"—she jerked a finger to the ceiling—"that sour old maid upstairs will be revealed only when you get back to Poland or wherever those two came from and ask some questions on your own."

Pursing her lips, Kalina said, "Although they both speak the language fluently, I don't think they are really Polish. There's a Cossack look about them. They are probably southern Russian or from the Caucasus somewhere."

Zuska's eyes glinted as with secret knowledge. "You may be on the right track there."

With mock irritation, Kalina shook her cousin by the shoulders. "Something tells me you know more than you're telling me. Come on, no secrets, remember? Did old Anusia tell you something about her past?"

A wicked smile was her response and then, "That's for me to know and you to find out."

The cousins had talked often in the past weeks about their native land, Zuska extracting a solemn promise from Kalina to return to Jaslo and say hello to Hania, Mashko,

Anya, and anyone else who was lucky enough to be still alive.

Now she cocked a brow and said, bubbling, "I'll bet that the real story will burn your ears off." Again the merry laugh, which, whatever its cause, brought joy to Kalina's heart.

"Maybe you *will* be queen of Poland, after all." Zuska finished, and the two women fell into each other's arms, giggling as they used to do when growing up together.

Next morning Anusia appeared with Zuska's breakfast tray as usual, her florid face showing no signs of the ravages of yesterday's weeping. The matter of the picture was not mentioned, and her manner toward Kalina was as frosty as it had ever been. But soon there was no time to think of anything but Zuska, for Litka's daughter began the serious business of dying. Hemorrhages became more frequent, and the little flesh that remained on her once luscious body seemed to melt away before Kalina's sorrowing eyes. The beautiful face became almost transparent, and there was a look of another world in the blue eyes.

Anusia fetched a priest. "She's a great sinner and needs to cleanse her soul." The priest, a sober young man from Homestead, bent over the dying woman and prayed in Latin and Polish, Zuska responding faintly from remembered childhood prayers. "Sometimes the holy oil works a miracle," Anusia remarked as she and Kalina listened from the hallway.

But there was no miracle; no cloud from heaven descended to heal the ravaged lungs. Zuska Olkonsky's life had run its allotted course. Anusia gave the priest five dollars, and he left.

At midnight on a Sunday in early August, she fell into a coma, from which she roused occasionally to mutter in Polish or lift a hand as if pleading for help. Anusia sat at the bedside, holding a crucifix to the dying woman's lips. "Mama, Mama," cried Zuska, grasping the woman's hand. Anusia sobbed aloud and Zuska murmured, "Don't cry, Mama. I'll be good."

There was more mumbling as Zuska regressed into the past. Kalina had heard somewhere that when a person dies, his whole life flashes before him. So it was no surprise when, in the midst of the general incoherence, she made out the distinct word—"knee pants."

Her cousin was back on Mulberry Street with her beloved mama where, with Kalina, they had sewed from dawn till dusk on the factory pants. Desperately, Kalina longed for Zuska to rouse once more; she wanted to ask her just how many dozen knee pants she had done in one day. Three dozen, four?

Kalina fell to her knees to pray for her cousin's soul. She could see no movement beneath the covers. All breath was gone. Suddenly Zuska's voice rang out, strong and firm, and she lifted her head a few inches from the pillow to say, "Kalina darling, when you get to Jaslo, look up a Cossack they call Yurek. He's got a crazy scar on his hand. I loved him just like you love your Max."

Kalina waited a full hour for her cousin to say more, but, as the hall clock chimed two, Anusia snapped, "She's gone. I'll fetch the doctor to make out the certificate."

The pall from the Homestead Works of United States Steel was so thick at noon that the motor jitney that came to drive Kalina to the railroad station was forced to turn on its headlights. They had buried Zuska just an hour before in the pretty little Polish Catholic cemetery on a hillside a few miles out of town. A maple tree hung over the grave, and Anusia had planted geraniums on the mound of fresh earth.

Memories of another burial in Brooklyn haunted Kalina. This time there was no sweet Max to comfort her.

Kalina climbed into the vehicle, and as the driver piled her luggage on top, taking his time about securing it with ropes, she glanced hopefully at the house for a glimpse of Anusia. Her sister-in-law had vanished into her bedroom upon their return from the funeral, and despite Kalina's repeated knocks, did not reappear to say good-bye.

Anusia had insisted on paying for the funeral. "She was the mother of Stefan's son," she said crisply to Kalina. "My brother provides handsomely for me, and I know he would want it this way."

The woman, who had unaccountably formed an almost passionate devotion to the brazenly sinful Zuska Olkonsky, also vowed that she would see that the grave was given proper attention, with fresh flowers monthly set in jars, and that she would have a photograph taken of it and sent to Stefi Murav as a remembrance of his mother.

Chapter Eighteen

Verdun, France, February, 1916

"Max O'Hara's the name. *Je suis Americain!*"

The young French officer gaped at the tall redhead who loomed up on the other side of the wooden table and with a weary gesture poked a finger under the edge of his blue helmet. Thoughtfully, he rubbed the chafed skin of his brow, and lifting a long brown cigar from a saucer, blew a puff of aromatic smoke toward the ceiling.

After a moment, he glanced down again at the metal tag in his hand, holding it up to the spirit lantern at his elbow. "Are you telling me that you are not this Oscar Wagner whose name is on this dogtag?"

"Yep," responded Max. "I took it from a corpse." A grin crossed his freckled face. "It came with the uniform."

The officer grinned back, and tipping his field chair back against the mud wall of the dugout, he said in English, "OK, Yank, sing the Star Spangled Banner."

Max O'Hara cleared his throat and promptly burst out in a strong baritone. "Oh-o, say can you see by the dawn's early light, how so proudly we hail —"

The torchlit subterranean room erupted into shouts and laughter. "More, more," cried out men in French and English. It was a welcome diversion from the tedium of war. Even the glum faces of the German deserters, lined up behind Max and whom the officer had been processing since early morning, broke into grins. The redhead in the

354

mud-caked field-gray uniform of the German army had proved without a shadow of any doubt that he was what he claimed. Not even the most abject and dispirited Boche deserter would dare to dishonor his Vaterland by singing the American national hymn. Even under torture. And certainly not with that comically distinctive American accent.

The officer waved Max aside. "I'm sure the tale of how an American civilian got mixed up with the Boche is fascinating, and were we in a cafe drinking cognac and had—as the poet says—'world enough and time,' I would gladly ask you for your story." He shrugged as only a Frenchman can. "But I regret that I must forgo the pleasure for the moment."

The released American's next stop was a second table where he was expected to reveal all he knew of the Germans' secret military plans. As a prisoner of war since last March when the Boche had picked him up after he had been thrown clear of the blown-up houseboat and had walked right into their trenches near Verdun, he could tell the French little they had not already learned from the throngs of other deserters. He had been too occupied with keeping body and soul together, scrounging for food, that in a retreating army, was in scarce supply.

Ever since the New Year and the launching of a renewed enemy campaign to capture the ancient fortress town of Verdun—the last bastion to be taken before the Kaiser's troops could march through the previously ravaged province of Champagne and onto Paris itself—German and Austrian deserters had crossed the lines in ever-increasing numbers. Reasons for the mass flight had included an exceptionally severe winter, poor or nonexistent rations, and—probably most compelling—low morale among an army that had lost more ground than it had gained since the war had begun in August, 1914.

In the seventeen months since the beginning of the war, the German army had penetrated fifty miles into French territory and had been stopped by the combined Allied forces at the banks of the Meuse. Each kilometer they took had been speedily recaptured by the French and British forces.

It was a stalemate, and the situation would not improve until more airplanes were in the sky.

That's what Max heard from an American pilot whom he stumbled on in another part of the meandering dugout. The man was drinking English ale and eating French bread and cheese around a table with five others of his countrymen. Max also learned that the dugout was actually the sub-dungeons of an ancient Roman fortress and that a body could get lost forever in the torturously winding caverns.

"Your bones will be discovered centuries later in the middle of still another war," said the American darkly, rolling his merry blue eyes in mock horror and pointing ominously to a whitish pile in a corner. The man's name was Larry Jackson and he came from Detroit. Bending his tall frame over the table, he shoved a bottle of ale toward Max. "You look like you need this, Red."

Grinning his thanks and bemused at his luck in bumping into friendly faces after more than a year in German hands, Max lifted the bottle to his lips. The stuff was rich and dark. Setting the ale back on the table, he wiped his mouth with the sleeve of his tattered gray German tunic. The others were dressed in snappy blue French uniforms with medals of all kinds and shapes covering the tunics. Several wore the *Croix de Guerre*, the highest award of the French government.

Noting his gaze, Larry bragged, "The shiny cross is for downing six German planes. Figure I can cash 'em all in when I get back home and buy myself a wife and kids and a house in the suburbs." He cocked his brows. "Always wanted to hobnob with the swells."

"Jake Epstein, Brooklyn," said a wiry pilot with snapping black eyes and a bristly black beard covering his chin. "You better get rid of the Heinie outfit if you don't want to get shot at."

Jake didn't look over a hundred pounds and looked more like a jockey than a pilot, but he shook the newcomer's hand with a grip that made Max wince.

"Were you by any chance a boxer in good old New York?" asked Max, rubbing his hand.

"Sure thing, Red. But I gave it up for flying."

Measuring Max with his eyes, Larry fingered his blue lapel. "How do you think the Irishman would look in one of these?" He leaned over the table to say intently, "Ever been up in a plane, fella?"

"Don't rush the guy," snapped Jake. "You might scare him off. Wait til he's got a couple weeks' good grub and drink in his gut." He grinned at Max. "Jackson's always recruiting."

"Got to replace the dead," Larry replied sourly. "Flying's one business that has a big turnover."

His interest was pricked, but Max decided to change the subject before he found himself in a mess worse than the one he had just left.

"It's a long way from Detroit, Larry," he said lightly.

"You said it, Red, but lots of us are over here." Larry's arm swept the table. "I'm nuts about flying and here I get the chance and a free airplane to do it in." He grimaced. "Though we invented the things, most Americans are still not wild on airplanes."

"Especially our government," cut in Jake. "But so many guys want to fly for France and England that plans are afoot to form a special brigade of Yankee flyers to fight the Hun."

Max's face lit up at that, but Jake lifted a hand and shook his head vigorously from side to side. "We'll talk about it later. Right now, drink up." He shoved another bottle at Max.

Max's eyes devoured Jake's homely face. "Ever been on Mulberry Street? Can we talk about New York sometime?"

"Why not now," said another, whose name was Don Brown and who came from Cleveland. "We got nothing to do till daylight."

Someone offered Max a Turkish cigarette, and lighting up, he joined enthusiastically in a boisterous discussion about the "good old U.S.A." To the exile, who hadn't seen his native land for thirteen years, each word was music to his ears, sweeter than a choir of angels. The men, on the other hand, seemed overjoyed at having a brand-new listener.

Max was amazed to hear from Larry that a man named Henry Ford had built a factory in Detroit and, with a technique called mass production, was turning out a motorcar that every working class family could afford to buy.

"Horseless carriages are no longer only for the rich," said Jake. "I got one of Ford's tin lizzies in the garage back home. It's not the most gorgeous hunk of junk in the world, and it comes in one color—basic black—but it goes twenty miles an hour on those crazy Brooklyn streets and it cost me all of three hundred bucks."

Max's mind slid back to the shiny red automobile that Libby had so proudly presented to him at the height of their love affair. At the time it seemed the most marvelous thing in the world to him, the symbol of all he ever dreamed of.

Jake kept up with the latest in stage plays and musicals and described, with sinuous gestures of his expressive hands, the luscious figures of the Ziegfeld Follies girls with whom he claimed to be on intimate terms.

Sensing perhaps that a man who had not seen America for such a long time had something to hide, the Americans did not press the recently repatriated prisoner for his life story. The old rule of the road, reflected Max: Don't ask questions.

Cagily, however, he revealed just enough to stave off questions that, in his weakened state, he might inadvertently answer to his detriment. Even men with such worldly devil-may-care sophistication might look askance at a man accused of murdering his mistress. More than anything else right now, he wanted desperately to keep the friendship of these easygoing Americans.

"I was involved in the labor movement in Pittsburgh. Something happened and I had to leave in a hurry." He grinned and lowered his eyes, permitting them to imagine what they pleased. "The Boche grabbed me while I was on a boating trip in Champagne."

Larry nodded soberly. "We've all got our closet skeletons." His blue eyes swept the table. "Somebody else's war is a place to go when there's no other placé to go." He flashed a wicked grin. "Sort of like the French Foreign Legion. For all we know, Jake over there is an ax murderer."

Jake intervened. "Was it rough being a Hun prisoner?"

Max shrugged. "The civilians I've seen are a lot worse off. Women and kids are eating dead horses and dogs and robbing corpses for boots and clothing. The German airplanes bomb anything that moves. Sometimes it's an Allied soldier, but sometimes it's a kid or an old lady."

"I thought you were in Germany for a year," Don remarked. "You mean to say they bomb their own people?"

"I was at Mons right after they went through the first time."

New respect filled the eyes of his listeners, but they said nothing. An orderly appeared with two fresh, crusty French loaves, and they all set to devouring them with the peculiar passion of those who know that every bite might be their last on earth. With the day they would once again invade the skies over Germany. Some of them might not return. Tomorrow night, there might be an empty field chair—or two or three—around the table.

Escaping the POW encampment had been easy as taking candy from a newborn babe, Max told Jake in answer to his question. "I was assigned to burial detail in an open field. The fools of sentries were frantic with trying to stem the tide of deserters, and I simply threw down my shovel and ran off into the night." Ruefully, he looked down at his tunic. "This once belonged to a poor sucker who never made it across the lines."

With the help of numerous bottles of ale and hours of friendly talk about hometowns, sweethearts, and the latest in fashions and politics, Max felt that he had somehow been transported by magic carpet to the busy streets of New York City. Even the interlude with Kalina had not given him this heady feeling of belonging, a feeling he had sorely missed during his long exile. But then, he thought wryly, when he had been in his beloved's arms, there had been no time or inclination to talk of anything but love.

For the first time since arriving within the French lines, he permitted himself to think of Kalina. Much as he enjoyed the camaraderie of the American pilots, he must not be diverted from his plan to seek her out. He had never permitted himself to believe that she had died when the houseboat had been hurled out the water by that German shell.

Unharmed but for a scratch or two, Max had survived. Miraculously. Never a religious man, Max now prayed each night that the deities that dispensed miracles with a frugal hand on a hapless world would save a very special one for his Kalina.

It was taken for granted that Max would bunk with the American pilots, so when they rose and walked out of the dugout into the predawn dark, he followed them out and across a field crisscrossed with shellholes, trenches, and tangles of barbed wire. Remembering the hazardous journey from Belgium to Champagne with Sidonie, he fell at once to his hands and knees, preparing to slither through the dangerous terrain while praying that a stray piece of shrapnel would not catch him unawares.

Larry yanked him to his feet. "Up like a man, Max. The war stops at night." He peered skeptically at the bright moonlit sky. "Unless some crazy Hun pilot gets himself drunk and decides to make a midnight swing over the lines while the Allied pilots are down. It's happened. Some of those guys are real daredevils. Think they're immortal, I guess."

No airplane was in sight, and the men—themselves more than a little tipsy—walked the half-kilometer or so to the airdrome from which the British and French aviators flew to meet the enemy. It was set in the lee of a cliff and was camouflaged in a haphazard way, Max thought, by up-rooted trees and rocks laid upon the canvas hangars.

"How do you keep the German fliers from dropping bombs on your hangars?" asked Max. "Despite the camouflage you're pretty much like sitting ducks."

"We get them first." Larry pointed to some rocks that Max had presumed were more Roman ruins. "Antiaircraft. It's not very accurate, but it makes an awful racket and the smoke from the popping shells confuses everyone."

He chuckled. "Besides, they'd rather meet us in the sky. They like to chase around in and out of the clouds, playing at hide and seek."

No more than you do, reflected Max, beginning to comprehend what drove these men to risk their lives four thousand feet above the ground.

They were a daredevil bunch, adventurers all, preferring an exciting life that promised danger to a safer but infinitely more dull existence on the ground. Although parachutes were used by flyers and passengers in zeppelins and observation balloons, the fighter pilots disdained them.

"A parachute adds too much weight and hampers your freedom of movement," Larry told Max. "Besides, if you're hit, there's no time to bail out."

A few who had managed to parachute-jump from a burning plane were strafed by enemy pilots while they dangled helplessly in the air.

"I'd rather go down with my plane," concluded Larry.

After a wait of what seemed like a minute but was actually three hours, Max awoke from a dreamless sleep to the roar of motors warming up. He ran outside into the winter sunshine to see a line of ten airplanes on the field, all with propellers whirling. The place swarmed with men,

361

some of them mechanics still tinkering with the engines and some pilots — French, British, and American — waiting, helmeted, goggled, and decked out in heavy woolen uniforms. Parachutes were humped on the backs of one or two.

He whipped round as a hand fell on his shoulder. "Come with me, Max. I'll show you my machine."

It was Jake, his frail figure encased Eskimo-like in insulated pants and jacket. The parachute on his back seemed to weigh him down, but Max remembered the strong handshake. The man was made of sturdy stuff.

Max followed the man from Brooklyn to a snappy-looking plane, which the wiry Brooklyn pilot explained was a French Nieuport. "I call it 'Bébé,' " he said, grinning and smacking the sleek frame with his hand as one would a favorite dog or perhaps the rounded bottom of one's sweetheart.

Six skull-and-crossbones "kills" were painted on the fuselage. "Today I'm up for Number Seven," Jake grinned, climbing into the single-seater cockpit. The last thing Max saw as his new friend taxied to get into position for takeoff was a lifted hand, thumps up, for victory.

The planes flew east into the rising sun in a smart V formation like a flock of geese heading south for the winter.

Max ate some coffee and rolls in the hangar. After breakfasting, he roamed around the airdrome and talked to the mechanics and guard personnel. The planes grounded for repairs came from England and France.

"Americans are kind of slow about getting into the aircraft industry, but I hear that Packard is gearing up with something that'll put all these babies out of style," cracked a grease-covered mechanic named Bob Venable, who came from a little town in Oregon. "Maybe when we get into the war too, they'll start hustling."

"Think America will actually go to war with Germany?"

Bob shrugged, then flashed a gap-toothed grin at Max. "Ever handle a screwdriver?"

362

Max said he certainly had and for the next few hours was happily employed as a mechanic's helper. His head was deep inside the engine of a small one-seater called a Sopwith Pup when Bob yelled, "They're back."

Everyone ran out onto the airstrip to gaze into the sky, and along with the others, Max shaded his eyes against the brilliant sun. The air was cold, the February temperature near freezing. Fleecy clouds gamboled through a dazzling blue sky like lamps in a pasture, thought Max. Too bad he couldn't enjoy the view.

He had been sweating inside the hangar, with all the motors going full blast, and now he felt a sudden chill go through his bones. He strained for the distinctive shape of Jake's little Nieuport.

Beside him Bob counted as the Allied planes circled to land one by one. "One missing," he said laconically. "But sometimes it takes a while for all of them to get back."

"How long?" inquired Max anxiously.

"Hard to tell. Minutes to hours."

No one left the field. The missing Nieuport showed up ten minutes later with a German Fokker on its tail. Jake Epstein's *Bébé* was trailing black smoke and, as his wings dipped and he began his downward spiral over the field, a shout arose. "Bail out, Brooklyn! Jump!"

Abruptly, the burning Nieuport halted its downward plunge and flew into a fleecy cloud. For a long, agonizing moment it was lost to sight. Then, emerging on the other side, it flew directly into the path of a bright-red airplane that seemingly came out of nowhere.

Only the tail fin and an oblong on each side of the fuselage had been left white to highlight the rows of black Maltese crosses that ticked off the "kills."

Max tried to count the crosses but stopped at ten. There seemed to be three times that many.

"My God," swore Bob at Max's shoulder. "It's the Red Baron. Only a brazen devil like him would come right into our lines."

Max turned. "The Red Baron?"

"Yeah. Full name is Manfred von Richthofen. Some damn Prussian aristocrat. Paints all his machines fire-engine red, whether Albatross or Fokker or whatever. Even if he's only borrowing it for a sortie, he splashes red all over it. No camouflage for him. But I got to admit he's wicked in the sky. He seems to lead a charmed life."

The blood was pounding in Max's ears. Manfred, here? A flyer? What happened to the cavalry of which he had been so proud? Suddenly his friend's words spoken in a Polish forest flashed into memory. *My God, how marvelous, to soar like a bird!*

"I know the guy—" He stopped. How could he explain to these patriotic American flyers that he was once "best friend" to the infamous Red Baron?

Both fell silent, watching tensely as Jake Epstein clambered out of the cockpit. His bundled figure dropped like a plummet for a few heart-stopping seconds, and then the watchers exploded with a collective sigh as the white parachute billowed up.

They heard the crash as the stricken Nieuport divèd into the bordering trees and sent plumes of smoke upward, enveloping momentarily both Jake and the red plane.

"Well, that's one plane the enemy won't get to show off as a prize of war," Bob remarked.

As Jake continued his float to earth, Max prayed to the patron saint of flyers, whoever he might be, to spare the little guy. Jake swayed as his billowing shroud swerved suddenly to the east and the river, upon whose banks German guns were mounted.

The Allied machine guns started chattering from the rocks, but with incredible daring, the Red Baron zoomed down to a few yards from Jake's floating shape and blasted the Brooklyn flyer with two machine guns mounted behind the red propellers. Jake's hands fell limp at his side and he slumped before the eyes of the men watching from below. A puppet on a string, thought Max, in agony.

The parachute was also hit, and instantly the voluminous silk collapsed around the falling man. The doomed

364

flyer was instantly lost to sight in the trees that had been his *Bébé*'s tomb. The red plane dipped and skimmed the treetops as if making sure that his prey was really down.

Max glimpsed the goggled head of the Red Baron behind the windscreen as the Fokker headed up again and pointed east. Did he imagine it, or was there a jaunty wave of the hand as it sped away? Could there have been a white-toothed smile? He imagined the Red Baron proudly painting still another cross on his fuselage.

Bob launched into a string of profanities, the gist of which was that a man who would shoot an unarmed human being dangling helplessly in the air was the spawn of the devil and a subspecies that even God himself would not own up to.

As he hopped into the ambulance along with the medical team to search for Jake in the woods, Max felt his heart turn to stone within him. The flower of Prussian nobility, the man with whom he had broken bread as a trusted friend and to whom he had confided his inner heart, was now his implacable enemy. The war no longer belonged to the French, the British, the Germans, the Russians. It was everybody's war. It was America's war. It was Max O'Hara's war.

They buried the boy from Brooklyn next morning in a five-hundred-year-old Gothic church, with high vaulted ceilings, stained-glass windows, and statues on the walls painted in bright colors. Jake had not been a religious man, and since no one could locate a rabbi in any case, his pals asked the local priest to say some words, figuring that all prayers went eventually to the same place.

The priest obliged in both Latin and Hebrew—"just to make sure," he said. Little girls in white dresses placed flowers on the wooden casket. Before they wrapped him in his shroudlike parachute, his American friends placed a small American flag between Jake's hands.

That night in the dugout there was no talk of America; the jolly camaraderie of yesterday was gone. Larry cradled his ale and remarked gloomily to Max, "No matter how often it happens, and, God knows, a pilot is killed almost every week, it still hurts like the very devil when it's someone you've lifted a glass or two with."

"I guess you can never get used to death, even when it's all around you," responded Max. His thoughts were not on Jake but on Libby Hughes, whom he still saw in his mind now and then as a bright, lovely being whom he had once adored.

One name was on every tongue—The Red Baron. The daring Prussian had downed fifteen Allied planes, and was a folk hero in his own country. " 'Ace of aces,' he's called," Larry told Max. "His kaiser has given him every medal in existence including the Blue Max."

"Blue Max!" Max quirked his sandy brow. "Can't say that I appreciate my name being bandied about that way!"

"Too bad, friend," said Larry grinning in return. "It's made of blue enamel, but where the 'Max' part comes from, I can't say."

Later in the dormitory Larry produced from a box beneath his bunk an assortment of photographs, some printed on postal cards to send home to loved ones from the front. Most of them displayed the handsome face of Manfred von Richthofen, who was sometimes pictured with his brother Lothar. "The townsfolk take them from dead Germans," he said. "They bring good money now as souvenirs and will jump in value after the war, no matter who wins. They also have a variety of helmets, boots, and uniforms."

Max stared at the cards, thinking of the photograph of Kalina that Manfred had teased him about in the Carpathians. He gave a dry laugh. "Hmm," he murmured, "the new brand of professional beauty."

There were several of an especially compelling picture of the Red Baron in which the pale eyes seemed to gaze out at the world with a kind of sardonic humor. The notorious Blue Max decoration hung on a ribbon around his collar. Tiny eagles were set between the arrowlike, inward-pointing arms of the Maltese cross.

366

He glanced at Larry, who was riffling among the cards and smaller medals in the box. "Got a Blue Max in there I could look at?"

"Nope. Far as we know, the Baron's the only one to get one as yet. Guess we'll have to tear it from around his bloody neck. He's never been seen without it in the sky."

Larry was happy to let Max keep the photograph. "Look at it long and hard, my friend," he said. "Make sure that next time you see the murdering devil you'll know him."

Max nodded glumly. "I've got the bastard's face memorized." He had no intention of telling this American, or anyone else on earth, that his acquaintance with the infamous Red Baron was already one of long standing or that the war between Max and his erstwhile friend would be a strictly private one.

In the morning the American pilots and mechanics quartered at Verdun were ordered to Luxeil, a town at the southern edge of the western front, where they would form the nucleus of a separate squadron composed entirely of Americans. It was to be called the Lafayette Escadrille in honor of the courageous marquis, who had sacrificed his fortune and a life of ease in France to help the American colonies gain their independence from England in 1776.

Hoots and hollers of joy greeted this announcement, and with a beaming face Larry turned to Max as they walked out to the military cars that would drive them to the train. "Are you with us, Red?"

Max nodded. "You bet." All night the dangling figure of Jake Epstein had moved in and out of his fitful dreams along with the laughing, sardonic face of Manfred von Richthofen. "I'd like a crack at the Red Baron myself." His fists clenched at his sides.

"You and every Allied pilot in the sky," said Larry, pounding his fists together with a smack. He raised his hands and covered his face. His shoulders shook as he wept silently for a moment. "God, when I think of how much Jake wanted to be part of this American squadron—"

When he lifted his face, the American's eyes were filled with such pure hatred that Max flinched, stepping back as though from a blaze. Hate was an emotion he had never allowed himself to feel. He had despised his German captors for their unthinking cruelty to civilians and their prisoners but had excused it because they were simply following orders. Like all soldiers in any war, they were automatons. Automatons were not permitted to have feelings.

But, as they rode through the ravaged countryside to board the southbound train, he felt within himself the beginnings of a vengeful fire that seemed to sear his very blood. That fire was hate, he recognized, and would not be quenched until he had met the Red Baron face to face.

In happier times the town of Luxeil had been a spa, its lovely hillsides threaded with hot springs once used by Roman caesars and, since then, by every crowned head of Europe and their retinues. Luxurious hotels looked out on a breathtaking panorama of steep mountainsides, clear blue lakes, and fleecy skies.

The pilots were installed in a handsome villa adjoining the hot baths, together with the French officers. They dined like epicures at the finest hotels. A pair of well-appointed automobiles were always on hand to transport them from place to place. A small army of servants darted obsequiously about, tending their needs.

"I feel like a king," said Larry.

"Or a calf being fattened up for the slaughter," said Max, grumbling. He felt ill at ease at the pampering, but in the weeks that followed, the man from New York who had started out in life as a tenement "rent baby," luxuriated in the kind of life he had dreamed of a child.

There was given to the pilots, he was forced to admit in pensive moments, more than a touch of the concern that is given to a person whose life is coming to a close. An aging, rich relative, for instance, or a fatally ill child.

In spite of the months of internment in Germany, he passed the medical exam with flying colors. "A bit on the thin side, but that's all the better for flying these flimsy contraptions you call airplanes," pronounced the doctor.

The comradeship of the other men was for Max a rare, exhilarating experience. During his long years of exile, he had of necessity made few friends, von Richthofen being the exception. Even as a child he had been a lone wolf, never joining the gangs that infested the streets. The easy friendship and quick understanding he found with Larry Jackson and the others, both pilots and mechanics, was the kind of closeness he had felt so long ago in Homestead with Stan Lesko and Gus Koval.

The name Max being too Germanic for their tastes, and since there was another Red in the group, the Americans called him simply "Yank."

He found himself developing a special intimacy with Bob, the mechanic from Oregon, who had grown up on the streets also. He was a tall, rangy twenty year old with straw-colored hair and an engaging grin, with a sweetheart back home whose picture hung over his bunk. "I'm over here to make some big money," he told Max, "so's we can be married in a year or two."

All of the pilots were bachelors, and all were more than receptive to the overtures of the young women of the town who flocked around the Americans. Although his sweet Kalina remained forever in his heart, Max was not averse to an hour or two of pleasure with a pert, young French girl. But when the time came to paint his beloved's name on his plane, he drew back. When he was given his own training Nieuport, he splashed the fuselage with red, white, and blue stripes, calling it simply "Yank."

"I guess he's been unlucky in love," quipped Bob.

Torn with anxiety over Kalina's fate, Max was forced to open a chink in his armor of privacy by requesting the French commander to use his military resources and telephone a certain convent in Auvergne and inquire if Mrs. Stefan Murav was there with her children.

The answer came within a day. "The lady in question," the smiling commander said, "repaired last spring to

369

Switzerland with her children."

It was when he was flying up above the clouds and mist into the sunlight that Max O'Hara shed his earthly burdens and felt ultimately at home with himself. In those times he caught a glimmering of why men risked their necks at flying when they could be safe and sound below, both feet solidly upon the ground. It was a feeling he had had once before in his life when he was shoveling slag into the blast furnace and felt himself a little god.

There were times, however, when he flew across the border toward Switzerland and glimpsed the towering Alps in the distance, that the image of the beautiful face that he had pushed to the back of his mind along with the rest of life outside the Escadrille would not be denied.

It was in those times that his hand gripped the stick until his knuckles whitened.

Although shelling from the front rarely extended this far south, an occasional enemy plane zoomed from the east or north, arrogantly dipping down to strafe anything on the ground, be it man or plane. The antiaircraft crews were constantly on the alert, but on a particularly murky summer morning when the air above the field was thicker than a London fog and it seemed that nothing could possibly get through the murk, a lone plane darted from the other side of a mountain and, flying low, dropped a bomb squarely on Max's red, white, and blue Nieuport.

Bob Venable had been fueling the engine at that precise moment, and by the time they got to him, he had been immolated. As Max ran out to the field, he took a piece of shrapnel from his own antiaircraft in the fleshy part of his upper thigh. No one else was injured, and the marauder got clean away.

Numb with grief, Max lay in bed with his leg in traction, a concerned Larry at his side. "When you first get into this racket," commented the man from Detroit, "you think that your own death is the worst thing that can happen. But nothing is further from the truth. The hell of it is seeing your friends go, one by one."

It was July before the doctor would permit Max to leave the infirmary, but it was only to order him to Paris for further surgery. "I've done all I can, but the bone was shattered. There's a man at a clinic there who's done a lot of work on this kind of injury. If you ever expect to walk properly again, you need to have it done immediately."

"Will I fly?" Max asked anxiously.

A typical, physician type of shrug was his answer.

The Paris clinic was situated in a stone villa in a charming little town called Les Andelys on the Seine a few kilometers from the city itself. Set at the foot of still another château built by Richard the Lion-Heart during his stay in France, it was surrounded by orchards and chestnut trees and provided a retreat from the war, not only for men with physical wounds like Max's, but for many whose minds and hearts had been touched by shock or tragedy engendered by the war.

Max's operation was soon after his arrival on the first day of August. He awakened to see a familiar face bending over him. "Wanda?" he muttered through the cotton that seemed to fill his mouth.

She nodded, smiling broadly. "Fortunes of war? Remember what we said when we met at *Villa d'Este*?"

He tried to answer her smile but managed only to retch into the pan she placed swiftly under his mouth and dozed off again.

When he woke again some time later, he saw a seemingly familiar man, his wide-browed, earnest Scottish face studying some papers in his hands.

Still befuddled by anesthetic, Max mumbled, "Are you who I think you are, or are you some kind of mirage?"

"I've never been anyone but myself," responded the doctor cheerfully. Then, "How's our patient?"

"I'll live," Max replied laconically, "but what are you doing here, Hardie? Last time I saw you was at Carnegie's estate, and you were being chased out of the country by Stefan Murav for giving him a stillborn son."

Alec chuckled. "In a way I'm grateful to the man.

371

Canada became a gold mine for me. In a few years I had enough money for me and Wanda to come over here and study psychiatry. What I always wanted to do in the first place."

Taking a stethoscope from around his neck, Alec came near and applied it to Max's chest.

"I have a hole in my leg, not in my head," yelled Max indignantly. "I don't belong in a mental ward."

"Easy there, guy, I can't hear your heart for all the noise you're making with your mouth." After a moment, he withdrew his instrument and said calmly, "That's a mighty reassuring heartbeat for a man who's supposed to be dead."

Max frowned. "Is that what everyone — what Kalina thinks?"

"I'm afraid she does."

At that moment the door burst open and a very excited Wanda burst in, her brown eyes aglow with excitement. "Oh, good, you're awake! And more sensible than the first time I saw you, I trust."

"I thought you were in Switzerland with Kalina," Max burst out. "Is she all right?"

"Fine, fine." Wanda dimpled. "And so is your little son, by the way."

"Son? You mean that she and I—"

Alec pursed his lips and waggled a finger at Max in mock disapproval. "It's the kind of thing that's likely to happen when two people persist in making love for weeks on end."

Choked with emotion, Max could only stare at the two of them and repeat over and over, as though it were a word he had just discovered, "son—son—son." Tears filled his eyes and spilled over onto his cheeks.

Her own dark eyes moist with happiness, Wanda perched on the edge of the bed and, taking Max's hand in hers, swiftly related the events that had followed the blowing up of the houseboat in Champagne. Wisely, she skirted over the matter of Kalina's being out of her head for a few weeks, telling him only that all had arrived safely and in good health at the convent in Auvergne where Dunia and Stefi were in the care of the nuns.

Max lay back on the pillow, his big hands over his eyes, his brow deeply furrowed as he concentrated on believing the seemingly incredible. Upon hearing that Kalina had not gone directly to Switzerland but instead had crossed the dangerous wartime Atlantic to visit her dying cousin, he groaned aloud.

"When Zuska died, she came to Paris to have me deliver the child," said Alec. "It was an extremely difficult birth, but when she left a few months later for Vienna to visit Franz Josef on her way to Switzerland to join her children, both mother and child were blooming with health."

"Vienna!" Max exploded, rearing up before he dropped back again in pain. "That's right in the middle of the war." He scowled at Alec. "How could you let her go?"

The Scotsman curved his mouth in a wry smile. "Your son's mother has a very strong will. Besides, the emperor sent an escort of three armed motorcars. No harm will come to her."

"And none has, thank the Virgin," broke in Wanda fervently. She squeezed Max's hand reassuringly. "I've just placed a telephone call to the Hofburg palace. When it is returned, we will wheel you out right in your bed and let you speak to her yourself."

The three friends talked of old times and better ones to come for the ones they all loved until Alec announced that it was high time for both the Hardies to get back to their duties and left the patient to his much-needed sleep.

But not before he extracted a solemn promise that the very second the telephone rang with Vienna at the other end, they would awaken him. "OK," said Wanda, laughing, "but military calls have priority, so it might not happen for a day or two."

A day or two! Giddily, Max gazed out the window at the twilight over the Seine. His heart was pounding so fiercely he wondered if he would get a wink of sleep before that wonderful time came when he would actually hear Kalina's voice. Oh, the wonders of the telephone!

But when they wheeled in another man to keep him company in the hospital room, Max O'Hara was sleeping like a baby.

Chapter Nineteen

Vienna, August, 1916

The night was unbearably hot and humid and Kalina flicked a hand to the back of her neck, lifting the heavy chignon away from her perspiring flesh. She bent her head over the chess table, reading for at least the hundredth time an official-looking paper which the emperor had given her an hour before.

"It can't be true," she murmured in a strangled voice. It was the same thing she said each time she read the document, as if by denying the existence of the piece of paper, she might somehow make the fateful words disappear.

The words had become an incantation. Her finger rubbed the embossed seal at the head of the letter. Unquestionably the eagle of Imperial Germany.

She met the eyes of the Austrian emperor. His were soft with compassion, hers glazed with longing. "Are you sure there can be no mistake? Have you checked your sources again?" She drew in her breath. "Sometimes officials will write anything, make up a story, just to close the case"— she gave a dry laugh—"to get rid of someone who's been a pest."

He shook his head. "Please, my dear, don't grasp at nonexistent straws. How fervently I wish I could say there was any hope. Nothing in my life since my own dear wife fell by an assassin's hand has given me more unhappiness than to bring you this sad news. But you see before you the authenticated signature of the German commandant of the camp in Strasbourg where your Max was a prisoner of war until—"

"Until he was shot trying to escape," finished Kalina flatly. Her eyes fell back to the letter, but she did not read. The words were engraved on her mind. Pressing her fingertips to her closed eyes, she recited, "He was supposed to be burying the dead but somehow got mixed up with a band of deserters." She fingered the metal tag that had come with the dispatch. There was a number on it, which the letter stated had belonged to a certain Max O'Hara, picked up in the war zone on the Meuse in March, 1915.

The record was specific. It had been raining for days, and the body were rapidly decomposing by the time they got around to burying it, but several other prisoners who had known the tall American had verified the identification, remembering distinctly the clothes he wore. The shirt had a hole in it over the heart and the trousers were ragged at the ankle, resembling a fringe.

"The shirt was red, but the trousers were blue home-spun." Kalina closed her eyes, invoking the image of Max behind the wheel of the houseboat. For the past hour, ever since the footman had brought the letter, the emperor had been trying with little success to explain to the bewildered woman why her lover had been held as a prisoner when he was neither French nor British nor Belgian but a citizen of a country officially uninvolved in the war.

"The German troops were retreating at the time," he said. "They had little time to stop and question every solitary human being who popped up in the middle of their lines. And perhaps he himself was confused. You said the boat was blown out of the water and that you yourself were disoriented for weeks."

At that moment a moth flew into the open window and the footman began to chase it round the room. Kalina and the emperor watched the antics of man and insect as they darted about the chamber in a kind of frenzied dance.

Near hysteria, Kalina succumbed to a fit of giggles.

Abruptly, Franz Josef thumped a fist on the chessboard. "For God's sake, man, desist. That bug's the only thing in this godforsaken place that seems happy to be alive."

The panting footman retreated to stand stiffly at the door. Rising from her chair, Kalina exclaimed, "Oh, don't say such a terrible thing!" The letter from Germany fell to the floor. She came around the table to throw her arms around the emperor's neck from behind. What were her troubles compared to his? His armies were losing the war, his loved ones were dead, his high officials not to be trusted, his advice no longer heeded. All regarded him as a senile old man.

He reached up to draw her hand to his lips, holding it there. "You speak too much of death," she said brokenly. "You are only eighty-six today. It is not fitting that a Hapsburg should be so morbid on his birthday."

"A Hapsburg is fit for nothing," he said morosely. "Except to be born, and after a life of futility, to die." A dry laugh escaped him. "As expediently as possible."

Then, in a chillingly dead tone, "The Hapsburg who dies young does the world a favor."

Kalina fell silent. The mood would pass, and in the morning he would be his old cheerful self again. Until the next bitter spell. The doctors had dosed him to the gills, but he weakened with each passing day. He had lost all interest in affairs of state, and except for Kalina and his minister of war, he saw no one. As for the war raging on all fronts, he seemed to have forgotten it.

The aged head dropped to the chessboard, scattering the pawns, and soon Kalina heard the loud breathing that told her he had fallen into one of his frequent dozes. Carefully extracting her hand, she walked to the window. Not a leaf stirred in the courtyard below, dark shapes moved about, a door opened and closed, emitting a fleeting shaft of yellow light.

Lifting her head, she gazed out over the city. Seemingly untouched by the war, life, on the surface at least, went on in the City of Song. People walked arm in arm, talking of this and that along the tree-lined Ringstrasse whose lights encircled the inner city like a diamond necklace. The opera, the ballet, the riding school—all the gay attractions that made the city a mecca for tourists—carried on in a curtailed manner. Curfews, shortages of fuel and electricity, and the loss of strong young men to the war had taken their toll.

What suffering existed went largely unseen and unnoted by a monarch engrossed in his own misery. Within the crooked, narrow cobbled streets that wound behind the gay night spots and cafés lived those who were starving. Food was in short supply, the emperor's troops must be fed first. Many had given husbands and fathers to the Imperial armies. Many would not return.

What whimsical fate had decreed, Kalina wondered, that she, an American, be stuck in the middle of someone else's war. She felt a kinship with the sad-eyed women in the huddled houses of Vienna. For the first time since she was sixteen years old, she found herself without a man at her side. Her rightful husband was wandering round the battlefields of Europe, a raving madman. Her sweet, adorable Max, the love of her life, lay moldering in an unmarked grave somewhere in Germany.

"Look at the silly moth, flying to his death." Awakening with a jerk, the emperor squinted up at the crystal chandelier. Turning, Kalina watched as the light brown insect flew directly into a fluted lamp and, with a last desperate beat of its tiny wings, perished in the flame.

"We are all insects," Franz Josef said.

Smiling at his childish petulance, Kalina seated herself once more across from the emperor. She picked up a pawn but simply toyed with it. Neither was interested in the game.

He had summoned her from Paris a few months after Michael's birth in November. The telegram had been brief and imperious. "I am dying. I need a friend."

She had come immediately, arriving in the midst of a

378

January blizzard and finding him exactly as he had said. Dying. He seldom left his bed. A few weeks into her visit, he had revived and become more himself, but since his ailments were of long standing and terminal, the doctors had assured her that any remission would be strictly temporary.

Upon hearing the story of Max's disappearance and apparent death, Franz Josef immediately launched an investigation. "May take months," he had warned. "Military bureaucracy is almost impenetrable, no matter if it's a Hapsburg cracking the whip." He had flashed a rare grin at the time and tweaked his bushy sideburns with a leer. "I presume, Madame Murav, that you also want me to catch your philandering husband."

She nodded, bristling. "Stefan is not philandering; he is simply unbalanced at the moment. Whatever his state, it would be most helpful to know if he is alive or dead."

In February she spent a few weeks in Switzerland with the children. It was a pleasure to tell them that no less a dignitary than the emperor himself would find their father and bring him home where he belonged.

Both Dunia and Stefi were enchanted with baby Michael, although Dunia, now a sophisticated eighteen, had rolled her brown eyes and said, "Where did all the red hair come from? Both you and Daddy are dark, and from what I studied about heredity, dark genes are dominant."

She had said no more than that, and Kalina had decided, given the worry about her father, not to trouble the girl with the story of her Mama Kalina's love affair. In any event, the chances that Dunia would remember Max were slim. She was only three when he left Pittsburgh and had not, to Kalina's knowledge, ever set eyes on him.

One day, when the war was over and everything was back to normal, she and Dunia would have a heart-to-heart talk about life and love and why people sometimes did things that might appear wrong to the world but were right to the heart.

First things first. Max must be found. And almost as an

afterthought — Stefan too, of course. At the time, Kalina did not let herself think what she would do when and if both were found alive. She would think about that later, too.

Her slipper brushed against the letter from Germany that had fallen to the floor when she had run to comfort the emperor.

Sometimes life seemed, she thought, like a kaleidoscope, filled with a mess of jagged, little colored fragments. The more one strove to bring order to it, the more it seemed to whirl around in its own chaos.

The emperor seemed lost in thought, holding a knight in his hand and staring at it mindlessly. Driven by a sudden, irrational impulse, Kalina stooped, picked up the letter, and running to the fireplace a few feet away, laid it carefully on the unlit logs. Then, taking a long match from the box on the marble hearth, she put it to the paper. It flared up and turned to ash within seconds.

"Something on fire?" Franz Josef lifted his head, sniffing.

Kalina hurried back to the chair. "Nothing, Your Majesty. Let's get on with the game." It was an idiotic thing she had just done but of a sudden, she began to laugh. She had disposed of one little crazy piece of the kaleidoscope.

The face of the footman at the door remained impassive. The odd behavior of his monarch and his guests was none of his concern. When a soft knock sounded at the door beside him, he sprang to open the door.

Mary Lesko entered, and after curtsying to the old man, said to Kalina. "We must leave for the opera, Kalina."

The old man scowled. "Nonsense. We've just begun the game. Sit down."

Promising with a smile and a kiss on the withered cheek that she would return long before midnight and take supper with him, Kalina left with Mary. Franz Josef took up his cane and, with the footman at his elbow, made his slow, meandering way to his own rooms where he would drink cognac and sleep, awaiting her return.

Halfway down the long corridor, he turned. "I'll place a telephone call to Strasbourg and speak to the German Commandant in person."

Kalina smiled and blew a kiss.

The performance that night was to be *Madame Butterfly* and Mary was to sing the role of Suzuki, the maid. Since the Puccini opera demanded a small cast and simple settings, it had become a mainstay of the wartime repertoire.

The Homestead girl had established a secure position among the international group of singers and had already received an invitation to audition for the Metropolitan in New York.

Tonight was to be a benefit for war relief, and the emperor having granted her reluctant permission to leave the palace grounds, Kalina went happily to don her cloak and fetch Michael from his crib beside her bed. Except for the hours when he slept and she was entertaining the emperor, Kalina never let the baby out of her sight. Nine months old, he had just begun to crawl about and make cunning sounds, which none but a doting mother dared to call speech. Tonight he would be with her at the opera. She always sat in the royal box high above the auditorium, and if he should cry, it was a simple thing to retire to an anteroom.

Kalina adored her baby to distraction. He was blessed with a sunny disposition. Her heart ached as she thought of Dunia and Stefi far off in Switzerland, deprived of Michael's cunning baby years.

Now, as she lifted him from the covers and held him close, she resolved to leave Vienna immediately. Tomorrow. The trains were crowded, but the emperor could easily get her a compartment to cross the border. Michael should be with his brother and sister. They should not miss a minute of his growing up.

She had promised the emperor to remain only until his investigation into Max's disappearance had borne fruit. It had taken seven long months. She had often thought, but had not dared to voice it, that the old man had known the truth for months but, fearing the loss of her companionship, had deliberately withheld the information from her.

Rage began to grow within her as thought became almost certainty. Hapburgs have died without me for five hundred years, she thought. So can this one.

The driver was new. "Felix is sick." Respectfully, he tipped his visored cap. "I am his brother, Jan."

The sudden change disturbed Kalina, but she was reassured by the sight of a second man in the uniform of the Palace Guard, two guns in holsters. The big Benz automobile was heavily curtained and bore the Imperial flag at the front and rear. They were as safe as money and power could make them.

The city swarmed with petty criminals, skulking around every corner, ready to pounce out from every dark alley or shop door at anyone who looked even remotely as if they carried money. And there were the eternal anarchists, who despite the war they had wanted, continued to stir up trouble.

As she took her place on the cushioned back seat between Mary and the nursemaid Agnes who held the blanketed Michael, Kalina felt a sense of unreality envelop her. She was dressed up in furs and satin and going to the opera as though this day were like any other! As though a part of her heart had not just been cut out by a few words in a letter.

Everything about her—the street, the auto, the lights, the people they passed—had the detached appearance of objects on a stage that one watches mindlessly, knowing that it was all a sham. The cold hard fact of Max's death had not yet become a part of her sensible mind. She was forced to accept intellectually the words on the paper, but her heart went its own way.

The two men slid in front. Kalina heard the gears mesh and the purr of the powerful engine as they moved smoothly through the streets toward the opera house. Michael became restless in Agnes's arms, so Kalina took him and quieted him. The movement of the automobile always disturbed him. As she took the baby, Kalina noted that the usually cheerful nursemaid seemed drawn and agitated.

"Are you ill, Agnes?" she inquired. "If so, it is not too late to turn around and take you back to the palace. I am perfectly capable of caring for the baby by myself. He is no problem. He likes the lights and the singing."

The Croatian girl sat up straight, and with an anguished glance at Kalina, screamed, "No, no, please stop. No-o-oo—" She clawed with her hands at the glass that separated the driver from the passengers in the rear, but just then the auto skidded round the corner and raced down an alley at a frightening speed, throwing Agnes against Kalina and the baby.

Mary bolted up. "This is not the way to the State Opera House, driver! What are you—"

Her words were swallowed up by the grinding screech of tires as the vehicle slammed to a halt and hurled everyone in the back seat to the floor. Mary gasped, the baby wailed, and Kalina's heart lurched to a stop. They must have hit something. Why doesn't that fool Agnes stop her screaming?

Frantic, she untangled the blankets from around Michael's little body and held his face to hers. She felt under the blanket for signs of injury. At once, the back door was thrown open and the driver thrust his head inside. "Don't scream, ladies, and you won't get hurt." The guard stood at the other door pointing a gun at them.

Kalina scrambled back up to the seat with Michael, while Mary sat on the floor, dazed but seemingly unhurt. The driver dragged Agnes into the street and took her by the shoulders. "Off with you, girl," he told the nursemaid. "Remember, one word to anyone about this and you die."

Heedless of the weapon jabbed into her back, Agnes shouted into the auto at Kalina. "Madame, forgive me, pray for me. They made me. They threatened to harm my parents in Croatia if I didn't help them. They need money for the cause, a lot of money, and they promised that no harm will come to you or Michael."

"Enough!" The enraged driver slapped the girl across the face. "Now be off!"

She scuttled off into the dark and the guard climbed into the back seat and sat down between the two women. Kalina had pulled out her breast to quiet the hysterical baby, modestly drawing her satin cloak over the suckling child's face and her nipple. The man beside her smiled broadly. "A beautiful boy, Madame Murav. How much do you think your husband will give as ransom for the two of you?"

The church bells of Vienna were striking midnight when the footman touched the emperor on the shoulder. The old one had drunk more than his prescribed quota of bedtime cognac before stretching his skeletal frame on the army cot that had been his bed for many years. Yawning widely, the footman gave the royal shoulder another shake.

It took three more tugs and still another cough, this time in his ear, before Franz Josef opened his eyes. He sat up straight, blinking. "Is it midnight? Has Madame Murav returned, then?"

"No, Your Highness, but there is a person on the telephone."

Abruptly, the emperor came wide awake. "Ah, Strasbourg. The matter of the American prisoner of war."

"No, sire. He says his name is Dr. Alec Hardie, and he is calling from Paris. The matter concerns a certain Max O'Hara."

The emperor drew his royal brows together. "I placed no call to Paris and I know no one by that name. As for Max O'Hara, he is dead. We received word this very day."

The old man collapsed back down on his cot. "Awaken me again when Madame Murav returns from the opera."

When the footman returned to the telephone in the Imperial offices, Paris had hung up. Wartime regulations cut off any calls of a nonmilitary nature to three minutes.

He shrugged. Why would anyone in Paris be calling Vienna? The two cities were at war.

The Benz headed out of the city, taking a circuitous route through dimly lit alleys and back streets. Here, unlike the gay thoroughfares around the palace, no one was about, the houses were dark and shuttered. A helmeted policeman stood on a corner but Kalina had no intention of screaming or making a fuss. The young man between her and Mary seemed to have an itchy finger on the trigger, and, despite the fact they were being taken for ransom, she could not take the chance that he would not shoot her—and the baby—in cold blood. Or perhaps, becoming frightened of discovery, shoot in panic.

And what about poor Mary, innocently caught in the conspiracy?

A clock chimed solemnly in the city and commenced to play *The Blue Danube* on the carillon. The guard began to hum and then to sing along in Serbian. Nine o'clock. They had left the palace at half-past eight. The guard began to stamp his feet in waltz time as the carillon went on and on.

The evil-looking gun lay on his lap, but Kalina squashed a fleeting temptation to snatch it up while he was engrossed in his song. If it came to it, could she kill?

Squeezed into the corner of the seat with her eyes closed, Mary was alarmingly quiet. But as the guard reached out to touch her face, she drew back and slapped him. "You scum, pretending to be a patriot, yet you're an animal like the rest."

There was the rap of a knuckle on the glass as the driver turned round. His shout filled the auto. "None of that, Basil. You know what Yurek said. No monkey business. Nobody, not even a filthy-rich Murav, will pay for damaged goods."

Rubbing his cheek, Basil leaned back and winked at Mary. "Just a little harmless fun."

A short distance into the countryside, their captors exchanged the easily recognized Benz for a motorized ambulance with large red crosses splashed on the roof and sides. Inside were two cots, and after ordering the women to lie down and go to sleep, Basil bolted the doors from the outside. He then joined Jan in front and they drove again at a very high speed, accompanied by a continuous jangling of the alarm bell. The men commenced immediately to talk in loud voices over the noise of the bell.

They spoke in rapid Serbian. Years before, on her first visit to Vienna, Kalina had, of necessity, learned to speak the melodic language. So had Mary. Many of the palace servants, as well as shopkeepers in the city, were Serbs. The men either didn't know or didn't care that their captives might understand what they were saying.

Listening intently, Kalina learned that they were being taken deep into the mountains to a rendezvous, there to await the delivery of the ransom that they were confident Stefan Murav would send without delay for the release of his wife and child.

The money was to be in the form of gold—bars or ornaments, anything would do—to be sent to Russia to keep the national treasury from collapsing. The progress of the war was being hampered by a lack of funds; if Russia lost, Serbia, which had sworn allegiance to the Czar, would be swallowed up again by the Austrian empire.

A Cossack named Yurek, a high officer in the Imperial Russian army, was the mastermind of the plot. It was a common name—"George" in English—Kalina reflected, thinking fleetingly of the Yurek who had filled poor dead Zuska's last thoughts. The name was probably fictitious, in any case.

After a time, the bells mercifully ceased, and the men fell silent. The ambulance motor labored as if climbing steeply. At one point, they stopped, but the men did not get out. They spoke in low voices with another man, who filled the tank with gas, and then drove off again. The road became much rougher; apparently they were now in the mountains north of Vienna. They must surely be well across the border by now in Bohemia, the land of the Czechs and Slovaks.

Beyond that lay Poland and Jaslo. Odd, Kalina thought, that I should be going home in such a manner.

Her rambling thoughts turned to Stefan. Obviously, he was alive and reasonably well and in control of his senses. This Yurek, who had engineered the kidnapping, must know where her husband was. Cossacks were no fools. This clever Yurek would not likely waste his time demanding money from a dead man. Logically, Stefan would be in Poland if he were anywhere. He had not died on that mountain in Auvergne as Franz Josef had been telling her for months. Had the emperor kept news of her husband's whereabouts from her, just as he had probably withheld the report of Max's death until forced to reveal it?

Kalina's mind became a centrifuge, in which her thoughts whirled round and round. She longed for sleep.

Mary dozed on her cot. Michael slept also, having taken the breast still another time since their capture. Kalina was accustomed to a midnight supper with the emperor, and she had eaten little dinner. A nursing mother needs food regularly, continuously. And drink. Were these reckless young Serbs aware of such intimate female needs? Both appeared too young to be fathers. She must also get some sleep, or her milk would surely dry up.

So Kalina fretted, her eyes staring at the ceiling that looked as if it had been in more than one battle. The worn fabric covering was pierced with holes through which the moon shone bravely, like little stars, as if assuring her that God was still in his heaven and keeping a paternal eye on all his children.

Her mind at ease, Kalina slept.

She awakened to a raging thirst and the harsh glare of a bright sun in her face. The doors of the ambulance stood wide open and a voice said in Polish, "Oh, what pretty

387

prizes you brought us, Basil. And three of them. Well done, comrade."

The speaker was a red-faced woman with a white kerchief tied in a loose knot under her chin. She wore the blue smock and white blouse of a Cossack woman. Both garments were very dirty, and she reeked of sweat.

Kalina and Mary stumbled out into almost unbearable heat that seemed to come in waves from the rocky plateau to which the ambulance had brought them. Tall, rocky peaks loomed on all sides, like a fortress.

Michael had awakened, and being both wet and hungry, began immediately to wail. Before a terrified Kalina could protest, the baby was snatched from her arms by one of a group of women who came running from a confusion of mud and wattle huts and tents dotting the plateau.

"My baby," she shrieked, lunging after the woman. But he had been swallowed up by an admiring crowd and was handed from one to the other, each exclaiming in a high, feminine voice. "Oh, how sweet — what a carrot top — he is famished, see how he sucks my finger."

Her son being obviously in no danger from the adoring women, Kalina turned to the red-faced woman. "Please, I must give him the breast."

"Sure, sure," she replied absently and, placing her big workworn hands on Kalina's satin cloak, flicked it rudely from her shoulders. Walking away from the group, the woman buried her face in its luxurious folds, swaying back and forth and emitting a kind of chanting moan of pure joy.

Other women closed round Kalina and Mary, and to Kalina's horror, began to undress them both. Carefully, the rows of buttons were released from Kalina's taffeta gown and Mary's *peau de soie*. Even their undergarments were slipped off without dispatch, and when they both stood naked except for their slippers, they were pushed down none too gently to the blistering rock, and these were taken off also, along with the long silken stockings. Mary wept softly, her head in her hands from shame, but Kalina faced her tormentors proudly, her black eyes defiant.

All the garments were passed around; each admired with awe and exclamations. Enraged, Kalina rose up and shouted, "Yurek will hold you all responsible for the shame you have brought to me and my companion."

A shout of laughter erupted from the edge of the plateau where a band of men had just emerged from the trees at the foot of the mountain. They had obviously been bathing in a stream, for they were naked to the waist and their flesh and hair glistened with wet.

The tallest of them walked slowly and with an air of authority toward the naked women, the others following at a short distance. He was obviously their leader and seemed every inch to fit the part. His hair was dark blond and fell to his shoulders in broad waves, a pair of deep blue eyes twinkled merrily in a face as brown as a nut. Arrogantly, he crossed his arms across a broad chest that bloomed with a fuzz of hair somewhat darker than his head. Although his fine, high nose and noble bearing betrayed mixed blood, the flowing sateen trousers and the curved dagger at his belt showed him to be a Cossack.

Halting his march a scant few inches from Kalina, he dropped his eyes to appraise her from head to foot. A muscle twitched in a face whose handsome good looks were marred by a jagged scar that ran from his left brow to the corner of his wide, sensuous mouth. The other men crept up behind their leader, grinning lewdly, but none spoke a word.

Whimpering with fright, Mary covered her breasts with her hands, and even Kalina, brazen until now, felt the blood warm her neck and face in a blush, as she felt the heat of the man's intent perusal. Mary started to weep in earnest and cowered against Kalina's back.

"They won't rape you, Mary. Their women are here. Cossack women always follow their men to war."

The tall man spoke. "You know us well, Kalina Olkonsky of Jaslo. When I saw you last, you were a little pigeon with no breasts."

She started. "Look up a Cossack they call Yurek," Zuska had said. "Kiss him for me."

Could this be Zuska's Yurek? But surely he was too young to have wooed the girl so long ago. Her heart was beating wildly. If this were the same man, she might be able to use the coincidence to advantage.

But she said merely, "I know that a soldier of the Czar is honorable and will do nothing to offend his sovereign."

At that moment, the red-faced woman came out of a nearby hut, carrying an armful of clothing. Thrusting them at the captives, she stood in front of the tall man and hit him in the chest with her fist. "God will strike you down in your sleep, Yurek, for gaping at a married woman with lust in your eyes."

Turning to the men behind him, she yelled, "Go to your huts, you lecherous donkeys, or I'll set the women on you."

Picking up a rock, she whirled it round and round her kerchiefed head as if to hurl it into the crowd, and the men scattered, laughing and hooting but running very fast.

As for their leader, his face was flaming. "I have no wife to comfort me at night, Sura." He grinned sheepishly, like a boy who has been caught looking at erotic pictures. Sweeping a hand toward Kalina, who was rapidly donning wide peasant skirt and blouse, he muttered, "Even you, old mother, whose bed no man has warmed for many a year, must confess that—"

Kalina's sudden cry of amazement cut him off. Suddenly gripped by the conviction that Zuska's Yurek and the man their captors had discussed in reverential tones in the ambulance were one and the same, she exclaimed, "Are you the Yurek who masterminded this foul plot to snatch an innocent child and his mother and"—she drew Mary close—"a leading prima donna from the State Opera, a girl who has no thought of war or politics, to this desolated place?"

He flashed a wide-toothed smile, the sheepish look vanished, and he bent almost double in a mock bow. "Yes, Madame, I am." But quickly straightening to his full height, he assumed a stern expression and continued soberly, "I am also the Yurek who will protect you and your companion Mary Lesko from my men."

He turned and walked away but shot back in a loud voice for all to hear, "Not *all* of them have their women at their sides."

Distractedly, Kalina ran to the hut where the women had carried Michael. He must be fainting with hunger by now. She had last fed him in the ambulance sometime in the dark.

The interior was dark but cool, and a small fire burned under a samovar. Someone drew her inside and handed her a tin mug of hot tea. "Drink, little mother, for the milk in your breasts."

Stunned at the change in their manner, Kalina sank to the earthen floor, joining in the circle of women who were eating their midday meal. Thick chunks of black bread lay on a spread cloth. There were also dried fish, goat cheese, and figs. Picking up the little knife on the cloth, she cut herself a hearty wedge of the aromatic cheese. The tea was rich and generously laced with honey.

Her baby nestled in the arms of a dark-eyed young woman sitting directly at her side. Michael was fast asleep and smelled sweetly of mother's milk. The woman turned and smiled. "I have a little one of six months, a daughter." She pointed to the corner where five or six bundled-up babies were asleep. "She is happy to share her food with the son of Kalina Murav."

By evening, Kalina was assigned to a spacious hut built against the forested slope. The cots were none too clean but Mama Sura, who also lived there, informed her there was water aplenty in the forest where she would be free to wash both herself and her linen. Mary would eat and sleep with the younger, unmarried girls, some of whom were Cossack sweethearts. Others were sisters, daughters, or even mothers of the men, who came along to tend them if they should be wounded or fall ill. Sura's two sons had trained here under Yurek and were now fighting on the eastern front for Mother Russia.

As she saw Mary being led away, Kalina was beset with anxiety. How would this city-bred girl fare with these rough, peasant women? Despite Yurek's bold assurances, she feared that Mary would fall prey to a dashing young Cossack.

But in the early evening as she walked to the stream to fetch water for Michael's bath, Kalina spied Mary with a group of women sitting around a blazing fire in a cleared space between the huts. Some of the men were preparing to dance, and the women gathered around, as is the custom. She remembered from her childhood the excitement of the vigorous Cossack dancing. Hardly an evening passed without the sound of their voices raised in song and the sight of their bodies twirling in the dance.

Dressed in a white blouse and flowing, red peasant skirt, her long hair in braids down her back, Mary was engaged in a lively conversation with the others, and even from a distance, Kalina thought she did not look unhappy. The two women had been intimate friends for many years, but to her knowledge Mary had never had a love affair, her music studies having consumed all her time and devotion.

But she's thirty! The thought struck Kalina with amazement. The slender, blue-eyed girl was no longer the little nursemaid she had hired in Pittsburgh to care for Dunia.

That first night of her captivity among the Cossacks Kalina did not go out to watch the dancing but lay on her cot inside the hut with Michael at her side. The men and women around the fire sang a folk tune she had heard in her childhood.

Cry the willows, I planted by my brook, cry my heart for my love has gone to war—

Mary Lesko's rich contralto soared above the powerful masculine sound, and Kalina found, much to her astonishment, that here among these warlike people, she had found a curious kind of feeling that she had known in Pittsburgh within the sheltering circle of her own family.

She searched for a word to describe it, ultimately

deciding that it was that elusive thing called "contentment."

That night her sleep was deep and dreamless as a child's. Must be the mountain air, she thought, when she awoke feeling more refreshed than she had since the weeks following Michael's birth when she had lain in the Paris clinic, Alec and Wanda tending to her every need, and experienced that glorious feeling of fulfillment each time she gazed on her love child and put him to her breast.

For all its romantic aura, Vienna was hot and close in summers, freezing in winter. Here, in the Carpathians she had known in her early years, and, despite the fact that she was actually being held captive, she felt free as a bird.

Rising quietly and leaving Michael asleep in his blanket, she padded out of the hut and toward the stream to wash her face and hands. Returning refreshed from the icy water, she was caught by the splendor of the rising sun against the northern mountains. She stood a long time, lost in thought. Jaslo lay a few hours' ride to the north. Perhaps the men who took her and Mary back to Vienna might be persuaded to travel to her native village before heading south to Austria. A little money in their pockets might work the miracle.

Some men emerged from the huts and climbed upon their horses. Yurek was among them, and as they passed her, he reined in. "We go to Jaslo to meet your husband, Madame Murav."

She looked up, startled. "But why not take me with you? I have not seen my husband for more than a year. I thought him dead, and now that you assure me he is alive, I am frantic with anxiety for his health. When I saw him last—"

Impatiently, the Cossack flicked the reins, the hawkish face darkened. "Out of the question. Jaslo has been the vortex of enemy action. There are Germans everywhere. No one is safe, especially pretty women. Furthermore, if Murav delivers the gold as promised, my men and I must go immediately on to Moscow to present our prize to the Czar."

He loomed over her a moment longer on his shaggy Cossack pony, gazing down at her, and under the tall sheepskin hat his blue eyes were dark and brooding, a sharp contrast to the merriment she had seen there yesterday as he had looked upon her naked. A long, crimson cloak they called a "burka" was flung carelessly across his broad shoulders, reaching to the short pony's flanks.

Abruptly, he lifted his hand as in a salute, and with a shout, led his men out of camp. Kalina stood, rooted, until the last hoofbeat had died away, wondering when she could give him the kiss she had promised Zuska? It must be on the lips of course; her cousin had never recognized any other kind. Even when her affectionate cousin greeted other women, the lips met — not cheeks or brows as with less fervid people.

Kalina found her blood warming at the prospect of fulfilling her dead cousin's last wish. A deathbed vow is after all more sacred than any other.

Beside her she heard the gravelly old voice of Mother Sura. "Yurek is a fine man. A great leader and an honorable one. He will keep his word and restore you to your Vienna."

"I have no wish to return to Vienna," Kalina responded with asperity. "My children are in Switzerland, and my husband is in Jaslo."

Turning, Sura placed her hands on Kalina's shoulders. "I knew your mother Hania well. She married a man who is my cousin." She smiled, her weathered face becoming a network of tiny wrinkles. "Would you like to see your mother, child?"

"More than anything else in the world." Kalina's black eyes widened with excitement. "Do you know where she is? Can you take me to her?" She took the woman's hands in hers with a pressure that hurt. "I was told she was with the Cossacks in Russia and that any attempt to contact her would be fruitless."

Through the years Kalina had written often to her mother, but the letters had been returned unopened. A letter to Pan Mikolai had been answered by a note from the local priest: "Hania Olkonsky has disappeared into Russia."

To the people of Central Europe, the word "Russia" meant the end of the world. Many hapless travelers were swallowed up in that vast country that stretched from the Baltic to the Black Sea and far to the east where lived the Tartars, Huns, Mongols. Going to China was less formidable.

"Hania is not in Russia but in the Caucasus, deep in the southern mountains." Sura said, "but the journey to her village is long and treacherous. You must ride through bandit-infested mountains. Many men must accompany you."

"I will pay handsomely." Kalina's heart was beating wildly and she clutched the woman desperately. "Please, arrange it for me, Mother Sura."

At that moment a farm wagon appeared at the head of the road and a clamor arose as women poured from the huts. The rock upon which the encampment was placed was barren, and all supplies and food were brought in by wagon from the farms below. A few goats grazed in the near forest and supplied milk for the children.

"I must go," Sura exclaimed, wrenching free of Kalina. "There may be meat or fruit that requires care in the unloading, and it is my job to see that a fair distribution is made among the huts."

Kalina returned to the hut to fetch Michael who no doubt wanted his breakfast. With the child at her breast, she joined the women on the road. The wagon was filled to overflowing with enormous bunches of white grapes as big as apricots, and it was some time before Sura completed the task of apportioning the luscious fruit among the huts.

When at last the wagon left, Kalina followed the woman to a group of younger women, Mary among them, who were setting barley loaves to bake in a stone-lined pit under which a fire had burned all night.

"I must see my mother," she pleaded, "As I have said, I

395

will pay handsomely—whatever is required."

The woman grunted, then pursed her lips. She shook her kerchiefed head in a disapproving gesture. "Your money, Madame Murav, will be of use, but what is required is men with both skill and courage to escort you. Best wait until this war is over. Guns are everywhere, and airplanes with bombs."

Kalina flared. "My mother will be dead when the war is over."

"So might we all," snapped the woman. Then, softly, "When I saw her last, Hania was blooming like a girl."

"Perhaps Yurek will arrange it."

Sura's eyes flashed with anger. "Do you think Yurek is in love with you?"

"Of course not. I have known him but a day. But there is a connection—" Kalina hesitated, doubting whether the fact that her cousin had loved the man when she was a girl of ten would impress this crusty peasant as a "connection."

"A connection, eh?" The woman turned to the women at the oven. "This fine lady already has a *connection* with our Yurek. What do you think? Does she have a chance to get into his bed? Will she conquer him as she conquered our doddering emperor?"

Blushing furiously, Kalina ran back to her hut. Let them laugh and have their sport. With or without Sura's help, or even Yurek's, she would find a way to see her mother. She evoked the image of the little globe in the sitting room at home where the Caucasus appeared as a mountainous neck of land between the Black Sea and the Caspian. Green and yellow were its colors, green for the high mountain ranges, yellow for the arid, low places in between. Many great, thriving cities were in the Caucasus—Tiflis, Baku. The Caucasus was not as frightening a place as Mother Russia.

Stefan had been there many times in the days when he peddled his armaments. She would make *him* take her there.

But curiously, the thought of visiting her mother with Stefan as he was now seemed unthinkable. Hania thought her daughter a rich and famous lady married to a rich and handsome husband. Stefan was still fabulously wealthy and retained much of his youthful good looks, but given his present instability, added to his idiotic claims to the Polish throne, he was not a man to make one proud to be his wife.

Certainly not a man to present to a mother one has not seen for more than twenty years.

No, resolved Kalina with fresh determination, when she met her mother at long last, it would be just the two of them, mother and daughter, face to face.

Chapter Twenty

The days passed swiftly—cool dawn, hot noon, soft dusk, and starry, velvet night following one upon the other in comforting regularity as in a chain. For the women, life in the Cossack encampment was much like any other. They gathered wood for the fires to cook the rare piece of meat or the fat fish that abounded in the mountain streams. At these same streams they washed the linens and garments for themselves and their men, beating them against the rocks with sticks as women did in villages all over Europe.

For Kalina, who thoroughly enjoyed the companionship and the talk that accompanied the washing, the life was happy. She recalled the long stretches of loneliness on Rutherford Drive, just her and Anusia and the maids in the big house. Sometimes, just to talk, one was forced to walk down long, gloomy corridors and knock on the door.

Her lips twitched in merriment as she evoked a mental picture of herself and Anusia at the banks of the Monongahela beating their satin sheets with sticks.

In truth, save for the fact that they were ringed by towering peaks instead of wheat or barley fields, the huddle of dwellings on the plateau appeared in every way a village such as one might find in any part of central Europe. Children ran about, men shouted impatiently for food or drink, women gossiped at the doorways of the huts. In the soft autumn evenings, there was often dancing about the bonfire, after which young couples drifted into the shadows to couple and banish, for a fleeting time, the war that crouched beyond the mountains.

For Kalina, as with any woman with a year-old baby, the long summer days had few idle moments. Any anxiety over the safety of herself and Mary soon vanished; they would be released and returned to Vienna the moment word was received that the ransom had been paid. She was free to come and go into and out of the forest as she pleased. There was no way out of the isolated place except by the rutted road, the entrance to which was guarded by sentries with guns.

Except for the daily drills in which the soldiers engaged, there was no reminder of the war. An occasional airplane could be seen circling high above, ducking in and out of the clouds in an eerie game of hide and seek. The men assured her, however, that the jagged peaks made it too dangerous for the pilots to fly low enough to drop a bomb.

The regiment was here to train recruits, who came and went with regularity as they were deemed fit for battle. Every Cossack youth was bound to serve the Czar from the age of eighteen until he was thirty-eight. Michael especially loved to sit upon the ground and watch the intricate maneuvers of the men in their colorful uniforms atop their shaggy little Cossack ponies, their sabers flashing in the sun.

Two months passed as in a dream, and now it was a cold November. Rain fell almost every day, the forested mountains turned red and gold and then finally wintry brown. Old Sura put her nose to the wind and promised snow within the week.

Inside the huts the stoves were lit, and Kalina was issued winter garb—a woolen shawl and a pair of trousers lined with sheepskin to ward off the blasts of a Carpathian winter. Michael went about in sheepskin too from head to toe, reminding her of Eskimo babies whose pictures she had seen in geography books.

Max's son was thriving, his little cheeks as fat as a chipmunk's, his legs long and muscular. The rough terrain discouraged him from the usual crawling on all fours, and by his first birthday, he walked upright, swaggering about like a banty rooster to the delight of all. He was a captivating child, tall for his age, with a lively glint in his light blue eyes and a roguish smile.

One wintry evening, Kalina sat in the hut, persuading Michael, newly weaned, to drink goat's milk from a cup. She was quite alone, almost everyone in the camp attending a wedding celebration in the spacious regiment headquarters building. She was grateful there were none to watch her clumsy efforts, for each time she placed the cup between his lips, Michael angrily batted it away or closed his mouth so tightly the milk ran down his chin onto the floor.

Of a sudden, the door opened and a tall fur-clad figure stooped to enter. It was Yurek in his boots and burka. He was breathing deeply and rapidly as if he had just been riding hard. She had not heard the ponies, but then Michael had been making such a noise.

Entering swiftly, he closed the door behind him. "You've got more milk on the floor than in the child," he said laughing. Then bending with astonishing grace for one so big, he picked up the mug and held it to the boy's mouth. "Now drink this, young man," he said in a voice that managed to be authoritative without being harsh.

Startled by the new, firm tones, Michael became still and drank, his baby eyes round above the cup, the little fists, which moments before had been pummeling Kalina's thighs, hanging limp at his sides. Gently, Yurek wiped the white-rimmed little mouth with a nearby cloth. Then picking him up, the Cossack swung the baby high up into the smoky rafters and down and around until Kalina pleaded with him to stop lest the little bit of milk that had gotten inside the tiny belly come up again as easily as it had gone down.

Yurek sat down by the stove, his booted legs crossed beneath him as if he meant to stay, and lit a cigarette from a pack in the pocket of his burka. It took some minutes to calm down the excited child, but Kalina finally managed to settle him atop the pile of skins that was his bed. He fell asleep instantly, and returning to the stove, she lifted a cup from the rack on the wall over the samovar.

"Some tea, Yurek?" Her voice was thick in her throat. He smelled of masculine sweat and tobacco and loomed as big as a bear in the little space.

He reached for the steaming cup, but as she made to draw her hand away, his other hand leaped up to capture it. His hand was warm and strong on hers and she felt a tiny sense of loss when he released her.

"Drink with me, Olkonsky."

Tucking her legs beneath the heavy woolen skirt, Kalina sat down before the stove, facing him and keeping a respectable distance. The warrior code among the Cossacks forbade the drinking of liquor when in training or in combat, so there was none in the camp. But now Yurek drew a flask from the lining of his burka and poured a few drops in his cup and then in hers.

"*Chikhir*," he grinned. "The local wine, much preferred to the Russian vodka."

Following custom, they consumed three cups of tea laced generously with *chikhir* before they spoke of serious things, the man being first, also according to custom. "A fine boy, Madame, my compliments." He seemed a little tipsy, and Kalina wondered if the *chikhir* had not left its fleecy nest more than once during the long journey from Moscow. "But I am forced to say that he resembles your husband not at all, and I have just had ample opportunity to observe Mr. Murav at length in Jaslo."

The wine was more powerful than she had suspected, for to her astonishment, Kalina said unthinkingly and in a perfectly natural voice, "He was not conceived by Stefan Murav."

He belched loudly, also according to custom, before he said, seemingly not at all surprised by her announcement, "Who is the lucky redhead then?"

"Was," she said tonelessly. "He is dead, and his name is of no consequence to anyone but me."

"Quite right," he responded. "A beautiful woman has the privilege of many secrets." He flicked his eyes to the corner toward Michael. "But one day your child might want to know."

Seeking to change the subject, she said, "For a bachelor, you have a way with children."

Lowering his eyes, Yurek twirled his empty cup between his hands a long time before he replied, "My wife and two sons were slaughtered by the Germans. One of their airplanes bombed our village. It is a few kilometers from Jaslo where you were born."

Impulsively, her hand reached out to touch his in compassion. Quick as an adder, he grasped her by the wrist and drew her to him with such force that her head fell into his lap, her body stretched across the space between. Cradling her by the shoulders, he lifted her face to his and kissed her on the mouth. At the touch of his wine-sweet lips on hers, Kalina's blood flared up in a rage of passion she had not felt since she had lain in Max's arms.

More kisses followed, each more ardent than the one before, but when his hand slithered under the neckline of her blouse to cup her breast, Kalina bolted upright, pushing him from her wildly. Hot-eyed with desire and desperately seeking to control her breathing, she said in a trembling voice, "I am a married woman who has had too much wine, I fear."

He stood up, towering over her. "You are a married woman who has not lain with a man for too long a time." Lifting the stove lid, he spat into the fire. The coals lit up his face, making a molten river of the ragged scar.

"We leave for Jaslo in the morning. Prepare yourself and the child," he said in a staccato voice. "There will be snow, so ask Sura for extra sheepskins. A pony will be provided for you. I trust you can ride."

She nodded dumbly, and he replaced the stove lid with such a bang that Michael awoke and started to cry. As she passed by him to pick up the baby, he took her arm. "Your husband eagerly awaits you there."

Ignoring the wailing from the corner, Kalina gazed long and hard at Yurek before she lifted her face up to kiss him full upon the lips. "That's for Zuska," she said, darting off to tend her child.

A smile transformed his face, which a moment before had been glum. "Zuska? Who the hell is Zuska?"

The baby in her arms, Kalina rejoined him at the stove. "My cousin Zuska Olkonsky left with me for America when I was ten and she was twelve. She remembered you fondly and begged me on her deathbed to kiss you if I should happen to see you when I visited Jaslo."

Yurek guffawed, and struck his brow with the flat of his hand. Then, bringing his hands together, he lifted them above his head and executed a little dance around the stove. Facing her again, he whooped, "Zuska was a brazen, little towhead who had breasts at twelve and ideas of a woman twice her age."

"She loved you very much, and never forgot you, Yurek." Kalina said, giggling. "As with children, you obviously have a way with women too."

Sobering, he said, "It is sad to hear that one so vibrant as your cousin is dead. We must talk of her sometime —" He paused, looking deep into her eyes, and seemed about to say more when the door burst open and the women returned from the wedding feast. Kalina moved away from Yurek into the shadows but not soon enough to prevent sharp-eyed Sura from seeing her flushed face as well as Yurek's broad smile.

Later, as they prepared for sleep, the old woman snapped, "You're being returned to your husband not a moment too soon, Madame Murav."

"Mr. Stefan Murav is no longer in Jaslo."

The priest stood in the door of the village church, holding it open with one hand. His black cassock was torn in several places, and one lens was missing from his spectacles. He shook his head from side to side, and the

403

eyes that met Kalina's were lackluster. The man had eaten little for the past few days, and the effort of talking to this excited woman was rapidly draining the vestiges of his strength.

Regretfully, the American industrialist who aspired to be the king of Poland — a smile flicked across the priests' pale, wan face — had departed without leaving word where he could be reached.

"Your husband left immediately after he and the Cossack Yurek completed their negotiations for your return," the young man told the woman who had said she was the mad American's wife. Although, reflected the priest, nothing is as it seems in these chaotic times. "At midnight I left him sleeping on the floor behind the altar, and when I looked for him after early Mass at six, he was gone."

Kalina frowned and chewed her lower lip in annoyance, but her eyes were anxious. "Was he in good health?"

Another wan smile. "As well as any of us, these days of shortages. He seems to have secret resources. Some say he deals with the Germans."

Exasperated, Kalina turned round to face the road, where Yurek and the twelve Cossack warriors, who had been assigned to escort the ransomed women to Jaslo, remained astride their ponies along with Mary and Michael. It had been snowing relentlessly since dawn, and already the snowpack reached well above the shaggy fetlocks of the animals. The beasts could travel no further. Kalina herself was chilled to the bone and near exhaustion, Michael had developed a troubling cough and the twelve Cossack warriors were impatient to complete their mission and rejoin their regiment.

She turned back to the priest. "Father—"

"Gomulka," he said. "I am truly sorry I cannot offer you shelter in the church. Every inch is taken." Drawing aside, he flung the door open wide and motioned her inside. "You can see for yourself, Madame."

Kalina stepped inside, her heart beating like a triphammer. Like most every building they had passed on the road into the village, the church had been severely damaged by shells and bombs from German airplanes. Boards hastily nailed together covered gaping holes in the walls, and skins and fabric covered the blown-out stained-glass windows. Women, children, and a few old men sat around samovars set over charcoal fires in cauldrons. The crowded scene reminded her of the railway terminals she had seen where crowded travelers waited days for trains.

As a child she had worshiped in this little church, sitting primly on a hard bench, rosary in hands, silent and unmoving. Exactly as rows of wide-eyed evacuated children were sitting at this very moment against the wall.

In those long-ago days she had worn her Sunday-best blouse and skirt, freshly washed ironed. These little ones were wrapped in rags, and their stillness came not from any fear of discipline but from hunger.

Walking through the densely packed church was clearly impossible, so Kalina remained at Father Gomulka's side, gazing avidly at the altar that miraculously was almost intact. Just a few nicks in the pink marble marred its pristine beauty. The brightly painted statues of the Virgin and the saints, before which she had whispered her childish prayers, looked down upon her from their niches as benignly as they had twenty years before.

Welcome home, they seemed to say.

Despite the grief of seeing the village of her memory ravaged beyond belief, tears of joy welled in Kalina's eyes.

Her church, her people, her village.

She was home at last.

"Is there an inn," she asked the priest, "or a hostelry where we may sit out the storm? I have a child and female companion."

He gave a dry laugh. "Nothing. What is not rubble has been commandeered by the troops, both theirs and ours."

"Kalina!"

Yurek loomed impatiently in the doorway, so covered with snow he seemed a ghost. "We must not tarry here. The ponies need rest and fodder and drink."

An old woman spoke up from the floor. "I know you from old, Kalina Olkonsky. The manor house that saw your birth still stands. Your father Pan Mikolai sits inside alone, sour and embittered. He drove out all who would shelter there."

With an exclamation of surprise and delight, Kalina stooped to peer into the woman's face. "What is your name, mother?"

"Sophie. I was a dairymaid when you and Zuska were still at breast."

Reluctantly, Kalina left the old one and hurried back outside with Yurek and the priest. "Perhaps your husband is still at the train," suggested Father Gomulka. "The depot is almost as crowded with refugees as our church. Mr. Murav spoke to me of arranging passage for Switzerland."

"Very likely," replied Kalina with more confidence than she felt. "We will proceed there directly."

Confound that Stefan! Why must he confuse their plans by disappearing in this maddening fashion? She took the priest's hand and shook it warmly. "Thank you, Father, for your concern. My husband is brilliant but often unpredictable." She pressed her lips together in a gesture of annoyance. "His mind does not work as ordinary men's. But we will find him, never fear." Glancing back into the church, she said, "I only wish we could be of some help."

"Care for yourself and your child, Madame," the priest cautioned, squinting first at the sky, then at the horsemen. "I suggest you return to the Cossack encampment in the mountains before the snowpack makes the trail impassable. The German troops will return to renew their attack the moment the storm is over." Sighing, he spread out his hands. "Our little village has unaccountably become the fulcrum of the tug of war between the Austrian and German armies and the Russians. Both sides have come through here many times since early spring, flattening our houses, eating our beasts, consuming all our stores of food and grain."

Yurek swore an oath. "Pardon the profanity, Father, but

where are the Czar's Cossacks? A regiment was assigned to Jaslo."

"Dead to a man," was the terse reply. Taking off his damaged spectacles, the priest rubbed his eyes with the backs of his hands like a child. "Not even the Czar's bravest warrior can stop a German tank with his saber, nor the fleetest mount escape the guns and bombs of the Kaiser's airplanes."

Still cursing roundly under his breath in rapid Russian, Yurek hustled Kalina back out to the road and onto her pony. His handsome face was grim. They continued along the narrow road, Kalina riding in front alongside Yurek, and had gone but a few meters when she exclaimed, "But this is not the way to the train!"

"We are not going to the train, which, in any case, will not run in this weather." He flashed a broad smile. "The loving reunion with your husband will have to wait a bit longer, Mrs. Murav." He flicked his eyes at the passing countryside where charred sticks showed where houses had once been. Corpses of men and breasts littered the fields and ditches, their frozen limbs flung out grotesquely.

It was a scene that a mad artist might have painted in a delirium, thought Kalina.

Like the priest, Yurek scanned the blizzardy sky. "If the priest is right, the moment this storm clears, the airplanes will be back in force, scouting the terrain in preparation for the ground troops. Let's try the manor house. Surely the great Pan Mikolai will not bar the door to his own beloved daughter."

"Beloved!" Kalina echoed. "I doubt if he will even remember me."

When a short time later they reached the manor, there was, ironically enough, no door to bar. The front of the house stood open to the elements. Although not as heavily damaged as the rest of the village, the great house of Kalina's childhood was hardly more than a skeleton. No smoke came from the holes where chimneys had once jutted from the roof, the many-paned windows were smashed in, the tall, branching trees that had shaded her as a child had been chopped down, probably for firewood.

They rode their ponies directly inside, where the father Kalina scarcely knew sat in the great kitchen amid the rubble of his former splendor. He was rocking back and forth in a wicker chair, a rifle across his lap, two large black dogs at either side.

A wide-bore cannon, exactly like the ones that had disturbed her sleep years ago in the meadow of Carnegie's estate, was mounted directly in front of him, its yawning mouth pointed at the intruders. Cobwebs shrouded its rusted iron surface.

Reining in, Yurek's eyes crinkled before he burst into an uproarious laugh. "A cannon, is it, old man?" Contemptuously, he kicked the gun with his booted foot, knocking it off its precarious base. It rolled onto the floor. The dogs leaped up, snarling. Touching the hilt of his pistol in its holster, the Cossack grated, "Call off your dogs, old man, or we will roast them for our supper."

Pan Mikolai rose up and pointed his gun at Yurek, but adderlike, the Cossack drew his saber and struck the weapon from the withered arm. It fell to the tiled floor to join the cannon.

"Kill me, then," Pan Mikolai said defiantly, "but the Germans will slay you all when they return."

The ragged figure stood proudly before the gathered warriors, and for a moment there was a flash of courage and nobility, a haunting remnant of what had once been. Dismounting, Kalina flew to her father, flinging her arms round his scrawny neck. "Pan Mikolai! It is I, Kalina, Hania's daughter. We do not seek your death. We beg only food and shelter for the night."

The old man drew back, his rheumy eyes peering at the fresh young face so close to his. Kalina withdrew her arms but continued to hold both his hands tightly in hers. Almost dizzy with fatigue, she closed her eyes, striving desperately to banish the present, if only for a moment. Mentally, she evoked a vivid image from her childhood.

The man who lived in memory had been tall and proud and strong, he had swaggered around the house and fields, attired in a splendid silk brocade blouse and crimson trousers trimmed with gold thread. The maidens had thrown flowers at him.

Opening her eyes, she forced herself to gaze upon the real man, not the dream. The rags that covered his thin bones emitted an overpowering stench, and as he seemed to recognize her, the tears flowed from his eyes, making runnels in his dirt-encrusted face. "*Chleb*," he muttered and slipped senseless to the floor.

"He wants bread. He is starving," Kalina said.

Yurek produced *chikhir* from his burka and forced a few drops down the old man's throat. Then, propping him in the chair again, he left with his men to search for food.

Mary Lesko came forward with Michael, placing him in his mother's arms. Kalina held the child aloft, close to the old eyes. "Your grandson, Father."

A smile wreathed Pan Mikolai's seamed face. "So many die, but God always sends the new little ones to take their place."

"Leave us, Mary," Kalina said. She glanced at Shamyl, the young Cossack who stood shyly at Mary's side. During their stay in the encampment, he and Mary had become lovers. "Ask Yurek to spare Shamyl to help you make some of the rooms fit for sleeping tonight. Fetch some snow to melt down for water so that we can bathe."

Alone with her father at last, Kalina pressed him for news of the people she remembered. Enlivened by the *chikhir* and the promise of food, the former lord of the manor chattered amiably with his long-lost daughter, answering her questions as best he could. Anya and her husband Mashko, the old servants who had been so dear to Kalina, were dead of good and natural causes long before the war.

Whatever he had become, Pan Mikolai had been a good master and landlord. Not a single person who lived in his domain had been forgotten in his memory.

In sad tones, Kalina told him of Litka's death and Zuska's, but when she mentioned her mother Hania, he spat upon the littered floor. "That one was my darling, my favorite, and she betrayed me by running off to Tiflis with a Cossack."

Tiflis! In her excitement, Kalina rose up and paced around the room several times before returning to her squatting position at her father's knee.

Tiflis was the capital city of the Caucasus state of Georgia. Sura had said the journey was long and treacherous, but Tiflis was not some hidden, rockbound village in the high mountains but a thriving metropolis, a trading center. The city could easily be reached by taking a ship across the Black Sea. Stefan had done it many times in his commercial travels.

"Your husband travels to Tiflis," the old man murmured. He closed his eyes and seemed to sleep, the wine working in his old veins.

Kalina shook him by the shoulder. "Was Stefan here?"

He nodded, without opening his eyes. Then, after a while, he said quite clearly. "One day he will be king of Poland. He has gone to Tiflis to get the papers."

Within the hour the men were back with some barley meal they found in the vast cellars and five wild hares they bagged in the forest. By nightfall a fire blazed in the great white porcelain stove, which was as tight and warm as ever. The samovar was gone, but Kalina heated water in a pot for tea. Into a second pot they threw the skinned and chopped hares, adding some carrots, turnips, and potatoes the men had found in the root cellar behind the house.

Some tallow candles were found, and a table laid with fresh linen from the press. Pan Mikolai awoke and darted into a pantry where he had hidden the few pieces of silver remaining. The servants had taken anything of value they could load on their farmcarts as they fled before the Germans.

No food had ever been so succulent, Kalina declared to Yurek as they feasted. There was no sugar for the black tea but *chikhir* made a splendid substitute. Afterward, as Cossacks must, the men danced around their sabers on the floor, their flying bodies defying gravity, and sang the bawdy songs of their native villages.

For Kalina, sitting happily at Yurek's side, her child asleep on a pile of skins, the twenty-two years since she had last seen her childhood home dissolved like smoke from a chimney drifting into the clouds. In her heart she became the child she had been. And, like a child, she determined not to think of Stefan or even of her children far away in Switzerland with strangers.

This time, this night, belonged to Kalina Olkonsky.

The future stretched before her like a vast, impenetrable forest. Like a child, she would wait until morning to think about the future. It would come soon enough.

When the men had tired of dancing, Mary Lesko rose up and sang an aria from *Carmen*. Her rich contralto rang out in the seductive aria, *Habanera*, in which the teasing cigarette girl from Seville seeks to cast her spell on the lovelorn soldier Don Jose.

Love is like a wild bird—

Mary danced around the room, in and out of the shadows, lifting her skirt provocatively, her lovely face flushed with wine and song and love. Her lover Shamyl followed her with adoring eyes, and when she had finished to thunderous applause, the young warrior leaped up and carried her off upstairs in his arms.

"I always thought it poets' talk," Kalina murmured to Yurek, "when they write of lovers having stars in their eyes."

The bedrooms on the upper floors were largely as they had been, seemingly untouched by time and war. The room where Kalina had slept with her mother and Litka and Zuska was on the top floor beneath the sky. It was a small gabled room without a grate, but heat came from the kitchen through a slatted hole in the floor and had ever been warm and cozy, even in the coldest winter.

The brass headboards were as golden as she remembered, and in her heightened state, the flowers on the wallpaper were fresh and bright. Like the statues in the church, the sacred pictures on the wall gazed down at her with welcoming smiles, and the crucifix, with its brittle dried palms attached to the back, hung in reassuring permanence over the bed.

Yurek had carried a stub of candle and hot water from the kitchen for her ablutions. Towels and the fragrant soap of the kind her mother had made from rose petals and tallow still lay in a drawer in the walnut sideboard. After bathing herself and Michael in the porcelain basin, Kalina lay upon her mother's bed and nursed the child until he fell asleep in her arms. She placed the candle in its saucer on the nightstand. The window was boarded up, the glass having been blown out by the recent shelling, so she stared at the ceiling, her belly full, her heart content.

She did not hear Yurek returning until she felt the kiss on her cheek. Quietly, he wormed the baby from her arms and placed him upon the other bed, covering him with his warm heavy burka. Turning back to Kalina's bed, he stood gazing down at her, his heavy-lidded eyes veiled. Conscious of her exposed breast, she hastily drew her blouse together with her hands.

"Leave it," he said quickly in a tight voice. Bending down, he flicked the embroidered peasant garment back again from her breast.

He kissed the warm flesh; then, with an indrawn breath, he reached out a hand to snuff the candle.

"No, leave *that*!" She laughed shakily. "I want to see you when—"

She blushed furiously, realizing that she was being brazen. Could she assume he wanted to make love simply because he kissed her breast?

"When what?" He sat on the bed and deliberately lifted the homespun blouse up from her skirt so that it covered her face.

"Yurek, please, I cannot breathe."

"Answer me," he teased, "or I shall smother you in your

412

bed." Tightening the cloth around her face, he said with mock pretended menace, his voice low and threatening. "Say the words. Beg me to love you."

Her muffled voice came quickly. "Love me, you beast, love me, love me." The word flowed from her tongue like water down a hillside.

At her insistence, he undressed before her eyes so that he stood naked as she had been naked when first they met in the encampment. One by one, his heavy garments dropped to the floor—the flaring thigh-length shirt, the flaring trousers, the scrap of undergarment. Taking up his gleaming saber, he flicked it round and round his head, executing a graceful and lascivious dance around the room, stepping lightly so as not to waken Michael. Then he laid the weapon on the floor beside the bed, ready to be taken up if danger lurked.

Kalina caught her breath at the magnificence of the man. Rock-hard muscles rippled in the flickering candle gleam, the dark hair, which grew so abundantly on his head and chin, covered a chest wider than she had ever seen, tapering suddenly to narrow hips between which the swollen manhood nestled invitingly in its nest of dark hair.

At the sight, her blood surged into her throat, and leaping up like a wild thing, she clasped him by the hips and pulled him toward her with such force that she thought she heard the old mattress heave a great sigh.

The flesh of these two had known other flesh, had many times been drawn to the exquisite pleasure of the senses, and had been long denied. Kalina spread her thighs wide in feverish welcome, and swiftly, impatiently, guided him to her.

His strong hands cupped her buttocks, lifting her lower body so that they were as one flesh. Her long slim legs curved to receive him. The world dissolved into pure sensation.

They coupled quickly, their surging lusts spiraling together, until maddened by the coiled tension inside her, Kalina screamed for release.

413

They exploded together with a violence that left them gasping.

A scrap of verse from the books she had pored over under Aunt Litka's vigilant eye flashed to mind. *Gather ye rosebuds while ye may, for old time is still aflying.*

One takes love when it comes. The flesh must have its due. The poets speak only truth, she reflected for the second time that night. And once again, she mused that her longed-for homecoming was vastly different from her imaginings. And once again, she reflected, she was far from unhappy about it.

They lay side by side, recapturing their breath and awaiting the resurgence of sweet desire. After a time, she said, "As a girl, I feared the Cossacks. The old ones called them devils and warned us that if we were ever caught by them, we would be ravaged until we died."

"Are you dead?" he murmured, nibbling at her ear.

"If so, it is a death far sweeter than life itself."

In half-teasing tones, he told her then that all Cossacks were not as brave and fine and good as he and his warriors. "There are wild ones who come down from their mountainous lairs and prey upon the innocent in the valleys and farms. "Alas," he said, "because of their kind, our people are known throughout the world as savages."

But, as they coupled a second time and she felt the fierceness of the man within her, Kalina thought the word "savage" too mild for what was taking place on her mother's bed.

They talked of Zuska. "Did you take her maidenhead?" asked Kalina.

He reared up. "Woman, I am no savage beast. The child was only ten though"—he chuckled wickedly—"she had these hard little breasts that she flaunted at every man in sight."

"I remember that she left off wearing her undershirt and petticoat, much to her mother's horror," murmured Kalina.

Toward morning, the winter birds began to call outside,

and rising, Yurek tore a board off the window and peered out. "The snow has stopped," he said. "The sun is pale against the hills. We must be up and gone before the shelling starts."

As if magically evoked by his words, there was the immediate sound of thunderous bombardment and a chatter of machine-gun fire. Kalina was reminded of the woodpeckers of her childhood that had awakened her in the summer mornings.

The house began to shake as from an earthquake, and frightened, Kalina hastily dressed and picked up Michael, putting him to the breast as they ran downstairs.

A mangy blanket round his skinny flanks, Pan Mikolai stood in the snowy yard, looking up at the sky. "Airplanes," he shouted, "swarming like gnats."

Bundled up in sheepskin, the baby in a sling across her breast, Kalina joined her father. "We are off, Father. Please come with us. You will surely be killed."

The buzzing in the sky intensified, and, as Kalina watched in horror, one dipped low and flicked it wings from side to side as if signaling. "That's for me," Pan Mikolai said laconically. "They want me to take shelter elsewhere. I imagine they mean to bomb the manor house to prevent its use by the Russians."

Whipping round to face her father, Kalina wailed, "So you *are* a collaborator as they claim!"

All her affection of the night before seemed to vanish. There was no time to say the scathing words that were on her tongue, for instantly, Yurek came with the ponies. Mounting quickly, they headed away from the manor and out of Jaslo.

Her child was screaming in fright at the noise, and his very life was in danger from the bombs and machine guns. A shell burst in a nearby field, sending bits of shrapnel high into the air. Fearfully, Kalina drew her cloak more closely round the child.

Finding the road already choked with tanks and caissons bearing heavy guns, they took to the forest. The few people remaining in the houses scurried into hillside caves or cowered in ravines, fearing for their lives. A young woman with two small children clinging to her skirts scrambled into a thick-branched tree by means of a little ladder left there for the purpose, then reached down to lift her little ones to safety.

Silently, the Cossacks rode in single file, Yurek at their head, Kalina behind him, their sure-footed ponies lifting their fetlocked feet instinctively away from scraps of barbed wire or long-forgotten animal traps.

The bombardment never ceased, and the airplanes dipped and dived, then flew up to dip and dive again. When the riders stopped to rest at a rise, fires could be seen far below where the bombs had found their mark. The sun was high in a cloudless sky when they came at midday to a small rock plateau. Here the eye could see into Austria to the south and the Ukraine to the east. They had passed the place, Kalina remembered, on their journey from the encampment to Jaslo just a few days before.

"Return swiftly to the regiment," Yurek ordered his men. "You will be called to fight the renewed German offensive. I cannot ride with you, for I must take the women to a place where they will be safe from bombs and German guns." Pausing, he flicked his eyes toward Kalina. "I swore before the Czar to see that Madame Murav is returned to her husband's arms. He is in Tiflis, so we travel east and south."

"Tiflis!" Kalina gasped, her eyes wide with excitement. "I did not dare hope that you would take me there!"

"It is nothing," he cut her off. "If Murav were in darkest Africa, I would be bound to travel there." A faint smile accompanied this remark.

Some of the warriors winked and snickered softly at each other. It was clear from their knowing glances that they considered a journey of such magnitude—Tiflis or Africa—to be above and beyond the call of duty, even for a Cossack, who is noted for his fierce devotion to his Czar.

As the crow flies, the city in the Caucasus was, at the

least, eight hundred kilometers over bandit-infested mountains and deserts where fresh water is not around every corner. And these two were no crows.

Surely, there was somewhere near at hand, their faces clearly said — Vienna perhaps — where their brave leader could deposit his ransomed ladies.

Reddening, Yurek snapped, "I appoint Shamyl to serve as leader until you reach the encampment."

Riding forward from her place at Shamyl's side, Mary reined in close to Kalina. "I do not choose to go with you to Tiflis, Kalina. I will stay with Shamyl."

"But Mary, that's a preposterous idea," Kalina stuttered, clearly shocked. "Why would you —"

"I love him," Mary interrupted. "I need no other reason." She cast her eyes to the ground, and slowly a blush suffused her face. "Without the man I love, any life, no matter how safe and filled with comfort, is unendurable."

"But, my dear girl, your Shamyl must go to battle!"

Kalina cast an imploring glance at Yurek, but the Cossack Yurek remained silent, deliberately turning his mount around so that his back was toward the two women. Clearly, he wished to separate himself from the discussion. A Cossack warrior is free to love whom he pleases; it is no concern of the leader.

But Shamyl spoke up boldly. "Cossack women follow their men to war."

More bewildered than angry, Kalina reached out between their ponies to grasp Mary's hand, holding it tightly in hers. "Mary Lesko, you've been blinded by passion. You are no camp follower. You are an opera singer."

But as she sat her mount proudly, high fur hat on her dark braided hair, sheepskin jacket and trousers covering her slim figure, her pretty face brown from the sun, the girl from Homestead could not be distinguished from the many other women whom she had known in the encampment.

Her voice when she spoke now was loud and uncompromising. "I care no longer for the opera. I care only for

Shamyl. Perhaps you find this difficult to comprehend, Mrs. Stefan Murav, but he is the first man to whom I have yielded my heart and body."

Breathless and close to tears, the girl added, "I want to live before I die. I do not fear the battle."

There was a small silence. The ponies shuffled their fetlocked feet and snorted, eager to be on with their journey.

Finally, Kalina said firmly, "My dear girl, I forbid it."

At that Yurek turned round, his face set in hard lines. "My God, Madame High and Mighty, let the woman go in peace. She is neither your 'dear girl' nor your chattel for you to give leave to stay or go."

Facing Yurek with blazing eyes, Kalina shouted, "But she was ransomed too. You vowed to the Czar to restore both of us."

His reply was cold, brooking no further argument. "The vow, as well as the ransom, concerns only you and the child. Any friend or companion who had the bad luck to be captured with you is not part of the bargain." Smiling at Mary, he added, "But perhaps Mary does not consider her experience bad luck."

Mary favored him with a grin and a wink.

An airplane with a Maltese cross painted on its tail buzzed overhead, circled once, and flew away. Yurek flicked his reins. "Enough of this foolishness. We are in danger here. Come, woman."

With that, he grasped Kalina's reins and turned her mount around, breaking her grip on Mary's hand. They rode away from the others, down a steep slope that required all of Kalina's attention to her mount. She heard the echoing hoofbeats as Mary rode off with Shamyl and the Cossacks toward the south.

It was near dark before Yurek spoke again. They made camp at a roadside shrine in a spacious grotto containing a wooden shelter, a crude, open-sided roofed affair. But it had a firepit and, while Yurek gathered kindling and got a blaze going, Kalina nursed Michael and prayed on her knees before the statue of the Virgin.

She prayed for Mary's safety. During the long hours of riding down the mountain toward the Ukraine, the first shock of the woman's defection had worn off. She was following her heart. As she herself had so wisely noted, to be safe is often to be dead. Happiness carries risks, but also great rewards.

Love weaves its own sweet cocoon around lovers, reflected Kalina, thinking of herself and Max at *Villa d'Este*. The world had been crumbling about them, but they had been oblivious to all but their own bliss.

Even in her greatest triumphs at the opera, when admiring audiences had thrown roses at her feet, Elena Lesko's daughter had never seemed so happy. Tears crowded into Kalina's throat as she evoked the image of the sweet young girl who had played cowboys and Indians with Dunia in the snow, and went about the house on Rutherford Drive singing at her tasks.

As they ate their meal of dried meat and biscuit and drank the tea brewed by Yurek on the fire, Kalina was withdrawn and pensive. Wisely, knowing her grief, Yurek kept his tongue and, more wisely still, did not press himself upon her when they rolled up in their blankets alongside the fire.

Kalina spoke but once. "I wish I had kissed her goodbye."

Contrary to her expectations, they did not travel due south through the Ukraine toward the great Black Sea port of Odessa on its southern flank to take a ship for the Caucasus. Yurek explained that the vast sea, which lay between Europe and Turkey on the south, was infested with German submarines.

"Besides," he added with a sly grin, "I was never much of a sailor."

"Nor am I," she quipped, remembering the journey to America at the time of Zuska's death.

That he was a landsman and superb at that was proved as they plunged deep into the vast Ukraine. It was in the prairielike land that Yurek had been born, and wherever they stopped, the peasants were friendly and open-handed with food and shelter. Yurek's father had also been an officer of the Czar and, early in his life, had taken his wife and son to Poland. Yurek and Kalina spent a quiet, restful week with the aged grandparents, who invited a host of relatives to a feast in honor of the visiting native son.

No one raised a brow at her or questioned her presence at Yurek's side. She was Yurek's woman; they accepted her as one of them.

Kalina became hardened to the saddle until it seemed that she had known no other life. Her pony whom she named Darling—much to Yurek's chagrin, for the pony was a stallion—became as her child.

As for Michael, the child thrived on life in the open. They spelled each other holding him in the saddle, and Max's son found his greatest joy in riding between the big man's legs. Unfortunately, the child had inherited his father's fair complexion and suffered much from sunburn and blistering of the nose.

Spring came early to the Ukraine, and winter was soon left behind in this southern land as they rode across sunny plains, fished in bright rivers, and felt the gentle winds on their faces.

"Surely Stefan will be gone from Tiflis," Kalina said at one point.

"We will find him." A smile tugged at the corners of Yurek's mouth. "If it takes the rest of my life."

Each night they made love, falling asleep instantly in each other's arms beneath the stars, their lullaby—and Michael's—the gentle murmur of a river or the soft rustling of branches in the wind.

It was a mindless, wonderful existence, and Kalina dreaded the time when it must end. Her emotions were in a kind of centrifuge. She was anxious for the reunion with her mother but not so anxious to see her husband once again. As for parting from her Cossack lover, which must perforce accompany whatever joy awaited her in Tiflis, she drove it from her mind.

Sharing her distress, Yurek seemed in no hurry. Many times they tarried at a lovely spot for days, he also acutely conscious that the end of the journey meant parting from each other. Forever.

More than two months after they had left Jaslo, the travelers came to Tiflis. It was an early day in March of 1917, and they stood upon a hill and gazed with mixed feelings upon a city of minarets encircled with a girdle of trees.

The sky was blue. A few light clouds floated, silvered by the rays of a warm sun that caught the greens and reds of the roofs below and turned the clouds into glimmering opal.

Yurek turned to face Kalina, his eyes bleak, his face grim. "The journey is done, Mrs. Murav."

Chapter Twenty-one

Tiflis, City in the Caucasus
March, 1917

"Murav?"

The old Turk with the red fez on his bald head screwed up his eyes and laughed. He turned to his companions in the bazaar, all of whom, like himself, were seated around a brazier and smoking long-stemmed pipes. "They search for a certain Murav."

Smiles wreathed the faces of the men. Some nodded, others laughed outright, doubling over and waving their pipes about.

"Yes," Kurek repeated in Turkish, somewhat angrily. "We seek a man named Stefan Murav. He is an American and is reported to be residing in Tiflis."

Kalina huddled against Yurek, tightening her arms around Michael as, seemingly out of nowhere, a small crowd materialized and filled the narrow street. A woman regarded Kalina broodingly from coal-black eyes above a veil that covered her nose and mouth. Tiflis was a city of myriad ethnic groups, people converging from all over the Middle East on the great trading center.

Everyone was laughing, some of the men slapped their thighs, the women giggled behind their Muslim veils.

"The Cossack seeks another Cossack. Perhaps they are brothers," chortled the Turk.

His face like a stone, Yurek drew his saber and pointed it

422

at the old man. "No one laughs at Yurek of Poland, who travels on the great Czar's business."

Sobering quickly, the old man drew back and bowed so deeply that the long black tassel of his red fez brushed the cobbles. "A thousand pardons, great Yurek of Poland. Surely you know we laugh not at you but at the man who declares himself king of Poland and who has been shot by a woman even as he stepped foot in this land. The man you seek is in the hospital of the Red Cross at the far end of the city."

They had ridden through the night, Yurek paradoxically becoming anxious at the end to deliver his ransomed prize to her rightful custodian. All Kalina's pleas to seek out her mother, Hania, first were unheeded by Yurek, who said in the curt tone he had adopted the last days of their journey, "My orders are to give you back to your husband. This I do. Nothing else."

Reasoning that their imminent parting weighed as heavily on her mind as on hers, Kalina took the rebuff mildly, but her heart was sore. Was their romantic idyll to end on a sour note? Could they not part amicably?

It was with relief that she spied the giant Red Cross splashed above the facade of the tall, white hospital in the more spacious Russian section of the sprawling city. They were afoot now, Yurek having left the ponies in a khan, or caravan stop, at the outskirts of the city. The hospital was cool and smelled of disinfectant, a welcome and comforting change from the odors of the teeming city.

"I'm a sight," Kalina whispered to Yurek as they stood in the foyer for a moment or two, waiting for their eyes to adjust from the brilliant midday sun to the cool, dim interior. "What will people think? What will Stefan think?"

Her sheepskin garb was soiled and tattered by their months of traveling. Yurek had sternly declined to stop at one of the bazaars that dotted the city and purchase more suitable garments, and, having no cash of her own, Kalina could do nothing but bow to his command.

"He will think the truth," he said now, unsmiling, "that

you've been living with a wild barbarian of a Cossack."

The day being warm, she had removed the tall hats from herself and Michael, and while Yurek had settled the beasts in the khan stables, she had combed and braided her tangled hair in a neat coronet atop her head.

The young woman in starched, immaculate white looked up from her papers as they approached. Her face under the white cap stiffened, and she fixed wide, china-blue eyes on Kalina. Drawing a photograph from a drawer in the long desk, she gazed quickly at it, then at Kalina. Shoving the photo into the pocket of her uniform, she hurriedly came around the desk.

Kalina shrank back, wanting desperately to vanish into thin air. She cast her black eyes to the tiled floor as if expecting it to open up and swallow her, sheepskin and all. Would Yurek draw his saber if they were asked to leave, she wondered. He had been so touchy all day.

But the nurse smiled broadly, extending a hand to Kalina as if she were a visiting diplomat. "Welcome to Tiflis, Mrs. Murav. We've been expecting you for weeks. My name is Jane Fadden. Like you I am an American."

The nurse giggled, covering her mouth with her hand and rolling her eyes as if enjoying a huge, private joke. "Mr. Murav will be beside himself." She spoke English with a broad, Midwest American accent.

Kalina's eyes flew up to meet the clear blue ones of the American nurse. This was no joke. "How do you know me?"

"By this." Jane Fadden held the photo aloft. Kalina gasped. It was one of those "professional beauty" postal cards that had been so popular before the war. She gazed at it, dumbfounded, a kind of sadness in her heart. The face that graced the photo was young and beautiful. She had not seen a mirror for many weeks, and quickly a hand went up to her cheek. Its porcelain smoothness was gone, wind and sun having done its brutal work.

"Mr. Murav ordered it kept in the desk so that, the moment you came, I would know you." The blue eyes flicked back to the photo. "I must say it's a startling resemblance. But come, your husband would be furious if he knew we stood here chatting while he waits most impatiently upstairs."

Michael had awakened, and setting him on his feet, Kalina took his hand and followed the nurse through a maze of corridors. Yurek walked silently a few steps behind as if already distancing himself from Kalina.

The place swarmed with visitors. Many, like themselves dressed in furs and sheepskin, squatted on the floors or sat on chairs beside the narrow beds where lay the wounded of many ethnic groups. Noting her glance, the nurse said, "The war still rages in Armenia and Turkey as well as in the mountains that encircle Tiflis. Ships dock every day at Black Sea ports, from which they come to us by train." Sighing, she paused to point into a children's ward, where many lay swathed in bandages. "The need is very great."

"Are there many Americans here?" Kalina asked as they walked up three flights of stone steps. The hospital reminded her of her beloved *Villa d'Este* and an overwhelming sense of déjà vu enveloped her.

"Ten of us are stationed here in Tiflis hospital," she said, "counting Dunia—" She stopped and pushed open a door. "But here we are."

Dunia!

Kalina whirled, but the woman was gone with a wave of her hand. Surely she could not mean *her* Dunia. She was in Switzerland with Stefi. How could she be here?

Murav's welcome was far from the cordial greeting Miss Fadden had led Kalina to expect. As they entered, he sat up in bed and roared, "It's about time, Madame. Where have you been?"

Quickly, Kalina stepped to the high bed and kissed him on both cheeks. "The journey from Jaslo was very long, Stefan. But I am anxious for you. Are you recovering?"

Little Michael, frightened at the big, black-bearded man with the loud voice, scuttled to Yurek's side and wrapped his small arms about the Cossack's long legs.

425

Ignoring both Yurek and the child, Stefan barked to a tall nurse who was scribbling on a notepad at the foot of the bed. "Leave us, woman." His wide lips parted in a grin, but his amber eyes remained hostile. "My loving wife is here to care for me."

Slanting a wry, half-amused glance at Kalina, the nurse dropped the notepad on the side table with a little thud and left.

"Hand me my robe there on the chair," her husband barked at Kalina in the same tones he had used with the nurse. She watched in silence as her husband covered his white hospital gown with a rich, blue-and-red-striped smoking jacket trimmed with velvet. "Now lift me up and put some pillows behind my head so I can sit in comfort."

It took some minutes to get the pillows exactly as he wanted, at which point he waved her off. "Is Dunia here?" she asked. "Miss Fadden said—"

Again the imperious wave of the hand as if he were brushing off a fly. "Not now."

He hadn't changed a bit, she thought with mounting irritation, still the same inconsiderate autocratic person she had married. His wound must not be serious, she thought with some relief. He has plenty of strength to shout as he always had.

Conscious of Yurek looming behind her, she decided to postpone any personal talk until the Cossack concluded his business with her husband.

His craggy, scarred face impassive, her lover spoke in stiff, formal tones. "By order of our beloved Nicholas, Czar of all the Russias, I hereby return your wife and child for which you paid so handsomely."

Murav smirked. "Cocky devil, aren't you? I trust you enjoyed the long journey in the company of my sweet Olkonsky." His amber eyes glinted lewdly at Kalina.

Yurek's hand touched his saber and his scar turned red, a sign, Kalina had learned, that his anger was at the danger point. She turned heatedly on her husband. "Were it not for Yurek, your son and I would not have survived the terrible journey from Poland."

"*My* son? You insult me, wife."

Stefan's heavy brows lifted almost to his hairline, and he opened his mouth to say more, but at that moment, his work done, Yurek whipped around and bolted for the door. Exasperated at her husband's boorish behavior, Kalina darted after him. He was nowhere in sight, and when she got back down to the foyer, Miss Fadden reported that she had not seen him.

"He must have used the fire escape." She dimpled. "I could hardly miss such a tall, good-looking Cossack."

Outside, Kalina stood on the portico, and shading her eyes with two hands, peered up the sun-baked boulevard. Not a sign of a sheepskin-clad figure. Running down the concrete steps, she started up the sidewalk, but realizing how foolish her actions were, especially with a heavy child to carry, she retraced her steps. "Damn the man and his Cossack temper. He is as intractable as Stefan. Damn all men for their mulishness."

Yurek would go to the khan, of course. She couldn't imagine him at one of the plush hotels that dotted the modern part of the city. She would seek him out tonight to bid a proper farewell.

When she got back to Stefan's room, a girl in a fresh white blouse and green skirt was bending over him, holding a lighted match to a cigar in his mouth. Probably a nurse's aide, thought Kalina, hoping she was an American. But as the slim figure turned around, Kalina nearly swooned from shock, clutching the doorknob desperately for support.

It was Dunia but a vastly different more mature Dunia. The long brown hair that had reached past her hips was gone. In its place a shining mop of curls hugged her shapely young head like a well-fitting cap. She wore bright-red lipstick on her mouth and in her hand she held a burning cigarette.

Dunia took a long drag on her cigarette before she said in a remarkably cool voice, "Mama Kalina, so you *are* here! I thought Daddy was teasing me again." Playfully, she bent to peck her father's brow but made no move toward the door to greet her mother.

Setting Michael on the floor, Kalina flew into the room and caught Dunia to her. As she was pulled into her mother's arms, the girl began to weep. "Oh, Mama, we were so worried about you! Stefi and I thought you had died. We got no letters, nothing—"

The women clung together for a long time, neither speaking, their tears mingling on each other's cheeks until a voice from the bed cried, "My chest hurts, Dunia. Put me down flat on the bed again."

Wrenching free of Kalina's arms, the girl tended her father. Michael had walked up to the bed, and placing both hands on the white coverlet, peered curiously at the big man with the thick, brown beard as though he were a new kind of bear. The sun came in the tall window, turning his crop of red hair to flame. Prone once more, Stefan took the little hands in his own and returned the child's intent stare. Finally, he said in a mild, sweet voice. "The boy is handsome and strong. You've done well, my darling."

Kalina's heart leaped for joy. As she had expected, Stefan Murav would take Max's child into his home and heart. There was much good in the man who had driven whole governments to think of war; like any human being, he was a mystifying mix of good and bad. But his love for children was constant.

"Oh, you darling," Dunia cried, swooping Michael into her arms. "He must be sixteen months old now!"

Dunia's eyes met her mother's over Michael's head, and Kalina knew there need be no words, no long, tortured explanation for the child's existence. That he was not her beloved daddy's offspring was obvious to Dunia.

Stubbing her cigarette out in an opal ashtray, Dunia said in a trembling voice, "I am a bastard child too, Mama Kalina. Michael will be my brother in every way. Since I was scarcely older than he when Max O'Hara went away, I do not remember the father. But all I've heard from Alec and Wanda pictures him as a person possessed of high ideals. I am happy that my brother's father has been cleared of that dreadful murder charge."

"A very pretty speech, daughter," laughed Stefan from the bed. He winked at Kalina. "This one is barely twenty, but she wants to turn the world upside down." He snorted contemptuously. "You know how it goes, 'the poor shall be rich, the rich become poor, the desert shall blossom as the rose—' "

"Oh?" Kalina smiled at Dunia's blushing face. "Are you a reformer then, Dunia?"

Michael started to wriggle in Dunia's arms, so the girl said quickly. "We'll talk later, Mama Kalina. Right now I want to show off my new baby brother to the others and give him some lunch." She hesitated. "Is he still at breast?"

Kalina shook her head. "No. He drinks quite well from a cup. And he'll consume anything that isn't nailed down."

Closing her mind to her wish to see her mother as soon as possible, Kalina shed her sheepskin jacket and, clad in the peasant blouse she had worn for months and which had worn thin by frequent washings in Ukrainian creeks and rivers, she settled in the chair at the bedside. For the remainder of the long, warm afternoon, she and the husband she had not seen for a year talked of many things.

When he inquired of Zuska and Anusia, she told him that Stefi's mother had died well, with a priest, elaborating to his obvious pleasure on Anusia's competent and loving care for the sick woman. She omitted the episode in the bedroom when Anusia had gone out of her head.

When he was recovered and out of the hospital, she mused, she would force him to tell the plain, unvarnished truth about himself and his older sister.

Perhaps then, too, she could dissuade him from his mad delusion about one day becoming the king of Poland. Dunia might be of help in that regard. She was mature now, fully a woman. Surely she would have some influence on her father, who obviously adored her.

He seemed so rational at this moment, talking quietly of family matters. As so often happens with those who have narrowly escaped death, he seemed in many ways to have become a different, more rational person.

His face brightened at her account of her recent stay in

Vienna, comforting the dying Franz Josef. "That bit of charity will be helpful when you are queen of Poland."

Her heart sank. His madness was not completely gone.

Concerning her time with the Cossacks, he asked only if Yurek had become her lover. She answered simply in the affirmative. He seemed pleased at that, too. "Your affair will put us in good with the Cossacks in our kingdom."

When she questioned him on his unannounced departure from Jaslo before she and Yurek had arrived there, he said, "The last train was due to leave that day. The Germans were coming, and I wanted to fetch Dunia and Stefi from Switzerland and bring them here with me."

To her great joy, Stefi was in Tiflis, too, in a house on the outskirts of the city. "He lives with Dunia. They are quite comfortable." A gleam came into his eyes at that, but he brushed off further questions on the matter by launching into a long and somewhat rambling speech, that sometimes became a harangue, about his reasons for being in the Caucasian city.

At various times in the afternoon, the nurse entered to check his temperature and examine a wide bandage around his chest. Food arrived, but he waved it away. In their life together, Kalina had learned to expect the unexpected from her husband, but what he had to tell her now approached the incredible.

The Caucasus, it seemed, was the last link in the chain of puzzles to be unraveled concerning his claim to kingship. Here, in these very mountains north of Tiflis, he had been born. As had Anusia too. An unknown village in the high Caucasus north of Tiflis was the key that would yield the final answer.

"There is a shining river, and a cave with a mossy fringe about the entrance," he said dreamily. "A woman dressed in black dwells there. It was she who told me of Stephen Batory."

"Batory?" she exclaimed. "The man who ruled a united Poland five hundred years ago?"

"The same. He traveled widely and passed through this land, scattering his seed into many willing wombs. One of those seeds thrives in my veins."

"Stephen Batory?" she murmured.

Aunt Litka had drilled her well in history, so it was with little difficulty that Kalina recalled the famous king. Of all the strong men who at one time or another had driven the conqueror from Polish shores, Stephen Batory was the most beloved, the most fondly remembered. His life had been adventurous and romantic. It was perfectly possible that Stefan's outrageous story could be true.

"Why did you not mention the name before?" she asked.

He grimaced. "The less you knew the better. Besides I wasn't sure myself until last year when my operatives verified my birthplace. When the ship that brought us and our parents to America sank in the Atlantic, all papers were naturally lost. I was only two or three as I told you."

"But what about Anusia, was she not seven or so, a perfectly sensible age? Surely she knew what city or town in Poland you were living in just before you sailed."

He shook his head. "She's never been able to remember a thing, claiming that the catastrophe drove everything sensible from her mind. And when I prodded her about it through the years, she would fly into one of her irrational fits of temper."

Kalina pursed her lips and kept her tongue. As with Stefan's irrational behavior of last year in Auvergne, Anusia's "fits" might well have been staged for purposes of concealment.

"At any rate," Stefan went on, "my sister knows nothing of my birth. My parents were traveling in the Caucasus when I was born."

"And have you found your native village and your old woman dressed in black?" she asked softly.

His gold-brown eyes looked agonizingly into hers. "There are thousands of hamlets in the Caucasus, and every damn one of them contains a river, a cave with a mossy fringe, and more old women dressed in black than needs to be on this earth."

He told her finally, grudgingly of the wound in his chest, and the incident that had caused so much merriment at the bazaar. He had taken a ship from Odessa across the Black Sea, having won safe conduct from the German submarines that preyed in the waters, and as he stepped onto the dock in the Caucasus, a woman, whose husband and three sons had died in the war, drew a revolver and shot him without warning. "You are the devil, Murav. You and your arms have brought evil upon the world."

The woman was not arrested but applauded by many for her courage.

The wound was healing slowly, and the big man chafed at the delay, for it had been his plan to leave the two children with their grandmother Hania, and take a caravan into the mountains to seek out his heritage.

The shiny green 1908 Oldsmobile that belonged to Hania's husband Kirov, now off at the war, braked to a smooth stop before a terrace thickly planted with vines and flowering trees behind which lurked — so Dunia assured her — grandmother Hania's house.

Promptly at five o'clock, the girl had poked her head into Stefan's room but without little Michael. Kalina's momentary alarm at the child's absence was banished when Dunia reported him to be in good hands. "Very good hands indeed," she had repeated with a twinkle.

Expertly, smoking a cigarette as she drove, waving hands at this one and that along the way, Dunia sped at an alarming speed through the congested city and into the suburbs. They came at last to a prosperous-looking section that lay on a gentle slope at the foot of a gorge between two high mountains. The houses were of stucco and fieldstone and were surrounded by lush, green growth.

"Wealthy foreigners live here," said Dunia. "The climate in this region is mild and protected by the winds that buffet most of the Caucausus." She had the proprietary air of one who had lived here in this outlandish place all her life instead of a scant month or two.

The sun, which had blazed all day, had gone behind the mountain, and a soft pure light descended from a purplish

432

sky. Kalina stood at the foot of a steep flight of stone steps and gazed at the place where she would see her mother who had kissed her good-bye in 1894.

A lifetime ago. Would she even know the woman? She had never had a photograph, childish memory would have to serve. Surely the black hair would be gray or at least salt and pepper. She hoped it would not be snow white; that would be too much of a change. Silly of her, she mused, but she wanted her mother as she had been so long ago.

But sometimes war and suffering aged people prematurely, far before the proper time. Tragedy was no stranger to Hania Olkonsky. Little Pepi, the half-brother who had been born when Kalina still lived on Mulberry Street, had been killed in France, fighting for the Czar, Dunia sadly related. His father Kirov had not seen his wife for three long years; his whereabouts were not actually known.

If the daughter were thirty-three, the mother was probably fifty or more. Hania's husband was a Cossack, life with that fiercely independent people was hard on women. Kalina put a hand to her cheek. Its silky smoothness was gone, from wind and weather. Would her mother's cheek be rough and wrinkled?

In her dreaming state, Kalina never saw the tall figure running down the steps until she felt herself caught in a tight embrace. The woman smelled of flowers, verbena she thought, and the cheek that pressed so tightly on hers was smooth and firm as a ripe melon.

Swaying back and forth as one, they could not find words for a long time. Then, murmuring incoherently in Polish, Hania kissed her daughter on cheeks and eyes and mouth as was the custom in their native village. Gently pushing her away, the older woman gazed with brimming eyes at Kalina's tear-streaked face. "You are lovelier even than the photographs Stefan has given me."

Still dumbstruck, Kalina stared unbelievingly at a woman who could pass for thirty. Dark eyes were clear and bright, the richly black hair was drawn back smoothly from a face in which showed little of age, just a few laugh lines around the eyes and mouth. Hania's teeth were white and strong in the generous mouth of Kalina's memory.

At last she stammered, "You are my mother surely, but you look more like my sister." It was an inane thing to say, she reflected wryly, after so many years and so much yearning.

But it brought a hearty laugh from Hania. "It's the light, darling. In the morning when the sun is bright, you will see all the wrinkles."

A discreet cough from Dunia brought mother and daughter out of their trance. She plucked the mangy sleeve of Kalina's jacket daintily with one finger. "Do you think, Grandmother Hania, that you can find some more comfortable garments for Mama Kalina?"

"But of course, I imagine my long-lost daughter may be weary of her wintry Cossack attire."

Within minutes, Kalina was lowering her naked form into a porcelain tub of warm, fragrant sudsy water. She had not bathed in such luxurious fashion since that fateful last evening in Vienna, as she prepared for the opera with Mary.

For a fleeting moment, her own happiness dimmed as she thought of the young American woman who had cast her lot with the warlike Cossacks. What if Shamyl were killed in battle? What if, when the first blush of passion faded as it must, Mary found herself an unwilling captive among an alien people? What if —

Stop that, she told herself sternly. Life has no guarantees. At sixteen she had thought to love Max O'Hara forever. They had been so confident that their feet would travel the same road forever. Together. Now he was dead, leaving her to go the rest of life's long journey alone.

There was Stefan, to be sure, and her children. But without true love, a woman is only half-alive. To admit that is not to deny one's obligations. Yurek and she had shared a mutual passion, but now Yurek was gone. Theirs had been an *amour* that was doomed from the start.

Love is truly blind, she mused, as she covered herself with thick lather, allowing it to lie on her face and arms and legs and body until it grew hard and shell-like. Then, she sloughed it off, turning the shiny brass spigots on full force with first hot, then cold water, until her flesh tingled.

As Kalina watched the water swirl down the drain, she imagined that her life up to this point was disappearing with it.

Here, in her mother's house, she would go back in time in order to go forward. The past, while not forgotten, would be put in its proper place. Memories are poor nourishment for a vibrant woman of thirty-two. Thirty-three next month, she corrected herself, laughing aloud at her own vanity.

Hania had left her alone in the spacious tiled bathroom, and now, as Kalina emerged into the adjoining bedroom, a thick towel wrapped round her body, she found not her mother, as she had expected, but a selection of frocks laid across the snowy counterpane of the wide bed.

"There will be much time to talk," Hania had said as she had steered Kalina into the bedroom through a side door, avoiding the others whose voices could be heard in the main part of the house. "Now you must take an hour to transform yourself into the beautiful woman who's been a prisoner under that filthy sheepskin."

"But *you* married a Cossack," protested Kalina. "Did you never wear sheepskin?"

Hania giggled. "But of course, and thoroughly enjoyed it at the time. Here in Tiflis, however, we dress as Western-ers."

On the glass-covered dressing table, Kalina found jars of various soothing creams and cosmetics, glistening clean brushes, combs, and hairpins. Thoughtfully, Hania had pulled open little drawers to reveal other aids to beauty — ribbons, bracelets, necklaces, rings, brooches.

Through the years she had pictured her mother in a simple Cossack hut, perhaps on stilts along a marshy shore, or in the depths of a forest with wild beasts lurking roundabout. There had always been a kerchief on her head, an apron covering her simple, black peasant frock.

Now she gazed in mute astonishment at the spacious armoire packed with stylish frocks, the cool, inviting bedroom with its Persian carpet, gleaming furniture, wide windows opening onto a flagged court.

Why is nothing ever as we imagine it to be, she thought, laughing inwardly at her own naiveté.

At seven o'clock precisely, one hour after Hania had left her to dress, Kalina walked into the large dining room from which the babble of voices sounded. As she entered, all fell quiet as if stunned.

Kalina stood, proudly erect in the doorway, conscious that she was making a spectacular entrance. The gold *crepe de chine* she had chosen from her mother's frocks bore a Paris label and fell in a straight line from shoulder to midcalf. Underneath, the one-piece satin undergarment caressed her flesh. The new "emancipated" fashions demanded no corset or brassiere, so she wore neither.

But it was her hair that brought finally a shriek from Dunia. "Mama Kalina, you've bobbed your hair!"

"But how perfectly marvelous," exclaimed Hania, just entering the room with a tray of food. "The new short look is perfect for you." Placing her tray on an already crowded dining table, she came forward to embrace her daughter.

Wrapped once more in Hania's arms, Kalina stammered, "It was a mad impulse I'm sure to regret in the cool light of day." Nervously, her hand went to her head, fingering the curls at her neck.

"On, no, you won't," said Dunia, "Once a woman feels the glorious, luscious freedom of short hair, she never thinks for a moment of letting it grow back into the tangled mess she has suffered with since she was born."

She swung an arm around the room, which was filled with young women sporting a variety of hair styles. Some, like Dunia's, were cut close to the head; others were in the old style—long, braided, chignoned.

"Perhaps your courageous act will encourage some of these stick-in-the-mud friends of mine to do likewise," Dunia finished. "They won't believe me when I say that within five years or so, only grandmothers"—she looked impishly at Hania—"will be wearing their hair below the shoulder."

As Hania seated her in the place of honor at the head of the long table, Kalina found herself still a little dizzy from her rash action in the bedroom. She had picked up the shiny sewing scissors from the dressing table without a second thought and started snipping the long locks she had been brushing with such strenuous effort. It always took fifteen minutes to braid the long strands and arrange it neatly on top of her head in a coronet, and she resented the time it took.

Afterward, of course, she had been forced to bathe again quickly and then wet down the shoulder-length black hair so that it would stay in place. Fortunately the thickness of her crop disguised the widely uneven ends. She would ask Hania to recommend a hairdresser who could style it properly, thinning it and perhaps cutting bangs across her brow.

Somehow Kalina saw her new short hair as a symbol of a new life of freedom.

Chapter Twenty-two

The guests whom Hania had invited to celebrate her daughter's homecoming were for the most part young American women involved in war relief work in Tiflis and the surrounding communities. Some, like Jane Fadden, were nurses at the Red Cross hospital, others served the needs of the troops that still fought in the lower mountains against the Germans.

Their talk was loud and lively and, to Kalina's surprise, largely concerned with politics and social issues. All were violently antiwar, antimonarchy, antimale domination.

Dunia was the most outspoken; in fact she appeared to be the leader, at least if one were to judge by the way the others looked to her when a controversial subject became an argument.

Though she remained silent throughout most of the dinner, being happy to be here at last and among her countrymen, Kalina could not help remarking during one of the rare lulls in the conversation, "But you women cannot vote. How can your views possibly have any influence on events?"

Her response was a withering look from Dunia and a caustic, "You've been in Europe too long, Mama Kalina, hobnobbing with decadent aristocrats. By 1920 women in America will win their long battle for the vote."

"Or Dunia herself will march right into Congress with a shotgun," quipped another.

Enormously proud of her daughter, who seemed almost

a stranger, Kalina joined in the general laughter. The Dunia she remembered was a pouty adolescent, unhappy with everything and hating all adults including her own mother. With an inward chuckle, Kalina recalled Dunia's vitriolic comments about Mother Celeste at the Auvergne convent.

The tantrums of Dunia's childhood, she reflected, had been merely the foretaste of the strong young woman she now saw before her. Zuska's daughter would always be the rebel.

And paradoxically, though Stefan was not the girl's natural father, there seemed to be more than a touch of her husband's flair for power and the manipulation of people toward achieving his purposes.

Kalina herself had ever been concerned with the inequities of society but had taken the easier, more sedate path of rendering social service in the old-fashioned way. These young women, assuming the roles that only men had taken heretofore, would shake the world.

There was much talk of a revolution in Russia, one woman of Slavic extraction vociferously proclaiming her intention to travel to Moscow to march with the serfs who were about to throw off their shackles.

Fatigued by the excitement of a very long day, Michael had been put to bed before dinner, but now, as the guests sat around the table drinking quantities of coffee and munching fruit and cheese, Kalina heard his loud, masculine wail from somewhere in the house.

Hania led her to a small bedroom where she found her son standing up in a slatted crib, his little face flushed with indignation at being left alone. As she picked him up, cuddling and consoling him with soft words, she heard the child's voice against her face. "I want Yurek."

Kalina started guiltily. How glibly she had put Yurek out of her mind and hopefully out of her heart like a discarded toy.

In her blind egotism she had completely ignored the fact that Michael had adored the man. For months, Yurek had been the father Max's son had never known.

439

And with the knowledge came a terrible remorse. Only this morning she had gazed with sorrow along a sun-baked street, her heart aching for a man, who was even then striding out of her life, and resolving to bid him farewell in the evening.

Evening had come without a thought of Yurek, most likely waiting for her at the khan. She imagined him standing at the gated entrance, looking longingly up the road.

Shoving the sobbing Michael into Hania's arms, she said, "There is something I must do, immediately."

When Hania learned that she wanted to visit the khan to kiss her Cossack lover good-bye, the older woman shook her head. "No, it would be most unwise to do so, especially at night. In the morning, if you still feel you must visit him, I will have my gardener, who also serves occasionally as chauffeur, drive you there. The khan is a very dangerous place for a woman."

Mother and son fell asleep in each other's arms in the narrow bed alongside the crib. Awakening at dawn with an urgent sense of something to be done before the sun came up fully, Kalina climbed into the Oldsmobile and directed the gardener, a handsome Georgian native, to take her to the khan at the edge of the city.

Fifteen minutes later, she sank back against the leather seat. Her mission had been fruitless. She had walked around the crowded, filthy place, littered with both human and animal excrement, asking one man after another if they had seen a Cossack named Yurek. All shook their heads; all cast sly, knowing glances at her.

One said, his swarthy face wreathed in smiles, "Did he leave your bed, little one, without paying?"

Face burning, her ears ringing with the laughter of the men, Kalina fled to the safety of the Oldsmobile. Her mother's gardener started the motor, discreetly avoiding her eyes. What must he think of me, Kalina thought, her shame deepening. Hot tears filled her eyes and rolled unheeded down her cheeks into her mouth. But whether

440

she wept for sorrow at losing her dear, sweet, passionate Yurek forever, or at her own shame and remorse for permitting him to leave without a decent good-bye, she was not sure.

She could only hope that time, the great healer, would eventually close the raw wound that now bled so grievously within her heart and soul.

Stefi was waiting for her at the house, and as she gathered her son into her arms, Kalina wept afresh. At fifteen, Zuska's child was tall and gangly with arms and legs that seemed to go on forever. He had spent the night in the lower mountains at a camp for refugee children where he was a counselor. As Kalina ran her fingers through his thick brown hair, she came away with twigs and dead leaves.

"We slept in the open under the stars," he laughed. "It's the greatest fun, Mother."

"I know, son. I know."

He was too big for tears but not too old to kiss his mother on the mouth and hug her as if he never wanted to let her go. "Promise me never to go away again," he said, his voice neither high nor low, but breaking, as fifteen-year-old voices will, somewhere distressingly in between.

It was Dunia who finally took the matter of Stefan Murav's mad delusion of kingship in hand. It was the girl, not the wife who through the long years had suffered from the humiliation of his madness, took decisive action. Not even Hania, the mother-in-law who herself had seen many loved ones die, could face down Zuska's passionate daughter.

It was Dunia who, as her father lay dying, faced them all with scorn and fire in her brown eyes. "I intend to find the secret of my father's birth," she said, "if it takes me to the end of my days."

Hard, dry-eyed, she lifted her bobbed head, the sun from the hospital window turning its glossy chestnut to a dark honey gold. "Even if it takes my life as it has taken his."

Although the whole tragic affair took three short days, it seemed to Kalina, after it was over and done with, that an eternity had passed. It was a time when her whole life flitted across her mind like a kinescope, each frame standing for a moment in full view before moving on to let another take its place.

It all began a week after Kalina had arrived in Tiflis. They had been called to the hospital by a frantic Jane Fadden.

"Mr. Murav has disappeared!"

Leaving Michael in the care of Stefi, who had formed an almost fanatic attachment to his baby brother and proved to be the perfect babysitter, the three women—Hania, Kalina, and Dunia—had driven at breakneck speed through the cool morning. They arrived to find the hospital staff in turmoil.

Unwittingly, the American nurse had seen the runaway Murav leave. "Last evening, after dinner, an old woman dressed in black went up to Mr. Murav's room to visit him. She seemed harmless enough at the time—"

Overcome with weeping, Jane dropped her head into her hands. "It's all my fault. His physicians warned me that he might try something like this and warned me to be extra careful at the front desk about who comes and leaves."

Impatiently, Dunia shook her by the shoulders. "Well, go on. What about the old woman?"

"He'd left orders that anyone who wanted to see him was to be admitted, although it was feared that a new assassination attempt might be made."

"Stefan never feared death," offered Kalina. She paused, and then added thoughtfully. "My husband never feared anything in his life."

Drying her eyes with a handkerchief, Jane sniffed. "I asked the guard to examine the woman for hidden weapons and, finding none, told her to go on up."

"Yes?" Kalina breathed, knowing what was coming next.

442

Stefan was a master of disguises.

"Well, she came back down in a half an hour and, waving her thanks to me, went out the door. It was almost dark at the time. About eight, I'd say."

"Only it wasn't the old woman who departed but Stefan Murav in the black peasant clothes," said Kalina flatly.

They had found the old peasant woman safely in Stefan's bed, sound asleep and snoring loudly. She was attired in his roomy hospital gown. She was neither tied down nor gagged nor seemed in any way to have been harmed. But when questioned, she merely shook her head and spoke rapidly in a dialect that nobody at the hospital understood.

The police chief shook his head. "The woman was obviously sent by those who would see Mr. Murav dead. She probably told him a cock-and-bull story about knowing the site of his native village."

Kalina closed her eyes. "He spoke of a woman dressed in black—"

A search party was quickly organized, and the police took the woman in protective custody, placing her in one of the smaller wards with a guard at her bedside. At Kalina's request, everything was done for her comfort, but since she obviously was part of the conspiracy somehow organized mysteriously by Murav to help him escape from the hospital, she would be held at least until his safe return.

" 'Safe' is not a word one uses in connection with Stefan," Kalina remarked as they sat in a nearby café sipping strong coffee. "Providing he is found in a reasonable length of time, the damage to his wound might be so great that—"

Dunia set her cup down heavily on the table. "Go on, Madame Murav, say it. Say what is in your mind. Say that you want them to find my poor daddy dead. That would leave you free to carry on with Max again, wouldn't it?"

Beside herself with a towering rage fueled by anxiety over her father's welfare, the girl stood up, and pushing her chair back so that it fell, she bent her slim form over the

443

table, waving her fists in the air as if to strike her mother.

"You never loved him," she shrieked. "Don't try to deny it. You only wanted his money, the big houses, the fancy dresses, and all the rest. You were perfectly happy to let him sleep with your own cousin, whom you claim to love so much, right under your nose and produce a bastard child. At every chance you took up with a lover—first the Irishman, then a dirty Cossack whom you forced to take two whole months to make a three weeks' journey."

It was a long speech, delivered without a breath, and at the end of it Dunia collapsed, her hands flat on the table, her head bent low.

Rising up, Hania took strong hands to her raving granddaughter. "Child, please, don't spread your dirty linen in public."

The grandmother managed to get Dunia, now weeping hysterically, outside and into the motorcar. Kalina followed, her heart in a turmoil. How astonishing that the daughter she had thought so strong and mature should harbor such venom within.

Later, at home, as they waited for word of Stefan, Dunia apologized for her irrational behavior. "I am inclined to say things that I do not really mean," she said abjectly. "Half the time I don't even remember what I said. Besides, what you do with your life is your own affair."

She managed to bleak smile. "After all, this is the age of the new modern woman. We are free to bob our hair, throw off our corsets, smoke cigarettes"—she lit up from a pack which she had opened an hour ago and was rapidly depleting—"and have as many lovers as we want."

"Like your mother, you often act in haste and repent in leisure," said Kalina. Then, "Like the rest of us, I dare say."

They were in the front parlor, Dunia slouched, exhausted, in a velvet chair, Kalina on the sofa. Hania had gone to the kitchen to fix some soothing herb tea.

Suddenly, with the same lightning impulsiveness with which she had stormed at her mother in the café, Dunia rose and fell upon her knees before Kalina, placing her head in her mother's lap.

"I am so ugly, and you are so beautiful," she sobbed. "And you were away so much, even when we lived in Pittsburgh. You seemed to think more of your Homestead families than of me."

Kalina's hand reached out to stroke the soft curls. "Darling, you had Mary Lesko."

"I wanted you."

The girl fell quiet, and wisely, Kalina decided not to pursue the matter for a time. Dunia's problems were too deep-seated to solve at a time when other, more pressing matters demanded attention.

Hania ultimately persuaded the exhausted girl to lie down in the cool bedroom, promising to awaken her the moment any word of her father was received. Then, sitting down with Kalina, the two talked in quiet tones of Stefan.

"He seemed so well when I saw him yesterday," said Kalina. "Outside of a few snide remarks about my cropped hair, he was unusually calm in speech and manner." She sighed. "I should have known he was probably hatching his little scheme."

Hania took her hand. "Don't worry. His chest wound was almost healed, and he is strong and virile. I was shocked to learn that your husband was actually fifty."

"If only he would abandon his mad idea to find his heritage, to prove his claim to kingship."

With a kiss and a quick, "Get some rest yourself, darling. You never know what's ahead," her mother left to tend to household affairs, leaving Kalina in the sitting room alone. She sat on the green velvet couch, her head turned to the window, from which she could see the panorama of high mountain peaks. Stefan was up there somewhere, perhaps lying dead and broken at the foot of a steep canyon.

"He will most certainly head for the mountains," Dunia had instructed the search party. "Here is a map he planned to follow in his search for his native village. He had it drawn up by a cartographer who's studied the area."

445

As for the girl's wild accusation of neglect, not to mention her exaggerated ideas on her mother's adultery, Kalina had no easy defense. How to explain to one so young that there are many kinds of love, that what a wife feels for a husband is not so easily described to one who has never known that special kind of intimacy?

If she said, "I love your father in a very special way," the girl would laugh in her face. To the young everything is either black or white. Love is love, hate is hate. There is little in between.

This was no time, when her father's very life was in peril, to tell the girl that while her accusation that she, her mother, had married for money was true, her father's reasons for marrying Kalina Olkonsky had also little to do with romantic love.

Stefan, don't you love me, for myself?

Love! Ninny! I married you for your bloodlines. Bastard or no, a whelp of Pan Mikolai's is not to be disdained.

Of all the venomous words the girl had uttered, however, one sentence stood out from the rest. She had said that Stefan's death would leave her mother "free to carry on with Max again."

Dunia could not know that Max O'Hara had died a prisoner of the Germans. She would have to tell her, soon, about the letter that had arrived that last night in Vienna, just hours before she was taken prisoner herself by the Serbians.

Next morning, just past dawn, they found Murav, not in a canyon as Kalina had suspected, but atop a bleak rock a few kilometers out of Tiflis, tied to a dead ash tree. His tormentors had wound hempen ropes round and round his naked form, after which they had poured honey on him from head to toe.

"His entire body was swarming with ants and other insects," said the constable, "feeding on the honey. Vultures were already perched in the branches of the tree, waiting." The man shivered in revulsion. "Were it not for his loud and persistent screams, we might never have found him."

He cast a wondering glance at the figure on the hospital bed. "Your husband is a powerful man, Mrs. Murav. They don't make many like him." He paused reflectively. "Whether or not he is really of royal blood, he sure as hell got the stuff real kings are made of."

Everything was done. Specialists were brought in, the entire hospital marshaled all its talent and resources.

But, inexorably, Stefan began to die. Someone had thrust his father's little dagger, which he had carried with him on his flight, into his healing bullet wound, and in the hours before he was found, infection had set in.

The bites festered also, so it appeared as though he was suffering from the pox.

He was beset with violent chills alternating with an alarmingly high fever. He thrashed about so vigorously on the bed that, many times in the week it took him to die, the male orderlies were called to hold him down. Kalina forbade them to tie him to the bedrails.

"My husband will die as freely as he lived," she said, thinking of him not as he appeared now, bruised and broken, but as she had first seen him that day in the Pottsville Hotel, sitting so proudly by the window and she had thought him a Cossack.

"He is a Cossack," she said. "To bind a Cossack is to deny his manhood."

Her daughter and her mother cast anxious glances in her direction, thinking perhaps that she was confusing her husband with her recent lover.

But Kalina merely smiled. "It's a kind of secret thing with Stefan and me."

At first he seemed strong and hopeful, chattering at great length, making long speeches about his plans to pursue his search when his infection cleared. But toward the end, as he grew weaker, depression assailed him. He rambled, usually in English or Polish but more often in a dialect that nobody understood.

"Sounds like someone who is caught up in a kind of religious fervor," suggested the doctor. "What they call speaking in tongues."

His women spelled each other at his bedside, and one afternoon, after an especially long harangue in the strange tongue, Dunia fetched the old woman who had helped him flee. She was still in police custody.

"We're searching for someone who speaks her language," the police had told Kalina. "Perhaps then we can determine just who is responsible for torturing your husband." He shrugged. "There must be a thousand villages in these mountains, and each seems to speak a language of its own."

It was thought the attempted murder was the work of an antiwar group, who probably had also inspired the war widow to shoot him on the dock. Others conjectured that some Polish nationals may have taken Murav's kingship claims seriously and decided to do away with him, just in case he might attempt a *coup* after the war.

A hasty telephone call from Dunia brought Kalina and Hania flying to the hospital to listen in amazement to a lengthy dialogue between Stefan and the old mountain woman. For the first time Kalina began to take seriously Stefan's vision of the cave with a mossy fringe and an old woman dressed in black.

Could this hag lead them to Stefan's secret village?

But sadly, it was not to be.

His dialogue with the old woman in black drained the life from Stefan Murav, and that evening, as the supper trays went round, and the dying sun made the sky over the city a brilliant, flaming red—reminding Kalina of the sky over the Monongahela when the furnaces were at full tilt— her husband gave up his fight for life.

Hania fetched a Catholic priest, who administered the last rites. The man prayed in Latin, Stefan joining in with his own confused mumbling. Kalina listened intently, but the only clear word she could distinguish was "Anusia."

448

"He has expired."

The doctor stood up from the bed and faced the family. "I can find no pulse and his flesh is growing cold."

To think of such a vital man as "cold" was an absurdity, Kalina mused, as she came forward and took Stefan's big hands in hers for the last time.

Dunia spoke first, almost rudely. "Leave us, please, and do not come to take my father's body away until we send word."

Kalina sat on the bed, holding her husband's limp hand in hers as if she could, by touch of her own flesh, restore life to the dead.

Hania stood at the window, staring at the flaming peaks of the Caucasus. Both had seen death before; both knew that words were superfluous at such times, that to wail and weep or cry out in protest was to question the wisdom of the Almighty who both gives and takes away.

But the youthful Dunia had no such compunctions to be respectfully silent. Much to Kalina's relief, the girl had been strangely quiet throughout the week, had not wept and stormed as might be expected in one so passionately devoted to her father. When they had brought him in from the hills, near death, covered with blood from the insect bites, she had simply stared dry-eyed at him.

Now, pacing round the small, white-walled room, she began a tirade, her hands clasped together behind her back, her head high, her brown eyes sparking fire.

Not for the first time was Kalina struck by the strong resemblance between Stefan and his adopted daughter. A wild thought — could Zuska and Stefan have known each other in Pottsville? Hedy had said that Zuska had known "every railroad man between Philadelphia and Pittsburgh."

Was the story of an Italian street peddler fabricated to hide the fact that her cousin did actually know for a certainty the father of her child?

But no matter now. Dredging up the past almost always

came to tragedy. Witness poor Stefan's quest for his ancestry.

"I intend to do what Daddy gave his life for," she began. "I will find the secret of his birth. You never took him seriously, Mama Kalina. Like the others, you simply laughed at him when he said the blood of Polish kings runs in his veins."

"Stephen Batory," Kalina murmured. Her brows lifted. "It is entirely possible—" Her eyes gazed directly into Dunia's. "I imagine many Poles can make a similar claim. Kings are notorious for spreading their seed far and wide."

"Don't interrupt, please. For once, I will have my say." The brown eyes softened for a moment. "I always thought of him as a king. Like the kind in the fairy tales. He was so tall and dark and handsome and spoke with such a commanding voice."

While Kalina's own sin lay in thinking Stefan's quest a mad delusion to be humored at best, the man's own fault—a minor one to be sure—so Dunia maintained, lay in going about the whole affair in a fumbling, old-fashioned way.

Dunia spoke as a scholar might, addressing a scientific convention of peers. "All the business of secret operatives and special maps and traveling all over the place in crazy disguises was ridiculous. Paranoid, as the psychologists would say. In his fever to be secretive, Daddy never thought of doing the simple, sensible thing. Advertising in the public press, for instance, or consulting a public agency that makes a business of tracking down missing persons."

Despite being in the presence of death, Hania repressed a smile. "I imagine, like many men of power, your father trusted no one but himself and the men he paid good money to. Knowing Stefan as little as I did, I venture that he thought it a kind of game."

But Dunia was not to be cajoled. She remained grave and unsmiling.

As they left the room a half-hour later, Dunia cast herself upon her dead father's chest. She kissed him on the mouth. "I promise you, Daddy. You will be vindicated."

450

Stefan Murav's funeral was the biggest affair of its kind seen in Tiflis for many years. Six white horses pulled the flower-laden hearse, also white. A band of musicians in spanking white uniforms marched behind playing, Polish national hymns and folk songs.

Surprisingly enough, the sophisticated Hania organized the occasion, hiring everything that was needed. "A war-torn city needs a celebration, no matter what the cause. It's as you say in your American way—a shot in the arm."

Truly, it was so. People need circuses as well as bread, Kalina reflected, as she gazed, open-mouthed from the limousine that carried the family, at the throngs that lined the streets. The myriad bazaars had a record day for sales, hawking American flags, little carpet samples, geegaws of any kind as mementoes of Stefan Murav's passing.

"It's a kind of vulgar display," she started to apologize to Stefi. "But your grandmother says that in Poland a big funeral is a mark of great respect."

But to her great amazement, her son said quickly, "Daddy was a big man, he deserves a big funeral. He did many bad things in his life, if I am to believe half of what I hear, but don't we all?"

Not trusting the year-old Michael not to make a scene in the church where a solemn Requiem Mass was celebrated in full panoply, Kalina had left the child with Jane Fadden.

There was no trip to a cemetery, she and the children deciding to take the body home to America for burial.

Now, as they alighted from the limousine and were walking into Hania's house, Stefi put a protective arm around his mother. "I am the man of the house now, Mother."

Tears sprang to her eyes. During the three days since Sefan's death, she had had time on her hands, Hania taking charge of the arrangements. With Hania gone much of the time and Dunia off on her self-appointed mission to find her father's birth village, Kalina had given much thought to her future.

It would be devoted to her children. Michael of course was too young to be of much concern.

But Dunia was another matter. Her friend Lini still called her Merry. Kalina had seen letters from Switzerland on her daughter's desk, which addressed her in that way.

Dunia's natural, merry spirit must be restored. Her unbounded energies must be harnessed into wholesome paths. Politics perhaps, which interested the girl enormously. But first she must get an education. Marching down the street waving placards was well enough in its place, but if a woman were truly to change the world, she cannot sound like a fool.

College, to start with.

As for Stefi, he showed remarkable artistic talent. His sketches lay about everywhere in the house. An artist friend of his suggested Paris.

No. If one thing was certain in her presently chaotic life, it was this: Kalina Murav and her family were sailing for America. On the first available steamer.

And never, she vowed, *never* would she leave her adopted shores again.

Having run ahead, Dunia was already inside with some of her American friends, partaking of Hania's lavish after-funeral repast. Dunia was poring over the stacks of responses to the advertisement she had placed in the Tiflis newspapers.

As Kalina entered the dining room, she was met with gales of laughter. A deep frown shadowed her face at the unsuitable hilarity. Glancing up from the table, Dunia caught the displeasure on her mother's face.

"But Mama Kalina, you should read some of these crazy replies. Even Daddy would go into hysterics. They are truly funny."

After a cursory glance at the many letters forwarded by the newspaper, Kalina was herself forced to smile. Some claimed to be Murav's father, others to know of his mother, and many offered to lead the family into the hills to the exact site of his birth.

One, claiming to be the direct descendant of Stephen Batory, ancient kind of Poland, in fact, was the leader of a kind of club composed entirely of Batory descendants.

All, without exception, asked for money.

Dunia was undaunted. "People who've done this kind of thing tell me it's always this way at the outset. One simply filters the wheat from the chaff and carries on from there."

The noise of airplanes overhead brought them all into the street to gaze anxiously into the sky. Earlier in the war, Tiflis had been the target of German bombs, but in recent months the fighting had been diminishing in the Caucasus, the Czar calling many troops home to Russia to deal with the threatening revolution of the peasants against the monarchy.

There were three planes, all with German markings, but it wasn't bombs that fell on Stefan Murav's mourners.

They were being bombarded with paper.

It was a blizzard of huge paper snowflakes, the white leaflets floating down to cluster on tiled rooftops, clog the gutters in the streets, and catch in the branches of the trees like manna from heaven.

Stefi picked one up and read, haltingly, for his Russian was newly learned.

"Soldiers of the Russian army, throw off your shackles! Citizens of Tiflis, free your city. Fight no more for the czar. Tomorrow we march for freedom. Join us in the Square!"

The leaflets fell during the night and into the morning, effectively preventing any of the household from sleeping. Baby Michael especially was terrified of the motors, keeping Hania and Kalina busy throughout the night consoling him. Now, at dawn, he had at last fallen into an exhausted sleep.

"He remembers the time we had to flee Jaslo before the Germans," Kalina told her mother. "The planes were flying overhead with their terrible noise and machine guns even as we stood in the yard of the manor."

The two had spelled each other, having spent most of the night in the kitchen drinking coffee and talking in worried voices of the coming revolution.

"Rebellion has been brewing for twenty years or more," Hania told her. "Kirov spoke of it many times. Now I think it's really going to happen."

Kalina cast an anxious glance at the gray sky outside the window. "Do you think there will actually be fighting in the city?"

"No, Mama Kalina, of course not. The vast majority of the people here are against the tyranny of the Czar." Answering for her grandmother, Dunia entered, fully dressed, ready for the day in her white blouse and green skirt, a perky military-type American hat on her curls.

"They simply want the soldiers to stop fighting the Germans. As far as Russia is concerned, the war is over."

White-lipped, Kalina bolted up, took her daughter by the arm as the girl poured herself a cup of steaming coffee. "Surely you don't intend to go into the hospital today. I forbid it. Your life may be in danger."

Dunia frowned. "There's been fighting in the city before, lots of it, Mama Kalina. What if everybody left their posts at the first sign of trouble?"

She drained her cup. "Besides, I'm not a child that you can forbid me to do anything."

Rattling the keys to the Oldsmobile, she dashed out the door before either of the older women could say another word.

Scarce two hours later a Red Cross ambulance pulled up to the curb outside the house and two attendants carried Dunia inside on a stretcher. A band of revolutionaries had boldly commandeered the Oldsmobile, knocking the protesting Dunia down into the street directly in front of the hospital.

A worried Jane Fadden had left the front desk and picked her up. "The people are rioting," she said. "It's not safe for anybody who looks rich." She shook her head. "If

454

only she hadn't been driving that big car—"

Luckily, Dunia's physical injuries were superficial. The wounds to her spirit were deeper. "Idiots," she stormed. "They thought me a damned aristocrat. When I think of all the hours and labor I've put into helping them and their children!"

She had recognized one of her attackers as a soldier whose family she had given much aid and comfort to after he had been wounded in the mountain battles. "I brought them food and clothing, medicines—put my life in danger going down into that slummy native section."

"We must embark for America immediately," said a very worried Kalina. "Hania's friends tell her that the revolution is increasing in intensity, not only here but in Russia and all over. People in a ferment have a way of not distinguishing the innocent from the guilty."

Even as she spoke, marchers appeared in their quiet suburban street, waving placards and shooting guns into the air.

"You will come with us, of course, Hania."

The older woman shook her head. "No, darling. Much as your offer tempts me, I cannot leave here without my dear Kirov. If the war is really over for Russia, he will be coming home soon."

They were in the little library where Hania had been telephoning, making arrangements for a private motorcar to take Kalina and her children to the port of Batum on the Black Sea, where they could find a ship to take them to Istambul. From there they could sail by a circuitous route to America.

"I'm doing this only because you're so hysterical," she said to Kalina. "I hope you'll change your mind. I really think you'll be safer here than on the high seas, what with all those German U-boats crawling about beneath the ocean."

"No, Mother. If it's true that the Germans and Russians are making a peace, then there will be no danger at least in the Black Sea." Her black eyes were afire with determina-

455

tion. "I must go home. Surely you can see that."

Hearing laughter outside, Kalina peered fearfully through the lace curtain at the street. "There are men out there, sitting on the steps. They have a bottle and seem to be drinking." She clutched her mother's arm. "They've got Stefi! Oh my God—"

"Stop panicking, Kalina," laughed Hania, raising the window, and calling out in Russian. Turning, the men waved and shouted back.

"They are my friends and Kirov's," she told Kalina. "They will protect the house. My husband has long been active in the revolutionary movement."

To ease Kalina's mind, Hania called the boy inside. He was filled with news. "They say that Czar Nicholas and his whole family have been captured and the people have taken over all of Moscow." His face was aglow. "And, Mother, guess what? It is almost a certainty that America will enter the war within a month."

Two days later, Hania's family physician declared Dunia fit for travel. Except for a bandage on her wrist, where she had suffered a deep scratch, there was no visible sign of her harrowing experience.

Kalina feverishly began her packing. Her mother had generously provided clothing for all, not only frocks and shoes for herself and Dunia, but sturdy jackets and trousers that had belonged to her dead son for the fast-growing Stefi.

A Benz motorcar with a powerful motor stood outside, waiting in the predawn dark. The Oldsmobile had also been returned by Kirov's friends, who kept their vigil around the house.

All were gathered in the foyer, waiting for Dunia, who had not yet put in an appearance. Clucking her tongue, Kalina sought out the girl in her room. She found her standing before her open suitcase, a newspaper in her hand that had been torn in two. She was holding the pieces together, and her hands were trembling.

As her mother entered, the girl looked up.

"This is no time to be reading," began Kalina, irritated. "Now close your case, please, and come out immediately. The car is waiting."

The girl trained her clear brown eyes on her mother. "A French girl who works with me at the hospital had this, and when I saw it —" She hesitated and then went on uncertainly, "She collects pictures of flyers. It's a kind of hobby with her."

"Really, Dunia —"

"I wasn't going to show you this, Mama Kalina." She glanced down at the paper. "I even started to tear it up to throw it away. But you told me he was dead —"

Kalina frowned, exasperated. "Well, what is it? Who are you talking about, girl?"

"Here, see for yourself."

Taking the torn halves of paper, Kalina laid it on the bed and bent down to examine them. The newspaper was French and featured on its front page a photograph of a man in an officer's uniform. The paper was much wrinkled, and torn right through the man's face. But the caption beneath left no doubt as to the officer's identity.

American flying ace Max O'Hara, who has downed fifteen German planes, leaves a Paris nightclub with his fiancée, Kundry von Richthofen. Although a German, the woman is spending the war years in Paris.

Kalina never heard her daughter close her suitcase and leave the room. Her world was spinning. The newspaper was dated just two months before, on New Year's Eve.

Rage burned within her at the emperor but was quickly quenched. The man had been dead since November; he stood now before a higher judge. It was clear that Franz Josef had fabricated the story of Max's death, for whatever convoluted reasons she didn't want even to imagine.

Max dead she could live with. The memory of their love cut off at its height could sustain her through the long years.

But could she bear the agony of Max alive and perhaps loving another?

Sometimes of late she had pictured her heart as a corridor with doors on either side. Some were open wide. These led to her children, her mother, those she loved.

Others were closed. Stefan, Yurek, Libby, Max.

"Kalina!"

Voices called her from outside the room.

Woodenly, she turned to join her children.

She crumpled the paper in her hands, let it drop to the floor. Mindlessly, she rubbed the stain of newsprint from her fingers and slowly drew on her traveling gloves.

Fixing a smile upon her face, Kalina walked through the door to join her children.

Chapter Twenty-three

The Western Front, France
December 1917

After two solid weeks of winter rain and fog, the weather finally showed signs of clearing, and at their airfield close to No Man's Land, the *Escadrille Américaine 88* prepared for combat.

At noon, Max rolled out of his bunk and delivered a hearty kick to the protruding backside of nineteen-year-old Tom Alison, huddled under his blankets in the next bed.

Max moved to the window. "Sun'll be out in an hour or two."

A muffled curse from Tom. "It's a mirage. You overdid it on the cognac last night."

At thirty-five Max felt like an old man alongside Tom, who was nineteen and had yet to fly his first combat mission, having arrived from basic training at Luxeil only the week before. A natural flyer, the kid hailed from Dayton, Ohio, where the Wright Brothers had done their first experiments on flying machines.

"I've been in love with airplanes since I was ten," he had told Max. "But never had the money to get a machine of my own. Or even make one. Over here I can fly all I want to and get paid for it to boot."

He and Max had hit it off straightaway. They had spent the previous night drinking and talking of home in a local bistro frequented by aviators.

Max turned from his window gazing, and ruthlessly dragging the boy feet first out of bed, shoved him into the shower.

Within the hour the two aviators were in the hangar working with their mechanics on their brand-new monoplanes. New planes from various makers were arriving almost every day, and headquarters had sent them a machine called an A-1 Parasol. The very latest in design, the airplane was the smallest, trickiest, and fastest in the air, swift and agile as a hawk. So proclaimed the manufacturer's printed brochure.

Extravagant praise, reflected Max. Too extravagant for comfort. He was reluctant to give up his trusty Nieuport for something that had all the earmarks of being experimental.

Like exchanging an old wife for a new model, he said to Tom, just because she's younger and slimmer and more stylish.

The clammy, ghostlike fog, which hid the mountain tops and clung to trees in shreds and tatters and for which the Vosges basin was notorious, had dampened the men's morale, and now that a teasing sun could be glimpsed now and then behind the clouds, they were eager to be in the sky again.

Flying was Max's life. Known among the squadron as a "cut-up," he rarely spoke seriously, maintaining at all times a kind of jovial devil-may-care posture that led many to regard him as an adventurer. He had a fund of risqué jokes and was much sought after for parties and the frequent, champagne-cork-popping sessions that celebrated every kill.

"His kind make the best fighter pilots," his commander often remarked. "He's an old warhorse, who lives on the scent of battle."

Many compared him to Manfred von Richthofen, the legendary German ace known throughout Europe as the

Red Baron, who now had over sixty black crosses painted on his crimson Fokker.

Although it was the stated ambition of all Allied flyers to be the lucky one to bring down the notorious Prussian, many thought that if anyone could manage the seemingly impossible victory, it would be the tall red-headed American.

"They're a match," was the consensus. "It's in the stars."

With a conspicuous lack of modesty, Max agreed, often boasting that the gods would not let him die until his bullet had struck that damned Blue Max right in the middle where the decoration hung around the Heinie's neck.

"Get the Fritz," became the watchword.

Painted on a propeller shard, the words hung over his bed.

The New York boy was a dead shot and had an uncanny ability to maneuver his plane with acrobatic ingenuity, feinting and dodging like a prizefighter into a position where his adversary's machine guns could not reach him and then to shoot straight from the shoulder, cowboy style.

It was a style of combat which became known throughout flying circles as *à l'américaine*.

To Max it was simply the kind of survival strategy he had been forced to learn as a street boy in the slums.

The few who were permitted to drink with the American from New York and to glimpse the man beneath the facade, saw the streak of pure idealism that had driven him to join up and that now drove him to incredible exploits in the sky.

"He's a kind of Sir Galahad," his friend Larry had written in his diary. "A knight in shining armor, out to save the world."

Max laughed when he read the poetic lines, which were included in a letter from his friend's mother in Detroit. Larry had gone down over the lines, his body never recovered. None of the men Max had sat around the table with that first night when he had stumbled into the dugout at Verdun with the German POWs was still alive.

The Detroit flyer's mother had written Max, responding

to his letter of condolence, which he had sent along with the diary and his friend's sack of medals.

Unlike most of the men in the *Lafayette Escadrille*, however, Max kept no diary. He was never one to commit his intimate feelings to paper, either for his own perusal or for future publication, as was the intention of some of the men.

Long hours were spent at the desk in the wardroom, though, writing in his slow, laborious hand to adoring females in America.

Like all other flyers in the European war, he had become the idol of women the world over. Photographs of him standing beside his plane or frolicking with the squadron mascot, a lion cub named Whiskey, were printed on postal cards and in newspapers.

Hundreds of women sent him long letters, begging him for his autograph, promising him their bodies and hearts and souls if needed, anytime he happened to be in their cities.

Max took special joy in answering the letters from America. Mostly small-town girls, their words had a fresh, sweet naiveté about them that warmed his heart and softened the pangs of homesickness. They had names like Jenny, Becky, Dottie.

The French girls he met around the airfield and on his occasional leaves in Paris were jaded and sophisticated. They had names like Fifi, Jeanne, Odette.

The whole thing was fairly safe, he felt. His native land was a long way off, across a vast ocean. There would be no entanglements after the war.

If he should by some miracle survive the war—

But he never thought that far ahead. The future, like the scarred land that surrounded him, was a kind of nebulous No-Man's Land.

It was two hours before twilight on this late December day before the weather cleared sufficiently for takeoff. Max and Tom, along with five other American fighter pilots, would serve as part of a fighter escort for a group of a hundred Allied bombers, mostly heavier British Sopwiths, assigned to strike a giant munitions works just across the German border.

Night flying was rarely attempted, but for strategic reasons, the bombing could not be delayed.

The message from headquarters was "Now or never!"

With a good slice of luck, and minimal action from enemy fighters, there was plenty of time to get to the target, deliver the loads, and return. As a diversionary tactic, five other American pilots would fly to another sector of the front, joining their British and French buddies in a staged dogfight to steer the German fighters away from the area to be bombed.

But minutes before zero hour, Max's Parasol was declared unfit by the mechanic and he went up in his trusty Nieuport. He was much relieved. With the help of the scrappy single seater, he had sent twenty German planes of various makes to the ground in flames.

Quickly, he and Tom suited up. If it was winter down below, the weather five thousand feet up was arctic. Their flying costume was inches thick and many-layered. Wool sweater, leather jacket, fur-lined coverall, fur-lined parka, helmet, paper gloves topped by fur gloves, paper socks, fleece-lined boots.

Mimicking older aces, Tom sheepishly slipped a red-dyed woman's silk stocking over his head, letting the long leg dangle from beneath his helmet.

"For luck," he said.

An hour or so later, the bombs were dropped, and the sky over the Rhine exploded into flames as the incendiaries touched off mammoth stores of powder in the munitions plant.

To Max, observing through his goggles from a distance behind the bombers, the conflagration resembled the top of the blast furnaces of Homestead.

After the first gigantic burst, a soaring black pillar of smoke plumed upward, to be grotesquely silhouetted against the sunset.

Hell with the lid off, he thought.

He tried not to think of the poor bastards caught in the factories below, but smiling grimly, gave an affectionate pat to the barrel of his machine gun.

"There goes a helluva lot of rifles, bayonets, ammunition, and cannons that will never see the Western Front," he muttered.

The fighters continued patrolling until sunset, diverting antiaircraft and enemy fighter planes away from the formations of bombers swiftly heading home across the river. Max took some flak in his wings, but by diving low into a cloud bank, managed to escape a pesky German fighter that dogged his rear like a damn bluebottle fly on a stack of horse manure.

Max had long since lost sight of Tom's Parasol and muttered a quick prayer to St. Wilfred, whom he had invented as the patron saint of flyers, to keep an eye on the kid. He looked forward to more long talks with the guy from Ohio.

Although the low altitude and the clouds kept him safe from enemy planes which he could hear clearly all around him, visibility was now practically zero.

For a time Max flew aimlessly in circles, a wary eye on his fuel gauge. Eventually a crescent moon glimmered through a crack in the clouds, and by keeping an eye on it, together with his own innate sense of direction, he found himself over familiar territory.

His fuel was nearly gone, but, if necessary, he could glide to earth. With great relief he spotted a pinpoint of light below. The pinpoint grew into two parallel lines of lights, but he glided instead a little to the left, where someone was waving a lantern in a circle.

The rows of lanterns were a dummy landing strip, designed to fool the enemy.

Easing back his control stick, Max cut his throttle and peered down at the field, looking for the lantern and a familiar rocky outcrop shaped like a woman's breast, which he habitually used as a landmark.

But a clump of trees that should have been cut down, he

thought with irritation, blocked his vision.

Twice around he went, gliding lower each time. His mouth was dry, and conjuring up a tall glass of beer, he mentally lifted it to his lips.

As he spun around for a third and final try, he felt a jolt, then a grinding crash, as the Nieuport hit the turf nose first. The flying machine went careening across the field, tumbling over and over.

Through the thunder in his ears, Max heard the ominous rip of fabric and the crunch of wood as the struts gave way.

There was no fire, since the tank was as dry as a used-up well, and Max lay stunned.

Tom Alison was the first to reach the crumpled wreckage, and as he helped the medics drag Max from the cockpit, the boy cracked, "Dummy, you get out of Germany without a scratch and come home to run right into a damned high-tension wire."

Lying on the stretcher, Max grabbed the red silk end of Tom's stocking cap. "Thank you, St. Wilfred," he muttered.

"What's that?" Tom's brow wrinkled, and he pursed his lips. "Jeez, the old guy must have hit his head. He's raving."

"Old guy—I'll get your ass for that—"

Laughing along with his rescuers and holding tightly to Tom's hand, the downed pilot joked and sang snatches of bawdy songs all the way across the field and into the ambulance. It took a short-tempered nurse at the field hospital to put an end to it.

All attributed his euphoria to his narrow escape from death. They had seen it before. They could not even guess that the sight of Tom's grinning face beneath the damn red stocking cap was the cause of his hilarity.

It's all in a day's work.

Max O'Hara had repeated the stock phrase time after time as the names of men who had become his pals were posted in the wardroom as among the missing.

But it was only something to say to ease the pain. Like a prayer learned in childhood and recited long after all real

465

faith had gone. He never quite believed it.

Now, as he saw the Ohio boy safe and sound, smiling down at him, he knew he would never say it again.

The battle-scarred Nieuport, which had been Max's loving companion for six months of combat, was sent "to the cleaners," being usable only for salvage of various undamaged parts.

As for the dauntless pilot, who had come a cropper right over his own home base, all his visible parts appeared to be intact.

The base doctor shook his head. "Can't understand it. Your bones must be made of rubber. Except for that nasty cut over your right eye—"

"And a badly damaged ego," Max quipped. "If a guy's gonna catch it, he might at least bring a Fritz down with him."

"You'll never catch it," the doc replied, "at least not in the air. Max O'Hara leads a charmed life."

Since there could be internal injuries and hairline breaks that could not be detected by the naked eye, it was decided to send the American to Paris where a newfangled device called an x-ray was being used to take pictures of a man's insides.

Besides, opined the doctor, a few weeks of rest and recreation in gay Paree would surely not be wasted on a man of thirty-five who had been flying more or less steadily since April.

Forthwith, the week before Christmas, 1917, Max found himself once again aboard the Paris Express.

At six o'clock on New Year's Eve, Max strode briskly down the *Rue de la Paix*, the bells of Paris in his ears, hunting in a random kind of way for a place called The New York Bar, where the fellows at the hospital had assured him "all the aviators hung out" and which therefore was the only place to usher in 1918.

"That bar is also crawling with girls," they told him, winking and mouthing *le fille joie*. That meant someone young and pretty and who had a house with a room to herself where he could spend future leaves in easy dalliance.

Many of the aviators had a *marraine*, a kind of "fairy godmother" with whom they maintained a steady, monogamous relationship. Someone who would be there, for sure, when they happened to be on leave. A girl who would be faithful, like a wife.

"Stick to one. It's the best way to avoid disease," was the general opinion.

Max thanked his buddies for their advice but didn't tell them that he was not at all sure he wanted to be with flyers tonight or with the kind of girl who hitched up with crazy, wild, aviators.

He was in the mood for something different. Maybe some real Frenchmen, down-to-earth types, people who had never been up in a plane or perhaps had never even gone for a ride in a motorcar.

Horses. That's what he would like. Rent a horse and drive it through the streets like a king. Like the gendarmes with their cocky uniforms and funny hats.

He looked about for a livery stable but soon realized the absurdity of the idea. The chances of finding a livery stable in ritzy downtown Paris were about a hundred to one. They were always on the edge of town or in the slummier sections.

A legless man in a tattered French uniform sat on a corner atop a carpet-covered crate, peddling French tricolors and tiny American flags. Digging into his pocket, Max put twenty sous into the tin can, and helped himself to one of each.

Putting the flags in his tunic pocket, taking care to crisscross them in the accepted fashion, he resumed his walk. He stopped half a block downstreet in the front of a crowded bistro where "Yankee Doodle" was being sung, very loud, very much out of tune and in barely recognizable accented English.

"Yankee-ee Doodle went to town, a-riding on a pon-ee"
He hummed along. The French actually thought that

crazy little ditty was the American national anthem.

France was in love with America. It was in the air. *Amour!* Girls ran up to hug the fresh, vigorous, pink-cheeked doughboys in khaki, asking always, "Where you from, *Américain*?"

They were from all over the big country across the water. Michigan, West Virginia, Kentucky, Arizona. They had names like Jack and Wayne and Leroy.

A "bridge of ships" had brought them over, three hundred thousand each month at least. They would burgeon forth among the groggy, discouraged, weary Allied troops. Victory was within sight at last.

The war-weary French blissfully ignored the cold fact that the Germans were rumored to be within seventy kilometers of the city and had developed a nasty habit of lobbing at random nine-inch cannon balls from a gun called "Big Bertha" day and night.

Max didn't go inside to join the drunken choir. He had had a bellyful of saloons.

He longed to be inside a warm, smoky kitchen where sausages were frying and old friends milled about, laughing, joking, drinking bottomless cups of gritty coffee brewed in a cracked, blue-enamel pot.

Actually, he had to admit that he didn't know where he wanted to be, who he wanted to be with.

Max was in a mood for adventure. The madcap kind. *A ragpicker's cart, a girl.*

Struck by the blinding jolt of memory, his head began to whirl in an alarming fashion, and he stopped to lean for a moment against an iron street lantern, gazing absently up to the round electric globe. It was painted blue to dim the city against the German bombers.

Somehow the dismal color echoed his mood. He was blue, and if he didn't do something about it right away, he was in for a real attack of what he would call "the dumps" and what Dr. Alec would call "melancholia."

The girl who had run smack into the ragpicker's cart by the frozen East River eighteen years ago and had changed his life forever was in America now, far from the sights and sounds of war.

Promptly after he had been dismissed from the Air Service hospital, Max had traveled across the Seine to see Alec and Wanda Hardie in their psychiatric clinic. They told him an incredible tale of Kalina's adventures since that night in Paris over a year ago when he had tried to call her in Vienna.

"It's unreal, like a story you read in one of those pulp magazines," said Wanda. "She was captured, along with Michael and Mary, and held for ransom." She rolled her eyes. "I think Cossacks were involved, though Kalina said nothing about *that* in her letter. I heard it through the hospital grapevine."

Everything had turned out all right in the end, nobody hurt, except that Stefan Murav had died in Tiflis of a gunshot wound. After a happy reunion with her mother, Kalina and the three children had sailed for America, taking almost two months to get there in a roundabout, southerly route.

"That's all we know," said Wanda. "Mail is spotty, and the one letter from Pittsburgh was very short. The French censors don't like long letters since I understand they get paid by the piece and tend to put them aside in a separate pile for later reading." She grimaced. "The trouble is, more often than not, the letters stay in the pile for months on end."

"I suspect that pile will end up in a dustbin," added Alec gloomily.

Recovered from her thrilling adventures, the widow Murav, Max reflected wryly, was no doubt celebrating the New Year at a swank Pittsburgh soiree or maybe at a grand ball at the Schenley Hotel complete with fancy costumes and stacks of rich food, with some of her posh friends. Lillian Russell, Jim Brady—that bunch of swells.

Or was she maybe in the big house on Rutherford Drive throwing an intimate party for her children and the servants? Anusia, too, for she too was now a rich heiress, having surely copped a big chunk of her dead brother's nest egg.

Along with the grieving widow, who now, whatever happened to him in the war, was distinctly out of Max O'Hara's class.

He had saved a hunk of cash from his flyer's pay, but even if he sold all his box of medals, it would probably pay for less than six months of upkeep at the Murav menage.

Max imagined the family circle. Dunia, now a lovely debutante, all decked out in fringe and feathers, maybe waving a silver cigarette holder in her dainty hand. The women were all smoking now, just like men. The cigarette would be Turkish, the best kind.

Stefi would be a lad of sixteen or so, he figured, a beanpole. They would offer him his first glass of wine. He would drink it bravely, his dark eyes watering, but he would hold it in his mouth until he could spit it out in the nearest potted fern.

There would also be a little redhead, toddling about on the thick carpets, in and out of the grown-ups' legs. At midnight, frightened at the shrill noise of horns and clappers, and the people yelling "Happy New Year" at each other, he would cry and run to clutch his mother's leg.

A fine snow had been falling since morning, coating the city with a charming white, shrouding the ravages of shells and bombs that appeared more frequently than he remembered from his last visit to the city.

Something was happening to the snow, and it started to come down in icy, hard pellets, a fiendish mix of rain and snow. It fell sharply on his nose and cheeks, bounced off his bemedaled tunic, and wilted the brave little flags.

Abandoning his flying jacket for the night, Max had dressed up in a spanking-new American uniform, complete with medals and silver wings on his tunic, hoping to impress any pretty girl who happened to catch his eye.

But the woolen cloth was thinner than he had expected, and suddenly feeling chilled, he whipped around to the street, resolving to pop into the nearest warm place.

As he turned, he ran smack into the outflung arms of a tall woman who seemed completely covered with a kind of silver-blue fur.

There was a gasp, then a pause, then a high, shrill squeal such as women make when pretending to be scared.

"Max O'Hara! What terrific, smashing luck!"

He blinked. Beneath a stylish silver fur cap, two blue eyes, made wider than nature intended with a painted black line around the rims, gazed up at him with wonderment and what could only be described as delirious pleasure.

Snow lay like dewdrops on long, fringed lashes, the lifted brows were arching penciled lines, her sensuous lips were painted a deep, glistening red.

She looked like a mannequin in a store window, but the effect on Max was electrifying.

"Kundry von Richthofen, you are a sight to warm the cockles of any man's heart."

Winking lewdly, she poked him in the ribs with her gloved finger. "I'll warm a good many other parts of your body too, you scalawag."

What luck, he thought. What tremendous, goddamn luck. An answer to a prayer — except that he hadn't prayed.

She was certainly no *le fille joie* but the sophisticated, worldly, madcap, easy-come, easy-go cousin of the Red Baron with whom he had tumbled happily in the Carpathians. She was the perfect woman to turn his thoughts completely away from the merry widow in America.

Kundry would stop the pain.

Pooh-poohing his suggestion that they squeeze into a crowded night spot, she took him immediately to her pension, a two-room affair in a quiet, expensive neighborhood near the *Arc de Triomphe*. Decorated in the fashionable Oriental style, the place appeared to be furnished almost entirely with plump satin pillows in brilliant colors, and rugs that once covered the bodies of bears and tigers.

At midnight when the bells rang out all over Paris, Max and Kundry were sprawled on a white bear rug, staring into a fire that crackled merrily in a blue-tiled grate.

They were naked and eating pearly green-white grapes from the south of France. Great bunches of the luscious fruit rested in a bowl at Max's elbow.

He drew his brows together and spoke with his mouth full, the sweet juice running down his chin. "How'd you manage this feast? Even aviators, who are pampered more than any one else in this war, don't get to eat grapes in December."

A secret cat-that-ate-the-canary kind of smile crossed her handsome face, from which the paint and powder had long since disappeared in the vigors of their love-making. She looked ten years younger without it, Max reflected.

"A woman alone must be resourceful."

There was also, she told him smugly, rich Brazilian coffee, heavy cream, butter, fresh-baked croissants, and fat sausages nestling in a porcelain pan, which Kundry promised to cook when they tired of making love.

"I've even managed some Russian caviar," she said, giggling, with a kiss. "Been saving it for a special occasion."

Not everyone suffered in a war, Max had long realized. There were many, like the crafty woman at his side, who remained unscathed. Others, like Stefan Murav, became fabulously rich on the misery of mankind.

His flying buddies, who came to Paris frequently on leave had given him black-market names and addresses. Anything, no matter how short the supply, could be gotten for money.

But Max was in no mood tonight to be judgmental. He would eat the grapes, the sausages, the caviar and enjoy every bite.

As he had expected, Kundry had driven everything from his mind but lust.

His love-making with Kalina had been the exquisite joining of kindred spirits who are merely using their bodies as instruments to express a kind of love that is, ultimately, inexpressible in physical ways.

The pleasure is there, of course. And a special kind of ecstasy not possible with women like Kundry.

But true love, the kind he felt for his lovely Pole, can never be assuaged. The sweet, sweet, desperate yearning continues until death.

Copulation with Kundry was an animal kind of activity. She did things to various parts of his body with her mouth that lifted him above the earth into a kind of floating, mindless place where he felt as though his body were separating from his soul.

Love-making with Kundry was hurting, bruising, feverish, wild, and frenzied.

"Yell all you want to," she said. "We are at the top of the house, and a garden stretches behind to a high wall. Besides, tonight, there will be so much noise outside that the little we make in here will be like a child's cry in the middle of the Atlantic Ocean."

She knew all the tricks, all the cunning devices he had only heard about from other men inclined to brag about their sexual exploits.

She rode him as a stallion does the mare.

She played games. "Pretend you're being hanged tomorrow morning for murdering my husband."

Responding to his questions, she talked a little of her cousin Manfred. "He's got a roomful of trophies—serial numbers of planes he's downed, pieces of propellers, even a whole engine from a Nieuport. He orders a silver trophy cup for every kill."

She laughed. "His silversmith had to make the last one of silver-plated lead because he was running out of the real stuff."

"Sixty or so," mumbled Max. "Amazing."

"Flying to kill is all he lives for," mused Kundry. "He never had a girl."

"I've sworn to get him," Max said thoughtfully.

"Huh, uh. Not you." Laughing, she ruffled his hair. "You couldn't shoot down someone you know."

She confessed to him, after they were both blind drunk, that she had been married at fifteen to a von Richthofen count who had sold her to his friends, that she had had three abortions, one stillborn child, and that she was forty-five years old.

Then, his own pain seemed as nothing and at dawn, when they came together for the fifth and last time before

473

sleep, he was tender with a woman whom he had misjudged.

"You must regard me as your *marraine*," she said, two weeks later when they parted. They stood on the railway platform, clinging together like sweethearts. It was raining hard, and she wore a glistening, blue raincoat, a pale-blue scarf covering her blond hair. People smiled at them in passing.

"Hold it, Ace!"

A photographer planted himself in front of them and snapped his shutter. Max frowned, resisting a mad impulse to tear the camera from the man's hands and throw it under the train. He didn't want the world to see him with Kundry von Richthofen.

Extricating himself with difficulty from Kundry's arms, he leaped onto the steps to board the coach. He began to sing. His heart was light. He felt as a man does who has just awakened after a long, purging illness to find out that he wasn't going to die after all.

From this valley they say you are going,
Do not hasten to bid me adoo-oo-o
Just remember the Red River valley,
And the poor bloke who loves you so troo-oo-o

It had been a rainy April, even for a region where the sun was mostly a stranger. Max sat glumly on the floor in the hangar, nursing a beer, listening to the mournful tenor of his mechanic, a rangy mountain man called Abel.

Back home, Abel played jew's harp in a hillbilly band in Tennessee and never ran out of songs and ditties.

The rain pounded like a metronome on the canvas roof; the louder it got, the louder Abel sang. "Yankee Doodle," "Over There," "Give My Regards to Broadway."

Water lay in a dirty, brown froth on the landing field, the puddles rippling with an occasional gust of wind. Nobody had gone up for three days, not since a twenty-plane dogfight right over Cambrai where the Red Baron had brought down two Allied planes, a Sopwith and a Spad, bringing his total kill to eighty.

A new death-grip offensive had begun on the Somme. Tanks were being used in force for the first time in combat. A million Americans filled the Allied trenches.

There were those who said, however, that unless the infamous Red Baron was knocked out of the sky, no amount of tanks or men or clever strategies would turn the tide.

"It's psychological," said Tom Alison, who had had a year of college and knew about such erudite things. "Everyone thinks the guy's some kind of a god. We all have a mental block about him."

"He's a symbol," Max agreed.

"He's also a helluva good shot and a genius with that cherry Fokker of his," grumbled Tom.

Although Max, according to the charts kept in the office, had gone up a hundred times and had been involved in almost as many dogfights, he had never spotted von Richthofen's scarlet beauty.

Unless you counted the first time, when he had watched the Prussian shoot Jake Epstein out of the sky.

Two days later, on the twenty-first, the rain had slackened, the morning was hazy but crisp, and a pale sun glimmered a heavenly welcome on the pilots of Escadrille 88.

Three flights of five planes each set out in close V-formation from various airfields toward the place where Intelligence had reported the Red Baron would take his Flying Circus for the day.

Max recited the directive. "River Somme, north of Paris, directly over Amiens, province of Picardy."

At precisely eleven o'clock, a time Max was to think significant eight months later in November, they met the enemy about a half-mile south of the river. Almost immediately a German flew at Max crazily as if to crash right into him.

Irritated more than angry that the plane was not red but

a bright blue with black stripes, he trained a machine-gun burst, then another, at the gaudy machine. His dead Nieuport had been replaced with a Spad, but he hadn't the heart to paint it red, white, and blue as before.

Grimly, he took a second or two to watch the burning plane zoom to earth. His twenty-first.

It was a mad dance of death, as the two opposing forces came at each other. Except for the shrieking engines and the barking guns it seemed like two sky-borne college teams coming together on a football field.

They told him later that below, in the trenches, men cheered and waved, watching the show. The circus lasted for thirty minutes, they said, but Max, in the thick of the milling planes, lost track of time.

Suddenly, as he concentrated on dodging bullets and a purple enemy Albatross that almost scraped his nose before scuttling into a cloud, he saw a bright-red Fokker headed in his direction.

Frantically, Max pulled on his stick, pirouetting in a kind of mad *pas de deux* in an effort to reverse his direction and get into a more advantageous angle for shooting.

That it was the Red Baron himself in the flesh behind the goggles, he had no doubt. Only one German plane was allowed to be painted that brilliant, garish red, and a double line of little black crosses in white painted squares marched on both sides of the fuselage.

Stay calm. He's not a god. Gods don't wear goggles.

As Max righted his machine behind the Fokker, he felt a splat of bullets on his tail. With dizzying speed, Manfred whipped round and appeared directly underneath Max's Spad.

Damn you! With a curse, Max spun up and around and down, twisting and turning at full throttle and coming once again to face the German. They were flying side by side, and Max turned his head to stare full into Manfred's face.

His hand went to his gun; the trigger was warm and giving. Manfred looked straight across and grinned. At his

476

throat between the open lapels of his fur jacket, the Blue Max glittered in the sun.

It was the same white-toothed grin he had flashed in that Carpathian hostelry four years ago.

Now tell your best friend in all the world the name of the girl you know who lives in Jaslo.

Bullets were whining and snapping about his head, but Max saw nothing but the handsome Nordic face.

Shoot! Now! Go hellbent for glory.

Pain flashed hotly in his upper arm where a bullet had found a home. More bullets hit the plane. He heard the ominous sound of fabric being ripped apart.

Still grinning, Manfred waved, then flew ahead. He had not touched his guns.

Slowly, Max let out his breath and released his own machine-gun trigger.

Tom Alison's little Parasol darted from out of nowhere, and, like an angry hornet whose nest has been disturbed, buzzed after the red Fokker.

An hour later, on the ground, Tom Alison was the hero of the hour. He would get five medals at least, maybe even the American Congressional Medal of Honor.

"I pulled the trigger and let him have it full in the face," he bragged. "He seemed to be asking for it."

"That damn Fokker went straight down, nose first," said another pilot. "I saw it, right after Tom fired."

There was some doubt, however, among the Allies concerning exactly whose bullets had snuffed out the Red Baron's life. An Englishman named Roy Brown was eventually to be given the credit and the glory.

But no matter, thought Max, he was gone.

Newspapers the world over carried the headline story, and next morning over a victory breakfast, someone read the following lyric tribute.

"Richthofen was a brave solider, a clean fighter, and an aristocrat. May he rest in peace."

"You too, Jake," Max grunted.

In the momentous battle Max had added two more to his shining record, making him second only to Eddie Rickenbacker as the top American flying ace.

His arm wound took a month to heal, and then the powers that be decided to ground Captain Max O'Hara.

"You'll be far more useful on the ground, training recruits," headquarters wrote. "Men with your experience and maturity are as scarce as hen's teeth in the flying corps."

"Maturity," Max thought sardonically, "could be translated as 'old.' "

Although there was some loose talk that the big Irish-American had lost his nerve — one or two pilots claiming to have seen him flying cozily side by side as at a damned tea party with the Red Baron and making no move to shoot — the communiqué from the top made no mention of it.

It was high noon on the eleventh of November, 1918, when Max leaped from the railway coach onto the Charleroi platform into a kind of bedlam.

A smiled creased his face. It had also been bedlam four years ago when he had first come to the Belgian town. But now, though the ravages of war were still very much in evidence, the stalwart people who had so valiantly held off the Kaiser's juggernaut were dancing, singing, getting drunk — all the wild, frenzied Mardi Gras kind of things people were doing in Paris, London, New York.

The few bells in the little town that had not been melted down for armaments rang out bravely, their measured strokes thin in the crisp, cold air. A gust of wind tore Max's soft beret from his head and sent it spinning into a water-filled ditch.

Stooping to pick it up, he plunked the soggy thing back on his red thatch. A few days before, when it became absolutely certain that the Germans would surrender, he had taken off his uniform, stuffed it into a duffel bag, and put it with the rest of his belongings to be picked up at some future date.

He had bought a suit of clothing such as a lower middle-class French merchant might wear — long, skinny trousers and a jacket fashioned from a kind of scratchy checked wool, dark blue shirt, and of course the pesky beret, which refused to stay on his thick hair.

"A perfect bourgeois," Tom had remarked, when he had dressed in the morning. "But why the hell you want to masquerade as a Frenchie for a couple years beats me." A dreamy look came over his youthful face. "As for me, I can't wait to get back home."

Grinning wickedly, he added, "That flyer's get-up'll be an open sesame at any armistice shindig."

"Somehow I'm not in a mood for—" Max paused, trying to think of the words to tell the kid just how he felt but, giving up, said merely, "It's something I have to do, Tom. Some unfinished business."

That unfinished business had brought him to Charleroi, rather than Paris where Kundry awaited.

Darling, I'm giving the most smashing party when the armistice finally comes. Lots of the rich international set. Later, we can be alone, of course, as long as you want.

Another sex orgy with the blond dynamo was definitely not part of his unfinished business.

The road to the château where he had spent those few days in 1914 with the Belgian girl, Sidonie, and her dying grandfather was filled with merrymakers, and it was with some relief that he took off through the woods toward the rocky outcrop where he remembered the shattered building was.

"The girl's gone back home," Wanda had told him. "She was in Switzerland for a time with the Murav children, but when they were collected by their father, she decided to come back to Belgium to render what aid she could to her countrymen."

Max was worried about her. The war had come back, again and again, to the region, some of the fiercest fighting taking place during the last great German offensive about the time he was in the air hunting down the Red Baron.

Maybe the place had been demolished completely by now. Bombing had been fierce and undiscriminating at the end.

But it stood, tall, turreted, and as full of shell holes as he remembered. The sun had come out after a cloudy morning, mellowing the old pink stone and what red tiles were left on the roof. A clutter of rain-soaked sparrows chirped from a nearby tree.

Ironically, despite the battered look about it, a kind of splendor hung about the ancient de Chambre home, like an old queen standing tall and proud amid the ruins of her past.

Except for some men busily engaged at some repair work on the wide front doors, no one was about. Seeing him approach, one waved a hand toward the back of the château.

"They're in the cemetery."

He heard the singing before he saw them grouped around a kind of monument in the center of the little ancestral burying place, where he and Jimmy Nelson, RFC, had placed the body of grand-père de Chambre.

The voices were high, light, airy. The sweet, ethereal voices of women and girls. The party was small, three layers deep, white-garbed nuns and old women in black. The few men wore black armbands on their sleeves. One or two of the sleeves were empty, and one veteran leaned on a tree, his crutches on the soggy ground at his feet.

Anxiously, he scanned the group for Sidonie. She was short, he reminded himself. He would have to wait until they all filed out.

Apparently, he had arrived at the close of the little ceremony, for as he stood uncertainly, his hand on the wrought-iron gate, a procession of little girls in white dresses marched past him solemnly, two by two, toward the château. Their heads were bowed; their hands folded devoutly together in prayer. The flowers they had brought now rested on the graves along with tiny French flags stuck into the mounded earth.

Once clear of the cemetery and into the little wood, they began to run, their laughter ringing clear. They wore no coats and must be cold, he thought, smiling at the pretty

480

sight and liking the sound of girlish laughter.

The nuns followed them, also two by two, eyes cast to the ground as is their custom. At the very end, one glanced up and met his eyes.

"Max!"

"Sidonie?"

His answer was a hug and a hearty kiss on both cheeks. When she drew back from his arms, her eyes were moist. "Oh, Max! If you knew how much you've been in my thoughts and prayers—"

"So you're the one who got me through this war with all my parts intact."

Overjoyed at finding her well and obviously happy, he pulled her to him once again, uncaring that people had stopped to gape at them.

After another long embrace, she turned and addressed the others. "In spite of his French clothing, this is Max O'Hara, the great American ace, who once befriended me and my grand-père." She cast adoring eyes on a very embarrassed Max. "He saved my life."

"Vive l'américain!" an old man shouted, waving a tiny American flag. Others took up the call, and soon Max found himself being kissed by everyone in the cemetery including the novices who had turned back from the wood at the commotion.

Max thought it the perfect Armistice Day celebration.

"We were hoping that an American doughboy would happen along," remarked Sidonie, as they entered the château by the back door. "But in my wildest dreams I didn't think it would be you."

After returning to her native land from Switzerland, Sidonie told him over tea and biscuits in the vaulted dining room, she had fulfilled a childhood desire to become a nun.

"I entered the Order of Mercy in Mons, but since their motherhouse had been bombed to the ground early in the war, I invited the sisters to join me here at Charleroi."

The château was now the permanent home of the order, which devoted itself to caring for the sick. It was also, for the time being, a hospital.

Sidonie conducted him through the vast place, stopping at the doorways of once-lavish bedrooms that now contained cots lined up so closely there was barely room to walk between them.

She handed him a cloth mask to cover his nose and mouth. "It's the Spanish flu. Only a few of these are war casualties."

"Reminds me of *Villa d'Este*," he said, softly.

She smiled. "Kalina is now in America, thank God."

"Where did the money come from?" he asked. "Did you dig up your grandfather's treasure?"

She shook her head. "No. We dug for weeks but couldn't find a trace of it. Somebody else must have discovered it. Probably a shell crater may have unearthed it."

Much of the money was a bequest from Jimmy Nelson, the British flyer they had helped to escape the German patrols.

"Back in April, I got a cable from the War Ministry in London," Sidonie informed him. "Jimmy Nelson had been shot down over Germany and had left his accumulated military benefits as well as a large sum in insurance to me."

She began to weep. "He was an orphan and had nobody else in the world."

With the aid of a local priest who considered himself an expert on finding buried treasure, having long been an avid reader of pirate stories, not to mention the earnest and continuous prayers of the nuns, Max found the treasure that the Viscount de Chambre had hidden from the Germans.

It was in the cemetery between the grave where the old man lay himself at rest and that of his beloved wife.

"But we never thought to look in such a place," exclaimed an admiring Sidonie.

She insisted on giving the tall American half of the money realized by the sale of the silver and jewelry.

"*Grand-père* wanted you to have it. He had an instinct

482

about people."

The Belgian girl he had met on the road to Mons at the outset of the war never asked him how he would use the money, nor where he was going the Sunday morning in December when they embraced for the last time on the Charleroi platform.

"Unfinished business," was all he said.

Chapter Twenty-four

Pittsburgh, June, 1922

A storm had been brewing for an hour, and now, at ten, a thick, gray curtain covered the sky over the Monongahela, bringing a kind of twilight to the vista of river and mill.

Kalina stuck her head out the window of her third-floor bedroom. To the east, purple thunderheads were massed like an army as if ready to march on the hapless city. Yellow lightning streaked a jagged path through the clouds, and she flinched, her thoughts returning momentarily to the days when a flaring in the sky meant enemy bombardment just over the ridge.

But instantly the fear was gone. Five years in America had all but banished the remembered terror. Kalina had made a determined effort to remember only joy.

"Heat lightning," Anusia had snapped at breakfast. "It won't turn into rain. Always this way in June."

Forthwith, ignoring the repeated flashes in the sky as well as the gloomy forecast in the morning paper, her sister-in-law had sent the gardener and the housemaid Becky into the front parlor to move all the furniture into the foyer and pick up the carpet for beating on the clothes line in the yard.

Anusia's "spring cleaning" was in full throttle, the annual orgy of turning the house upside down having begun promptly on April first with the appearance of the first robin, and would—if past years were a barometer—last well into August.

Kalina was occupied with her own kind of upheaval, having turned out all the bureau drawers, presses and armoires in preparation for packing. She had been at it all morning and had sent Michael into the yard to play, along with his chum Jason, with instructions "not to bother Mama unless it is an emergency."

From time to time, the rhythmic thump-thump of the girl's whisk as it hit the accumulated soot and dirt of a Pittsburgh winter echoed through the house. Being the only servant these postwar days, carpet beating was only one of Becky's many duties. She also helped Anusia in the kitchen with the meals and kept an eye on seven-year-old Michael.

The brand-new electric vacuum cleaner that Dunia had presented to her aunt for Christmas leaned against the wall in the cleaning pantry, unused, itself sporting a layer of dust. Anusia had not taken to the newfangled contraption any more than she had accepted electric light twenty years before.

With a sigh, Kalina turned back into the room to face the open suitcases and the clutter of clothing. Already a niggling headache was teasing behind her ears and the thumping from the yard wasn't helping a bit. With a last look at the sky, she lifted the damp curls at her neck. At least the storm would break the oppressive heat for which the Pittsburgh summer was notorious.

Tomorrow, she would leave this house for a prolonged stay in Arizona with Stefi, who was there for his health.

"Absolutely no thunderstorms in Arizona," Stefi had written, "and not enough rain to fill a teacup."

Kalina hoped her departure from Rutherford Drive

485

would be a permanent one.

A flash of fierce, bright lightning lit up the room, and Kalina tensed, waiting for the thunderclap. The voices of the children in the yard came shrilly in the silence. Kalina moved toward the door. She must fetch them inside before the rain started. Michael was hardy and could withstand a soaking but Jason was sure to develop a cough.

But as she reached the first-floor landing, the beep-beep of the postman's whistle sounded and she turned instead toward the front door, worming her way with difficulty between the heavy parlor furniture that filled the space.

At that moment, the expected thunderclap broke with a noise like a locomotive hitting the side of a hill. The big house shook, and instinctively Kalina put her hands upon her ears. She saw the shadowy hulk of the postman leaning against the glass panel to the side of the heavy front door.

He was peering inside. He rapped impatiently, once, then twice.

After shoving a few tables aside, Kalina finally reached the door and flung it open. The man's arms were filled with brown envelopes, and in his hand he held a fistful of letters. He was sweating profusely.

"Sorry to seem in such a hurry," the man said, "but this is my last delivery, and I'm anxious to get back to the post office before the storm hits." He cast an eye upward. "Looks like a bad one."

"I beg your pardon for taking so long about getting here," Kalina laughed. "But as you see—"

She swept an arm inward to the clutter, and the postman raised a brow. "At it again, is she?"

Nodding, with an exasperated roll of her dark eyes, Kalina took the pile of mail from the man's arms and watched as he climbed back into his high-sided motorized wagon before shutting the door. She understood his anxiety to avoid the storm. The new postal wagons were prone to mechanical breakdowns, and the postman had often been heard to speak longingly of his departed team of horses.

Kalina placed the stack of mail on the nearest marble-top. Inside the official-looking envelopes were annual reports from corporations in which Anusia held stock. The woman collected them the way some people collect teacups or china dogs. The reports came almost daily, and since she never discarded any of them, her second-floor bedroom resembled the periodical room of the Carnegie Library.

As she flipped through the letters in her hand, her face brightened as she saw the two she was expecting. One from Stefi, postmarked Phoenix, and one from Wanda in Detroit. But another thunderclap, even sharper than the last, caused her to drop them on the table and sent her flying through the kitchen into the yard.

"Michael, Jason!"

Cupping her hands round her mouth, Kalina stood on the small back porch on which fat drops were already falling heavily. The yard was very large and overgrown with trees and bushes. They could be anywhere. They were strictly forbidden to leave the yard, but knowing little boys —

She called again but another thunderclap drowned her out, and this time the rain began in earnest.

A familiar "choo-choo-choo" and the sight of two very dirty and bedraggled little boys emerging from the hedge along the wrought-iron fence brought a relieved smile to her face.

"We were playing train, Mama," Michael cried as he ran toward her across the grass.

Jason was close behind. Although six months older than seven-year-old Michael, he was half a head shorter. He was a quiet, thoughtful boy, a perfect playmate for the more boisterous Michael. The boy's father had been killed in France in 1918, heartbreakingly just days before the armistice. His mother, a frail creature, had taken to her bed at the news and had seldom left it since.

The family physician, who also served the Murav household, had brought the boys together. "The lad is being neglected," he told Kalina. "His mother leaves him to rattle around all alone in that big house while she pines away upstairs."

He shook his head. "I've given up on the mother. I can find little organically wrong, but the boy needs companionship and a normal routine."

As the man had anticipated, the upshot was that Kalina visited the woman, a Mrs. Sponsel, begging her permission to let Jason visit Michael daily, using Michael's own loneliness as an excuse.

At first the boy came every day, and then, yielding to Michael's pleading, Kalina put another little bed alongside Michael's in the nursery, and soon she had two sons to care for.

"Just until I get my health back," said Mrs. Sponsel gratefully.

Immediately, Anusia complained about the cost of "another mouth" until Kalina pointed out that hiring a nursemaid to keep Michael amused would have cost ten times the measly amount of food consumed by the thin little boy.

Jason Sponsel had become part of the family, and it was only natural, in due time, that Jason would accompany Mrs. Murav and her son to Arizona. Maybe the western sun would put some color into his pale little cheeks, Kalina thought.

"When I think what a year in Arizona wouldn't do for me," his mother had whined, casting a hopeful glance at Kalina.

But Kalina pretended not to hear. Her charity had its limits.

Now, taking the boys into the kitchen, Kalina peeled off their wet pants and shirts and sat them down in their undershirts and drawers at the table, snatching a sweater from the hook behind the door and draping it loosely across Jason's skinny shoulders.

She was reaching into the icebox for cold milk and apples when a wet and very breathless Becky appeared at the door staggering under the weight of the rolled-up parlor carpet on her shoulder.

"Sorry, Madame. I meant to bring the boys inside, but there was this carpet getting wet."

"You did the right thing," Kalina chuckled, picking up one end of the carpet and walking with the girl into the foyer. "Little boys dry much more quickly than parlor carpets." She grimaced at the heavy thing. "If that thick chunk of wool ever got wet, it would take ten years to dry. Besides," she added, "the boys are really not your job."

Hurrying back into the kitchen, she heard a loud crunch as Michael bit into a crisp red apple. The juice ran down his chin and made little spots on his cotton undershirt.

Her heart turned over as she bent to plant a kiss on the firm, round cheek of Max's son and her only natural child. After the hectic first years in wartorn Europe, when she had fretted about uncertain meals and the constant traveling, he had grown into a sturdy little boy with a lively crop of red hair like his father's, but, thankfully, only half the freckles that had made Max so brown.

He had also inherited the harum-scarum nature of the street boy she had met on New Year's Eve in 1900.

If only his father were here, she thought with a pang. Whatever his pressing reasons for remaining in Europe long after the war was over, Max O'Hara was missing the most precious years of his son's growing up. Years that would never come again.

But with two active youngsters in the house and her continuing social work in Homestead, there was little time to brood on Max's continuing absence, and now Becky reappeared to plunge back into the rain, which had become a veritable cloudburst, thundering on the windows with almost demonic ferocity.

"Clothes on the line," gasped the maid.

Leaving the boys, Kalina flew out after her, welcoming

the wet coolness on her warm flesh as instantly her cotton housefrock clung wetly to her warm body. The downpour hit her head like an open spigot, and she was grateful once again for the mad impulse that had made her take scissors to her long mane so long ago in Tiflis.

In minutes she and the maid were back, carrying the overflowing wicker basket of laundry between them.

"I'll have to wash them all over again," mourned Becky.

"Oh, surely not," panted Kalina. "Just a quick rinse."

"She says the rain is dirty and picks up all the soot in the air."

There was a conspiratorial exchange of glances as mistress and maid walked down the narrow steps into the cellar. They always talked this way about Anusia, referring to her simply as "she," as one talks about a kind of wicked witch.

"Hang them in the cellar and light the gas on the cellar stove," Kalina suggested.

"She'll can me for sure," exclaimed the girl. "Last time I did that, she showed me the gas bills."

"She" should have come down to help, Kalina thought with irritation. But "she" was up in her room, closeted with her financial papers and annual reports. Maybe wielding the special silver scissors with which she clipped the coupons from the stock dividends that had come in the morning mail.

Her brother's will had left Anusia fabulously wealthy, with seats on countless boards of directors worldwide, Although a small army of New York lawyers dedicated themselves to running the Murav empire quite efficiently, Anusia felt she had to keep "a finger in."

Predictably, as so often happens with people who become obsessed with money, her sudden wealth had turned Kalina's sister-in-law into a Scrooge. She carped about household expenses to an unreasonable degree.

Kalina bore it patiently, but during the past months, as her escape from the house became a certainty, her patience had begun to show a ragged edge.

She herself was comfortably fixed, wanting for nothing material, but she depended for her money on the trust funds Stefan had set up for the children. The will had been blunt.

"Since my wife will undoubtedly remarry, and my beloved sister will surely remain alone, I leave the bulk of my estate to Anusia Murav."

Anusia had also been given the house and, as before Stefan's death, continued to manage the servants.

At present, there was only one, the cheerful, big-boned Becky, who like Laura so long ago, had come straight from St. Joseph's Orphan Asylum across the river in Allegheny and was glad enough to have a home, a room of her own, a clean bed, and all the food she could eat.

There was little danger that Anusia would "can" the girl or that, like a whole series of maids before her, Becky would run off to a factory or department store. "That's for girls who don't have to put all their pay to room and board in some crowded rooming house," she said. "This way I can put some money aside for the future."

"Besides," she added, with the cynicism of orphanhood, "Miss Murav don't bother me. There's always one like her anywhere you go."

Back upstairs, Anusia stood, arms folded across her skinny chest, staring stonily at the two boys, who having polished off an apple each, had started on a loaf of fresh baked bread. The obesity of the time of Zuska's death was gone; Anusia had reverted to her natural gauntness.

She looked up as Kalina entered. "Milk costs money. Between the two of them it's half a gallon every day. I think we should buy a cow." Angrily, she pointed a finger to a whitish puddle on the wooden table. "Not to mention what they spill."

This wasn't the first time a cow had been mentioned, and with great difficulty Kalina kept a straight face. Quietly, she went about wiping up the spill with a kitchen

491

towel and sending the boys upstairs to the nursery to play.

"A cow brings its own problems," she said calmly. "I wonder how Mrs. Boggs next door would react to the mooing, not to mention the smell of manure."

Characteristically, Anusia didn't bother to respond to such a point of logic but countered with, "The woman sent her maid again to complain about Michael's drum. She suffers greatly from the megrims."

At the sink rinsing out the milky cloth, Kalina felt the brown eyes boring into her back and bit her tongue to keep from lashing out. Why start another argument? Tomorrow she would be gone, out of sight and sound of Anusia Murav.

"It's in the attic now, in the Poor Relief bag of outgrown toys," she said flatly.

Mrs. Boggs had also complained bitterly about Michael's little terrier, Sparky, who, apparently under the delusion that the grass was greener on the other side, persisted in digging holes under the fence at a spot that led directly into Mrs. Boggs's prize roses.

"There are no fences in Arizona." So Stefi wrote.

She had taken Sparky to Elena Lesko for her grandchildren, telling a tearful Michael that the long train trip would surely have killed the puppy.

Upstairs, she found Michael and Jason on the nursery-room carpet, building a village from a boxful of brightly colored wooden blocks, and repaired to her bedroom, a few steps down the hall to resume her packing.

The room was unbearably stuffy, but the rain still beat mercilessly on the window, which Kalina thoughtlessly had left wide open when she had fled downstairs and which Anusia had thoughtfully closed. But not before the curtains had gotten wet, she noted, spreading the lace apart to dry on the sill.

As she resumed her packing, Kalina silently berated

herself for her continuing resentment of what Anusia called "mothering" and what Kalina chose to call "interference." A woman of thirty-eight, a mother herself, scarcely needs the kind of tyrannical mothering Anusia offered.

Although she hated every inch of the dark, old house on Rutherford, Kalina had taken up residence here with the children upon her return from Europe after the long sea voyage in 1917. Living here with Anusia in the house where Stefi had been born and where Dunia at least had been a child, would restore the sense of family that they had missed during most of the long years in Europe.

She really longed to buy a house in the country, away from the smoke and grime of the mills. But Anusia was enraged at the mere suggestion of selling "Stefan's home" and, unexpectedly, Dunia took a liking to the gloomy old place.

The twenty-year-old girl had also surprisingly formed a strong attachment to her spinster aunt.

"She's really a dear if you give her half a chance, Mama Kalina," she remarked.

To Kalina's continuing amazement and delight—for it kept Anusia out of her life considerably—the attachment had not waned with time but rather strengthened. It was Anusia and Dunia at the Women's Suffrage League Tuesday afternoons; it was Anusia and Dunia at the picture show downtown at least once each week.

Dunia drove her aunt to the stock exchange in Pittsburgh to watch the quotations on the board, settling her ecstatic relative in Dunia's new Stutz Bearcat automobile, which had marvelous balloon tires and a canvas top that could go up and down to suit the weather.

Ironically, sometimes Kalina felt left out as the two women sat in the little downstairs sitting room, once her favorite, but which they made their own, sipping sherry and laughing as Dunia regaled her aunt with stories of her school days in France and Switzerland.

Five years passed, and Kalina found herself entrenched.

Michael adapted easily, loving the big yard with all the bushes and trees, perfect for playing hide and seek and cowboys and Indians. Inside, his joy was the long, highly polished banister, perfect for sliding down—a dangerous little-boy pastime that even Anusia's repeated scoldings failed to curb.

Stefi began art studies at the prestigious Carnegie Institute and had done very well. His senior exhibition had received good notices by the critics. He had a future in art.

But then Zuska's son had fallen ill, spending the entire winter of 1920 in bed with a nagging cough and congestion in the lungs. On a physician's advice, Kalina packed the boy off to Arizona to the sanatorium where Elena Lesko had recovered from her tuberculosis.

It had been raining that June day too, last year, as the doctor swung an arm toward the window down which the water streamed, just as it was doing now.

"He needs a dry, bracing climate. He should sleep in the open."

How she had longed to accompany Stefi to the wonderful American West, where she always imagined the "real America" to be. But she herself had come down with bronchitis, probably from the strain of nursing Stefi, and it was a full year before her plans to visit came to fruition.

The letters!

In her pensive, introspective mood, Kalina had completely forgotten the letters she had left in the foyer. Scrambling to her feet from the floor, where she was kneeling over Michael's suitcase, squeezing in the last of the little pants and shirts, she bumped right smack into Anusia, the top of her head hitting the stack of annual reports in her sister-in-law's arms.

Instinctively, Kalina rubbed her head. "Oh, dear Anusia, I am so clumsy—"

"It's nothing."

Backing off, Anusia assumed her avenging-angel pose, narrow, deep-set eyes inscrutable, sallow face set in rigid lines, long, thin body tense.

"Here are your letters."

"Thank you for bringing them upstairs. In the confusion I forgot."

Sweeping her eyes over the disheveled room with disapproval, Anusia snapped, "Stefan would have forbidden you to send his son off to the wilderness among wild Indians and God only knows what kind of people."

Kalina set the letters on the high bed. "Arizona is hardly wilderness, Sister. It's part of the Union now. Since 1912. There are houses and schools and churches and policemen. Everything needful for a civilized society."

Moving to the window, Kalina cast her eyes down to the street. The rain was softer now, the wide street was completely inundated, the water reaching over the curbs, swirling in wide concentric circles around the sewer on the corner.

She closed her eyes. Patience. This was an old argument, one which had been repeated many times since Stefi had gone away. It was a ritual between the two of them like a stageplay one repeated each night or a choreographed dance whose steps are rigidly set. Each sentence, each turn of phrase, each word. Always the same.

But it was a ritual, she realized, that Anusia felt compelled to repeat.

"As for Indians, they are no longer wild, as you put it, but are living on reservations. Quite peaceable, I understand."

"The boy needs to be here, where his roots are."

"A person carries his roots with him."

"Eventually, he will tire of his painting—it's hardly a respectable profession—and should be here where I can direct him toward taking over the Murav Enterprises."

Kalina turned from the window and fixed Anusia with a direct gaze. "Stefi is not interested in business."

They spoke the next sentence together, like a verse choir. "If you had sent him to Harvard as I suggested, he *would*

495

be interested in business."

At this point Anusia, offended, usually closed the argument, sometimes by abruptly changing the subject, more often by flouncing out of whatever room they were in.

This time she darted to the window, throwing it up. "Oh, there's Dunia now. I was becoming concerned about her."

Her voice brightened. "And she's got some young people with her." Leaving the window open, Anusia ran to the door. "I must prepare some refreshments."

Anusia left, and Kalina thrust her own head out the window, taking deep breaths to clear her head of the unpleasantness the woman had put there. Three young people were clambering out of the bright-red auto, the sound of their chatter and laughter echoing in the street.

As if sensing her mother watching from above, Dunia looked up, waved. Her smile was wide and happy. Although nearly twenty-five, the girl showed no inclination to marry and start a family of her own, being perfectly content to live at home.

A quick check on the boys in the nursery found them both fast asleep on the floor, thumbs in mouths.

In the bedroom once more, Kalina settled down to her letters. Anusia would be occupied with Dunia and her friends for the rest of the afternoon, and if she were lucky, Michael and Jason would sleep for an hour or so.

Reaching for the letters, she settled back on the floor to read, the chaise and chair still being covered with unpacked garments. She slipped her finger beneath the flap of Stefi's letter, but, as Anusia's shrill voice came up through the heat register from the kitchen, Kalina found her thoughts wandering back to her sister-in-law.

Leaving this house would solve another problem for Kalina. No more would she be tempted to put Anusia in her place by telling the domineering woman of her suspicions concerning Anusia's true parentage. Despite the continuing lack of evidence, Kalina could not shake herself of the notion that Stefan and Anusia were not really brother and sister.

Part of her feeling came from the troubling episode in Anusia's bedroom at the time Zuska died and she had caught the woman spying on her and her cousin through a hole in the ceiling.

She would never forget the strange, babbling words that had tumbled irrationally from Anusia's mouth.

His mother was a whore. She was traveling with a man not her husband, who called himself a count.

In the next breath, she had mentioned that her "uncle" was taking her to America to be a slavey to him and his ten children.

That her sister-in-law harbored a secret about her past Kalina had no doubt. Even Zuska had hinted at it, suggesting just before she died that Anusia had revealed the truth to her. But maddeningly, Zuska had taken the knowledge with her to the grave. "I'll bet the real story will burn your ears off," she had taunted.

Her playful cousin's reasons for being mysterious about it were characteristic. She loved to goad people. But, to be more charitable about it, she might have wanted to shield Anusia—of whom she had grown fond—from Kalina's revenge if the truth were known.

Once, since returning to America, Kalina had tried to ferret out the truth from her sister-in-law. The woman had flared up into a rage and had come near to striking the younger woman, doubling her fists and thrusting them into Kalina's very frightened face.

"You are determined to steal my inheritance with your vile suspicions," she had shrieked.

Dunia had sprung to Anusia's defense. "You deserve to be punched in the face," she stormed at her mother. "It doesn't matter whether Aunt Anusia is really Daddy's sister or not. In her mind she *is* his sister, and Daddy always treated her as his own flesh and blood."

Dunia had stared into space, then added slowly, "As he

497

treated me. You know, Mother, I'm not sure who I really am, either. Sure, I'm Zuska's daughter, an Olkonsky by heritage, sharing your blood. But as for the other side, I have no idea who my father is. You say he was some Italian named Victor, a no-account street peddler, but my mother was a prostitute. I could be anybody's daughter."

She had said the self-damning words with a complete lack of emotion. Kalina felt strongly, however, that, deep within her heart, the girl was anything but emotionless about her history. She would probably live with that underlying conflict until a time when, no longer able to bear it, she would erupt into a delusion as had Stefan.

Not for the first time there flashed through Kalina's mind the teasing idea that Stefan had actually fathered Dunia during some scandalous assignation in Pottsville.

But, to Kalina's enormous relief, Dunia took no action to uncover her real family roots. It would be simple to take a train to Pottsville and ask some questions. People in small towns had long memories. No gossip ever died.

But the investigation the girl had launched in Tiflis concerning Stefan's ancestry had borne some fruit, though of a distinctly unripe variety.

It had taken well over a year for the refugee search organization to respond. The report was brief, but little was resolved. The priest who had given Stefan last rites had notified them, enclosing the official report with his own confirming letter.

Kalina's heart thumped even now as she recalled the morning the news arrived. Armistice Day, 1918, and they had all been celebrating. The mail was late.

Anusia came close to discovering their scheme, having picked up the letter from the foyer table. She felt it her privilege to examine thoroughly every piece of mail that entered the house.

"Oh, a Tiflis postmark!" She turned the letter over and glanced at the return address. "From a Reverend Takich."

Entering the foyer just then, Kalina had said lightly, "He

is one of Dunia's friends from the refugee group."

Anusia had frowned. "Strange, she's never heard from any of them before this."

When questioned later by her aunt about the letter, Dunia made up a story about Jane Fadden getting married and Father Takich wanting to tell her the news. Anusia had looked suspicious but said no more about it.

The official report was short, a few paragraphs, answering point by point specific questions asked by Dunia in her application.

Yes, Stefan Murav's father had been a high czarist official; yes, he had visited the Caucasus in the 1860s; yes, he had fathered a child by a local woman in a remote village; yes, the woman's family had claimed descent from Stephen Batory, a Hungarian who had become King Stefan of a united Poland.

The mother having died, Mr. Murav had taken the child upon his return to Poland and soon after departed for America in the company of his wife, a certain noblewoman, a countess.

Concerning Anusia Murav, there was no record or memory of an older child accompanying Captain Murav in the Caucasus. It was suggested that the family make inquiries in Poland concerning her. The manifest of the ship that had foundered off the coast of America in 1870, listed a child named Anusia, aged seven, traveling with an uncle.

It was possible that the uncle was Stefan Murav's father, which would make Anusia a cousin rather than a sister.

Or, perhaps—this from the priest—Anusia Murav was another bastard child of Captain Murav.

Any further investigating on the Murav lineage insofar as it concerned King Stefan of Poland who had reigned from 1576 to 1587 must perforce be carried on in Poland, or preferably Transylvania, now part of Romania, where the great and beloved king had been born.

In a postscript, Father Takich hinted that he would be

deliriously happy to be of help in tracing Stefan Murav's forebears in Transylvania. Genealogy of Polish noble families had always been his great love, he said, and he himself took some pride in the fact that he sprang from aristocratic loins. Provided expenses were paid, he was certain that he could uncover the secret knowledge which had so possessed Dunia's father during his lifetime.

They were to write if interested.

Although Kalina was willing to hire the priest for such a mission, her motivation springing from a desire to clear Stefan's memory of madness more than from a vicious impulse to humiliate Anusia, Dunia was curiously indifferent.

"No," she had said firmly, as she and Kalina talked through the night about it. "Auntie deserves all the money in the world. She saved Daddy from drowning or disease on the ship. She loved him. If it hadn't been for her, he might have died in the almshouse, or been sent back to Poland."

The scene in Anusia's bedroom at the time of Zuska's dying was still vivid in Kalina's mind. "Sometimes I'm convinced that Anusia herself went a little mad when the ship went down," she told Dunia. "She became convinced that the little boy to whom she had formed an attachment during the voyage really was her little brother."

"You may be right, Mother," Dunia replied. "But being right doesn't justify hurting people."

As it had turned out, nobody got to be the king of Poland. The land of Kalina's birth, that had been coveted by so many through the centuries, was now a republic, much like the United States of America. It even had a president.

A photograph fell out of the letter from Arizona. A thin but grinning Stefi squinted into the sun. Behind him loomed a quaint old-time Spanish mission building.

A girl named Heidi had taken the photo, he wrote. She's a whiz with a camera, he continued, and wants to make photography her career when she is cured.

Cured! Kalina's heart ached for them, and for all the precious young ones afflicted with the scourge of tuberculosis. The doctors said there was no real cure, only remissions, gained at the expense of constant vigilance throughout one's whole lifetime.

Heidi was of German extraction, and her father had suffered greatly from the anti-German hatred during the war. His silversmith shop had been smashed in by an angry mob and all the artifacts stolen. He died from a heart attack a few days later, and now his widow worked in the sanatorium kitchen.

Kalina stared at the photograph for a long time. One day Stefi would marry. She never permitted herself to think that his lungs would not strengthen.

She wanted grandchildren from Zuska's children. Maybe there would be a little girl with golden hair and blue, blue eyes. But, at twenty-four, Dunia was in no hurry to wed. "Mama Kalina, why do you think a woman absolutely has to have a man to make her happy? That's old-fashioned. The day is past when a woman must wrap herself around a man like a cocoon. I may never marry, like Aunt Anusia."

No, not like Aunt Anusia, Kalina mused. Her "merry" Dunia would become old in time but never embittered.

Wanda's letter merely confirmed the arrival day after tomorrow of Kalina and the boys at their home in Detroit. Three-year-old Mary Helen was on pins and needles, reported her mother, waiting for Michael and Jason to play with.

The childless Hardies had adopted the orphaned daughter of Mary Lesko and her Cossack lover. Shamyl had fallen in the last bitter fighting of the war, and Mary had lived only long enough to bring their infant daughter to Paris, staggering half-dead from hunger and exhaustion into the clinic, where she expired days later from the

501

Spanish influenza, then rampant all over the world. The privations and horrors of the war had left her weakened, Alec had said.

Poor Mary Lesko, to die so young—

But so many had died in the flower of their youth in the war to end all wars. Others had been granted the fullness of time. Stefan, Millard Hughes, Carnegie. Just yesterday Kalina had stood at the graveside as they lowered the pink-and-white beauty of Lillian Russell into the grave.

Zuska, Libby, now Mary. All the beautiful ones.

For Mary at least it was a world well lost for love. The glowing face of her longtime friend and companion on the mountain near Jaslo as she had ridden off with her Shamyl would remain in Kalina's memory forever.

"It'll be so grand being together again, talking over old times," Wanda concluded.

Old times. They would talk of Max. "He loves you very much," Wanda would surely say, "but he has this thing to do in Europe, what he calls his unfinished business."

She and Wanda had spoken many times on the telephone after the Hardies returned to America. And before that, there were numerous letters.

There had even been a letter from Sidonie, now Sister Jeanne d'Arc, who had reported that Max was using his half of the very large amount of money realized from her grandfather's buried family jewels to set up orphanages, hospitals, and the like, in ravaged parts of Europe. He had put the bulk of it, however, in solid longtime investments, establishing a foundation that he called "The Mulberry Fund."

Immediately, she cabled Sidonie, requesting more detailed information about Max. Her cabled reply was lengthy, assuring Kalina of Max's well-being and of the fact that he had not forgotten his child in America.

The unfinished business was being implemented by an organization called *The Mulberry Fund*. Max told Sidonie that the name was a kind of secret between him and

Kalina.

There was more about Max wanting to play Andrew Carnegie for a year or so. Sidonie added that Kalina was supposed to understand that too.

Kalina's lips tightened at the memory of Sidonie's words. The old Scotsman had taken twenty years to give his money away. She and Max couldn't afford twenty years. He was forty now, she almost that.

He was probably taking time, now and then, to philander with women like that Kundry von Richthofen, whom he denied categorically ever being engaged to.

Oh, yes, he had written, at long last. In 1919, a year after the Armistice. She remembered every line, for it had been short and to the point, in the way of a man who is not comfortable with putting his intimate thoughts on paper.

> Don't expect me for a year or so. I forgive you for
> that Cossack fellow Yurek if you forgive me for
> Kundry. You played at being Cinderella, now it's my
> turn to be rich and famous like Carnegie. Okay?

"Do you lose much Murav money if you remarry? Maybe we can live in sin. Only joking, darling Polack."

For months she had expected him, gazing out the window to the street a hundred times a day it seemed. Even at night she'd leap out of bed and run to the window at the merest sound of a motor stopping at the curb.

Anusia and Dunia made little jokes about it. "Give it up, Mama Kalina," her daughter said. "He's never coming back."

But stubbornly, Kalina went on hoping. If she slackened her window-watch during the day, at night she indulged in fantasies of their joyful reunion. Max had never been in this house. What if Anusia opened the door? Would she snap at him?

Would they kiss in the foyer, with Anusia watching?

Where would they sleep the first night? Surely not in the high bed where Stefan had possessed her body, and which still bore the sagging imprint of his heavy body on the other side. Not to mention Anusia downstairs, creeping about, listening. Maybe she could drill a hole in the ceiling directly below, on the second floor, to make the listening easier, as she had so comically done when Zuska was ill.

Unthinkable.

They would simply have to go to a hotel. A posh one, The Schenley in the East End, or maybe the William Penn downtown.

Perhaps they would rent a small house, with a little yard for the children, somewhere out of the city, just until they could decide where to live. Much depended of course on Max's line of work. Now that he was rich, would he return to the labor movement? From what she heard from Elena Lesko and Anna Mielchek and her other Homestead friends, conditions had not improved a great deal since 1903.

The days turned into weeks, the weeks into months, and when there was still no word from him, the enormous, incredible hurt never ceased. How could he stay away when she needed him so?

It did little good to tell herself that beneath Max O'Hara, the newly wealthy man of the world, there breathed the heart of the street kid who had been a rent baby, who had made his own way from the age of eight.

While she had basked, during those early years, in the glow of Aunt Litka's love and concern and Zuska's companionship, he'd had no one. He had learned to live alone in his cigar-factory cellar with all those barrels and crates of stolen stuff.

It was only logical that he would want to give the money away himself. A street kid trusted no one. Maybe she should have gone back to Europe, hunted him down, insisted he come home and do his duty to his son, if not to her.

From the time when he could first comprehend such a thing, Kalina had told little Michael about his absent father.

"He's doing some important work in Europe, across the ocean," she'd said, showing him the photograph of Captain Max O'Hara, American ace, one of hundreds distributed by the American Air Services.

The picture held a place of honor among the others on his little chest of drawers. Grandmother Hania, Auntie Zuska, Uncle Stefan, Auntie Anusia were also there.

He bragged to all his friends at kindergarten about his daddy who'd been a flyer and had shot down so many German planes.

But when Jason came along, with his very own photograph of his daddy who was dead, Michael began to worry.

"Is my daddy dead, Mama?"

"No, darling, of course not." A stricken thought flitted through her mind. Maybe he *is* dead, an accident or disease, how would we know?

"Jason's daddy is dead. He says my daddy must be killed, because he isn't coming home."

In the shops or on the street, the little boy pointed to any red-headed man who happened along, asking in his childish treble, very loudly, "Is that my daddy, Mama?"

Eventually, in the way of children, he stopped asking.

"Well, so you're actually going to do it!"

Dunia stood in the door, munching a piece of Anusia's special cheesecake. Puckered lines furrowed her smooth brow, but her brown eyes were inscrutable. Her early prettiness was gone, but she had what the fashion magazines called "style." Strong face, well-defined features, intelligent eyes. At forty she would be handsome.

"Another meeting, darling?" asked Kalina, noting the leather briefcase in one hand.

Dunia sighed. "Yes, boring as usual."

"Why do you bother?"

"You know I am very interested in improving the conditions of the poor."

As with Anusia, this discussion was one with which Kalina was all too familiar. Dunia's idea of social work was heading up committees, shuffling papers on a desk in a downtown office, holding luncheons for her stylish friends, and staging huge benefits at which society folk dressed up and gorged themselves on rich food.

In exchange for which a large donation of money was hopefully forthcoming.

Dunia never went into Homestead to see for herself. She knew the poor only by hearsay.

Best to change the subject, Kalina reflected. No point in arguing on the last day mother and daughter would see each other for a long time.

"Your frock is lovely, dear. That Italian silk looks very cool. And the red flowers do so much for your complexion."

A frown clouded Dunia's face once more. She glanced down at the knee-length, beltless dress that clung damply to her slim figure. Her slim fingers plucked distastefully at the fabric as she tugged the fabric this way and that over her bosom and thighs.

"I sometimes wish we could go back to the old days when a woman could hide her ugly shape with all those frills and ruffles." She smirked. "That bustle idea, for instance."

"Ugly! Why darling, you are anything but—"

Her daughter's lack of confidence in her appearance was also a problem that Kalina had failed to resolve. Perhaps when the girl was older— If she would only fall in love. Many quite eligible young men had pursued her with an eye to marriage, but she consistently remained indifferent to one and all.

As eager as her mother to avoid conflict on this day, Dunia said, "I do wish you would stay at least until our midsummer gala is over. With Lillian Russell gone, you are just about the only one left in town who could do the kind of hostessing that these affairs demand."

"Noblesse oblige." Kalina chuckled. "It's a kind of flair that combines humility with nobility. Aunt Litka taught me that on Mulberry Street. We used to practice at it, using crusts of bread and weak tea and lining up chairs with pretend guests."

Dunia came into the room to stand in front of the armoire mirror, scowling at herself and looking backward through the glass at her mother.

"Oh, Mother, how do you do it?"

"Do what, dear?" Kalina closed the last suitcase. "There, that's done. The new, light clothing is so wonderful. Twenty years ago we had all these voluminous dresses, the corsets, the feathered hats—" She sighed. "Took almost a whole railroad coach just to carry the luggage."

Impulsively, Dunia turned round and dropped upon Kalina, who was just getting to her feet. The two women fell upon the now-empty chaise, embracing, laughing, weeping.

"You don't have to worry about how you look, Mama Kalina. You can wear anything." cried Dunia, "Even in that old cotton housefrock that you've had for years—"

"I think it's the chocolate ice cream stains from the time Michael had his first cone—"

They were silent for a time, each wrapped in her own thoughts of parting, of life, of love, and of the past.

"Where are the locomotives, Mama?"

"Don't be such a question box, Michael dear. Mama is busy. Why can't you be quiet for a minute, like Jason?"

Kalina walked rapidly behind the porter pulling the cart with their luggage, completely oblivious to the Grecian elegance of the vast railroad terminal in downtown Pittsburgh. In former, less harried times, she had seen and duly admired the marble pillars and vaulting, stained-glass dome and often wondered who on earth ever had the time or leisure to fully appreciate the splendor.

507

Neither did she note, as she might have on another, less hectic occasion, the fellow travelers who smiled at the charming picture made by mother and two sons, one on each arm.

"But one so dark, and one so red," a fat old woman exclaimed as they passed.

"One so bothersome, and one so calm," Kalina muttered to herself in response.

The porter turned around, his face sober under the blue visored hat. "Follow me right through the iron gates, Madame. I have your ticket, no need to stop. And please hold on tightly to the children. The locomotives are a few feet from the platform and sometimes blow out steam from the sides."

Women of Mrs. Murav's position in society never traveled without a maid to care for the children, relieving her to enjoy the scenery, but Kalina was not inclined to include a fourth person on this pilgrimage. Becky had been eager to go but was afraid she might get homesick for Pittsburgh, and Stefi said there were lots of girls in Arizona who would make excellent nursemaids.

They walked a long way down the wooden platform, Jason gaping open-mouthed toward the top of the huge shed with its trails of smoke and steam. Stefi had written that they now had electric locomotives to pull trains up and down mountainsides.

Kalina thought she would miss the smoke. It was part of the excitement of traveling.

Michael continued to pester her with questions. "What makes the trains go? Why does the man wear that funny uniform?" But he was sensible enough not to wait for answers.

It was hot, and already Kalina's hair was curling damply on her neck beneath the close-fitting linen cloche. She resolved to take it off once they were on the coach. Her frock was of cool lime-green linen, sleeveless, beltless. Thinly strapped alligator sandals covered her feet.

She shivered at the memory of the high-top boots of yore. Not to mention gloves, corsets, all the instruments of torture with which women were once inflicted.

"You look like a girl of twenty," Dunia had said admiringly. A charity luncheon which she "absolutely" had to attend prevented her from accompanying her mother to the station.

"No matter, darling. We said our good-byes last night," said her mother. She needed no more tears, she thought gratefully.

Suddenly, the porter stopped as another of his kind emerged from a little officelike shed on the platform. The two men conferred; both glanced back quickly at the little family. Both nodded, the first porter disappeared into the shed, and the second picked up the shaft of the cart with one hand.

With the other hand, he lifted his hat and ran his fingers through his hair.

Michael tugged at Kalina's hand, half-dragging her toward the cart.

"Mama, is that my daddy?"

"Of course not, darling. Now come on, behave. Remember what I said, there are lots of red-headed men in the world. Look out, you'll run right into the cart."

But he wasn't listening, and with the surprising strength the boy often displayed, he pulled her toward the cart and the porter, who turning round suddenly, threw his hat into the air.

Speechless, Kalina watched as Max O'Hara, disguised as a porter, swept his son into his arms.

They were well into the countryside along the Ohio River, heading west, before Max and Kalina could talk. The two boys were huddled at the windows of the seats across the aisle, staring at the passing farms, counting cows and barns, as Max had sternly instructed them to do.

509

It was to be a contest, a dish of chocolate ice cream for the boy who had the highest count. But Kalina had a feeling that, in this contest, both the children would be winners.

Judging from the way they took to the tall man with the red hair — silvered now at the ears and temple — the association of man and boys promised to be a happy and long-lasting one.

Man and woman had not kissed — a porter and stylish female traveler embracing would have caused a commotion — but their eyes and hands were joined.

Kalina was the first to speak what was in her heart.

"How could you stay away so long?"

"It wasn't easy. I wrote you." His eyes were sober.

"I could have married." Huffily.

"But you didn't." The old cocksure smile.

She moved to join him on the facing seat.

Nothing had changed. They were nearly forty, but the magic was still there.

They ate a catered lunch in their seats, Kalina being reluctant to risk the elegant dining salon with two little unpredictable boys. The excitement of having a daddy materialize so suddenly had finally ruffled even Jason's equanimity, and he too could not be still for more than five seconds at a stretch.

Ultimately, nature took its course, and the boys fell fast asleep on their pulled-down seats.

As they clung together across the aisle, Kalina's head on Max's blue-uniformed shoulder, he spoke with some impatience.

"I've been in town for a week, waiting for you to leave Murav's house. I couldn't bring myself to enter that house and kiss you for the first time in seven years under that roof. Or even on Murav's porch, or on his sidewalk —"

Her instinct had been right. "I understand, dear."

We could have met somewhere else, she thought.

But the unworthy thought quickly vanished. The reunion had been perfect. Max had done it right, as he had done everything right, from the very beginning of it all, when he had picked her up from under the ragpicker's cart.

They were crossing the Ohio River on a long iron bridge somewhere in West Virginia when she said sleepily, "I hope we've heard the last of your 'unfinished business,' Max O'Hara."

Chuckling, he cast a wary eye across the aisle where his son slept, arms entwined, with his young friend, Jason.

He sighed. "Somehow I get the feeling that it's just begun."